THE SECRETS
WE CARRY

A novel by
Megan Noel Opava

This book is a work of fiction. Any references to historical events, real people, or real places are used fictitiously. Other names, characters, places, and events are products of the author's imagination, and any resemblance to actual events or places or persons living or dead is entirely coincidental.

Copyright © 2022 by Megan Noel Opava

All rights reserved, including the right to reproduce this book or portions thereof in any form whatsoever.

Cover design by Megan Noel Opava

ISBN 979-8-9869615-0-7

To my Dad.
Adam Michael Opava,
Who helped me every single step of the way.

Chapter 1

1

The pale yellow phone on the kitchen counter rings, just as the water in the pot froths to a boil.

When I see the blocked ID on the screen, I immediately know. It's too dark for this time of day. My stomach sinks and I'm a thousand pounds heavier.

I tug on my leggings still sticky from my workout this morning and take a deep breath.

"Hello."

"He said you would know what this is about."

My best friend walks in smiling, but her face quickly lines with concern once she looks at me.

Clinching the phone, I hurry to the window above the sink to see the sky turning a light orange. The floating stained glass flower hanging in front of the window is no longer projecting light. The noon sun is far too dim as the silhouettes on the sink fade to nothing. I remember from the wildfires here in California, what the absence of shadows and a dark sun means. I've never experienced one in the middle of Santa Barbara though.

I stare at the glowing sun that looks like a dull fireball floating in the sky creating no sun beams. Ash and smoke begin to snake up on the horizon line. Panic starts to boil inside me. I knew this time would come, but can we anticipate something is going to happen when it's this incomprehensible? The mind refuses to grasp it, and in doing so we seal our own fate. Here it is now and during all those trainings, I never believed it was coming; not really. I so badly wanted to validate my importance, and the group recognized I was special. I want to prove myself to the world that I'm capable of more than our society allows, but now that the time has come I feel selfish for hoping I could be a part of something revolutionary.

And yet, as the first few seconds of this event unfold, I find that I am excited. It's my time to be brave. To be extraordinary.

"I thought we had more time," I say.

"Stop talking on this line. Just do what we said. Goodbye and stay safe."

The line clicks and goes dead. The long droning beep of a dead line will be the heart monitor of the world stopping.

The room is filled with steam and smoke. I taste campfire on my tongue, but it's toxic.

The smoke smell continues to get stronger and the orange sky is deepening in vibrancy.

"Miranda! Move out of the way," Kelsey pushes me away from the window to close it. Her skirt brushes my legs that now feel like stone. She turns the stove off.

I know she's waiting for me to speak, but I can only stare out the window with the phone pressed against my face.

A dull repetitive voice pounds through my head.

Fire is coming.

Fire is coming.

Fire is coming.

2

"Miranda! What's happening?!" Kelsey screams, clenching my arms with her stubby fingers. She jiggles and her blonde curls sway. It breaks my heart to see her pouty face wrinkled with confusion and fear. She looks like a baby who heard a loud noise and doesn't know what to make of it.

The skin on my arms hurts as I'm being moved rapidly forward and backwards, but I can't take my eyes off the sky that gets oranger by the second that's deepening into a red. I don't feel like I'm in my body anymore. Everything is interacting with myself outside of myself. It's like I'm a spectator of my own body. I see things happening and I feel them happening, but they must be separated on a neural level I'm unaware of. I start to detach and watch my body as I float above so I don't have to deal with the real world.

"Miranda!" Kelsey slaps my face. Her wedding band she never took off snags a strand of my hair.

Energy shoots through me as I come back to reality, "Kelsey! Oh my God! It's happening!"

"Wait, what?! What the hell are you talking about? Are you sure you're doing alright?"

"Do not imply that something is wrong with me when you can clearly see out the window for yourself that the world is turning orange. I'm not supposed to do this..."

"Do what?"

"I can't leave you here to die. It's not allowed, but I can't possibly leave you here. Chaos is coming."

"Miranda," Kelsey reaches her arm towards me apprehensively.

I swat it away.

"We need to go now! You have five minutes to grab whatever you don't want destroyed forever. I'm going to get the car ready."

"Why should I listen to you? Are you having another episode?" Finally there's a clip of fear in her voice.

"You know I've been good for years. This is real. This is really happening. Just pack."

"How am I supposed to just pack everything in five minutes? What do I bring? I don't understand what's going on."

Kelsey trails me as I sprint through our living room with walls covered in paintings and family pictures and pictures of us since we were kids and stumble into my bedroom.

I'm on autopilot now.

I grab the fraying cord attached to the attic door.

"Why can't we just wait it out. Someone in charge will do something any minute," Kelsey tries to reason. "Also, what's happening? Why do you seem to know?"

"Goddammit, Kelsey, just listen to me."

"You're being crazy."

"I'm needed Kelsey. You wouldn't understand."

"Oh I wouldn't understand? You are always one step ahead of me. And now you think you're so far ahead as to know what's happening."

"Oh my God, Kelsey if you would just listen…"

The house shakes as if a small earthquake passed through or a large plane has flown overhead. I jump out of the way as my lamp crashes to the floor knocking me into Kelsey's arms.

During that one second embrace I see the true terror in her eyes. I must look crazy right now. I feel like a lunatic myself. Fires are spreading and my house is literally shaking around me, but I still question if all this is happening. I went to the trainings and I was educated and I knew what the future held, but never during any of that did I actually feel like any of it was real. It's like reading grotesque headlines on the news or listening to the doomsayers who are scientifically valid in their screams, but our detachment as a society prevents us from truly believing. Until something's tangible and irrevocable do we listen. Even then, it seems too absurd.

"What the hell was that," Kelsey says. One shoulder of her flower blouse is hanging down revealing her nude bra beneath and her neat appearance is following her emotions into dishevelment.

"I'm sorry Kelsey. You now have four minutes. Pack now," I try my best to exude calmness; The type of calmness that's been trained into me.

Like a tornado just touched down, the windows blow inwards as a deafening boom goes through the bones of the house and through mine. I'm knocked onto the floor as everything crashes down. Across the room, my obnoxious Victorian style dressers plummet to the ground shattering and sending splintered projectiles around the room. I cover my face as my belongings break around me and I try not to let myself break with them.

I wish I could move faster, but becoming frantic will not make me move any quicker. It will only serve to distract me. I repeat the words I heard drilled into me over and over again.

Breathing deeply, I brush the dust, glass, and debris off me. The drills I was hesitant of and dreaded are now coming in handy.

Kelsey moans next to me pulling my attention away from the chaos to the fact she still exists hopeless by my side.

I try to be a robot like I was told to, but I suddenly see myself in her place. I have no idea what's going on and just as I thought my friend had spiraled into madness my house is on the verge of demolition. I'm the most terrified I've ever been.

Thinking of her is giving me strength because knowing she'll get hurt is too much to bear.

I reach for her and instead of seeing a distraction I see my best friend.

"Go Kelsey," I nudge her and turn away.

I reach back for her, but she's at the door. She looks back and we run into each other hugging. I pull away to grab for the string on the attic door.

She leaves, but pauses at the doorway. "You're going crazy again Miranda. There's no way what you're saying has any validity."

"Just go!" I scream.

I throw duffle bag after duffle bag through the latch letting them fall to the floor as puffs of dust fly off them each representing the falling of different parts of my life I will never see again. I sneeze.

In the attic the duffle bags are stacked orderly next to the latch ready to go at a moments notice. I shove the final bag through the hole and climb down. I grab as many will fit in my hands. The bags pull my fingers so hard they turn white and go numb, but I don't let them give out.

I look at my watch and it's 12:03. Seven minutes since I got the call. Three minutes and I need to be out.

"Kelsey! You have two minutes!"

I'm dripping sweat as I run back and forth carrying, dragging, and lugging the last of the bags into my truck. I throw them in the bed of my truck under the windowless cover I installed preemptively for this moment.

My watch reads 12:05.

I'm going to run out of time. We're going to die and all this will have been in vain.

I hurtle back into the house, through the garage door, through the living room and into the kitchen. I know this will be my last time seeing my home, but I have no time to say goodbye. I drop to my knees in front of the sink, and although I don't have time for emotions I become vividly aware of how cold the tile is on my skin and how it will be the last time I'll feel it. The colors are more vivid and the textures are more prevalent and I notice the way my house smells and the places along the counter that have been touched more than others and the way the clocks in our house don't make a ticking sound. I slide my finger along a tiny crack we never fixed from a glass vase Kelsey dropped when we first moved in. I had the vase since I was a teenager, but we laughed. We laughed because we both escaped manipulative relationships. We were just happy to be together. Nobody was there to yell at us or belittle us. She grabbed some wine and opened the cabinets. We pulled out anything that reminded us of them and was breakable. We stepped over the the broken glass and went to our metal fire ring outside. We lit a fire and threw the mementos one by one into it. There was no rage any longer. We drank wine and laughed with joy at our newfound freedom.

  I yank the cabinet doors open and scatter junk onto the floor surrounding myself in a mess. I punch with the energy of a burning society trying not to die and the drywall in the back crumbles revealing a hidden compartment. Warm blood trickles down my arm as I reach in and pull out my dusty backpack. I wipe a few rat pellets off the top feeling lucky they didn't turn my pack into bedding.

  I make sure the revolver and the maps and water tablets and other gear I may need are inside.

  I run through the house unaware of any of the love and effort we put into it over the years. Everything in here that holds so many memories will be gone forever. An invisible rope snags me in my attempt to not acknowledge this other blow of pain. Everything I know will be gone. Everything Kelsey and I built as we were rebuilding ourselves will be gone. A photo of us on a boat smiles down at me. She picked me up from a random street and on a whim we stayed on an island for over a week. She just left her husband a week before that and when she picked me up, it was minutes after the last time I would be alone with mine. She saved me that day. I want to take it with us. We felt the most freedom we ever had that week. Before the knot in my throat bursts into tears the invisible rope lets me go.

  "Kelsey! We need to go NOW. I'm leaving in 10 seconds!"

  The engine roars to life and I press the garage button above me causing smoke and a dim orange light to pour in. It gives the appearance of a garage door opening and smoke billowing out from someone attempting suicide, but in reverse as our society is crumbling upon itself.

I feel a strange sense of relief at the thought of everything I know disappearing. It's not like I'm one of those that want to watch the world burn, but maybe one of those that want the hurricane to hit. What I want is to finally live up to my potential. I always knew there was some secret that would need my help eventually.

After we left those relationships I became more determined and Kelsey became peaceful.

"I'm coming!" Kelsey bursts through the door covered in bags just thrown together leaving a trail of sentimental items behind her.

"Throw them in the back and put that blanket over them. Hurry!"

"I'm trying Miranda! I'm not you. I can't move that fast," She huffs and looks at me in disbelief.

"This isn't me just being crazy. It's real! There's nobody to help us. We're on our own now. I just need you to listen to me without question."

"Yeah of course, you're always the boss." Kelsey looks at me like I'm a stranger and not her best friend she's known since she was six. She continues to follow me though.

I ignore her comment.

Smoke fills the truck as she opens the door. Kelsey's coughing and panicking and trying to do what I say, but she's a bumbling mess and wasting precious seconds. She slams the door and runs around the truck jiggling as she plops inside.

It wouldn't be fair to say I'm not also coughing and panicking, but I focus my energy on keeping her safe and making her listen so I don't run the risk of getting caught up in my own head. She can be mad at me for now, but I know what I'm doing.

The moment I hear her seatbelt click, I slam my truck into reverse and skid out of our home. I leave streaks on our drive way as I drift out. I'm letting myself panic. I can't do that.

I look at our home one last time. One long minute. The nice green yard with splatters of dandelion yellow is already turning into a hazy memory.

With a calming breath I drive off at a normal speed.

I don't want to attract too much attention, repeating another mantra I've been told at least a hundred times.

My stomach sinks deeper with each housing development we pass. Dogs are barking and parents are yelling and babies are crying. I will never see this suburban lifestyle again. It will cease to exist.

I want to tell Kelsey to pay attention to these moments, but I can't tell her what's going on. I'm already breaking a rule by bringing her with me.

The smoke's getting so thick I can almost feel the resistance against my truck, but I know it's my imagination. The heat is cooking us inside like helpless children in a cauldron. My entire world has a dark orange filter as the ash rains down heavier.

I keep the windows rolled up and turn off the vents.

"Reach under the middle back seat. Don't let any of your bags show under that blanket. Everything has to stay covered."

Kelsey reaches back with one hand straining to open it.

"I can't. It's too heavy with everything on top."

"Push your shit to the floor and jump back there if you need to. Do it now. Grab the two black bags on top," I say exasperated.

Kelsey clambers to the back pulling my hair with her.

"Ouch! Careful," I snap at her clumsiness. I take both hands off the wheel pulling my long hair into a ponytail. I nearly veer us into a ditch.

She finally gets the middle seat open and grabs the black bags. She looks at three small oxygen tanks that are hidden beneath them. She inhales sharply and moves even slower. It looks as if she turned into a soft white statue.

"Kelsey!" I yell.

She throws herself back into the front breathing hard as the color is leaving her face. She opens the bags and pulls out two N95 respirators.

"Be ready to put yours on and help me with mine. I can't take my eyes away from the road or my hands off the wheel again. The traffic is getting busier and we don't know who could be watching."

"You must be able to hear yourself right now," She doesn't sound condescending or mean or harsh. She's genuinely concerned for me.

We turn out of the neighborhood and drive through the outskirts of the city.

"We need to go faster," I say under my breath.

"Then why don't you drive faster?"

"I can't," I speak up. "We need to blend in. Whatever is going on around us we need to do as well. We need to get away from the city center."

The buildings are getting smaller and fewer in between as we drive further from the city.

They always said to get out of the city, but besides a superficial vacation here and there I never listened and nobody else does either. It takes disaster to knock us out of our humdrum life of consistency, patterns, and boredom. Now I don't have a choice.

Another thundering boom comes from the city center. The truck lurches forward slightly or that could be my imagination again. I press the gas going faster than I should be.

"I can only remain so calm. Remember breathe. Just breathe. You can do this. Don't be so helpless. You aren't weak. You know how to breathe. Don't be so helpless," I say barely audible.

"What?" Kelsey asks.

"Don't worry about it."

Empty cars are pulled over sporadically. They're surrounded by people who stare into the area I'm trying to separate myself from as fast and as calm as possible. They look like a movie set standing the exact same way with one hand holding their shirt over their noses and another hand over their eyes even though the sun isn't shining, but the smoke is stinging and they're only following what muscle memory tells them to do when our eyes hurt.

A mother falls into a coughing fit pulling her son down with her as she grips his little fingers cutting the circulation off.

A young teen screams at her phone for whoever she's trying to call to "Answer already!"

The smoke from the fires thickens. The heat is becoming unbearable.

3

"Kelsey," I try to say calmly, "I'm going to talk things through to myself like I do when I need to sort my thoughts."

"Why don't you talk to me. You know you can always do that," she cares so much for me.

"The only thing you need to know right now is that I've got you."

She rolls her eyes, but then glances at me with worry.

We've been on the road for hours now. At Los Alamos, we take the 135 connecting the 1 so we don't drive through the heart of Santa Victoria.

"More people escaped than I thought. Well, I don't know if they're escaping or just traveling to another city and/or trying to get to family. I have to keep an eye out for The Nothings and hidden stops. I know where they'll be on the highway. At least I think so. They could be anyone. They could be the car behind us right now."

"You sure you don't want to organize your thoughts with me?" Kelsey asks as if I need help untangling my own head.

"I'm fine. You'll see. Stop doubting me."

Heading north I drive a large circle around Santa Victoria. I pass a neighborhood where everyone in the whole place seems to have gathered at the church. The priest is yelling about Revelation.

I pass through a town where nothing out of the usual go to work, fill on gas, go to a shopping mall type of life is happening.

With only social media to go off of, people don't know what to feel. Their listening to the reactions of a few resulting in entire towns having similar outlooks. The reality of what's happening obviously hasn't settled in yet. Anywhere.

Mostly we pass a lot of fields.

How would they know? I wasn't even told everything. That's bothered me, but I don't have the time to dwell on it right now because I'm too busy listening to orders without the whole story. I feel slightly like a pawn right now, but mostly I feel honored to know anything at all. I only wanted to feel like I was a part of something important and bigger than what everyone else was doing. I feel important. I was chosen to be a part of this. I'd probably already be dead if I didn't receive that phone call.

"Are we in Santa Victoria?" Kelsey mutters.

"We're in Guadalupe. Big cities and military bases are an absolute no. We can't be too careful."

"Are you sure you're okay?"

"Yeah, stop implying that I'm not. We're going to make it."

Off in the distant east there's an orange glow that turns into a deep and ominous red as I am directly west of Santa Victoria. Unfortunately, I predicted correctly. That area is gone.

For a second I hear the agonizing screams from the east, but I'm miles away from those fires so I know that's in my head. I smack the side of my head trying to shake the sounds out, but they stay put somewhere in the back of my brain where nightmares live.

Kelsey reaches over for the wiper fluid to clear away the ash raining down again, but the last drops sputter out.

The hours feel like minutes and the minutes feel like days. I keep driving through the changing colors and the changing air quality.

Kelsey's laying against the window wide eyed. She hasn't pestered me with many questions since we left. Usually I can't get her to shut up, but right now I yearn for her gentle and curious voice. She stares out the window.

It can't be comfortable with her respirator pushing into the glass and pressing into her face like that, but she doesn't move. I figured it's better we wear them right now so we don't get any permanent damage from the smoke and ash and besides there's not many people out right now to see us. I wish we could snuggle and watch TV. The world needs me though.

I turn my eyes back to the emptying road ahead as I drive further from the city. The sound of my breath going through the filters of my mask are nearly as loud as the chaos in the cities during this silent part of the drive. The condensation building up inside my mask tastes salty.

A sign tells me there's a town ahead.

"Kelsey," I reach for her leg. "We're going to pull over for gas. I don't want to pull from our gas reserve until we're forced to."

I exit into the little town. The air's only a light yellowish-orange here. The air quality's much better. There's no ash snowing on the hood of my truck and even better, there's no embers floating like dandelion seeds in the breeze to start another massive burn.

"We have more time to travel than I thought Kelsey," I say as if she knew the itinerary. The extra time gives me hope we'll make it. I lick the salty condensation away from my mouth as I take the suffocating mask off.

"Go ahead and take yours off."

Kelsey lets the moisture sit there as she stares ahead. She doesn't seem to believe me, but at least she's listening.

"Stick these under your bags under the blankets," I hand her my mask.

The gas station is straight ahead and the pumps seem to be deserted yet there are cars everywhere in town. The larger restaurants and shopping centers downtown we pass have packed parking lots full of people standing outside as if waiting for an eclipse. They're waiting for the media to tell them what to do.

"Why are they standing around?" Kelsey asks with a scratchy voice.

"They're waiting for someone to tell them what's happening."

"Shouldn't we be doing that?" She glances at me. The stress of the last few hours has made it look like she hasn't slept for days judging by the bags under her eyes and her slow, tired movements.

"I know what's happening. Just trust me."

It's probably my mood she's picking up on and I feel even worse for keeping secrets.

A deep rumble vibrates low in the Earth.

"Another explosion. They're getting bigger and stretching further out."

"But you know what's happening?" She doesn't believe me.

"Yes. Stop asking so many questions. I need to focus right now." I reach over and rub her back, but I don't feel her soften beneath the weight of my hand like normal and it breaks my heart to see her this upset. At least I can take her into safety with me and out of the fire zone.

I worry at the repercussions that may happen from bringing an unknown into the Haven, but I couldn't leave her behind.

In front of the dingy, small town gas station a group of men are looking suspiciously plain in sunglasses while talking too normally. They look as obvious as under cover cops in cargo shorts.

If it weren't for my hyper vigilance right now I wouldn't have noticed them. They blend in almost too well or maybe it's paranoia.

"Miranda."

"Yeah?"

"Those men are staring at us."

So they are suspicious.

Barely moving my lips I say, "Don't look back at them. Don't look to the back of the truck and just hope to God everything's covered.

[pause]

If anyone asks we're on our way to San Francisco to our parents to stay with them."

As normal as possible I slide out of the truck. My knees nearly give out from the constant clenching. I close the door behind me, swipe my credit card, and start pumping. I go through the steps of pumping gas in my head so I can perform them naturally now that people are watching.

I know how to pump gas, I've done it a thousand times, but when's the last time I thought about what I was doing. I wished I paid more attention to this mindless task because now that I have to do it normally it's so hard.

There's a small parking lot out front with litter instead of leaves. A fast food bag rests on the tiny grassy area where nobody cleans up after their dogs. The gas station itself couldn't look more boring. I'm at the last pump.

"HEY!"

I ignore the call. I don't have the energy to talk to anybody. Mostly I don't want to interact with members of The Nothings. If they are them.

"HEY!" The one woman out of the group yells at me.

I try to pretend I don't hear.

"Hey! Miss, are you from around here?" She jogs towards me. The men keep us in their periphery like men at the beach who pretend they're not staring.

"Hi," I force a smile, "I'm not. My sister and I were on our way to our parent's house in San Francisco. We've been camping out on the coast for the last week. Crazy weather right? Is there a wildfire or something in the distance?"

"Uh … yeah … weird weather today." Her demeanor screams suspicion as she inches closer to the truck. She pulls her sunglasses down to see into me better. She walks around and stretches her neck to look inside. She hones in on Kelsey inside the truck and leans against the window breaking every social rule of distance.

"What do you think this weird weather's from? It's so orange and smokey. Must be a fire in the distance. Do you know anything?" The lady asks.

I'm hoping Kelsey's freaked out melancholy can be pushed aside and she can appear normal.

Kelsey shakes her head and gives her a smile, "Oh hello," she reaches for the driver's side door and rolls the window down manually. "Sorry, I was just day dreaming. We've been camping all week and I can't wait to get back home."

"What do you think of this color? Maybe a nearby wildfire like your... sister guesses?"

"No clue. You?" Kelsey puts on her innocent expression she wears so well. She looks normal enough. Her face is pale and puffy, but she's fine.

The pump has to be the slowest pump I've ever used as my tank is only half full.

The lady leans her body between me and the truck peaking into the back committing an absolute crime of social norms, but I feel compelled to let her. A gold necklace around her neck with a cross and a tree charm dangle from her neck. When she turns back around with her dark sunglasses back on and hands on her hips I notice the outline of a pistol.

"What's with all the blankets?" She asks. Her fingers twitch near the butt of her gun. If she's trying to be discrete she's failing miserably.

"Why are you asking so many questions?" I chuckle. "At least take me on a date first," I stupidly chuckle some more.

That was a dumb thing to say.

"Those ocean breezes are cold. Obviously." More laughs. "We throw them on top of our camping gear so we can just grab them if we get cold on the drive. I usually like to drive with my windows down, but this smoky haze is forcing me to keep them up. Anyways, we have to get going, our parents are expecting us. Nice to meet you."

I over explain and blabber like I always do when I get nervous. I'm about to start explaining my explaining, but Kelsey's cough breaks me out of it.

4

My body looks calm and as normal as any person on any day, but my heart's beating a mile a minute.

"I think we should try the interstate. It'll be slower, but I believe those people are..." I begin.

"You believe those people are what?" Kelsey stares me down.

"Let's just say there are different . . . umm . . . check points you could say that we want to avoid right now."

"Please Miranda, what's going on? You're scaring me," She begs. "You're not even trying to be believable this time."

"It's not like I could get away with lying to you anyways. We'll take Highway 1 the rest of the way. When we get close to San Luis Obispo I'm going to take a detour. It's a smaller town, but it's better to be as safe as possible," I say more to myself as I think aloud.

I drive through the town's downtown watching everyone congregating outside along the sidewalks like waiting for a church to open. There's no smiles here. It appears as if people are on the verge of running off, but they're glued to their city as their ignorance doesn't allow an answer on where to run to. I watch a group fixated on their phones then look up with panic. Then they go back to scrolling frantically.

We merge onto the highway. Luckily the traffic has thinned out since the last time I tried the road earlier today.

"I believe most people will head east, but who knows? Will people try to stay where they are or wait for someone else to take charge? Will people drive to the country? How many will actually get out. What will the death count be? I can't believe the time is finally here." I say under my breath working through my thoughts. I'm getting lost in my head.

"You look a million miles away Miranda," Kelsey says half questioning.

"I keep asking myself questions I can't answer. I just need to focus on what's happening right now. If you see me this distracted pull me out of it again, Okay? It's not helping me anymore," I turn my attention back to the road trying not to think of anything else, but moving forwards.

"It never helps you."

"Don't critique the way I think right now."

"I'll help you," She sounds relieved to have anything to do to help.

Although the air around us is still orange, it isn't as deep a red and the smoke isn't as thick as it was. We don't bother putting our masks back on. It's best to avoid stares or possible groups of The Nothings looking at us. I slow down adjusting my speed to fit into the flow of traffic.

A couple hours later the 1 and the 101 join up together, but before we get to San Luis Obispo we drive northwest along the Los Osos Valley Road. Signs of civilization pitter out. Fields stretch out for miles. Finally the traffic is gone. Hardly anyone is out.

The silence makes itself too known. It pulls down on me like a chain.

Just as soon as the weight came it lifts when I see a vulture swoop in front of the road. I return my attention to navigation and roll the windows down. I don't see any ash or smoke. The air's clean here.

I'm in some vortex. The fields and hills fly past me in never ending patterns of greens and browns. The road floats under me in colors of tan and the sky above flies past with colors of light blue and white streaks. It all morphs together. Occasionally I feel distant tremors that take me out of the spell of the vortex. Within no time, the tremors become a part of the ride I'm on.

"Why did we lie to that lady?," Kelsey asks breaking the silent void.

"I promise I'll explain everything once we're there. We only have a couple more hours to go."

"Please just tell me something," Kelsey pleads with her helpless doe eyes and I nearly start talking.

"If anyone talks to us we're on our way to San Francisco. I guess with the orange skies, there must be some wildfires we haven't heard about. We aren't worried. Only if we're asked, everything in this truck is camping gear. It'll be obvious it isn't if the wrong someone were to see what's inside so keep everything covered. Better yet, no one will notice we have bags with us."

"Are we going to be okay?"

"I believe so," I let out a long slow breath bumping along the dirt road watching grass and barns fly by in that steady vortex pattern. "There's been an organization for many years now with goals that aren't completely understood by anyone I know. Not even the people within my group know. There's a high possibility we would be stuck somewhere along the road to where we're going if we didn't leave the minute we did."

"This sounds delusional." Kelsey doesn't sound accusatory or irritated. Her voice is sweet and when I glance at her I see her eyes have a thin teary film over them.

I turn my attention back to the road. Last thing I want to do is crash into a deer when we're this close to safety. I know she wants to ask more questions, but she doesn't. Her forehead's going to have permanent worry lines in another hour if she doesn't relax.

Kelsey watches the cows. Usually she's one of those that gets excited every single time she spots a cow, but now they might as well be gas pumps. Every blade of grass brings her further away from the life she knew.

"Thank you," She says so softly I don't know if she muttered it or if it was my hopeful imagination.

I grip the wheel harder preparing myself for anything that could be hidden on this road.

5

The open fields are turning into houses and driveways.

"Miranda," Kelsey turns around. She's been sitting with her knees folded against her chest. She must have lost circulation by now.

"Where are we going? What's going on?" She asks.

"We're so close. We're in a little town; Morro Bay."

More houses and restaurants and gas stations reveal themselves as we drive further into town. The Pacific Ocean is glittering blue to the left of us.

"It'll be a straight shot once we get onto the 1."

"They made a roadblock! They found us!"

I slam the brakes and skid across the road.

"It's a line of cars waiting for the gas pump," Kelsey says.

Cars are zooming in and out of a grocery store ahead so I drive around the long line and head for it.

"Why are we pulling in? I thought you said we have to go or we'll die?" Kelsey still doesn't believe me. She seems more worried about me than by the world around her ending.

"It'd be suspicious if we keep driving when every other car is getting supplies. We have to blend in." I ignore her tone. "Not just news of the explosions, but how many places are burning must have reached the internet." Even with prior knowledge I'm shocked by the unfolding chaos.

The cars are parked double and triple on the side of the road. People are yelling at each other and driving into cars to push them out of the way screeching and denting other vehicles. It's difficult to navigate.

I was told this would happen, but I didn't expect it to look like this. Reality's always a hundred times more intense than the worst things you can imagine solely because they're real.

A bag of flour smashes against my windshield as I pull into the parking lot and a lady screams at a car that narrowly avoids crashing into us. I try the windshield fluid, but it's empty. The screaming lady gets in her car and drives over the grass medium. I stick my head out the window to see and enter the crazed lot.

"Listen to me," I grab Kelsey's shoulders once I'm parked in front of the grocery store. "I need to go inside to help us blend in. Someone could've been following us. And maybe I'll get some information on how much the public knows at this point. I don't know who's watching. Guard this truck. Do.

Not. Let. Anyone open these doors. Go on your phone, but don't use the internet. In fact turn your phone on air plane mode. Look as if you're scrolling. Look terrified. No matter what you do, don't glance at anything on the internet. Don't send a text or make a phone call. Don't answer any phone calls."

I put my phone on airplane mode.

"This is life or death. Please listen to me."

"Yeah, okay."

"A gun's in the glove compartment. Don't take it out, unless someone's breaking the window. I'll see you soon. Did you hear that? Don't take it out unless someone is physically breaking in."

Kelsey's eyes spring open like an owls. She's never left the cities of California and is terrified of any weapons because of that.

"Kelsey do you understand?" I squeeze her. I'm inches from her face pleading with her. I feel desperate.

"Yes," She stutters.

She at least believes something terrible's going on.

I step into the chaos. Everyone's running between cars with carts full of food and others carrying as much as their arms will allow them. Most are carrying more than they can and cans of this and packages of that are filling the parking lot as they spill out of people's arms. It's almost comical the way the food's flying around. It's like I'm in a cartoon. Carts are strewn across the parking lot not too dissimilar than the cars. A mother's dragging her children with one arm and pushing an overflowing cart with the other. A lady in a bleach stained shirt runs in front of me. Her hair's in a plastic bag and the bleach smell burns my eyes. A couple in bathing suits run out of the store with beach bags full of food. I expect a director to call "Cut!" any second.

"Let's go," a guy ushers his crying wife inside an electric car. They won't be able to charge it soon.

This doesn't seem real.

Every bit of my body wants to run in a different direction and my mind's trying its best to keep up, but I need to be focused and calm.

My mind may need to be focused and calm, but I need to appear as panicked as everyone else. That's what I was told to do. I got this. Blend in. Get information. Listen to your surroundings. Look panicked. Be calm.

"Wait! Don't leave me alone. Let me go with you!" Kelsey yells out.

"I need you to stay with the truck. Just blend in. I have to go."

"Miranda!"

I keep walking.

"The end is here lady," a man in a dirty cloak with a backpack full of food tells me. He grabs my arm with his fingerless gloved hand, "The end of times. God's coming back."

Two carts knock into each other, but they don't acknowledge each either. They continue running with their carts.

A person in a black hoodie is spray painting the front of the grocery store. White paint drips down posters for tomatoes and pineapples. It reads OrDer ThroUGh ChA...

I step inside before they're finished. Nobody's at the cash registers. I stub my toe on a can of green beans and stumble around spilled cereal as I enter the chaos. At least there's no violence yet. People are running in different directions. I run to the cold section knowing there'll be food.

It doesn't matter what I get as long as I blend in, in case anyone is following us.

I grab steaks and beef and chicken wings and pork chops. This section's full of food and empty of people. They're running past with cans, boxes, water, and strangely a lot of toilet paper. I run towards the exit. When I get to the front I realize I should grab water as well. Who panics and only grabs cold meat?

God damnit Miranda, blend in. You're smarter than this. You came in here so no one would follow you when you pass the grocery store. Don't be obvious now. Don't be a fucking idiot.

I run down the aisles looking for water. On the third aisle I see it and bolt into the circus that's the largest crowd. I'm trying to figure out how to make my move so I can get out of here. People are shoving each other in this mass that doesn't resemble humanity anymore. Just chaos. There's no order, but patterns emerge as the stronger and more desperate are able to get what they need.

"I have five children at home!" A lady yells at a man in a business suit.

"Fuck your children!" He pushes her aside. Hard.

She kicks the back of his knee knocking him into other people who are trying to fit as much water as they can in their arms. People have left their carts to grab water, but others are coming in behind them and swooping their carts away. The man falls to the ground as the people push him. A person runs behind me and straight into the crowd of people stepping on the back of the man as he struggles to get his hands beneath him. It's a scene you only see on the news, but it's happening right in front me. Another person steps on his hand and he lets out a startled scream as he struggles to stand, but everyone's out for themselves and his cries are muffled by their panic. The woman jumps out of the crowd with three large packages of water bottles. She looks back at the crowd and then to the floor where she sees the man she kicked. He tries to get up, but people continue to trample him.

She turns to go back and help as he makes eye contact with her and he screams "Help me, you dumb bitch!" but she darts off bumping my shoulder on her way out.

"He wouldn't let me get water. I have kids," She tells me hanging on to the last bit of humanity as she tries to explain herself to a random stranger. As if I could give her permission to leave a man to die.

I look to my right where those cheap gallon juices are. Those are mostly water. I hug the meat to my chest and hook my hand into a couple of them and run out.

I didn't help the man, but he wasn't a good person to begin with. It's not like these people will live much longer anyways. I have to think about the greater good.

His screams are gargled, "Please, my mother's waiting in the car." A big woman steps on his back to get to the higher shelf. He can't say anything. She leaps off and barely audible he says, "She can't take care of herself."

I look down at him. He's dying. He wouldn't let that Mother get water though. I need to help him.

I start back, but everyone in the store's running towards the water. I'm pushed into the shelves by a girl in a bikini. I can't see him anymore.

I go in anyways. I try to push my way in, but I fall to the ground. Someone trips over me. I'm going to end up like that guy if I don't get out. I lunge out of the crowd and run the hell out of there.

I hurry back to the truck while people are running past me in all directions. My breath comes easier in the open space. At least people haven't started yanking supplies from each other out here because they don't know what it looks like inside yet. The people coming out feel like they're home free.

A man in a white button up and a black tie is talking to Kelsey. I nearly drop everything to run over.

I'm barely able to hold everything in my arms. Once I'm close enough I yell, "Hey! I got the only food left and some water! Everyone appears to be heading east so let's go!" I scream my words hoping to startle the man away from the truck.

The stranger turns to me with greedy eyes, but he says nothing. I keep walking until I'm face to face with him like he isn't a caricature of menace.

"Where are you going?! Oh God, I don't know what's going on. The food's almost gone. Everyone's going east. Are you going east? Do you know what's going on? Oh my God, we have to go," I open her door and throw the food on her lap pushing the man aside as I make sure her door's locked. I rush to the driver's side.

An old women with a hunched back walks by with glazed eyes muttering about when her son will be back.

The man walks away as if he were going to work while talking on the phone. It's mostly hidden, but I can see the top outline of a pistol in his waistband.

I throw the truck in reverse and then drive, but I'm forced to slam on the breaks throwing Kelsey into the dash.

"What the hell? Do you want to die?!" I scream at the man blocking our way. It's the fingerless glove guy. "Kelsey put your fucking seatbelt on."

He says something, but I can't make it out.

"Move!"

He doesn't move. He continues to speak.

I back up a little to drive around him.

I'm fixated on him as I drive slowly past. He pulls his pack of food off and carefully pulls a small stone tree souvenir type toy out of his backpack. He holds it towards us, but not like he's giving us something, but like he's presenting something holy to be admired.

I head for highway 1.

"Go ahead and throw those groceries in the back," I tell Kelsey.

"Who was that man? He kept asking me questions and wouldn't go away," She asks.

"The one dressed in the black tie?" I forget about the gloved man switching my attention to this potential danger. "What did he ask you?"

"I don't know. A lot."

"Think Kelsey, think. What was he asking?" I'm on the edge of my seat brushing the steering wheel with my chest. I'm going to burst.

"I umm…" She fiddles with her fingers and looks out the window.

"Kelsey come on. You can do more than look out the window."

"That's not fair."

"I'm sorry. I just need you to think."

"He was asking where we were headed. Who we were going to. Some other things. I don't know," She grows exasperated. "He asked if I knew about OTB or was it OTC? I don't know."

"OTC. He asked you about OTC?" My voice rises in volume, but I can't help it.

"Yeah, I think so."

"Oh God. No."

Kelsey looks out the back window. "Is he following us?"

6

The Pacific Ocean has been on our left since we left Morro Bay. The land went from rolling green hills with seal covered beaches to tight mountain roads hanging on to the side of cliffs. We slowly climb higher and higher in elevation. Fields of cows and seagulls fly by the windows. For a moment I saw zebras far off in a field. I need some sleep.

We passed a few stores where a bunch of people were milling around. None of them looked panicked. Then the road got twistier and more dangerous. We inched along. Some turns were fine, but others were nearly 180 degrees and ridiculously tight. It didn't help my fear of heights.

The grasslands and pines turn to redwood gulches and mountains.

We drive for another hour in silence.

"Kelsey! They have a gas station!" I pound the steering wheel.

Kelsey jumps, frightened at the sudden loud noise.

"Didn't mean to startle you. Anyways, I know we'e almost there, but let's fill up." I smack the steering wheel with excitement.

I feel lighter and almost completely safe. I know the road we need's down the way and there's nobody else around. I don't think I've ever felt this relieved. As long as nothing stops us from here on out.

I pull into a tiny little neighborhood/shopping area called Pacific Valley. Actually, I would call it a group of homes. There's only a couple little shops and some raggedy signs advertising Jade.

"Do you see how expensive the gas is?! Jesus fuck," I yell to no one in particular. "Oh wait. It doesn't matter. It doesn't matter how much it'll be. If normalcy comes back remind me never to come here for gas," I try to make a joke, but I fail miserably in my hurrying state. My laugh comes out as a ragged and forced cough.

Nobody's outside. Curtains are drawn and the doors are closed to the little shops.

A curtain moves, but it's snatched shut again.

"We need to get out of here. That could be anybody," I nod at the window and clench the steering wheel until my nuckles turn white.

I pull back onto the road thankful to be away from the traffic.

"Where are we going?," Kelsey whines. She rotates her wedding ring. I threw mine off a boat when we went on a tour of The Channel Islands. We were supposed to throw them off together.

"Actually this is our turn," I pull onto a dirt road.

We travel for another hour on this bumpy and sandy road. The trees and bushes are tan from drivers kicking up dust. The road must've been graded recently because it isn't terrible like I was warned it could be. I never had to use four wheel drive until the end.

We drove through hills and mountains and valleys. The roads with massive steep drop offs weren't my favorite, but I pushed forward even when I felt like I wanted to puke. And when puke did come, I swallowed it. I looked out my window and saw deep gorges filled with redwoods a thousand feet down. I snapped my eyes back to the road and concentrated on driving and not the fact that at any moment we could tip over if I moved a hair to the edge. The edge didn't have barriers. It was ready for me to fall into. My stomach squeezed every time I glanced over.

I turn right down another dirt road pass tall pine trees and then take a left along a ridge where I can see the ocean in the distance. We're high above the ocean. It's glittering in the sunlight and a huge bird flys over head, I'm scared shitless of falling off right now so the beauty is only background.

I take a few more turns and I believe I'm at the spot.

I stop the truck in a field of grass. I pull my map out of my wallet and look it over. I followed the turns exactly. This has to be it.

"Where's everyone? Where's anything?"

I step into the clean air and take a deep clean breath in. There's no smoke. I look back down at my map and then fall to the ground accepting this must be the place. I let the juicy grass kiss my body and the dirt cushion my sore muscles as I let the biggest breath of air out. We're high on a mountain top vulnerable in the open, but safely inside the middle of nowhere.

The sound of a UTV rumbles over the hills like a warning call on the mountain. The foreign sound in this majestic landscape startles me and I jump squinting into the distance. The driver peaks over the hill, but all I can see are semi automatics slung over his back and dark sunglasses.

"Please tell me they didn't find the Haven."

Chapter 2

1

Before I can make out who's on it, a man yells, "Miranda you made it! Fuck me sideways, this shit's wild!" Within seconds he's next to us. He flies out in a blur of flannel and tackles me into the truck. "Damnit Miranda we made it! Almost everyone's already here. We're going to be okay!"

He grabs my hips and yanks me into the tightest hug. I resist for a second, as I haven't been able to fully breathe for more than a minute since that call and this feeling of normalcy shocks my system. I feel I still need to run further. He keeps squeezing until I finally let myself melt into his chest. It feels so nice. I smell the sea breeze, bay leaves, and redwood forests on him. He's grinning like a wild man; a really cute one.

How can I not smile while looking at his huge, handsome grin?

We made it.

"Cody, I'm so happy to see you." I look at his dimpled smile and fall back into his arms pressing my face into his sweet smelling scrubby neck. He's so warm and I feel cocooned in his arms.

The passenger side door closes and he jerks violently.

"Who the fuck's that Miranda?"

"I'm sorry, I know we weren't supposed to bring anyone else, but she's my best friend and she's my roommate so she was right there when I got the call. You know how important she is to me. We've talked about this."

"I wouldn't say we talked," his grin turns to stone.

Kelsey walks with lead in her shoes, her eyes glued to the gentle grass blowing in the breeze. She leans against the hood kicking her feet in the dirt.

"You've got to be fucking kidding me babe?" Cody looks into my eyes. "Ah Jesus Christ you aren't."

He slumps his shoulders and turns to her.

"You must be Kelsey."

Kelsey avoids his glare.

"Well, fucking A you're already here so bring it in." Cody shrugs and opens his arms wide. With hesitation she comes over and when I step in we fully embrace each other. For a minute it feels like introducing a friend to your family in normal circumstances. I feel Kelsey let go of some of the tension and her breathing nearly returns to normal. The tall grasses brush my thighs. I can feel the mountain air blowing across my skin and swirling through our hug. The birds are singing and the butterflies and bees are hard at work. It's unrealistically picturesque.

"You weren't being crazy Miranda," Kelsey pulls away.

"Did you tell her something?" His usual joyful voice has an edge to it.

"I didn't. Just that I knew what was happening."

As with any major traumatic event, does one ever feel like it's real? At what point will this be implanted in my brain as something that's actually happening. It feels like we're going to go on a merry hike and meet up for lunch the next day, but instead I'm hours away from any town. Away from our home. I know it's happening and I've been told it'd happen hundreds of times, but knowing isn't believing.

"Alright ladies, let's get this shit show going. Park your truck in that oak forest. We're way too exposed. It'll give coverage from anything that might be looking down. I'll meet ya cuties over there."

I turn in a circle looking across the mountain top. We're high on a ridge with open skies without a single cloud in sight. Running water gurgles and splashes just out of view in the canyon below the trees.

Cody practically skips away. He's full of jittery energy. It's comforting to see him as his usual self.

Kelsey and I look at each other acknowledging there's no going back now. I know she has a million questions.

2

A jumble of other cars are parked under the oak trees. We know we won't be leaving anytime soon so we don't need to worry about blocking each other in.

The oak tree's branches climb down to the ground so low I can reach the acorns. They look like giant ancient bonsai trees. It's beautiful and mysterious. Some of the branches are barely hanging on ready to return to the soil once again.

"Let's fucking go ladies!" Cody pulls up speeding and laughing.

I walk happily over caught in his gaze.

"You're everything this movement needed," Cody says.

I feel like I'm on a mission and everything's going right. We're winning the quest. All we have to do is do what we're told and follow our assignments and the game will be over and everything will go back to normal. And the normal will be far better than ever before.

We haul our belongings into the UTV. I leave the survival gear in the truck knowing I won't need it down below. I also want my truck to be ready just in case. I wish I could move my truck so it won't get blocked in, but I can feel without asking that's not an option.

"Fuck me, that's all that'll fit. I'll be right back," Cody drives away dangerously fast flying over unseen bumps.

"Miranda?" Kelsey asks.

"Yeah?" I almost feel calm again.

"Are we safe here?"

"Yes," I grab her hands watching the terror and emptiness in her eyes float away into something harder and more determined.

"Will you please tell me what's happening?" She may not look as lost, but tears are waiting for the cue to jump out. "The obvious of what I know is I'm not supposed to be here."

"I know you just want to know what's going on, but I just can't yet. Like Cody said earlier I wasn't supposed to bring you with me. I have to talk to some people first."

Kelsey steps closer, "Thank you. Seriously, thank you. I'm so scared. I feel like I'm going to hurl. I thought at any moment all day I would just lie down and wait for the news to tell me it's all okay and you're just crazy, but here I am still standing and something terrible is actually going on."

"I can guarantee you I'm just as terrified. The only difference is I was expecting this. Not as soon as it happened, but I did. I had training. I had information given to me. I was so scared coming out here I felt like even my toes and fingers wanted to scream and run away, like getting hypothermia, but for terror. I wanted to dissolve away into the driver's seat never to come out again, but then I didn't really believe all this so that made going easier. And having you with me."

"Oh that makes me feel a lot better Miranda. Also why didn't you tell me you had a boyfriend?"

Cody's UTV echos above the canyon rumbling the air around us.

"The mountains play tricks on my hearing. It sounds like it's coming from several places at once," Kelsey says.

"Whooooo!" He yells as he jumps out and grabs the rest of our bags.

I climb in beside him and he yanks me closer making me giggle. Kelsey gets in the back with the rest of our bags. Cody finally drove gently as he slowly weaved through the trees.

If only the trees could talk.

We descended in elevation until the oak grove gave way and we were in a sage brush clearing where a road was cut. We drove through it soaking up the bright yellow sun.

"The sky isn't obscured out here," I gesture to the sun, "There's no more ash."

"I can only imagine, love. I've been out in these God damn beautiful mountains for a while now. Were the fires bad?"

"I'll tell you later." He grabs for my thigh and I weave my fingers through his hand.

We continue driving until a steep redwood forest comes into view. A road has been dug out of the side.

"This fuckin' mountain. Ain't it somethin' ladies?"

"It's beautiful," Kelsey says from the back staring at the massive redwood trees. She's wearing the first smile I've seen since she walked into our kitchen in Santa Barbra a million years ago or this morning.

"Not as beautiful as you Kelsey dear! Or especially Miranda here. Did y'all know this road was for miners?" Cody informs us. "There was gold in these creeks. Before them, the Indians were here. They altered the land to make it easier to live in. There were also loggers later on and even later the hippies from the 60s came through. A real famous one with a huge colorful bus and loud speakers rolled around and shook the world. Now it's us. We're the next big thing to happen. There's history here. There's some God damn magical energy here. It's ready for some fuckin' change and we'll give it what it wants. And we'll all be a part of it. Whoo-wee!"

Cody stops in front of a rock outcropping inside a redwood gorge where a creek flows and we're surrounded by bright green clovers. A small waterfall falls above and to the side of us crashing down with the forces of nature delicately in balance. It sprays me with a cool mist and the hot sun is blocked from the towering redwoods. Cody grins boyishly and jumps out leaving the UTV idling. He moves dead tree limbs and dead sage brush over revealing an empty space where the rocks overhang. I can't see anything inside. It's in shadows. He walks through little trickles of water as the beautiful waterfall flows to the side.

It feels like even the waterfall's alive here and acknowledges us. Everything feels like it has eyes. There's a feeling of intelligence in the land and I feel like I'm a stranger who doesn't belong.

I can't hear his footsteps as the water drowns it out.

A long slow scraping sound emanates from the dark abyss ahead. He bounces back into the light.

We drive into the overhang and we're immediately engulfed in darkness and humidity. Sound is different here. I can hear his footsteps clearly now as he jumps out and walks back to the entrance. A long echo hums with each step. I hear the gentle rustles of sticks and leaves as he puts the vegetation back where it was. I'm in an amphitheater where the music is the branches getting dragged across the floor and the echoing calls for an encore. Then that long slow scraping sound I heard earlier reveals itself to be a massive rock door. I have to cover my ears it's so loud.

If I thought it was dark before, I was wrong.

I can't see, but I hear him pounce into the driver's seat.

He pops the lights on and off we go through a long limestone corridor.

We drove for a good while until we reached a huge cavern full of lights. It's hard to determine speed when I can't see much, but the ride felt long. I have no inclination how far down we are.

I've heard of this shelter before, but I've never seen it and I can't help feeling scared after going through the damp, dark air. I know this means I'm safe, but there's something real unnerving about being so far away from the surface where life thrives versus this lifeless hollow.

The lights are abnormally bright in this giant 'room' it blinds me at first erupting my senses further.

People are talking, laughing, crying, and moving around in this huge, almost perfectly round, cavernous room. More hallways spiderweb away from the center. He parks the UTV against the wall in line with a couple other identical ones just inside the tunnel.

Couches and tables and rugs fill the room. There's what looks like a cafeteria built into the circular wall. I suddenly remember food's still a thing and realize I haven't ate and my stomach's in pain.

The ceiling rises forever except for this gigantic stalactite hanging from the center. It's like a geological chandelier. The same darkness I see when I look into that tunnel is in the ceiling.

Vertigo flushes over me as the distance up top is masked in blackness and the realization of just how deep in the earth I might be, floods over me making it difficult to breathe under the weight of it all.

If it weren't for the walls being made of limestone and the cave formations it would be a regular large gathering space in any building. Also, if it weren't for the occasional person crying. And that earthy wet smell.

I'm still sitting in the UTV taking the wildness in.

I had discussed this place and knew about it, but seeing it was something else. Feeling the stale cold air you can only feel when deep underground makes me feel like I'm on another planet. It's a different world down here. That smell that resembles nothing on the surface yet breathes of some life and also nothing but million year old water dripping on stone fills my nostrils. It's damp, but no longer humid. The air isn't musty or old, but it isn't the fresh air I'm used to, and yet it still smells clean, an ancient clean that holds secrets no one's supposed to find out.

I feel as if I was transported into another realm where an ancient society had once dwelled and this is their temple and here I am trespassing. It's hard to believe this was created by the Earth.

"It's beautiful," I say astonished.

"You're damn right it is!" Cody grabs my shoulder with his huge hand pulling me in squeezing all the worries away and planting a big wet, sloppy kiss on my cheek. "You know, you're so beautiful even standing under this weird ass lighting." The blindingly bright LED lighting scares the darkness away into the ceiling and tunnel.

I squeal delightfully in his rough embrace.

"Let's get some food in y'all's tummies. It'll only be a tiny snack since the kitchen's trying to get dinner ready. Then I'll show you to our room Miranda." He turns to Kelsey, "It wasn't easy, but I was able to string together two attached bedrooms when I came here with the bags so you can stay close to us. Your room is quite small even in cavern terms." He flashes her his award winning smile like this situation is the best it could possibly be and he was able to do God's work finding that room for her.

"You really owe me girls," He laughs. "Y'all best believe I'll cash it out."

3

We walk through an old wooden door with stained panels and dark metal fixtures. I'm ready to unpack when a speaker above our bed transmits, "Meet in the Big Room in one hour at 9:00 PM."

"I was excited to lay down," I say. "But I'm ready to go to work. I belong here."

My body feels sluggish and heavy. It wants to rest. My mind's running nearly as fast as it was when I was running away from the city though.

It's almost like a hotel, if a hotel were made of stone and instead of a bedside phone there's a speaker in the corner and instead of a clock there's more stone.

"Love!" Cody tries to get my attention.

"Yeah?" I look around in awe.

"Most people don't have private shitters let alone showers, but I was able to get this for us," He pokes his head around the blue curtain that's the only non grey item in the room. "Also most of yours and Kelsey's belongings are already unpacked. I had some of my people help. You'll be taken good care of here. You're important to everything we're trying to do."

He waits with his sweet grin until I give him a grateful smile.

"Besides the floors, walls, and ceiling being made of stone, it's a normal bathroom. To flush just hold this button down. It's like those water saving ones you see in campers," he demonstrates the eco-toilet like he himself invented it. I love how enthusiastic he is about every little thing. It's invigorating. He gestures to the mirror, "and here's a mirror and a working faucet and the shower here," he bounces the short distance over to the shower. "Its got hot water." He winks.

"Thank you," I stare at the shower anticipating feeling clean. The smell of adrenaline and stress is sticking to me.

"Wait. Someone was touching our belongings and going through it?" I whip my head around.

"Yeah, and anything else anyone can do to make this transition more comfortable just let me know. Nothing's too big. We're a community here," he's clueless to my concerns, but at least he's full of smiles as if it were any other day and not the end of the world as we know it.

It's like a medieval castle without the rich fabrics and colors. It's more like a clean hospital mixed with an abandoned castle mixed with a catacomb.

His candy smile makes me melt. I'm glad I stayed with these people, not just because I'm alive, but now me and him are together.

Kelsey walks through the door that joins hers and ours. "I guess everyone or everyone who's going to make it is here right?" Kelsey is still ignorant on most of what's going on.

"Must be. I hope not. I hope more can still make it in this region and it's not too late. There's more shelters..." I'm cut off by Cody jabbing his fingers in my ribs.

"I hope it isn't too late for more. You're beyond lucky you were able to come here. You'll learn more at this first meeting, but information is given out on an as needed basis. Please respect that," Cody looks serious, which isn't like him, "Let's get to the Big Room with some hurry, eh?" He playfully pushes his arm into mine.

"It's already 9:00? How do you know? You're not wearing a watch."

"It's past 9:00. Let's go," He grabs our hands like a kid leading his friends to his secret clubhouse.

We walk out of the door not locking it behind us.

Cody leans forward looking across me at Kelsey who's walking with her head held high.

"You need to watch what you're saying Miranda," Cody whispers not realizing Kelsey's always listening even when she doesn't look it.

"I'm sorry." I repeat the saying to him under my breath, "A need to know basis. Nothing more."

4

The Big Room's the engulfing cavernous room we first arrived at. The room's like a spider web with hallways branching off from the center. Rock piles, shadows, and little cracks are everywhere from the floor to the ceiling. There's less than a hundred people here.

"That's Jayne," I tell Kelsey like she would know how significant that is.

People are talking quietly in small groups. Most of them are fidgeting and waiting for something. For someone. For anything to put them at ease. It makes me feel like I'm not alone in how lost I feel.

"Who's that?" Kelsey asks us as we stand against the wall. She looks at Jayne, the woman who seems to stand the tallest. She has short, black, straight and perfect hair cut into a sharp bob. She's wearing a black leather jacket over a nice white blouse with dark blue jeans plastered to her legs with modest black heals. She's holding a microphone by her side and looks nothing less than a Bond Woman, but she would be James Bond and he would be the sidekick.

I look at my dirty clothes I haven't been able to change out of yet. It seems like everyone except her is covered in a layer of grime.

The people around surrounding her shuffle papers and clipboards and murmur importantly amongst themselves.

"She's the one running this mission. I've only met her twice. Once at a meeting and once in a random coffee shop near our home. I mean our old house. There's no home to go back to anymore. And no house."

"A meeting?" Kelsey asks.

"Yeah, this has been going on for a long time now."

"Why didn't you ever tell me?"

A stab of guilt grasps for my heart. I probably could've had her join and I know I've left her out in the past. Not on purpose though. They needed me in particular though.

"Cody!" Jayne yells over to us. "Come here for a moment!"

Without hesitation Cody leaps over at her command. He starts talking to her without her saying anything to him first.

It seems presumptuous to me, but I guess it's normal for them judging by her reaction. They seem pretty comfortable with each other.

She's nodding her head and they both start looking out at the room. Their eyes hover at different people. They talk to each other some then look at someone else and do it again and again.

"Cody knows her?" Kelsey asks me making me realize I was staring.

"I know who she is too."

"They seem close though," Kelsey looks at them inquisitively.

"Yeah. He's been working here full time now for the last month or so. He used to only come up here once a month for a few days, but the trips got more frequent and for longer times."

"Where'd you meet Cody?"

"He was a drug rep at my office. The reps used to take turns taking the therapists and psychiatrists out for dinner as a group where they'd tell us about some new drug they wanted us to try on our patients. Then it was only him coming by and he asked me out almost a year ago."

"A year? Is that how you got involved in this?" Kelsey gestures around at the rocky room. "Why didn't you tell me? I'm your best friend."

"I couldn't. I…

"was told not to tell anyone. Once we were official I wanted to tell you, but then he introduced me to this organization. They're amazing. They really are. You have no idea how happy I am you get to be a part of this movement. If it weren't for Jayne's vision we would be dead and I wouldn't have been able to spend the time I did with him. He makes me feel important."

"You've always been important to me," She says.

"It's not the same."

Cody walks back over smiling, "Let's take a seat. My ass is tired."

We head for the front row.

A hundred or so chairs are set out in front of a wooden chest where Jayne and a few other people are standing. Behind the chairs it's mostly a large open bare space. I can tell they're anticipating more people by the thousands of chairs stacked in the back near the UTV's.

The room is separated into three sections with eight tunnels branching off. Bright LED lights are attached to the walls making the room seem medically bright. The ceiling's in shadow since the lights can't penetrate that high, but they try to.

Looking across the room towards the entrance tunnel there are lunch tables to the left. They look like the kind you would see in High School. Beyond the benches is a long opening carved out of the stone looking into a large kitchen. There's a few people back in the kitchen moving like flies trying to make sense of a window.

The right side of the room looks more comfortable with sets of couches and rugs laid out. There's little side tables and coffee tables with books on them. There's a lot of tall wooden furniture like book cases, but with intricately carved doors. It looks like a furniture store from the early 1900s mixed with items that looked like they were ordered from a Sear's catalog in the 80s. Nothing matches, but it looks comfortable and inviting as it was likely designed to do.

"Hello everyone. . . . Can I have your attention please?" Jayne asks and the murmurs slow to a silence. She's standing on the little wooden chest.

"Thank you. I am sorry to inform you, but the Haven has been officially closed. We set up a road blockage at the entrance to our dirt road. Anyone who has not made it by now is either dead or compromised. After going over the roster of who has arrived there are three names I don't recognize. You all know the rules. I could have them executed as it could be a breach to our movement, but I trust all of you." Jayne lingers before continuing.

"I gladly welcome them since I trust your judgements." Her soft smile is powerful. "Two are kids and one is a woman.

"Those who brought the unknowns are responsible for them. And here is the big BUT, you are responsible for them so any consequences that arise will come back to you, but I trust all of you and I am happy you are here."

When she talks she has a way of pulling the gravity in the room towards her.

"As you should know now the United States as we know it is over. I have been told all the bombs unfortunately went off successfully around every large city in America. I wish I could have informed everyone who would listen, but then our existence would have been compromised. I only received the information half a day before it happened. By then it was too late for us to stop them. As far as I know our existence is still only speculation among them. We will save the world. We will not only bring back society, but we will reinvent it and make a better world.

"I need Lilly Whiteman, Mark Langlend, Cody Chen, and Miranda Haney to come with me. Everyone else is welcome to some much needed food and sleep. You deserve it and much more."

"Oh that ain't good," Cody tells me.

5

Everyone piles to the kitchen forgetting their complete exhaustion in place of hunger. My stomach gives me an angry kick for not joining them. It's nothing compared to the hunger trainings we had to endure to prepare for this moment though.

It's funny the type of social constructs that are embedded into our brains even when there's chaos and everything above ground's dying we still follow things as simple as forming lines. Their neighbors might be dead, but damn if they aren't going to make a line for their feed.

Kelsey looks apprehensive.

"Go ahead. You'll see me soon." I point to the line.

Jayne steps off the tiny chest and walks over with a presence that grows with the loud clomping sound her heals make on the stone.

"Follow me to hall Framing. You four and the rest of the people here will be considered the original group members. All of you live in hall Aero," Jayne informs us. "We will have the opportunity to rescue more people from the evil doings above ground once we are more established. We have to form a strong group of people who are on fire for this movement. There is no room for being lukewarm."

She turns and walks off with purpose, her heels clacking along the cold floor reverberating power with each echo and we hurry to follow being led through a bright hallway like scared soldiers through the spider web cave. Hall Aero is ridiculously full of light with LED bulbs every 10 feet. Even the rooms are uncomfortably bright and I couldn't figure out a way to turn them off. Hall Framing's more gentle on the eyes.

The lighting here alone already makes me more comfortable than other areas in the Haven.

"This is my office," Jayne says when we reach a door with a bright light above it. She takes her keys out, which unlocks a box to the right of the door revealing a keypad. Her key ring is full of nearly identical, unassuming, silver keys. A cacophony of locks clang open.

We walk inside past redwood tables pointing to the end of her enormous 'office'. Carved wooden chairs with red cushions line the tables. It's something out of a fantasy series. The stone walls are sanded and smooth. Her desk weighs the room down at the end with its sheer size and beautiful wooden carvings. The details are intricate and were obviously handmade with great care many years ago. Large book shelves on the right are leering down. There's another door to the left that blends in with the room itself, but it has a gold doorknob so it's hard to miss.

In place of a window behind her demanding desk is a large painting of the coastal cliffs in the area.

In stark contrast to the furnishings, the walls are plain grey rock. The light in here's warm instead of the cold bright lights elsewhere. My headache's already lifting.

I feel honored she's called me into her office with her. It makes sense. I'm not run of the mill; I have so much more to offer.

"Please take a seat," she gestures. Four chairs were pulled from the redwood tables sitting in front of her desk. Below us is a beautiful Middle Eastern rug with red and gold and black and cream colors in stunning handcrafted designs. She walks around it with the calmness and confidence of any stressed out leader. Jayne bends over and opens a drawer behind her desk.

The drawer slams shut and before I can recognize what's happening she's charging at me.

"Do you know what could have happened?!" She screams.

The cold metal of the end of a pistol presses into my temple.

The earlier composed woman looks utterly insane now. The cock of her pistol is as loud as an 18 wheeler falling off a cliff inside my brain. I feel death a hair away as I struggle to say something. Anything. I'm trying to say something.

Panic's rising in my chest, but I'm glued to my chair squeezing the soft red cushion tearing at a lose thread I found. A bead of sweat falls into my eye stinging it shut.

I try to turn my head to look at Cody, but she shoves the pistol harder into my temple. The only movement I can muster is my chest rising and falling as I struggle to breathe.

Words are now foreign to me.

Her breath smells rancid even though her outside appearance is fresh and the glimpses I manage shows me her poised, but outraged demeanor. She's clean on the outside, but something is rotting inside.

"Why the absolute fucking hell did you bring another person here?! You could have this entire place compromised. Everything we have been working for!" She flails her arms upwards and then grabs the other side of my face pushing the pistol into my face harder. Her porcelain face is now an inch away from mine

"You are supposed to be one of my trusted advisors during all of this! How many others brought people you asked? NOBODY! The only other two people are children! 10 and 12 years old from a single Mom and a single Dad. Explain yourself." She forces the gun so hard into my head it knocks me off the chair. I hit the red carpet feeling the stone floor beneath it letting my hands cushion the fall so I don't hit my head on the hard ground, but pain rushes through my wrists. I curl into a ball pulling my arms over my head trying to protect myself. The ornate carpet's scratchy. It's worn down and old. She's standing above me in her black heals straddling my shaking body.

"I...I...I...."

"I, I, I WHAT?!" Jayne waves the gun.

"I'm. I am sorry."

"You're sorry."

"When-when I received the phone call, my friend Kelsey, my roommate was with me. She's a good person I swear. Like you said I'm completely responsible for her. There's no way she's one of The Nothings. I've known her basically my entire life. She votes and cares and volunteers her time. She loves our country. Why would she want our government to disappear?" I try to sit, but it feels like a thousand pounds presses into my chest from the disappointment I caused and all I can do is cower as tears stream down.

Jayne squats with her knees on either side of my face. She waves the gun in front of my forehead swinging it like a pendulum.

"Jayne," Cody says in a gentle voice not making any sudden movements, but reaching out for her. "Please put that shit away. She's proven herself time and time again." Cody breathes deeply. "I'll also be responsible for this damn person because I trust Miranda and her judgement."

Jayne stops the pendulum motion and looks up at Cody, "Do not dare talk to me like you have any control over my reactions. You know how treacherous this is."

She straightens and goes behind her desk sliding the gun into the drawer with the grace of a queen during wartime.

She walks back around and sits on top of the desk looking at us as if we had just walked in and nothing out of the ordinary had happened.

As she's talking I stumble back into my chair. She looks at me with kindness and admiration again.

"The Nothings take up too much space at the moment to safely do anything," Jayne explains. "Washington DC is gone. Every capitol is wiped out. Every decent sized city is reduced to rubble." Jayne directs her attention to the other chairs. "Lilly, Mark, you came here directly from the heart of San Francisco. Because of that I had to make sure you got the call earlier than the others. How did it look?"

Mark's still shaking from the violent scene. He's wearing a brand new baseball cap and in a light colored button up. He looks like he stepped out of an inheritance catalog.

Although Lilly's face is white she speaks up, "We left within five minutes of receiving the call. Mark and I had practiced the drill over and over again. We were completely ready to go. We immediately grabbed our respirators knowing the bombs would start then loaded up in under five minutes. The city was still packed full of people going about their day to day lives when we left. We were away from the center when we felt the first shockwave. It lurched us forward and pushed us into a ditch, but Mark drove us out. When he's determined he can do anything. Within an hour the sky was turning orange as the fire was spreading from building to building. We drove the same speed as the other few cars around to avoid raising suspicion. We missed each successive explosion by five to fifteen minutes until we were in the outskirts that I guess weren't worth burning to pieces. The rest of the way we stayed clear of other major cities including the ones we weren't sure were big enough just like you instructed. I know for a fact we weren't followed. We filled up in north Big Sur, 45 minutes away at the last gas station. It appeared as if everyone had just received the news and didn't know what to do yet. They weren't even rushing to get groceries or gas yet." Lilly held her head straight and made eye contact with Jayne, but she was cleaning her finger nails out like the action was the only thing that would keep her alive.

I was still sweating.

"Good," Jayne looks at me. "Cody was with me as you know. He wanted to warn you sooner, but he and I both had faith in you. Before you tell me how it went, I have something important for you. I know perfectly well you are capable and have abilities others don't so I need you. I care about you Miranda and have high expectations I know you can fill. I apologize if I scared you. I just care about this movement. I know in my heart you are meant for greatness in this world and if your focus stays true you will accomplish wonderful things."

"This is what I have planned for you …" Jayne says.

6

"Are we doing the right thing?" I ask Cody as we walk back to our bedroom through the bright lights of hall A. We pass wooden doors that must have been stolen out of a castle or an old church. They weren't made recently that's for sure.

He stops and grabs my elbows to face him. "Look Miranda, there wasn't a single fucking thing we coulda done to prevent this shit show. The only thing we can do now is use this situation to make the world a better place. The world wants structure, not some chaos where everyone dies for no fucking reason. We're a part of something special."

I nod.

"Do you hear me Miranda?"

"Yes. We're a part of something special."

We open the door to our room and Kelsey's on our bed.

"Oh you're back!" She leaps up to hug me. I push her away and trudge to the bed and collapse. She looks at me with a knowledge only she can have of me. "You've been crying? Are you okay? What happened?"

I lay on the bed staring at the stone ceiling. "I don't regret bringing you. I love you. It'll be okay and before we know it everything will be even better than before. I just hate I let her down."

"What?" She mutters coming closer, but Cody puts a hand out and nods for her to leave.

"Are you ready for what you have to do in a couple days Miranda? You have to make sure you get this right. Jayne trusts you." Cody climbs into bed and wraps his body around mine.

"You don't have to worry about me. I'll never disappoint her again".

Chapter 3

1

I slept the entire first day only waking to eat and only waking to eat when Cody forced me to wake up. On day three I woke up early. At least I think so. There's no clocks so I'm not sure, but it had that feeling.

I roll onto Cody wrapping my arms around him entangling my soul around his. "I love you," I speak into his sleeping ear.

He stirs and rolls his groggy body to face mine. He wraps his arms and legs around me. "You'll be okay. I don't doubt," he breathes a sleepy breath, "I love you so much." We push our lips together and stay still like a photograph in a moment of peace.

Too soon I get up and get dressed.

I knock on the door that joins mine and Kelsey's room. This room was reserved for the inevitable situation where people bring their kids with them, but I guess we got it. Not as many people brought family members as first predicted, which makes what I did worse. I hope it doesn't cause resentment among the others.

"What's up?" Kelsey's voice is scratchy with sleep.

"We have to go. You're coming with me. Get dressed and don't worry about a bag. I have one for you. Hurry. Meet me in the hallway."

She's rushing and her half asleep body bumps about as I grab our bags and brush my teeth and make myself look somewhat presentable. I'll do anything else I need to do in the truck.

I'm not ready to go back into the chaos just yet, but I know I have the strength to do it.

"Don't die out there," Cody kisses me on the forehead.

"What?"

"I'm kidding love. I know you'll be back in no time or I wouldn't let you leave."

2

We're driving down the dirt road, but this time I blindfolded Kelsey as per Jayne's instructions.

I make a few stops and pretend to turn my truck around although Kelsey already saw us go up to the Haven, but I'm done with breaking rules so I just listen without question to the detailed instructions Jayne gave me. It's not worth potentially making her disappointed in me again. I won't make her regret putting her trust in me for this assignment.

Some indeterminate time later we pull onto Highway 1 and drive to that little shop and gas station. The only one for many miles.

No one's in sight and blankets and curtains have been hung in the windows. The sign at the door is flipped to closed.

I untie the bandana from Kelsey's eyes, "How are you doing?"

"I'd love it if I knew what was going on," Kelsey says annoyed. "Why'd you do that?"

"I had to. Jayne said we have to take every precaution. We can't be lukewarm with any assignment."

"Are you okay Miranda?"

"We're here to scout the area. You remember those checkpoints I was talking about and mentions of The Nothings right?" I ask.

"Yeah. You didn't answer my question though."

"We're here to make sure we're safe and to report any new information."

"Like what?" Kelsey asks giving up for now, but I feel her looking into my soul getting the answers for herself.

I feel good though. I'm ready for this. I've always been.

"I'm not sure, but we'll see. The owner and a family who works here knows Jayne and knows we're coming. They don't know much, but we guaranteed them safety and other future promises if they help us now. If anyone asks we're residents of this area." I grab her hand. "Let's go."

I look into her eyes to give her courage just as much as I need the courage by looking at my best friend and knowing we're here together.

I jump out of the truck ready for business. She flops out of the truck, but she looks as determined as I am.

"This should be easy. We're in the middle of nowhere so what could go wrong?" I ask.

3

The gift shop/convenience store/gas station is still mostly stocked.

Kelsey and I walk past the register past the food and beer and into their tiny little restaurant and take our seats across from one of the owners who had been waiting for us. Her big hands calloused from years of hard work are resting on the table.

"Victoria, have there been any suspicious people through here? People who asked a lot of questions? Seemed out of style with the rest? People who were obviously not from around here?" I'm going down the list of questions Jayne entrusted me with. Kelsey places her hand on top of mine to let me know I need to wait for answers between the questions.

"Are you thirsty or hungry dear? I can get you something," Victoria starts to stand. Her motherly presence already puts me at ease. She's the type of person who genuinely has a love for other people. She's an anomaly.

"No I just need these questions answered please."

"There was only one. He was asking about a safe place to go for his family. If I knew of anywhere. He told me the rest of his family died in explosions in LA."

"What was weird about that?"

"Miss, he kept asking question after question eventually asking about any fall out shelters for him and his daughter. He was getting real pushy and started talkin' faster so I pretended my English wasn't good and could no longer understa-"

A loud screeching sound roars from outside and four people in military gear pour out of a pickup. They storm the steps and pound on the locked door.

"We are the US military! Let us in immediately. We are here to help you! We know you're in there!" I shrink at their booming voices.

Victoria looks to me expecting me to lead them elsewhere, but I give her a nod and we walk to the door.

I go into character, "Oh thank God you are here! We heard the White House and The Capitol was burned and all big cities across the country are gone!" I stumble dramatically into one of their arms.

He pushes me away with open disgust. "Who's been through here? Has there been any unusual traffic?" He looks to me then to Victoria then to Kelsey.

"I am just so glad you are..." I try to get out.

He looks to Victoria and Kelsey, "What about you two?"

I look at them and Kelsey looks at me and then Victoria who is looking at the floor starts crying. Kelsey turns her head to the floor as well, "I can't get in touch with my parents or anyone. What's going on? Are you here to take us to a shelter?" She asks.

I pull Kelsey into a hug pushing out fake tears while I loudly say, "It is going to be okay. There are contingencies in the government," I look to the group, "Right?" I appear to be crying, but I whisper in her ear, "Why are you asking about a shelter? Choose your words wisely. That shouldn't have crossed your mind."

The biggest man steps forward, looks at us and decides to hand the card to me, "If anyone you don't know comes through here call us. We're trying to isolate who and what's in charge." He turns around and the others follow. He stops a few feet away and turns to me, "What's your name?"

"Melissa, Melissa Hanner Sir. Are you leaving?" I ask

"We'll be back Melissa. We will be back with more people. Umm. To help control this situation if you get my drift. We are trying to mediate the situation. Help us to help you."

And like that they were gone.

"Why didn't we tell them who we are? It's the military!" Kelsey raises her voice at me.

I slam my hand over her mouth pushing her into the counter in the store pinning her down. I smother her while listening for noises outside. She's muffling something under my hand. I shush her. Nothing has felt real since I got that phone call.

I listen. No sounds from outside.

I relax into one of the refrigerated doors full of beer. I was expecting a nice cold touch, but the power was turned off.

"Kelsey, they could have still been listening to see what we would have said after they leave. The military's gone. How do you reckon there's a military when the government has fallen, the cities are burning, and the largest and most populous military bases have been turned to ashes?"

"I'm sorry. I didn't know it was that bad. It's not like you told me anything. You always leave me out."

I turn to Victoria, "You are going to open back up. Open the windows. These are terrorist attacks and you want to help in any way you can. Kelsey and I are Big Sur residents residing here until we figure this out."

"Si," Victoria answers.

I look into Victoria's eyes, "We will double if not quadruple anything they promise and we will have the most wonderful, fair, and kind society after we clean up their mess. Do you trust us?"

"Si."

"Good. Open up. We need to get information from anyone we can."

"If I open up there's no hiding against looters or terrorists."

"You will be okay. You have us."

"If you say so sweetie."

4

Kelsey and I are in Victoria's guest room laying in bed trying to fall asleep. Old pink rose wallpaper that lazily holds onto the wall is discolored where the ceiling meets it. There's a smell of old mold, but it's not entirely unpleasant. It looks like the room in my Grandma's house I would stay in when I was sick and my Mom dropped me off.

Kelsey flips towards me, "I'm so scared. I've no idea what's happening. What is all of this? The government's gone? Are you serious? Who can we trust? Who are we with here? Who is Jayne really? What do you guys plan to do? It doesn't look like you are trying to help anyone. Tell me something. Please."

I lay on my back staring at the ceiling. "Kelsey, know I will protect you. Promise me you'll not tell anyone I told you anything including Cody."

"What do you mean?"

"Just promise."

"Okay you have my word," Kelsey reaches over where my hands are resting on my stomach and holds them. She looks at the side of my face as I continue to stare at that interesting ceiling where the mold creeping in has been painted over with varying coats of white through the years.

"There's a group. An organization. Much larger than us. But they're messy. It's chaotic. I mean they want chaos. They want utter anarchy. They want the people to choose their leaders in any manner they choose. If someone disagrees in their new society, they can murder the person. It's survival of the fittest and who is liked by most. Until that leader isn't liked anymore then someone can challenge them or outright murder them. To them, that's fair game. Complete and true anarchy is happening. Without a government or military they have a clean slate to do whatever they want. They believe in having nothing. As in no rules and whatever they can will to happen. Therefore we call them The Nothings. They believe in nothing."

"Where do you come in?" She asks.

"We have a vision. Okay. This vision's nothing like the previous democracies. We'll be safe. I promise you." I turn towards her and squeeze her delicate squishy fingers. "I need rest."

"Thank you for telling me something." Kelsey turns away letting her tangled blonde curls fall over eyes making her look like those old master paintings of soft baby angels.

The flowered covers smell clean. A slight smell of bleach wafts up, but it's nice. I wait for her to pester me with more questions.

As I'm drifting off, Kelsey says, "Miranda I know you think you're this really special intelligent person, but you need to remember to see everything around you."

"What the hell does that mean?" I ask half asleep.

"We're all people here."

"Yeah I know that. Jayne sees something in me though. It's no lie I'm outgoing and I have an influence other's don't."

"All I'm saying is be careful of your own head. I don't want anything to happen to you."

"Jayne told me herself"

"Miranda please."

5

"Miss! Miss! Come quick!" I bolt awake to the screams of Victoria banging at my door and trying to open the old wobbly knob. "The gas pumps are in rubble! There's fire! Please help!" She slams and falls into my door until her cries turn to sobs.

I wait longer listening for any other voices or movement before I move. I can't be too careful. She can wait.

"What are you doing? Go help her," Kelsey whispers.

"Hold on."

There's no other sounds except for Victoria's sobs.

Kelsey starts to stand, but I yank her back.

"This isn't you Miranda."

I ignore her listening intently.

I get up already dressed for the day.

I inch the door open and Victoria falls inward. I drop to the floor catching and cradling her in my arms.

"Tell me what happened. Slowly."

It feels weird. She's supposed to be holding me. She feels like a protector, but I'm forced to take over the role. I continue to prove to myself I am capable of this. I am terrified and uncertain, but for the greater good I find my strength.

"Those men dressed as military came back in the night and made the gas explode. Men in uniforms came here. It's only ruins now, but how are we to get supplies? You'll help correct? I hid and didn't say a thing. I didn't run out even though they were yelling about helping those that can give them any information that's different than what social media's spreading.

Miranda," She grabs my cheeks in her plump brown fingers, "There's no newscasters any longer. All channels are black." Her face is streaked with tears and her tight black curls are glued to her face with sweat.

"We have space for you and your family in the Haven. We just need to stay here a little longer. Please stay with me. You're strong. Do this for your boy," I say.

A guttural, primal, pain filled scream comes from outside.

Victoria dashes down her hallway towards the door pounding the house with every step she takes. She runs into a tall lamp and it smashes to the ground. I lurch into a run after her, catching her just in time, tackling her to the floor directly in front of the exit.

There's a loud crunch sound from underneath us and Victoria sobs uncontrollably. She is writhing under my arms. God, she's big. My skinny muscular arms are somehow enough to hold her. Her body feels like an oven and she's lurching with the force of a bull, but she has the terror of an old woman even though she's not that old.

Using all of my strength I manage to straddle her using one arm to try to keep her still and the other over her mouth.

"Oh Mary, Mother of Jesus that's my husband! Let me go!" She manages to cough out swinging her head to the right knocking me into the wall beside us and then to the left and again to the right. I push myself back on top trying to restrain her.

"Shhhh," I say. "You need to be quiet or they'll come in here and kill you and your boy. Do you want that?"

The screaming outside abruptly stops. Silence. The sounds of Victoria's laboring breaths dissipate. Her large chest heaves up and down rapidly, but she has stopped struggling.

The sound of tires screeching away carry death and relief.

"Victoria please stay calm," I try. I know telling someone to stay calm hardly ever works, but I apply pressure on top of her body until the rapid shallow breaths turns to slow sobs. "We need to wait a few more hours before going outside."

"He might be dying," Victoria pushes out words barely audible. "Why won't you let me help him?"

"You still have your phone right? Let's check the internet. That's if they're still up and running and haven't gone black like the news channels."

"Mommy."

Victoria throws me off of her with ease this time.

Her little boy is standing with a toy truck in his tiny hands. She grabs a hold of him as if those men could come in here and snatch him away right this second.

Kelsey joins us in Victoria's living room near the front of the house. The heavy curtains probably haven't been opened in some time judging by the discoloration from the dust on the once solid burgundy color.

"Oh my God. No...no...no," I say.

"What? What is it?" Kelsey asks.

Victoria's slumped in the corner on the floor. She has her small boy in her lap holding onto him as if at any moment he'll be taken away. Whenever I glance at her, she pulls him in tighter like I myself might cause something atrocious to happen.

"Are you sure you want him to hear this?" I ask Victoria.

He's stricken with terror and his cries are muffled in his Mom's chest even though he has no idea what happened. He's feeding off Victoria's energy.

They are terrified over there against the wall, but as much as I want to help I can't. I have to stay here to find more information. That will serve more people and them in the long run. I still feel like a terrible person though, but I cannot steer away from my training. I may feel bad in the moment and I may be hated by those who do not understand, but I need to stand strong with the knowledge I am helping the entire world.

"It's fine," she whispers.

"According to Facebook and Instagram, people dressed as the military are going through towns destroying gas pumps and killing anyone who's there or runs out. Only so many gas stations are left and people are flocking to them. My God, they're making themselves sitting ducks."

Victoria looks at the tilted crucifix hanging on the beige wall while gripping her terrified boy. She rubs the golden crucifix around her neck and mumbles a prayer.

"It's worse than I thought. We need to go. I'm not worried here since we're an hour and a half away from the nearest town and hours away from the nearest large bombing. I can't explain why they would come to your gas station, but it seems to be happening all over the continent simultaneously. It's still weird they would come way out here though."

A soft knock at the front door interrupts us. I cautiously tiptoe over the thinning carpet even though I want to sprint in the opposite direction, but I peek into the peephole.

"It's Cody!"

I pull it open and before I can breathe he's all over me, kissing my cheeks and neck. "I'm so sorry I let you walk into this danger."

Finally I feel a moment of grounding thanks to his presence. I allow myself to let go of "being in charge" and let him take command.

I might be bossy and act confidently, but actually being in charge isn't what I expected. Jayne shouldn't put so much faith in me. A leader should have no doubts and I'm drowning in mine.

"I'm so happy you're safe," He kisses me with as much fervor as our first kiss during what Jayne called a training. I prefer not to think about that day.

Cody walks inside, "Gather as many people as you can Victoria. Have them wait safely inside. Tell them not to bring anything. We've got everything they'll need. Even clothes.

"We'll be back in a few hours. I'm going to gather as many people as I can from both directions. Oh. And destroy your fucking phones and make sure everyone else does the same. You can no longer use 'em. They're compromised. I've received some troubling news after you two left."

Chapter 4

1

I'm gathered with the original group behind Jayne who's addressing the newcomers. They're sitting on the white fold out chairs spaced like a convention. Her speech is nearing its end. She's able to move crowds like a preacher. I love listening to her, but not as much as she loves to talk.

I'm just exhausted. My temper's short.

"I know you were asked not to bring any personal belongings besides those you can fit in your hand so I have stations set up that will give you new clothes, toiletries, and other necessities. Each of you will be assigned rooms down hallways Clarity and Demo."

"You are safe here. You can finally breathe. We have enough resources to last years, but we won't need to be here that long.

"If being blindfolded and tied frightened you, it need not be. We could not risk you knowing how to get to the Haven. That was only a precaution against The Nothings. We could not risk any information of our location becoming known. And we could not risk them hurting or outright murdering anymore of you. They will do anything to wreck havoc on this world. They are evil. This is a safe place. I have a few people here who will help you along. I am sorry about your loss. We will not let evil take over our hearts. The light will guide us through this apocalypse and those who crossed to the evil side will be left behind."

The locals we were able to rescue look terrified. We caravanned them up the mountain road in a big school bus that had been fitted for off-road use. It wasn't easy finding them, but as the day went by after Victoria's husband had been murdered locals drove down from their properties.

Children are crying and adults are crying and people are staring off into space. A few of them rub their wrists due to the restraints we were told to use. An old man stretches his fingers out in the wobbly way only people with arthritis do.

I understand the blindfolds, but the rope was too much. I didn't want to speak my concerns to anyone and risk it getting back to Jayne that I'm questioning her. It's not worth it. She's far more experienced than me and it's probably my own narcissism that makes me think I know better. Cody has spoken to me about it before.

"Everyone else follow me into hallway Framing," Jayne addresses everyone whose been here since the beginning. "Not the two children though, they can play with the others." She finds me in the group with her beautiful eagle eyes, "Kelsey is coming with."

Eight hallways lead away from the Big Room and the letters don't go in alphabetical order, but split themselves in half so A, B, C, and D are to the right of hall Heaven where the UTVs are. E, F, and G, spread out to the left.

She leads us.

When we reach her office there are candles lit around the room. It reminds me of a catholic cathedral or an ancient castle where members of the royal family and church meet.

It's nice to have gentle lighting especially since none of the bright LED lights have shut off. Not even at night. The bright lights have started gnawing away at my eyes and my ability to sleep through the night. I'm having difficulties judging time.

The redwood tables are filled with food to salivate over. I look at fresh vegetables, lobster, pasta dishes, and other meats. My stomach pulls me with excitement and I forget everything else for a moment.

Cody, Kelsey and I look at each other grinning like children and dive in. The space in between the tables form a runway with a throne room feeling to her massive desk.

I'm gorging myself on butter and delicious seasoned foods. No words are exchanged, only smiles.

After we get our fill and are sitting around laughing with one another, Jayne comes in. She walks onto her intricately designed red rug wearing a black pantsuit with those same black heels. She seems to cast a shadow over us even though that's not possible in this lighting.

She stands at the front in silence until all trails of conversations end and we're looking up at her. She didn't even raise a finger. Her presence alone made us quiet.

"You have all had to leave people behind. Even if it was not a choice because you could not call them or get to them before the bombs. We have all left people. I have specifically chosen this bunch to receive phone calls early enough to arrive here hopefully unharmed. Unfortunately, not all of them made it. It also showed me who can come through in times of high stress.

"But hey? This new world cannot take people who are weak or timid or afraid to act. We must have the most intelligent and creative individuals if we want to take the world back from the anarchist Nothings. And that's what each of you are, with your unique talents. You are important and special."

Jayne pauses for a long time.

I hear a drip far off somewhere in the cavern.

I catch her eye for a second and I know she sees me and I'm not just another person here.

"I believe we have a leak," She says. "Any ideas? Anyone?"

A stifled gasp comes from most of the members.

She stands there for what feels like an eternity. I can hear the sound of the clock hand ticking by although there are no clocks. I can hear the gentle breeze in the room although there's no air current down here. My mind is searching for any stimulus to focus on in this moment, but the room is stale even with the candles and food. The drip has ceased to make a sound. It's like the water could feel the tension and decided to pause its movement.

Jayne glides between the tables looking at each individual. She stops and looks at me placing a hand on my shoulder. My insides turn to mush. I know I've been nothing but obedient and loyal to her. She looks at Kelsey and moves on sliding her hand away each finger tip at a time.

I don't dare sigh a breath of relief when she passes us. I've seen her flash into this mood before.

She places her calloused hand on every other shoulder until coming to a stop at the end of my table.

"Ryan. Oh sweet Ryan," Jayne is baby talking this orange-haired man at the end. "How come the quote, unquote military showed up in Pacific Valley destroying the gas pumps directly after you were sent to Monterey and then returned here," She chuckles. Jayne smiles devilishly. She seems to be having fun with this or maybe it's just her way to assert power.

"I find it funny that an area that has such a low population they don't even have a single regular neighborhood had their pumps destroyed. We predicted at least a week of getting more gas easily. It's true we know how to pull gas out of the reservoir without their pumps so if you were trying to rid us of a significant amount of fuel I am afraid you failed."

Ryan hasn't turned around, but his freckled skin is now milky. I can see the individual blue and red veins in his forehead bulge as she continues talking in a beautiful haunting way. His skin is covered in goose bumps and little beads of sweat pop out of his hairline like ants through a crack in the sidewalk.

"Sure, maybe it was someone else. Right Ryan?" Jayne asks.

"Yes! It wasn't me! I swear to God. I did everything you asked." He squirms on the old red cushion and a thread pops in the tedious silence.

She smiles down at him and slithers inches to his face.

"Bullshit! That piece of old spit knows something!" Cody yells. "I've been suspicious of him. Something wasn't never right."

Jayne glances at Cody staying by Ryan's ear. "You have to admit it is weird they travelled from Monterey."

"No it isn't. They were headed this way anyways," Ryan pleads.

"How do you know where they were headed? Well, little to your knowledge I knew they were not going to come here. I got word from a trusted member up north who is on the inside that they were not going to go into Big Sur and not only did they travel into Big Sur they drove all the way to the south end traveling more than an hour out of the way."

"There's no way! I mean that's not possible. They were headed south like I told you. I only saw them in person from a distance."

She lifts her arm and reaches into her bra and pulls out a small revolver. With grace she brings it to rest between his eyes. She only holds it with one arm. He could easily knock her hand away, but doesn't.

She's just scaring him like she did to me. You can't convict someone on the actions of fake soldiers. It's messy and confusing.

He's shaking and his incomprehensible words spray spittle all over her arm. He won't be able to defend himself being scared shitless like he is. He can't get a single word out.

"Let's see Ryan. Leave the choice of the innocent or the guilty to a higher power. There is only one bullet in here," Jayne smiles as she pulls back on the trigger.

It clicks.

Nothing.

He squirms and she looks pleased.

Jayne laughs aloud as her head falls behind her and she swings the gun loosely. He could easily snatch it from her.

"Looks like you were lucky Ryan," Jayne yells as she tosses herself back towards him. "But are you lucky a second time?"

Her Cheshire grin is followed by another pull of the trigger.

It clicks.

Nothing.

"Please! Stop this. I swear I'm not working for them," Ryan pleads.

"Tell me the truth and I will stop pulling the trigger," Jayne says this as she slams the front of the gun into Ryan's mouth. Blood and a chip of tooth falls out of his mumbling frown.

Nothing.

She pulls it out. His dark red saliva drips from the tip of the barrel.

"Please believe me. I'm not one of them. Make it stop. All I said was you may want to check out the remote sections of Big Sur when they asked for information," He gurgles his words.

"You did what Ryan? You said you never spoke to them, but saw them from afar. So you lied."

"Big Sur's miles wide and miles deep. There's no way that helped them to know where you are specifically. They were going to kill me if I didn't give them something."

"Excuse me guys. Please escort this man into F3," she turns to the guards by the door. That's the first time I noticed them. They ate with the rest of us, but I didn't see them standing there.

He kicks and screams as they drag him off into a hidden door between two massive bookcases along the wall.

Jayne follows slamming the door behind her.

We're left alone.

Loud tortured screams reverberate around the stone walls like a choir in a church for the damned.

The screaming stops an eternity later. I look around the room and they look frightened. I feel frightened.

After a few moments of silence, a deeply wet sound comes from the door followed by crunching sounds. None of us say a word, but look around as if to say, "Is anyone going to do anything?"

The distant noises stop again.

"Are we supposed to leave?" Someone asks.

BOOM!

A gunshot rings through the door and into the room through our ears and into our minds rattling our brains. My insides are doing flips and my body boils filling me with a flushing heat. Now I feel true panic rising in me. I'm about to leave but...

Jayne walks out of the hidden door splattered in blood.

The guys walk out carrying a large bag unmistakably human shaped.

I don't want to look, but I have to see. I suddenly feel faint and dizzy. The heat's replaced by a rushing chill.

His head rolls out of the bag and they shove it inside like dirty laundry. His orange hair is now a dark red.

They drop him and return to their positions at the front door.

Blood seeps out forming into a puddle around the bag. Blood's soaking into the stone floor changing the grey into a dark red-black. It's like when you place silly putty on a surface and it slowly oozes away from the center as if it's alive and at any moment it will snap back. The blood continues to spread away gently though and will never snap back.

I can't believe I saw my first dead body and compared it to a children's toy. He did it to himself though. We all could have died from his carelessness.

Jayne walks casually back to the front, "You did not need to see that, but it is important to know to make the world a better place and make sure The Nothings can't prevail we have to be ruthless. We cannot let them think our kindness makes us weak. It is what makes us strong.

It will be rough at first. To make the change you want to see in the world, you cannot be lukewarm. You have to be on fire for your beliefs and willing to do anything for the greater good. I have chosen each of you specifically because I know you have the strength and the light in your hearts to know the difference between good and bad and fight no matter the immediate cost because you have the intelligence to keep the greater future in mind."

I can't tell what the others are thinking. For once, I can't read Kelsey.

"I know what you're thinking. What if this man was innocent? Right?" She asks while walking around the room standing like a warrior on the largest horse after battle giving her men a speech of resiliency and honor.

"I had hard proof before he walked into this dinner tonight he was one of The Nothings. He killed an entire family in north Big Sur when they would not stop asking him for help when he was on his way back here. That included three small children. He murdered in cold blood three children in front of their parents. Those were innocent lives we were going to save. He knew this and exploited that. He has compromised the trust we could have gained in communities up north. He is responsible for the deaths of innocent lives and at the same time dragged our name through the muck. He might as well murdered hundreds more because those hundreds that would have trusted us and followed us to safety never will now."

Her eyes meet mine and for a moment all I can do is admire her. The tension in the room seems to melt away. It's replaced with faith in Jayne.

"You can go to your rooms in hallway Aero now. Sleep well." Jayne's voice changed into a casual conversational tone.

Before we could leave, she named off ten people she wanted to stay including me and Cody.

Did I do something wrong? Did Cody?

2

Once the room emptied out, Jayne walked to the door with the gold knob. She pauses and looks back giving us a look that says, "Are you coming?"

We jump out of our armchairs and rush over. I trip over one of the corners of her decorative rugs trying to hurry in.

Inside the room, lit candles are scattered purposefully. It looks like a movie set for some seance. The candles in her office/dining space were paired with gentle electrical lighting, but in here it's only the fire. Eleven burgundy pillows are on the ground in a circle. The colors are warm. Plants are down here. They're dried out in vases and hanging on the walls, but plants nonetheless. There's no door I can see. It blends in perfectly with the wall. The room's an octagon and there's no points or podiums or direction of focus. It's like I walked into a real life mandala. Every piece is the exact same next to it. There's no hierarchy and Jayne lets us, instructs us, to sit on the pillows first. It's simple in comparison to her ornate office.

"I chose you all for a reason. You show promise, fervor, and passion. I have been able to trust you all for a long time or partners I trust with my life trust you. Although our meetings before the bombs were brief I took notice of each of you. I have been paying attention."

It feels good to have her approval. I thought I've been unnoticed or worse, held in contempt, but she notices me. She notices how hard I work. How devoted I am to seeing the new world through. She sees how on fire I am.

"I need to confess and be honest with you first and I expect you to do the same," Jayne sits on the pillow next to me. She rubs her thumbs against each other while seated criss cross. She had taken her heels off revealing perfectly red painted toenails. Her sharp black bob sways. "I tried. I tried hard to stop The Nothings. I did not want anyone to die. If I had it my way I would have continued protesting and moving my way into politics to change what I needed to. Unfortunately the ending was inevitable so we as a team need to take our world back. This is an opportunity that comes around less than once a lifetime. Less than once in several lifetimes. We have the opportunity to build the new government from the ground up."

"Jayne, I care for you so much and I think you're brilliant, but so are all these people and if we're going to kick this shit in the ass and start from damn near nothing then maybe they needa know more," Cody talks openly.

"That is a good point and in due time I will form an entire picture of what we are doing. For now, I want to focus on what we can control. Our ideologies will come through."

"Have faith things will turn out as they should as long as you are doing your part," She tells the circle.

"Its been a week since the first detonations went off which I know means there will be leaders popping up in every city. Our job is to capture them to see what they know and keep them hostage, but mostly to wait and see who is strong enough to claim power after them. This is an example of survival of the fittest. The fit will survive and we need them. Once they taste power they will want it again and I will give them the illusion of that. They will look anywhere to be noticed. We are picking the best fish out of the ocean this way. We are playing The Nothing's game and turning it back on them by using their anarchy Darwinian model to use the leaders that rise to power for them for us. Soon there will be no judgement or favoritism or unfair advantages. We will all be equal and living off the land." Jayne reaches for a remote in her pocket and turns on relaxing music. The octagonal room echos the sound in the dreamiest way. "We will take advantage of The Nothings mishaps. We will take some of their best to work with us. You cannot just rule a city and then be cast aside. These people will be yearning for something and it is our job to lead them on the right path. I have plans. And each of you are crucial to it."

Jayne instructs us in a relaxing voice to breathe in and out and watch our breath while feeling the rhythm of the music.

Before I know it 20 minutes had passed and we are departing.

3

I wake in the morning to the sound of the speaker above our bed softly projecting Jayne's voice.

"Good morning everyone. These two weeks have been extremely stressful and many of us have lost loved ones along the way. Do not worry. It will not be in vain. We will bring the people who did this to justice.

"Before you get out of bed lets breathe together.

"… in …

"… out …

"… in …

"… out.

"Slowly. If you feel your thoughts drifting away return to your breath and listen to the words I am saying.

"You survived.

"You are strong.

"You will make it through to a brighter future.

"You survived for a reason.

"You are safe.

"You are taken care of.

"You are meant for a greater purpose.

"Amen.

"Now slowly start moving around. Move your muscles and flutter your eyelids open. Stretch the neck and the back. It is too easy to get cramped down here and forget to move.

"Breakfast will be in the Big Room in 15 minutes. We have a big day ahead of us."

I feel calmer than I did pre-bomb. I know I need to do as much as possible to keep myself composed and strong during this so maybe that's why I feel better; since I'm finally trying my hardest. I'm finally doing the work necessary to feel peace in a literal fiery storm. I finally have a clear trajectory for my purpose in life.

4

We're in Jayne's office which sits the original members in the afternoon. At least I believe it's the afternoon. There's no windows or clocks just bells and Jayne's voice projecting from the speakers telling us where to go and when. I had breakfast and lunch with everyone in the Big Room earlier today where we introduced ourselves.

It has been a day of socialization. It's exhausting especially since Jayne told us we're representing the movement and whatever we do is watched so we have to lead through authentic example.

Kelsey leans over, "I miss sunlight and air that isn't stagnant."

"I know. Me too."

"I believe some of us may start working outside again," Cody drops in.

Jayne walks to the front sitting on her desk, "We have received good and bad news. The bad news first. People are continuously dying. Innocent lives are out there and we are helpless to aid them. We continue rescuing more nearby people, but an unprecedented amount are dying compared to the number we are saving.

The good news is the bombs have stopped going off except for small ones from random people. It is utter anarchy out there as evil has thrashed its tentacles onto the Earth. The cities that were bombed had leaders rise up immediately. They were facilitators of The Nothings. Their belief is people will continue fighting against whoever has taken power until the member the people want and the person who's the strongest is in charge. Almost all of the original leaders who were set up to take over have been overthrown already. It is moving faster and more dangerously than I originally imagined. Although that is what The Nothings intended, nobody can taste that kind of power and walk away. They will forever crave it. I am sure the members who were chosen thought they would be the leader everyone wants. Fortunately none of them died. I will need people to gather them from the closest cities; Santa Cruz, Santa Victoria, and Fresno.

The ten I talked to yesterday are too important right at this moment. It is not that the rest of your lives are dispensable, it's that I need their counsel right now. This could be deadly, but I will forever be in your debt and for what it's worth, I will admire your dedication to the cause and the power of good over evil. I won't forget."

People immediately start standing.

"I need three groups of three," Jayne says.

She pairs them off, but is one person short.

"Would anyone else like to join the last group that is headed to Santa Cruz to capture The Wolf. That is what this guy calls himself. I know, it sounds like a joke."

Nobody moves.

I'd volunteer, but I can't. This makes me restless. I get up to volunteer anyway, but then a tall and gangly younger man with a baby face, probably under 20, in the back of the room near the exit stands. He tugs at his collar a few times.

"Very well then, I am so grateful for your service to our cause. It will not be forgotten. The fight for good will forever be in your debt. You are brave and will be heroes when history is written. Go ahead and leave. My main partner, Isaac, is outside and will help you along. Safe journeys and God bless," Jayne radiates confidence.

"Who's Isaac?" Kelsey whispers.

"I've heard about him, but I haven't met him. Him and Jayne are supposedly the orchestrators of the Haven and the whole movement. He remains unseen to most. I have heard other people say he's always with us at every meeting or event or gathering, but nobody sees him either. I know I've heard more, but I cannot remember."

We finish our meals with the original members minus the nine who left when Jayne wants to talk to us again in the other room.

5

I sat myself in the same spot as last time between Cody and the empty pillow that Jayne fills.

"I would like to start assigning specific jobs to everyone and goal charts for everyone to use," Jayne explains. "This is our chance to change the country. We need to start off on the right foot immediately. This begins with the people here. Before we can move forward with job assignments I need everyone's personal identification papers. Everything they have from social security cards to birth certificates to passports to past job IDs." She looks to me, "Miranda, with your experience in psychology I want you to take the lead. Cody will work with you and will be the middle man for me and you so neither one of us needs to worry about scheduling times to meet. Lilly, I want you to help her. Anything she needs from you whether it's coffee or meeting with people when she doesn't have the time. We currently have 192 women, men, and children living here not including the original 46. That includes your friend Mrs. Miranda."

"I would love to. Can I ask you something?"

"Sure," Jayne looks at me with such kindness. I wish I could talk with only her. I have so much to learn and she's so close yet so far away.

"A lot of people have been talking about when they will go outside again. People are feeling cooped up and without the ability to turn off our bedroom lights and the hallway and Big Room lights never changing people are not sure what time it is. It seems to be getting under people's skin. I'm worried about their mental health."

"After all I have done for them they are complaining about going outside where all the danger, chaos, and death is. They do realize I am letting them live down here during a catastrophe and asking for nothing in return. I am not charging any rent even though it costs money to run this place. I am providing food for them. I am not just doing the bare minimum. Is this how you are feeling? Since you came to me? I don't believe the others are feeling this way or they would have told me themselves. Are you sure this is not a projection of your own?"

"Everything I am doing, I am doing for a reason. My ideas will show themselves true as time goes on. As of now, it is on a need to know basis."

"No, please I don't believe any of that. I'm perfectly content here, but everyone, not everyone, a few feel nervous to talk to you," I try to answer.

She gives me a sharp confused look.

"They're only nervous because you're the head of everything here and the movement and they assumed you'd be busy and some mistakingly thought you'd get angry, but I know that's not the case and I can come to you with complete honesty so I volunteered to convey that for them, but I'll let them know what you told me and clear up any confusion."

"Of course you can always talk to me. I have done enough inner work I can hear these things and know they are not personal against me. I suggest you learn from this as well. I know you are younger, but you have so much potential I want to see blossom. It is a potential that only a leader who comes around rarely has and I see that in you."

"Thanks," I know I'm blushing.

She continues to give everyone else their assignments.

As we are departing Jayne calls me, Cody, and Lilly back towards her.

"I want this to work. It needs to be organized. Ridiculously organized. As you are gathering everyone's personal identifications I want you to gather more information. Everyone will have their own folder where the identification papers will be kept. In this folder I want you to assign each person a set of nine numbers. I have already gone through the liberty of making one for you all and all of the original members still with us today even though I am busy. Talk to the people some. See how they are doing and what they feel about everything going on. See if they have lost anyone recently, where they lived, what they did before the bombs. Anything remotely interesting that makes them an individual I want you to write it down.

"If you would like you can make a questionnaire to save time, but at least take some time to feel them out face to face. Every six hours I want Cody to bring the folders to me so I can have a member start digitizing it."

"Aren't you nervous there will be resistance to giving over their paperwork?" I ask.

"They do not have to be here. We can take them off the compound and drop them off somewhere safely," she says. "Does that work for you?"

"Yes."

"Miranda, we need everyone to begin on the same playing field. Do you understand?"

Chapter 5

1

"Good morning," Jayne addresses everyone in the Big Room a few days after we complete the information gathering. My eyes are puffy and I'm barely staying awake as that arduous work left me with little time to sleep.

"With the hard work of my counselors here, we have assigned everyone jobs. I know this place has started getting chaotic with only having people volunteer to do jobs like cook and clean. The plumbing has started to clog and the kitchen area is filthy. We need order and we hope to provide that for you. I apologize I have not done it sooner, but I have been swamped just making sure this place runs and doing other crucial jobs nobody else sees.

"We have chosen different job categories and the leaders for each one. Each leader will use their own autonomy to decide how to structure their area. The people who know best are the one's living it everyday so I won't micromanage. I don't believe in that and I hope to be passing off more responsibility of mine onto trusted members in the near future. I want all leaders to come to my office in hall F once they design the new structure.

"We put you where we believe your experience and also personal interests align the best. You can always change this later. Nothing is set in stone. I am not here to make permanent orders, only to help you all reach your full potential and guide you along.

"I want you all to feel comfortable coming to talk to me, but do remember how much I do and please be respectful of times when I am taking breaks, but other than that please reach out. Please write me a letter and give it to one of the main 10 advisors I have here to give to me. I cannot have people walking up to me or giving me letters all the time as much as I want to hear from you.

"I will start with announcing the leaders so they can head to a large common area in hall F to commence planning. If I call your name, come to the front and a member will give you a structured packet to take with you. Once I assign you your job area I want you to stay together in this room until tonight when your coordinator can meet with you." Jayne talks into a mic on her small makeshift wooden crate stage.

She looks at her notebook and announces, "Dan Eibenhower, you will be the assistance to the head maintenance who is one of the members of the council, his name is Rick Keller. Come grab your paperwork and follow instructions from there. Dan Eibenhower.

"Carrol Wecker, you will be head of structural foundation/architecture. Carrol Wecker.

"Dakota Johnson, you will be head of the sanitation department. Dakotah Johnson.

"Charles Stroff, kitchen. Charles Stroff.

"Kylie Hanner, entertainment. Kylie Hanner.

"Andrew Billon, gardening and food inventory. Andrew Billon."

And on and on Jayne went.

2

I was sleeping hard when I woke harshly to being shaken. A hand was pressed over my mouth and I bit it as I kicked my attacker.

"Miranda. Miranda. Wake up," Cody whispered. I grew still at his voice and saw Mark and Cody above me.

"Hurry and get dressed. We have to go to hall F immediately," Mark Langlend, Lilly's partner, with the fuzzy mustache said quietly. "I was sent to get you both, but you wouldn't wake up."

"I don't know why she didn't just tell me," Cody says.

"She picked me Cody," Mark says annoyed.

I heard something fall on the other side of the conjoining door to Kelsey's. We turned our heads and waited. There wasn't another sound.

We walked out in silence. The lights were still on like always. The only way I could tell it's night or day is we've agreed you go to sleep after dinner. We walk through the brightly lit hallway Aero where the council members reside. It feels like it's the middle of the night. It has that eerie absence of sound only the hours after midnight have.

The bright lights in the stone tunnel reminds me of movies I watched as a kid and makes me feel like I'm in some lair. Door after door. It'd be easy to lose my way if I didn't pay close attention.

"Through here," Mark leads us through an inconspicuous door. It looks just like the others that lead to people's private quarters.

"I thought we had to go to hall Framing," I say.

"There's another passage. We don't need to go through the Big Room risking people seeing us," He answers.

The smooth stone turns to rough stone immediately after entering. The only light is coming from the open door. The door slams shut and so does my sight. I can't see the hand in front of my face.

I hear Mark grabbing for something on the wall. I can't see my hand in front of my face. Then I see a flicker and another flicker and suddenly a circle around us is glowing from a torch in Mark's hand.

It's the size of a normal hall in any house, but the stone is much rougher than the polished stone everywhere else in the Haven. The space starts to shrink and soon we're walking single file.

The ceiling dips increasingly lower. Eventually we're on our hands and knees. There's little tiny cave formations. The torch makes it look like the stalactites are moving along with us. They're swaying and dancing as if they're coming alive after decades of rest. I can't tell if they're angry for being woken or indifferent.

"Be careful for cracks and holes," Mark calls back to us no longer talking quietly. His voice sounded like it was echoing from ten different surfaces as if it came from the air around us and not from him.

I stop crawling to look at these little figures carved into the wall. I sit back on my heels so I can have both hands to explore and I start tracing the different images. Simply carved human figures are around a large swirling symbol. It looks like an abstract tree.

"Keep it coming Miranda," Cody says.

Most of the stone in the shelter has been dry, but you could still smell the dampness that comes with being underground. Here, the stones have a thin layer of water.

I continue crawling along with the guys. It feels like I'm descending deeper into the earth although I don't feel an obvious slope. I feel heavier or maybe I feel like there's more earth above me bearing down. There's a different kind of pressure surrounding me. It's harder to breath.

The stones look less like a pile and more like a roughly cut hallway again. What feels like an hour later, we get to a stone door with wood and metal fixings on it.

"Was this a part of the mining tunnels?" I ask.

"What else would it have been?" Cody asks.

3

We walk into Jayne's office through a door I never noticed behind her gaudy desk in the back. The door blends in seamlessly with the rest of the room; No door knobs or latches.

She isn't here.

Mark looks to Cody. "Jayne said you would know where to go once we were standing on this rug over here," Mark says as he walks to an animal skin rug to the right of her office near a book shelf. He sounded jealous that Cody knows something he doesn't.

I look at Cody confused.

Cody reaches for the side of the book shelf and starts pushing it open to the side revealing descending stone stairs. This time Cody reaches for the wall and lights a torch.

"My daughter's only six! Her mother died years ago, she's all I have!" A man at the bottom begs.

Jayne's at the bottom with a guy who went to Santa Cruz and a man in a black ski mask. They stand over a bulky angry looking man with a square face tied to a chair. He shoves a dirty shirt into the prisoner's mouth. The prisoner's asymmetrical face has a full beard and a scar across his cheek stretching from the corner of his eye down to the bottom of his jaw. Angry grunts pop out of his slobbering mouth.

The room's lit by torches. It's almost a perfect circle, but unlike the other public spaces the stone wasn't sanded as smoothly. It's like the entrance and exit to that tunnel.

The man's dressed in dirty rags, but even in this compromising situation he looks important. He isn't struggling against his restraints and in between those angry little grunts he stops and stares with pure hatred at the man in the ski mask.

The man in the mask stands unnaturally still and never breaks eye contact with the tied man.

His continued mumbles make me feel sorry for him. He's trying to appear menacing, but it's almost comical. He look's like he's out of a mafia movie, but then I'm snapped back to reality and realize this is a real person in front me. He doesn't look like a good person though.

"Who?" I look at the man tied up. My heart has a mind of its own when it comes to how fast it likes to go, but my mind is focused. I'm keeping my mind calm like I was taught.

Dressed in a dark grey pant suit with her shiny black hair hovering above her shoulders, Jayne says "The Wolf," like I should've already known.

A man steps from the shadows around Jayne.

"This is Ian Campbell. He is the only one that survived out of the three who left. He brought The Wolf to us and saw many members of The Nothings up close." Jayne looks like she admires this boy. He's the 19 year old with the baby face who volunteered at the end.

Ian straightens the puffy jacket he's wearing adjusting the zipper up and down a few times before he decides he's comfy enough to continue. He reaches for The Wolf's ropes and my stomach constricts as I look to the man in the ski mask to see if he's going to stop him.

Ian adjusts the rope on the man's side a half inch. Now it's more symmetrical looking. Although he touched the prisoner without asking, neither the man in the ski mask nor Jayne say anything, let alone blink.

"Hello Ian," I reach my arm forward to shake his hand.

He drops his eyes to my hands, looks back up and says "Nice to meet you Miranda Haney." Ian looks to Mark and Cody on either side of me, "and you two as well." He picks at the side of his pants barely pulling them up and pushing them down and back again in quick movements until I guess he finds himself comfortable.

I awkwardly drop my hand reverting my gaze to the man who is called The Wolf. His skin swallows the rope tied around him. It's too tight.

"Alright, what's with this fuckin' puppy name anyhow?" Cody asks. "Also, are we going to address the God damn ski mask or continue to pretend that's completely normal?"

"The Nothings refer to him as The Wolf, Cody," Mark says.

"Yeah, no fuck. But why?"

"He only just arrived. I wanted you three with me." Jayne says and then looks at the masked man, "Ungag him."

"What the hell is this?! What is this place?" The man asks full of rage. "Are you part of the OTC, Order Through Chaos? I tried. I fucking tried man. Isn't that what you all wanted anyways. Order through fucking chaos?! I got overthrown. So what?!" He goes on spitting brown muck with every word. His sweat and spit mix together to form this rotting smell that fills my nose and spreads into my eyes and into my mouth. The more he talks the more the smell penetrates the room.

The masked man steps in front of him and stretches his arm high and in a full swing he slaps it across his face wobbling the man shaped like a boulder back and forth almost knocking him over. The masked man immediately returns his arm to his side standing rigidly straight.

Jayne leans on her knees inches away from the man looking as professional and clean cut as always and kindly says, "Now what is your name?"

"Bitch!" He screams and spits on her face.

Before he can push a laugh through his maniacal grin the masked man undercuts his chin throwing him backwards. The lumbering man smacks his head against the stone ground and goes quiet.

Jayne bends over and checks his pulse while wiping his dirty spit from her face as if it was a rain drop and nothing more. "He's alive," She says indifferently.

"Jayne. Come on," Cody says. "Tell us who this muscle bound, tall ass, faceless man is in the mask."

"Don't be impatient with her," Mark smiles at Jayne who ignores him.

"It's Isaac," I say.

Jayne looks at me quizzically.

"It has to be Isaac. Who else would come down here you trust enough we've never seen?" I ask.

Isaac walks to the wall without swinging his arms at all behind the prisoner to a huge wooden chest with rusty fittings. The chest looks like it hasn't moved from that spot in a thousand years or more. He comes back with a black fabric roll. He lets it spill open on a table next to the man revealing terrifying shiny metal tools similar to what a dentist would use.

"You are so intuitive Miranda," Jayne smiles. "I am sure you realize this is to be kept between only the people in this room." She grabs my arm, but in a loving way.

I feel admired and stifle a small smile.

Isaac pulls the chair back up and reaches for a metal bucket next to him and throws water on his face.

The prisoner's consciousness is slapped into him as hard as it was taken away. He looks at us then focuses in on Isaac in his mask then the shiny silver tools next to him. The angry hatred has evaporated and now it's only fear.

"Now, what is your name?" Jayne asks with a smile too genuine for this moment. She moves gracefully around the room.

"Johnathon. Johnathon Davis," the man says swinging his eyes between Isaac and the table with its menacing shiny bits.

"What was that about OTC, Order Through Chaos? What do you know about The Nothings Johnathon?" Jayne stands in front of his chair with perfect posture while the three of us stand behind her almost dumbly compared to her nearly perfect demeanor.

Ian's messing with the length of his sleeves and Isaac hasn't broken eye contact with the prisoner.

"The Nothings?!" Johnathon yells back at her mocking her voice. He throws his head back almost knocking the chair back again cackling loudly.

"I know the OTC and The Nothings are the same group. Why do you pretend to have a goal when the goal is anarchy?" Jayne stands in front of him leering down touching his knees with hers.

Johnathon continues to laugh and Isaac picks a tool up.

Jayne does a flick of her hand and he puts it back.

"I've heard of you! I wasn't sure if you existed," Johnathon looks around. "Wow," he shakes his head in disbelief. "Here you are and here I am in some God damn death cave in who knows where. I can't believe you're real."

"Why do you want to destroy humanity?" Jayne asks him not moving from directly in front of him.

"Now why would I want to destroy humanity pretty lady?"

"Bombing the cities and murdering people in the government could be evidence of you wanting to destroy America." She speaks like a teacher reprimanding a student for something he knew was bad.

"No. You got it all wrong," Johnathon shakes his head and looks truly dumbfounded at that idea. "We're saving humanity. The OTC will save humanity. The world. The government we had would be the death of us all. It's the people's choice. I did it for my daughter."

"You weren't the people's choice." Jayne sings with a coy smile.

"I know. I thought I was, but I wasn't. The people wanted someone else. It's about freedom. True and unadulterated freedom. Strength and choice and passion will rule the new world. Don't like someone? Put someone new in charge. No voting, no hidden agendas, no paid off politicians will be tolerated."

"How do you plan on doing that?" Jayne asks.

"It isn't up to me pretty lady," He answers.

"Then who is it up to?"

"Maybe give me a little somethin', somethin' and I'll talk." He smacks his lips at her and attempts to thrust, but the rope is too tight so the movement looks like an awkward twitch.

Jayne looks at Isaac who picks up one of his shiny tools.

"I'll talk! Jesus! You catch more flies with honey than torture!"

Jayne nods to Isaac.

Isaac grabs one of his fingers. The man struggles to no avail to slip his wrist out of the rope. The man lets out a blood curdling scream followed by cursing Isaac repeatedly as he deliberately rips a nail off. Blood pours from the empty connection where the nail should be.

A smile flickers across Ian's baby face as he adjust his collar a few times.

"Let's try this again. I'm being nice here so work with me. If it isn't up to you, then who is it up to?" Jayne asks.

"The people. Of course," His voice strains.

"Who told you to take charge?"

"Why does it matter? The people decided I wasn't the ruler to be."

"Who told you?"

"Doesn't matter. You hard of hearing?"

Isaac moves towards him again, but Jayne stops him with a simple raised finger.

"You're a whipped little cock aren't ya?" Jonathon asks Isaac.

Isaac squeezes his arms into his sides more than he already was, but doesn't do anything else.

"Where are the people who told you to be in charge?" Jayne asks.

"This. This right here. This is changing the world. You create what you want. You choose the people who make decisions. If you can't hack it then you don't make it. The world will be stronger! Freedom and choice!" Johnathon yells to the stone ceiling teetering on ecstasy.

Before Johnathon could level his head, Isaac grabbed another tool glittering in the fire light and grasped his jaw open. Isaac straddles him and slips the tool inside his mouth. With too much intimacy, he yanks a tooth out.

Johnathon's ecstatic smile turns to screams of pain as he struggles to hold his mouth while being bound in scratchy rope as his mouth gushes blood down his chest and into his lap like spilled soup. Isaac gently caresses his wet chin before sliding off him.

"Tell me," Jayne's voice remains calm. "Don't keep running your big mouth or we will have to make it smaller."

Johnathon writhes and yanks his arms upwards against the strain of the rope. He looks like an actor in an electrical chair.

"Tell me," Jayne says. She looks bored.

In his jerking and yelps of pain, he sprays blood onto Jayne's face.

Almost in a trance of peace Jayne grabs her under shirt and pulls it up to wipe the blood off. She rubs the spot on her shirt and gives Isaac a nod.

Isaac squeezes the sides of his cheeks forcing his mouth open as he strains with huge pliers until a front tooth pops out. His screams sound like drowning gurgles as his breath tangles with his blood. Isaac holds his head backwards making him choke further on his own blood.

Like a spray bottle, his blood sprays out of his mouth in the air in a mist as he chokes and struggles to breathe.

"He's only brainwashed though," I barely say.

"What did you say?" Jayne turns around.

"Can't we help him? He was brainwashed."

"There is no helping him now. It's too late. He's too indoctrinated into their doom philosophy. He is not in line with what is good for the world."

"Tell me," Jayne turns her attention back to him while blood pours out of his mouth as his head bounces against his chest.

He gulps for air as the pain of his mouth fights against the relief of not gagging on his own blood any longer.

He looks at her with the same intense hatred he looked at Isaac with earlier. "They will murder you," He shakes his head. A bloody smile forms on his face. "No they won't. They'll murder everything you've worked for. This evil you're trying to push onto the world won't succeed. You're God is wrong. We fight for freedom. Pure, unadulterated freedom." He chuckles until it morphs into a full booming laughter mixed with a hacking cough.

"He's a maniac," Jayne states. "Just look at him. I would help him if I could, but I just don't have the power. At least not yet. We do not have the power to save someone like him. Yet."

Isaac brings a small knife to his wrist that is bound to the chair. He saws at his skin like stale bread.

"Oh God! Stop!" He screams.

I watch helplessly as the blade cuts through his skin and veins until the knife is stopped by the bone.

The screams intrude my every cell burning themselves deep into my memory. Those agonizing screams are going to live inside me forever.

"Tell us where they are or you are losing a hand." Jayne leans an inch from his face. She squishes her nails into his open wrist and claws at it. His insides squelch between her fingers.

Isaac has a hatchet in his hand waiting.

What's Isaac thinking? Is he enjoying this? Is this his duty? That mask drives me insane. I need to be able to read his face.

Johnathon whispers inaudibly.

"What was that?" Jayne says digging her nails in deeper.

Through pain and clenched teeth he says, "Go.

Fuck.

Yourself.

Bitch."

The man's neck trembles and every line can be seen through his skin as he strains to tell her off.

Jayne snatches the hatchet out of Isaac's hand and slashes it across his neck breaking her professional composure screaming. "Who looks like the maniac now?!"

Warm blood splatters across my face and everything else in the room. It reaches the walls. It smells like a rusty tool shed.

His head falls backwards revealing the gash making it grow larger with the weight of his own head. The screams and the rasping breaths and the straining finally stops. The silence is uncomfortable. The awful sounds replay themselves in my head.

I feel like I'm in a dream. The man's gash looks like a second mouth on his neck. He'll be screaming double for eternity.

Ian's rigorously cleaning the blood away and Jayne has disappeared. Cody pulls on my arm leading me towards the stairs where the door was left open by Jayne.

It looks like a stairway to heaven the way the light's shining down.

4

The next morning when Cody and I walked into the Big Room everything had changed.

Before, the kitchen was starting to make people sick and the Big Room was getting disgusting. There was no central authority to organize basic living necessities. Luckily no bugs or critters can live this deep in the earth except us. There was no order and people had been crying and yelling and laughing and cheering and cursing and every emotion in between.

Now, everything is clean and ordered and the atmosphere's more relaxing. Still full of heartache, guilt, and loss, but better.

I don't know why Jayne waited so long to properly organize everything. She let it get pretty bad. With all the chaos of the world ending, it wouldn't be the first thought to have, I guess, to think of the basic needs of everyone you're saving. It's comforting to see how much Jayne can organize and gather everything into working order though. It'd be chaos if it weren't for her.

The Big Room's so clean. It has order. People are looking happier and eating the food at the tables and couches scattered about. The people in the kitchen are moving with intention instead of anxiety. That one pesky light directly across the stage is not twinkling anymore either.

Everyone's moving slower than normal with bags under their eyes, but still happier. They must have stayed up all night to complete this turnaround. Yeah, there's still people crying and eating alone here and there, but the overall atmosphere is better.

Just one night and everything went from a terrible mess to being fully functional. People are chatting and milling about.

Jayne is phenomenal.

"Do you think they stayed up all night?" I ask Cody.

"Don't tell anyone I'm telling you any of this fucked up shit even though I think it's harmless and more people should know more especially my sweet love right here," Cody boops my nose and gives me a big sloppy, happy kiss in front of everyone. I happily blush.

I pull back giggling and look at him full of love, "I don't like keeping anything from each other. For these wonderful ideas to come to surface we need to go about this correctly, but let us not keep anything from each other. At all." I kiss his chest.

"Oh darlin, I don't know about everything because Jayne and everything we stand for has been so clear about taking baby steps or everyone could turn against us. It's a part of the bigger plan." The way Cody looks into my eyes makes my stomach mushy. "But, you're as much a part of this as I am. I don't want to keep anything from you . . ."

". . . God, you're amazing."

"Anyways, what were you saying?" I ask.

"It's not a big deal," Cody says with his big, beautiful smile. "But yes, almost everyone stayed up. The leaders had to fill out these packets sorting everyone into roles and then give 'em directly to Jayne. Then they had to assign jobs to everyone in their department. Everyone had to perform those jobs. They couldn't stop until right before the best fucking breakfast we've had inside this shitty hole."

"I want to explore the beautiful land above us with you when it's safe to do so," I hug him again. By the looks of it, everything is turning around and I'm thrilled to be a part of something so revolutionary.

"Fuck yeah," Cody answers.

We walk over to the line to get food and Charles Stroff, head of kitchen, is back there running the show complete with a chef's hat.

"Hey Charles!" I hope I don't disturb his flow. "This looks wonderful. Thank you." My plate is a piece of heaven full of eggs, toast, grits, potatoes, and grilled green beans.

"Hey Miranda! I didn't know you knew who I was."

"Of course I would know who you are. I remember talking to you that day. I was the one who told Jayne about you and this position."

"Thanks so much! I've made the extra effort in learning your name and hopefully more. I want to be a part of what y'all are doing. I don't know what it is, but from what I see it's something real special."

"Thank you Charles," I say with gratitude. "I'll see you around."

"Jayne sure did an amazing job," I say to Cody.

"What can't she do?" Cody's spilling food on his chest.

Yeah, what can't she do?

5

Later after dinner, the ten of us went into Jayne's peaceful room. We started discussing Santa Cruz.

"I do not want any of you to go, but this might be the most important project yet besides getting everyone here and my organization engaged," Jayne says. The light from the candles is relaxing. A nice change from the LED's that never turn off on this compound. "I would be forever in your debt if one of you would take three counsel members and 15 people who we welcomed into our compound to establish a base and start implementing some of the practices we have started here."

I start to speak, but Jayne puts her hand on my knee.

I'd like to get out of here and into the world again, but I know I am one of the most trusted members and I am needed for the management. I don't want to disappoint Jayne. When she looks at me I feel important and when I hear her message I know we'll change the world.

A woman named Mikaela Leandra raises her hand timidly, then eagerly she calls out, "Jayne, I'd like to go."

"You would like to go or you can do this?" Jayne asks looking into her soul to read it. Her previous calming and sweet vibes go serious during Mikaela's request.

"I know I can," Mikaela says.

"Why do you know?" Jayne asks prying. She has a way of getting into people's heads with a look and a tone of voice.

"I'm ready. I ran a warehouse pre-bomb. I know I can do this. I've listened to every word you've said. I was one of the first people to arrive here. My husband and I had set up different stations with supplies for ourselves on our way here ahead of time in case we couldn't make it in one drive. We have backups to backups to backups," Mikaela's on the edge of her pillow leaning forward across the circle. She nearly falls inside it. She catches herself and tucks her hair behind her ears. She bounces on her cushion smiling.

"Do you understand the weight of this assignment? It's the first time people will hear of us in an official manner. You have to recruit people in Santa Cruz. You have to move fast and with purpose and show the people they cannot live without our organization and rules. That we are here to make their lives easy and safe," Jayne sits with perfect posture and the calmness of a monk. "Is there anything? Anything we or I could do to help you succeed?"

Mikaela sits back and says, "I need my husband Austin with me. He's been half of the decision making behind everything. We're a team. Do you know him?"

"Do you take me for an idiot?"

"What? No? I don't know what you mean."

"Obviously, I know who he is. You guys sit together during dinner. I know everyone on the counsel. Very well," Jayne answers sharply.

"Yes, of course. I just m-meant . . ." Mikaela stammers.

"That sounds good to me," Jayne waves her hand.

Mikaela breathes, "I meant if you knew how efficient we are together."

"Yeah. Okay. He can go with you. It's fine." Jayne settles back into a comfortable seated position. "I am proud of you Mikaela."

Mikaela blushes.

I can't help feeling jealous. Why didn't she want me to volunteer?

6

Later that night after I had fallen asleep I woke to Jayne walking through the door.

Jayne kneels next to me and Cody stirs awake.

"Miranda, I would like to go above the compound and look at the stars with you," Jayne strokes my cheek.

"Umm," I look over to Cody.

"Sounds great love," and he flips back over.

I pull the covers back stepping out naked, "I'd love to go with you."

"Dress in something warm."

7

Jayne drives the UTV to the mountain ridge where I first arrived and shuts the lights off. It's pitch black. At least my time table is true. It couldn't be off by more than five or six hours, but most likely it's still the same. As long as it's the right day.

I let my head fall backwards as I watch the night sky. The stars appear one by one then tens then hundreds then thousands as my eyes adjust. I gaze in wonder at the Milky Way stretching across the black void.

God, is it good to breathe fresh air. Air that isn't stale and full of other's trapped smells, but one that is fresh and full of life. There's no hint of smoke left. I breathe it in romantically watching the night sky.

"Miranda," Jayne nudges me.

"Yeah?" I stare at the Milky Way and watch the stars closer to the bottom glittering from atmospheric disturbance.

I hear her nose sniffle and then sudden sobbing. I turn towards her, but I hesitate to grab for her and give comfort, "Jayne. Jayne, what's wrong?"

"I just need to cry." She grasps at me until we are hugging.

I wrap my arms around her and feel her melt into my chest. I allow myself to melt as well. Her tears against my neck are warm and I squeeze her tighter. I feel special she chose to me be a safe place.

I start remembering the people I left behind. The world I left behind. My career and my friends and my hobbies. The emotions I have been burying since that phone call, bubble to the surface. Before I know it I'm crying along with her.

We embrace each other under the stars for what seems like an hour as we cry. We sag in the seats of the UTV that took me underground so I could help save so many people's lives and possibly the world.

"Do you want to talk about it?" I ask.

"No," Her voice is muffled against my neck and long hair. "Do you?"

"Maybe later."

"I just needed to get it out so I can better serve those lost souls down there and the ones to come. You felt safe," Jayne pulls back. "You would think most people would flee to the country after nearly everyone in the cities were murdered, but they went there because that is where The Nothings or-" in a mocking voice Jayne says, "-the OTC, Order Through Chaos sent their people to establish order over rubble. There is nothing for them to survive off of there. That is why The Nothings, those evil people who believe absolutely nothing; No government or true order or religion or spirituality or a way of life or anything are . . . I forgot what I was saying."

"Why'd you send Mikaela and Austin to establish rule over Santa Cruz then?" I hold her hands.

"I don't want them to rule necessarily. I want them to bring the people in Santa Cruz to safety. I want them to be saved. We are the New World Order," Jayne stops talking and she snaps her head towards me. I see her perfect face and beautiful eyes even though it is the darkest sky I have ever experienced, but she's only inches away. "What do you think of that for our name? New World Order?"

"New World Order?" I ask.

"Yeah, as the name of our movement. I know in previous meetings and work functions we never put a proper name to us, but I don't know. I think with a name it will give us more recognition. More legitimacy. It will give people a word to say and recognize. A symbol. Something to unite us more easily."

"What about New World Freedom? Order sounds communist and controlling and we are trying to give people the freedom to pursue personal growth while also running a society that benefits from complete and utter organization at every single level. I don't like the word control so I'll say guidance. Through controlled guidance we will give people the feelings of safety and freedom they need." I look away from the stars and back to her, "Unless you think that is too close to what The Nothings want." I say Nothings as if it's a derogatory term for the people who want to destroy humanity through the belief of nothing; true anarchy.

"I love it," Jayne leans closer to me until I can feel her forehead pressed firmly against mine while she squeezes my hands.

I realize we still haven't let go of each other once since Jayne first grabbed for me.

"Cody has been my right hand man and he has only ever said spectacular, brave things about you. From what I have seen he is right and I want you to be my left hand woman. I want you both by my side as we enact the visions to make this world a perfect place."

"I would not dream of wanting anything else," I say as our foreheads are pressed against each other. Her hands are sweating, but I don't mind. The smell of fresh air and oaks and sage brush and open fields and the sweet smell of Jayne's hair tickling my cheeks calms me.

I am rejuvenated.

"There is much to be done. It might get ugly, but I need your faith to stay strong with the movement," she says. "Promise me that."

"I am on fire for this movement."

"I am serious you cannot let evil inside of you. You cannot let it influence your decisions. You must not be lukewarm."

"My heart will stay true. I promise."

She grabs my cheeks and says, "The world depends on us."

Chapter 6

1

In the morning Cody and I went to meet Jayne in the Big Room. The first thing I noticed was the stage in front of Hall Aero. Rick and Dan, the head maintenance and assistant walk up like shy children repressing smiles.

"Wow!" I exclaim, "This looks amazing!"

"Really? Do you like it?" Rick, a counsel member, asks blushing.

"Jayne will love it." Just as I said her name she walks out of Hall Framing. Anger flashes across her face when she notices the stage. I swear her face turned red.

She stomps in her heels towards us and in a hushed, strained voice says, "Who the fuck did this without asking me? Who came up with the bright idea of changing something so drastic without my consent?"

Rick and Dan look at each other frightened. "Ummm-I-Um . . ." They look down and fiddle with their hands.

"Rick. You are on my counsel yet we did not . . ." Jayne makes big air quotes as her voice rises, ". . . counsel." She turns to Dan, "You are assistant to Head Maintenance correct?" He nods quickly, "Then why did you not try to advise Rick here to communicate?"

Cody places his hand on her and whispers, "Jayne, the rest of the goddamn people are starting to stare."

He's comfortable with her. I don't see anyone else touching her.

Jayne closes her eyes.

"Talk to me next time. It looks great. It really does. Thank you!" Jayne is suddenly professional and calm, composed, and grateful. "Cody and Miranda, come stand with me on the stage now that there is room for you on this beautifully crafted stage." She looks at us sweetly.

A wave of happiness flows through me as I realize just how lucky I am to be in this position of the New World Freedom. Right by Jayne's side.

People are finishing breakfast. Jayne prefers to wait to talk after people eat because she told me they are happier and more likely to pay attention.

"Hello everyone! Can I please have your attention," Jayne projects. "We have received 78 new people this morning. They will be screened and assigned positions after breakfast. They will be meeting here at the stage and then finding their leaders after I finish talking." Jayne takes a deep breath as she looks up at the massively high cavernous ceiling. She drops her head and smiles with so much conviction everyone else smiles with her. "We are called the New World Freedom!"

Cody and I clap, which cues the counsel members, then the rest of the room erupts in cheer. Cody pumps his fists in the air and jumps. The cheers sound like a firework show.

"That was my idea Cody," I say proudly.

"That's fuckin' awesome babe."

His hand glides to my lower back and I'm filled with a joyous peace.

Jayne continues, "We are saving lives down here. Everything is running smoothly and even during the darkest of times we have found sanity and organization. I know a lot of you are feeling scared and don't know what is going on above ground.

"My counsel members and I have been meeting for years now to try and stop The Nothings. I know you're wondering, "If we knew about it then why did we not contact the US government?" We tried, but the tables were quickly turned on us and the NSA started stalking us, treating us like terrorists. Then they quickly began ignoring us and our pleas, so I expanded our operation since they wouldn't help.

"In case you have not heard, every major city has been bombed, killing nearly everyone in it and many who tried to escape were murdered. There is no government left. The president is dead and the line of succession has been all but eradicated. The United States infrastructure has been rendered useless in most areas. In the chaos, the major cities have been retaken by those from the organization who murdered millions destroying everything we know and love. We call them The Nothings since they believe in nothing. They do not believe in helping those around them, just murdering people in pursuit of power. They call themselves Order Through Chaos or OTC. Let me reassure you; There is no order when there is only anarchy. Many cities that were unharmed still had their government buildings bombed or set afire. Small towns were often spared. My deepest condolences if you had family and friends in the hot zones or in government work." Jayne bows her head.

"Why couldn't you stop it?!" A man in the back yells desperately.

The room rumbles with similar shouts.

She waits patiently for the shouts to subside.

"We postponed it as long as we could. We have been developing this safety bunker you are all residing in now. It used to be an uninhabitable cave with mining shafts waiting to swallow someone into its depths, but now it's the Haven. We have every supply people would need to live here for a long time and possibly a limitless time. We have solar and other renewable sources of energy. The series of roads we have above ground we will use more in due time. They were overgrown logging roads and horse trails. Many more of us are working in different states trying to save as many people as possible.

"Together with everybody doing their part, the world will go back to normal, but our previous "normal" of corruption and brutality and disorder will be improved upon."

The crowd settles.

"I want, no, I need everyone in this room to help us. We will have vengeance for our loved ones murdered, our buildings and properties destroyed, and we will regain our confidence. New World Freedom is about equality and making the most out of our lives. Everyone's voice is important. I want you to talk to my counsel and I want you to talk to me. All of us will be transparent with each other because a healthy society is built off trust." Jayne emanates vibrant confidence and it's clear she won the crowd's approval.

A man I've seen at every counsel meeting comes on stage and whispers something into Jayne's ear then leaves. His arms stayed unnaturally straight against his side. He moved like a wooden board.

"And on that note, I will take my leave and let you begin your daily jobs. Thank you for all your hard work!" Jayne's voice echos off the high ceilings and disappears through the hallways and the cracks in the rock until it's gone. The room fills with noise again from those we're saving.

I am filled with pride. Everyone here is safe. People are happy and and they believe in the greater good. I know there's people who are still sad and angry at the world because of OTC, but all I can see right now is blissful gratitude.

Chapter 7

1

"Miranda I need you to leave with Kyle for Santa Cruz. He arrived the other day and we need to rescue the people Mikaela and Austin have initiated," Jayne sits on the edge of my bed.

I feel like we are close now. Having her in my bedroom makes me feel like we have a special bond.

"Of course, anything you need."

"I am so sorry, but I need Cody to stay. I know you will be safe. Isaac will fit you for weaponry and gear. I am sending Lilly, Mark, three of the recruits that have been here the longest, and your friend Kelsey if you can trust her." Jayne waits for me to nod.

"Cody isn't coming?"

"and Isaac. He will lead the caravan," she doesn't hear me. "Kyle will ride with you to update you on everything you missed the other day since you could not hear their recounting of Santa Cruz."

"I don't want to be separated again."

She cuts me off like this conversation is her giving a speech she already rehearsed. "Each person will drive a large school bus. Your goal is to rescue as many people as possible that Mikaela and Austin have recruited. If there is any extra space, try to find more people in the smaller towns between here and Santa Cruz who did not head to the cities. Only on your way back are you instructed to grab random stragglers though."

"When do I lea-?" I ask.

"You are to leave immediately."

"I will be ready in an hour. I just need to pack and eat something."

"Everything you need is already in the bus waiting for you. Say goodbye to Cody and shower and meet me outside of your door in 10 minutes with Kelsey. The buses depart in 20 minutes. There are eight of them." Jayne hurries out the door.

2

I'm driving behind Isaac's bus with Kyle as we head north along the cliff sides of the Pacific Ocean on Highway 1 in our big yellow school bus caravan. It's a good thing we don't have to be conspicuous.

"Where is Mikaela and Austin living?" I watch the road intensely. I carefully drive around the curves which cling to the side of the steep cliffs. I have never driven this large of a vehicle before and this road is not the gentlest for first timers.

"Are you okay to drive? Not saying you can't," Kyle asks. His long surfer hair is blowing next to the open window. He's handsome for a younger guy and unlike Cody he is unaware of that fact.

"The city center is rubbish, but the outskirts aren't too bad. They settled into a castle of a church where they've brought other recruits in. We took daily journeys into the bomb zones to rescue stragglers. We sent scouts to gather people to live near the church."

"Why a church?"

"I'm not so sure. I mean it's on the edge of town. It's also crazy big. I think Jayne told them to choose a church though."

"Why?"

"I think . . . actually I don't know."

"What was it like when you first arrived?"

"Not pretty." Kyle grows silent for a minute. His young eyes look full of a weary darkness. "Not good. It's still chaos there, but order's coming back. At first people were only trying to kill us for supplies, but then The Nothings got suspicious of us and started attacking. Many died and many joined us. They'd always say roughly the same thing during these attacks, "We destroyed the entire country for controlling their citizens and now you're brainwashing them worse than the country did. It'll be easy to kill your measly little group." He mimicked the way they screamed the words. He had to shake himself before continuing.

"That's awful."

"I don't believe they ever figured out we were tied to a much larger group south of 'em. We started in a big ol' house near the church only recruiting those close by. Well, with our food supply we were able to feed people winning their trust. After a while we gave them weapons to defend the area. Anytime an attack would come from The Nothings or other scavengers they'd quickly kill 'em. We displayed their heads around the neighborhood warning groups that meant us ill-" his voice didn't alter like it should have revealing something so awful.

"You did what?!" I squeeze the steering wheel tighter as the cliff to the left of me kisses the road.

"No, it worked you see. I was unsure at first too, but Mikaela was right. We put up posters along with the heads telling people we have food, clean water, and other things. We can protect anyone. That we believe in equality, peace, and order. This brought new people in everyday. This also brought more attacks at the mention of food and such, but that only allowed us to extend our boundary by making the circle of heads larger and larger. Then the attacks almost stopped altogether. Eventually we were big enough to move into the city center, but there was no place to make camp so Mikaela had us take over the church. We gave people jobs and before we knew it, the place was running pretty smoothly." He looks proud, but I also detect worry.

"Was there any resistance to the job assignments or the food and supply distribution?" I ask.

"Of course. Jayne warned us about that."

"So what did you do with them Kyle?"

"Mikaela said some were members of The Nothings trying to turn people against us since their savage attacks didn't work on our organization," Those were obviously her words he repeated. "We added their heads to a spike and continued to grow our boundary. We didn't advertise who the heads were. We kept it quiet. Mikaela told us to just tell people somebody walked off when they went missing. It wasn't uncommon for people to leave so that's what we went with. When more heads popped up it meant we were protecting everyone from even more people who only wanted to cause harm and chaos."

"How do people feel about the plumbing and electricity not working?" I ask impressed at how quickly they won the hearts of so many.

"Instead of focusing on what we don't have, we tell 'em about this place in the mountains where we're from that has all the power and sanitation they need. We told them they would eventually be allowed to go there. And that they wouldn't have to work so hard once they were there. They're hopeful. They treat us almost like Gods," Kyle tells me with reverence. "The biggest massacre-"

"Why are we slowing to a stop?" I interrupt him.

"Isaac to team. There are rocks in the road that must have rolled from the mountain. Over," Isaac's voice transmits through radios he gave us. He sounds mechanic. I don't think I've heard his voice before until now.

I am trying to see around his bus when I see movement on the other side of the road in some bushes.

"Mark to Isaac. I hear you loud and clear. Do you need us to get out and move them? I would be happy to do that. Over."

"Do not get out," I say into the radio.

"Isaac to team. I already installed a rock plow onto the front of my bus. I am lowering it now. Over."

I can clearly see a group of people in the bushes now. More of them continue to appear.

"People are in the bushes. Over," I say.

"Kyle. Grab the machine gun under the seat. Don't let them see it and be ready by the window," I order.

Isaac's bus inches forward and a group of people jump out of the bushes and run towards his bus and back behind us.

"Now!" I shout at Kyle while reaching for my pistol at my waist. It feels good to be armed again. I'm not allowed to bring it below ground even though other people get to.

Kyle points the barrel out the window and empties the magazine at the people charging Isaac's bus. Two of them collapse, but one disappears in Isaac's bus. I hear shots go off around me, but I can't place their locations. Out of the corner of my eye a person tries to jump inside the bus. We both shoot. Mine hits a fraction of a second sooner knocking the person back off the bus and their bullet into the roof. More shots go off in front of me around Isaac's bus and back behind us. I'm scanning and waiting for the slightest of motion.

The gun fire peters out, but Isaac's bus still hasn't moved. I stand still trying to decide if I should get out when I see a body fly out of the side of his bus. The body lands on its head pulling its neck until the top of its head is touching the middle of its back. Blood is turning the grey road a deep black as blood pours from some unseen wound.

I am trying hard to identify the blood soaked face.

"Isaac to team. Is everyone okay?" The radio transmits.

Thank God it wasn't him. I can feel my heartbeat again and it's ready for more action.

The Secrets We Carry | 94

The radio goes off over and over again until everyone is accounted for. Isaac brings his big yellow bus to life and crawls forward moving the rest of the rock slide over.

We are on the road again.

I still haven't seen Isaac's face as the last time I was with him he was wearing a ski mask. There is no way I haven't seen him lurking in the background at meetings though, yet I do not have a fucking clue what he looks like. He was already in his bus at the front of the line when we headed north.

I spot another person hiding behind a tree on the side of the road, but we are going fast enough now so I don't say anything.

3

North Big Sur is probably empty since we saved everyone we could find and brought them to our Haven. Except for the people I spotted on the side of the road that is. We slow down again and I am already reaching for my pistol. I'm expecting another bloody ambush when I hear the radio.

"Isaac to team. This gas station's only missing the pumps. Doesn't look like any fires or explosions. We can get gas from the reservoirs so let's fill up. Let's be quick about it. Over."

I pull behind Isaac and finally see his face. I barely recognize it. How can that be? I mean it looks familiar, but I can't identify it. Actually no, I have seen it a lot. He's at nearly every meeting or event, but in the back and never says anything. So that's the infamous Isaac. A man with a face so plain he blends in everywhere seeing everything without being seen.

A few of us stand guard around the buses while the rest explore what is left inside.

Some return with arms full of candy and snacks from the convenience store. I didn't think it was a good idea to leave the close vicinity of the buses. People are smiling and picking through it like children.I listen to my colleagues becoming friends as they giggle like kids. There's an air of real happiness that nearly makes me forget the danger around us.

Kelsey walks over, "Look! Candy! How come the shelves weren't wiped out?" She shoves a chocolate bar into her mouth as she continues talking. I can't understand a word.

"Ah yeaaah, give me one a those," Kyle snatches a bar from Kelsey who happily lets him take it.

"This is definitely a win for us. We will take them when we can. I won't question it," I smile. "I want that one." I grab at my favorite chocolate bar. Kelsey knew the one.

"Sooooo good," Kyle says with crumbs falling into his long wavy hair. He dances a little jig.

"I'm going to ask the guys pumping the buses what they want," Kelsey says. She's wearing the first genuine smile I have seen her wear since the bombs. I tear open my candy bar and take the mushiest bite. The chocolate melts in my mouth and the sugar hits my brain. The familiar feel is comforting. I watch Kelsey bounce off to the others.

In ecstasy I go for another bite enjoying the sun when out of the corner of my eye I thought I saw something in the upper story of the bar window. I stop eating and reach for my pistol.

I go hard again.

"Alright let's fall out!" One of the men helping Isaac yells.

We climb into our eight buses and continue.

4

The miles are passing us by and the towns are empty except for a few sporadic movements.

The Pacific Ocean to the left of me pulls me into its vastness and I think of how small we are compared to what the Earth has been through. The mountains to the right of me stand relatively permanent against this brief moment of history. They have seen so much, but they still stand tall hugging the rough water with the road scarring their sides. That winding and terrifying road that makes my stomach drop.

We leave the wilderness. Although the town we're entering wasn't bombed, it was ravaged to pieces. The stores and gas stations have broken windows. In the relatively short time since the bombs, the sidewalks and parking lots and roads have already begun to grow weeds. Wildlife is everywhere.

"Isaac to team," the radio buzzes. "We're going to turn away from the main roads and head on into residential areas. Don't stop. I repeat do not stop for anything."

"Why're we doing that?" Kyle jumps onto his knees to look out the window better.

"I'm not asking Isaac. You're welcome to use the radio though," I hold it out for him to grab.

"I bet the main roads are blocked. No need to ask," he shakes his messy hair.

I ride his tail, turning into what was once a perfectly clean and proper neighborhood. The houses are not too dissimilar from the one Kelsey and I resided in. Lawns don't exist anymore. Nature is already taking it back. It seems the more an area tried to control its environment, the more wild and disorienting it looks now. The land was once conquered by man - the grasses cut, the bushes trimmed, the leaves raked, the weeds plucked, and the animals removed. And now all those years and generations of work have disappeared in an uncomfortably short amount of time. I'm assuming only a short time has passed. Time is weird in the cave.

I pass a luxurious light blue two-story house with boarded windows. A car is parked out front with a family of raccoons milling around it who scatter as our loud caravan cruises past. The front door lies in the middle of the once unnatural "lawn." A large plastic sheet is duck taped around the door as if its purpose was to seal off the house from the outside air.

Another house has a large gaping hole in it where a crashed truck hangs halfway out. The windows are shattered save for the one survivor at the top looking into the attic. I saw a glimpse of plates on the coffee table beside the truck. Possibly that family's last meal. Everything is wet and sodden inside and tiny weeds are poking up. The morning mist has helped turn their expensive rugs and leather couches into a type of forgotten soil where tiny plants are making new memories in place of the people before them.

Every house we pass screams a blood curdling song of sorrow.

Up ahead I see a beautiful beach house with double porches. In the tall grasses there's large wooden signs with painted words. The house is covered in blue tarps.

"THE END IS HERE," one sign says. Another beside it says, "GOD HAS COME." Another "REPENT." Another, "SAVE YOURSELVES, ACCEPT HIM." A large cross is clumsily nailed through the Earth's skin. Every entryway is boarded with more signs. Some of them say, "SAVE US GOD," "666," "RUN."

As we crawl through neighborhoods avoiding the cars that were abandoned haphazardly, we watch the ruins pass by our huge bus windows as if we were watching a movie. A dog runs out of the bushes barking at the critters on his lawn. Cat's are going in and out of houses accomplishing their errands. Deer are chewing on forgotten lawns as they say hello to their neighbors. Foxes and raccoons pour out of garages, houses, and cars leaving for work.

Another house with signs comes up. Graffiti and random splotches and splatters covers the first nine feet of it circling the entire house. The door had been painted black. The largest sign reads "Order Through Chaos." The windows have sheet metal over them and wooden planks over that. It's hard to tell while rolling past, but it looks like they were welded onto a metal frame that had been attached to the house. It's a modern fortress.

I take my foot off the gas as I pass a sign with a body behind it. I reach for my gun, but it's pointless when I see it's a lifeless sack. The corpse holds the sign up. 2x4s are holding the corpse up, but it's starting to look more like a kebab as it deteriorates. Flies and maggots party in the holes that rotted away once the birds slurped the eyes out and tore at the skin. More signs in the yard read, "DON'T TRUST ANYONE," "OTC WILL SAVE," "SURVIVE AND DIE FOR SURVIVAL." As I drive past each sign purposefully laid out on the edge of the sidewalk there are more bodies. These signs supported by corpses go on for three more houses. They read "GOVERNMENT GONE," "TRUE FREEDOM AT LAST," "WE WILL RISE," "BURN THE RESISTORS,"

"DON'T LET THEM LIE," and so on and so on, each with their own designated body. We pass the last sign that reads, "TAKE CHARGE" and I see the body supporting it in my giant side mirror as we drive by. Unlike the other bodies where the signs leaned on them, the last body appears to hold its own sign with duct taped hands. Someone had stuck bright red Halloween devil horns on it. Stuck into its thigh is an upside down American flag. The sign reads New World Freedom (NWF) inside a nuclear waste symbol. It was painted in bright red, which will forever look like wet blood by the way it dripped.

 That name is so new. Jayne and I had only told the rest of our members recently. How could they have already heard of it unless there is another leak?

 I know we are not alone. I can feel people staring at us through whatever rubbish and broken glass and boarded up windows they are hiding behind. Tarps litter front yards where they blew away and nobody was around to replace them.

5

"Isaac to team. Over," the radio buzzes.

One by one everyone answers him.

"We're about to stop. Meet me inside my bus when we do. Over."

We drive out of the neighborhood onto a long stretch of road further away from the ocean that has no buildings. The grass is green and there's cows out in the rolling hills.

Isaac slows to a stop. Kyle and I get out and climb into his bus. We look in the back and see that it's chock full of supplies. The others follow suit.

"It's gettin' dark," Kyle says.

Isaac's thousand yard stare breaks and turns to Kyle. He stands with his arms plastered to his sides, "It's late and I don't know what the roads ahead will hold. We will camp here for the night. There's a road leading to a large empty field 15 miles away at the next turn. The field is about three miles in. Any concerns?"

"We barely made headway today. We're moving too slow. The Nothings will know we're coming," Mark, Lilly's partner, tells him like he relayed important information we're not already aware of.

Isaac looks back out the window rubbing his pistol to make sure it didn't fly off his hip. "We'll try a different route tomorrow. It may work or may not, but we need to move faster. Oh and," he looks around us, "Don't use the radios for the rest of the night unless it's an absolute emergency. Also don't use any lights."

"Did you hear me?" He asks.

We nod.

"I hear you," Mark says.

"We've lost people on this drive before. There are hidden mines and road blockages set up for ambushes. Tonight will be the most dangerous part of the journey."

Chapter 8

1

The next morning we travelled along the highway for hours with no trouble. Kyle stared out the window in the same fashion as Kelsey's long unblinking stares she made when we first drove to the Haven. Vehicles lined the sides of the road, but we always had plenty of room to carry on.

Isaac's bus slams on the brakes causing me to swerve to the side barely missing him. Loud squealing and the sound of tires burning across the road roar behind me. I squeeze my eyes shut waiting for the sound of a collision, but nothing comes.

I prepare myself for an ambush.

"Isaac! Do you come in?!" I yell into the radio.

"Yes. Yes, I am here. Over," Isaac answers. He sounds mildly aggravated instead of ready to kill members of The Nothings.

"What happened?" Mark radios.

"The road is gone."

I step out of my bus to the view of a massive car pileup. Chunks of asphalt are covered in paint. "OTC" is written everywhere.

I jump when my radio buzzes and it's Isaac's voice, "Get back on the bus Miranda. I didn't say you could step off. This could be a trap."

Isaac walks out holding a can of white spray paint. He goes to a car and shakes the can and writes, "GO SOUTH 4 SAFETY."

The last bus in the caravan begins the awkward hurdle of backing up.

There isn't enough space with the other abandoned cars on the road to turn around. We're forced to drive dangerously slow in reverse until we reach an on-ramp with enough room to turn around.

Santa Cruz isn't too far away now.

"Kyle to team. Over," Kyle radios.

"Go ahead Kyle. Over," Isaac responds.

"I know the way to our people from here."

"We'll follow you then."

2

Kyle leads the caravan as he drives my bus. I'm more relaxed now that I am back with Kelsey driving her bus.

I see what looks like a face on a pole ahead.

It begins.

"Oh my God is that?!" Kelsey shrieks.

My stomach churns as we pass by a head so rotted you could barely tell it was ever a human before. It might as well be a cheap prop from a Halloween store, but then I remember with hellish clarity this is all real. What is left of the skin is hanging off the bones gently blowing in the wind like birthday streamers marking the way for a celebration. I can see the white of the bone under where its nose used to be until it was snacked on by hungry birds who don't differentiate humans as something other than another animal.

"There will be more Kelsey. Kyle told me Mikaela and Austin put The Nothing's heads on spikes." I lower my voice, "-and people who turned violent against them after joining them. Kyle said it was just The Nothings in disguise who tried to cause chaos within though."

"You believe that?"

"Even if it were other people who turned on them that means The Nothing's evil ways got to them."

"What happens if you decide you don't agree with something?"

"We are doing the most important work that has possibly ever been done. They chose me to be a leader alongside them."

"I'm happy for you."

I can't read her.

Another head lops into view with a sign beneath it that says, "THE." Another head with another sign ahead says, "NOTHINGS." We are driving off the highway past abandoned gas stations and old fast food restaurants and outlet malls. I wonder if some of these places will be like passing old and decrepit western towns in the future.

We pass another one that says, "OTC" then another, "MURDERED" and another, "YOU," "AND," "THIS," "COUNTRY." The sign that reads "COUNTRY" has a full corpse with its right arm outstretched pointing our way. We listen to the corpse and turn. The first head reads, "FOOD," then, "CLEAN H2O," "SUPPLIES, "SAFETY," "PEACE," "ORDER," "AHEAD." We drive on passing more heads staked into the ground.

"How is this peaceful?" Kelsey asks me horrified.

"Anarchy has caused nothing but misery. We will add true order back to society. There will be a society again. As long as you do not engage in the evil The Nothings do then there will be peace again. These people are not people anymore was what I was told. Evil has entered them and there is no way to save them, but to end their lives. I still wonder if there is anything we can do though." As an after thought, I tell Kelsey quickly, "You can not tell anyone I said that."

"It's okay to have doubts."

"The movement does not have room for people who are lukewarm Kelsey. We have to be on fire."

Six black SUVs pull out of parking lots blocking the road. People dressed in black and outfitted with military weaponry pour out.

"Announce yourself!" They demand.

I look past Isaac's bus to see Kyle walking out with his hands casually up as if he were at a concert. Watching Kyle excited to see them, immediately puts me at ease.

I can't hear what Kyle is telling them, but the guy that screamed is now talking into a radio. They return to their vehicles. Kyle turns around with a big cheesy smile and gives us a thumbs up.

We follow them to the parking lot of a huge church. It is stunning. Two tall towers and stained glass windows stand in stark contrast to the disheveled cheap buildings nearby. High eaves and relief sculptures cover the light beige building. It looks like it was plucked out of ancient Europe or my old art history textbook and dropped here. The entry has white granite steps leading up to a white entrance with two magnificently large wooden doors.

They remind me of the wooden doors with the ancient metal fixtures in the Haven.

At the bottom of the steps is a white fountain with a granite sculpture of Jesus. Except the Jesus has no head so now it's just a buff mannequin. It could be placed in a Rome pleasure house and nobody would know the difference. The water fountain is full of green and brown sludge drooping over the edges. People are walking around and some are even smiling and laughing.

A gas station to the left of the church in front of a large grocery store obviously has people living inside. To the right is a beautiful park. The fact it's no longer maintained and turning wild only makes it more beautiful. People are walking through it as if the world is normal again. Across the street are different restaurants, which looks like people's homes judging by the clothes hanging outside and the children's toys scattered around.

There's a touch of normalcy here or as much as you can get during the middle of an apocalypse. People want that feeling of normalcy so badly during any disaster they will try their hardest even if it's only a small pocket protected temporarily from the outside world.

After we park, we stand at the bottom of the granite steps. The SUVS drive off.

The doors burst open. "You made it!" Mikaela runs out, "Kyle! Oh my God you're back!" She jumps onto him flooded with joy. He embraces her.

"Where's Austin, that blonde headed goof?"

"I'm here you ol' fucker!" Austin yells from the top of the stairs. Him and Kyle meet halfway in a rough embrace. The kind of hug after not knowing if the last time you said goodbye would be the last. The kind you see between people whose family members are in the military, but now every single person in the country is experiencing it.

"I'm so sorry if I butcher your names, but there were so many," Mikaela looks to us. "You are Miranda," she points, "You're Lilly, you're Mark, Lilly's partner, and you . . ."

One of the newer members speak up, "It's fine, you probably don't know us. We were saved by the New World Freedom and were sent on this journey to further Jayne's great work," One of the members told her. "I'm Kelly by the way and these are my two brothers, Ryan and Jake. It's a pleasure to meet the infamous Mikaela and Austin." Kelly extends her hand. "You guys make a great couple."

Mikaela disregards the hand and hugs her.

"My pleasure. We will make this world the most beautiful perfect place together," Mikaela says.

She turns to Isaac and she stops smiling. She tucks her hair behind her ears, "I know you. I've definitely seen your face around, but I apologize I do not know your name."

Austin walks over, "Hold on, it's been a crazy time. You're-you're in Jayne's large counsel."

Isaac says with annoyance, "I'm Isaac."

Mikaela and Austin look aghast. "Isaac, Isaac?" Austin asks him.

"So you've heard of me," Isaac responds matter of factly.

"Uh . . . yes. I mean yes. It's a pleasure to meet you," Austin extends his hand too fast. His fingers wobble.

Isaac looks at his hand then begins to walk with his arms held straight by his side towards those two enormous ancient and beautiful wooden doors with relief sculptures above them displaying the biblical story of the fiery end Earth is to have. "Do you have food for us? We've had a long journey."

Austin runs up the steps and opens the heavy door letting Isaac in first and we pour into the main worship hall barely seeing anything until the door slams behind us and our eyes adjust to the sudden dimness. Candles are lit making the space feel warm. It's strange though. Something is off. Nearly everything religious has been stripped out of here so it feels naked. I check to see I'm still standing beside Kyle and Kelsey.

It was uncomfortably hot outside, but it's comfortable in here. Almost like when it's cold and your Mom wraps a blanket around you.

"Do you see it?" I whisper.

"See what?" Kyle asks in a regular volume.

Kelsey hooks her arm around mine and whispers, "I know. I still feel I have to whisper as if the energy or holiness or whatever still lives here."

"There's no signs of Christianity in here except for the stained glass. Everything is gone," I whisper.

"Oh yeah, that. You get used to it," Kyle says.

The pews are still here covered in soft red velvet with gold painted edges. Instead of bibles in front of them there are little packets of paper I don't recognize. On the alter a single planted tree replaces the pastor and other holy images. One cross remains and it's the one behind the tree. The stained glass covers the cavernous room in gentle colors that the flickering of the candles bring to life.

"It smells closed," I look around at the cavernous worship hall that's too empty.

"Smells like incense sticks," Kyle says.

"And something else. Like if heavy emotions had a smell," Kelsey says.

"Let's get some food," Mikaela says as she watches us enjoy the beautiful architecture and art of this building. "I know it's beautiful. You never get used to it," She says as she disappears up some steps to the right expecting us to follow her joyful gait.

3

We walk into a large room on the second floor. The walls are bland except for the outlines of old frames and crosses that used to hang: the ghosts of the religious symbolism that can never be replaced. The only unique feature is the long table made of a single giant tree taking up most of the space. It reminds me of the ones in Jayne's office.

"Please take your seats," Austin says leaning on one of the chairs relaxed. He has a similar vibe to Kyle.

People dressed in clean white clothes are carrying plates of rich food. My stomach growls at the smell of spices and meats and fruits. I sit myself between Kelsey and Kyle. Isaac takes one of the heads of the table. Mikaela takes the other with Austin beside her.

"All I have eaten since we left the Haven is canned foods," Kelsey says.

"We all have to make sacrifices, but tonight I wanted to make sure we had a true meal," Mikaela says.

The "servers" set an oven baked fish covered in herbs and soaked with butter, a broccoli and cheese platter with sauce from the fish, tiny potatoes sautéed whole, rosemary asparagus, shredded chicken in a bowl of Brussels sprouts, and a huge chocolate cake in front of us. I'm salivating.

"Please dig-" Mikaela isn't able to finish her sentence before we start grabbing for utensils to dig out the food. I forget my manners as I gorge myself licking the butter and herbs off my fingers enjoying every little morsel of food.

We look like animals. We haven't showered since leaving and we are strapped with guns across our wastes and shoulders. Mikaela and Austin only have a single pistol hooked to the side of their clean pants. Do they ever leave the church? They're so well groomed.

I finish my plate feeling the most satisfaction I have had in a long time. Several people dressed in fancy white clothes have been keeping our wine and precious clean water cups filled. None of them look a day past eighteen. They wait behind us along the wall.

"I understand the time's come for us to go back," Austin states.

"That's correct Austin," Isaac looks up. "From what I've heard, you've made quite a following here."

"At least a thousand. We even have some of the original people we travelled with. We lost some of them to the evils of anarchy though," Mikaela responds not disheartened, but with pride.

"People seemed happy outside when we first arrived. I heard laughter. It was almost as if everything was normal again except for the lack of power and the plants growing out of the concrete and roads and everything else," I say half laughing.

"What have you told the people about us?" Isaac asks.

"That we have people who are coming who are greater than us who can take them to a much safer and permanent place. We told them about the running water and power," Austin explains.

"Will we be able to leave tomorrow morning?" Isaac asks.

Austin leans back in his chair.

"Yes." Mikaela's hands are folded in front of her and her head is held high. "There is one problem though . . ."

4

I wake startled in the middle of the night to the sounds of screams that overpowered the screams in my nightmare. The streets below are alive with cries of anger, pain, and sorrow. A child's choking cry stabs my heart. I jump out of bed throwing the richly patterned covers to the floor. I run straight into the corner of my bed flying forward. Heat and sharp pain shoot through my knee as it makes contact with the old splintered wood flooring as I tumble to the ground. My muscles vibrate with tension. Machine guns, rifles, shotguns, and pistols are being shot in the street. Their rhythm matches the pulsing of my knee and then my heartbeat as their pace quickens.

I struggle to a crouching position over to the window. I pull the heavy red velvet curtain away. The top half of my window is a stained glass scene of Mary holding Jesus. Her face is pained as she looks down at her babe. I look down at the street.

It's night, but everything is orange. Someone's restaurant turned home is ablaze with flames reaching with urgency into the sky. A woman is screaming and crying trying to escape a man's grasp to go back into that burning house. Then whoosh, the house explodes licking flames into the street grabbing at stragglers and shattering glass in all directions. The woman falls from the man's grasp into the cold and wet overgrown grass into a sobbing fetal position.

Shadows of people dressed in black run through the street. One of the shadows fires their gun at a little shop. Another shadow runs past him shooting at the corner of the same building where somebody is firing back at them. One of our members slams a rifle out of the window of a gas station and tries to fight back. A shadow I can't see takes him down. The people in black hide behind a mixture of abandoned cars and our own.

I am tucked safely in the church on the third story. More people dressed in black and disguised by the night sky come pouring out the back of a large truck that just stopped in front of the church. They assemble into a line and swing assault rifles from their backs to their shoulders.

I push myself off the edge of the window with all my strength flailing backwards onto my tail bone. I roll hard onto my back as my breath is knocked out of me.

My window blows inwards raining colorful shards of glass. It's like a rainbow tornado eager to carry devastation. My cheek is hot. I reach my hand up and feel glass below my eye. It's wet with my blood. I pull it out and before tossing it aside I see it is the hand of Mary reaching for Jesus.

I scramble upwards throwing myself at my bag under the antique wooden bed. I yank my belt with my pistol in it and swing my semi automatic over my shoulder. I lunge for the door and hurry out. I don't know whether to go left or right. The hall is dark and there's a million doors. Where the hell are the stairs?!

I only have time for instant decision so I blindly run to my right. The plush middle eastern style carpets grip my shoes. They seem to project me faster down the hall.

I see a room with candle light ahead and run towards it hoping it's Mikaela and Austin or anyone who would know how to navigate this labyrinth of a building. I lurch into the room tripping over something barely catching my balance. My adrenaline is pumping as I look around and see nobody. I turn back to the door.

Lying there at the entrance is a massive pile of blood and guts. I move closer, but the blood is so thick I can't make the face out. The clothes are soaked in blood and entrails snake out of the man's stomach. He was cut open and left here to die.

I kneel to wipe the sticky hair and blood away from the face. It's Austin. Mikaela's husband. I scan the body starting to breathe harder, but I see no gun wounds nor knife wounds. Just one long gash revealing his entire inner torso. This happened shortly before we were attacked. Or while we were attacked. It's fresh. His body is warm to the touch.

"Oh God, I'm going to be sick." I turn away and retch into my hand. I slap the slimy chunks off my hand and look back. There's so much blood.

I try pushing myself up, but my strength escaped with my bile. I try to make this scene disappear by squeezing my eyes shut. Now that I know it's Austin I can see his blonde hair soaked to a dark red. Who would have done this? I walk around him slipping on his blood causing me to step onto his trailing intestines. The squishing pop the intestines make under my heel will haunt me forever. It was like popping bubble gum full of raw egg.

I take another step careful to place my foot between the mess of organs. I step over his head, but I slip and my shoulder bangs the door causing it to swing open smacking the wall.

I barely regain my balance and stumble to the door frame bracing myself on either side.

I can't stop dry heaving. The smell of puke and iron makes my head pound and my vision swirl.

Kyle appears with a continuous waterfall of tears. He grabs my bloody arm pulling me out of the door frame, "We need to leave right now."

We run across the centuries old carpet. We take a left passing five foot tall portraits of religious figures in gold frames. I throw up again splattering chunks inside a gold painted goblet on a pedestal.

We take a right and another right and we fly down the stairs.

We end up in the main worshipping hall where a small crowd of people who live in the church are listening to Mikaela on the stage in front of the little potted tree in front of the cross where the pastor used to stand.

They turn their heads as we run in, covered in blood.

"Fuck, everyone's here," Kyle curses under his breath.

Isaac runs over with his arms straight by his sides, "Miranda, we need to fight back. The Nothings breached our camp. Innocent people are going to die." He doesn't comment on the blood. I have a feeling he has seen much worse many times before.

We're safe inside while screams wail through the wooden doors. The gunfire had stopped sometime between Austin finding me and us joining the rest in the big room.

"You heard the plan, let's go!" Mikaela yells. She looks ready for battle in an excited, adrenaline junky, way. She must not know her murdered partner is lying in a pool of his own gore above her. "Grab weapons if you haven't already and let's go!" She runs to the front like she's the team captain and she's leading us onto the field. She throws the doors open letting the moist night air in.

I look around distrusting every face. One of them must be a member of The Nothings that got in here and killed Austin.

We charge after her bumping into each other, but moving as coordinated as a school of fish not knowing where we are going, but following the crowd. We move as one and leap down the white marble steps, past the headless fountain statue. I look around ready to defend our people. Nobody is shooting though. People are crying or screaming, but there's no fighting. A few sit as still as the dead around them.

A man stumbles by with a glazed look on his face.

I walk away from the group and into the street hoping to help.

An older man limps up to me with half of his face blown off. His right eye hangs loose in the socket like a paddle ball. I can see his teeth where there should have been soft cheek. He grips my shoulders digging his nails into my intact skin.

I try to pull away from him, but he holds on with his life.

The old man pulls me closer with shaking hands and whispers in my ear, "don't trust them."

"The Nothings?"

"Don't. Trust."

He falls to the cold black road bleeding out and not moving.

I drop to my knees gripping his hand that's going limp and ask desperately, "What do you mean? The Nothings?"

He doesn't respond though. He just floats lazily in a pool of blood. Bone and muscle try to hold their shape, but his skin betrays him and decides to depart from the inside of his face to melt to the ground. I can see the bones in his face, but his one eye that's still there seems to be looking into my soul. The good eye is trying to speak to me, but I can't understand it. It's warning me. I reach for his pulse feeling his hot wet blood. His temperature begins to plummet.

I let out a defeated sigh mixed with lost curiosity and reach to close his eyelid. I hold his hands to his chest. It's the best I can do or at least that's what I tell myself.

I stand ready to fight. There is nothing to do though.

They are gone. The enemy escaped. I wasn't able to help. I'm useless.

I look back to the church and see the words "Order Through Chaos" and anarchy symbols spray painted in red over the white marble steps.

People are walking around the street freshly bathed in blood. They walk with no destination while others are screaming for help and running around blindly. A man nearly pushes me over as he sprints past.

Isaac walks over to me, whispers instructions in my ear and leaves.

A shiver goes down my spine.

Chapter 9

1

Isaac instructed me and Kelsey to walk through the compound telling everyone there will be justice and work is being done to bring that about.

Hours have passed since the gunfight and Isaac and many other members have disappeared.

The sun is coming up. We've been up all night.

We talk to each person and tell them to meet in the church. We could have just yelled out from the entrance of the church for everyone to meet inside, but Isaac said Jayne would have wanted each and every person to feel important. It is necessary for each person to feel cared for especially by the high ranking members.

I am walking through the road when I'm snapped out of whatever I was thinking about by a wailing woman holding two children at a gas station. She is sitting in front of where the gas pumps used to be before they were destroyed. Her back is heaving up and down as she sobs uncontrollably. One of the children looks to be asleep and the older one is staring off into space with wide empty eyes.

"Excuse me?" I ask gently.

She does not look at me and continues to sob. The teenage girl staring off does not seem to sense someone walked up either. She's so skinny. All three of them are.

"Excuse me?" I try again.

They still don't react, but the smaller kid, a boy under ten, stirs from his sleep and looks at me. He tugs at his mom's shirt sleeve.

She looks around quickly and begins to panic more, "What is it Brendan? What's nearby?"

She grasps for her children as if she could hold them closer than she already is. Her eyes meet mine and she realizes I'm not a threat and starts crying again. A gentle cry this time instead of the deep sobs. A type of cry that will live inside her until she dies even on happy days.

"Who did? Why?" Her eyes show more red veins than white space.

"My name is Miranda. I am a member of NWF, New World Freedom, we are going to get you to permanent safety. I promise you."

She looks at me through tears that won't slow down.

"Is this your family?" I ask unsure of what to say when she does not say anything back.

"It is now."

"What do you mean?"

"My husband was murdered."

"I am so sorry. There will be justice for him," I realize I am following Isaac's script too much.

"No he was murdered," She repeats again.

"Yes, we will avenge him."

"No he was murdered."

The lady must be in shock. I look for another member to help me get her to the church.

She removes her arm from around the boy who's too big to sit comfortably in his Mom's lap and claws at my hand yanking me closer.

"He was murdered."

"I know. You said that. I am sorry," I look around for anyone, but most of the people have left for the church.

"He was murdered."

I decide to sit with her and I place my hands on her knees so she can still feel my physical presence and she can have both arms to wrap around her children. She's in shock.

"It was horrid," the young girl says pulling my arm towards her, obviously repeating what her Mom had been saying.

"What is your name?" I ask.

"My father was murdered. He wasn't just shot. They came inside and dragged him out. He was crying out for help and you guys didn't come and they cut his tongue off. Then they forced it back into his mouth. He choked really bad on it," she returned her gaze to a faraway nothing. Her face was blank.

"Oh God," I feel helpless.

2

Back inside the church, the large old worship room is packed tightly with people. The doors are kept open for fresh air. I can't tell who is bleeding and who only has blood on them. Blood is everywhere. I have lost count of how many people's blood I have on myself alone.

The smell is dizzying. If it weren't for the breeze coming in our combined smell would cause us all to pass out.

Kelsey, Kyle, and I are standing on the stage, but everyone's either sitting in the pews looking at nothing in particular or facing outside. One woman continues to stare at a stained glass window of the beast with "666" painted on his head surrounded by fire.

"Where is everyone else?" I make sure nobody else can hear me.

"They should be back soon," Kyle answers.

We look at everyone and then back at our feet. We're just waiting now.

"I have to tell you something Miranda," Kyle looks at me with dreadful urgency. His eyes are wide and cautious, but desperate.

"Yeah?"

"Everything isn't as it seems with Mikaela. I was hoping to all hell I was wrong, but…"

Kyle is interrupted by the rest of the members returning in several black trucks.

They come in hollering. They look ecstatic. Mikaela is riding in the bed of one of the trucks holding a semi automatic above her head in victory. They come pouring out of the trucks and over the top of the truck beds.

"Oh my God Kyle. I don't think Mikaela knows," I say suddenly remembering Austin.

"Knows what?" Kelsey asks.

Isaac walks to the edge of the headless statue with Mikaela beside him. Everyone in the church has already turned around and some have migrated outside. We follow suit.

"Attention everyone! We found the anarchists responsible for this slaughter!" Mikaela announces. She tucks her hair behind her ears and places her hands on her hips like a cheerleader.

"Who are they?! Let's kill them! Why?!" A cacophony of desperate people in shock scream out. The other half are silent or sobbing quietly.

Mikaela turns to Isaac and nods. He pulls his backpack off his shoulder and sets it on the ground as the people around him continue to yell out questions and threats. Mikaela and him reach into the bag at the same time and pull something out.

I'm having a hard time seeing what they are doing.

A disturbing hush spreads across the crowd and the three of us hurry to the front squeezing between the tight crowd.

Mikaela and Isaac are each holding decapitated heads as high as their arms will allow. Isaac's other arm is plastered to his side and his face is determined. Mikaela is waiving her other arm around in victory and smiling. The heads dripping blood have faces frozen in agony. They don't lower them.

"I think I'm going to be sick," Kelsey retches and begins to fall over, but Kyle holds her up.

The people around us look confused more than anything, but then it gets strange. A slow clap starts to resonate through the crowd until everyone is clapping and cheering. It's not sounds of happiness, but the sounds of tortured lives getting one small victory.

"I told you we would protect you!" Mikaela yells out.

"You didn't! You liar!" A man from the back bellows.

Nobody else joined him. The crowd waits for her response.

Mikaela yells back at them, swinging the head and splattering blood on the people in the front row. "If it weren't for us you would all be dead. Your rides to full safety and hope are finally here! There are busses waiting. The place of no violence and a new kind of freedom is in our future. We will finally be able to protect and provide even better than we have here. No more unnecessary deaths! This is what happens when we are left out here with no protection! Our goal is to not hurt anyone, but first we cannot let them think we will sit idly by!"

The crowd erupts in cheer with inter-dispersed crying.

Mikaela scrambles over the ledge of the green sludge fountain still holding the head. She pushes through the slime and climbs atop the headless Jesus statue. Dark red blood drips down the white marble as she hugs the muscular sculpture until she is sitting on its shoulders. She looks at the crowd as she squelches the decapitated head onto the statue's neck.

"Release the others!" She yells triumphantly.

Isaac nods at the trucks. Some of them get back in and drive into the lawn. They cut the engines and open the beds of the trucks.

Dead bodies of the enemies are piled inside.

"These are the bastards who killed our loved ones!" Mikaela yells like a true showman.

The crowd around me erupts in conflicting noise. A man next to me pukes and I jump out of the way, but some of it still splattered on me. A group has migrated to the church's steps and are praying. Most of the people continue to cheer.

Mikaela slides off the statue smearing the trails of blood like a watercolor painting and joins Isaac's side.

"Oh dear God," I look for Kelsey and Kyle.

They haven't left me. They're still beside me.

I look to Isaac, but his face gives nothing away for how he feels. He tells Mikaela something who turns back to face everyone.

"We will leave in the next hour to go to our new home in the mountains. Where you will be completely safe and part of a new revolution," Her voice projects.

I feel disgusted, but I also feel proud of our group. This will not happen again after we were able to take vengeance like that. As much as I want peace and how much we are preaching peace, you cannot have it when the other group is grotesquely violent. I feel pride within myself looking around at these hurting people knowing I will be able to save them.

"You are murderers!" A woman screams from the crowd.

Isaac whispers something to another member who journeys into the crowd towards the sound.

3

I'm in the church's large parking lot helping people onto the busses. A few of Mikaela's men who pushed the bodies out of the trucks onto the lawn of the church drove ahead. It looks like God smote the sinners at the church's marble doorsteps, but it was us who did his bidding.

Mikaela walks over smiling.

How can she not know about her partner Austin still? Isn't she wondering where he is?

"Hey Miranda. I am grateful I'll be able to take these people to real safety. Thank you."

"For what?"

"For coming here. For being a part of this."

"Of course." An idea pops into my head. "Mikaela?"

"Yeah?"

"Would you like to be in charge of driving a bus back?"

"I would love that! Who's bus would I drive though?"

"Kelsey's."

"Is she okay with that? I don't want to step on anyone's toes."

"You deserve it. You have earned more responsibility. Go let her know and tell her to come to me."

"For sure," Mikaela smiles bigger. "You know, between me and you I was lukewarm at the beginning, but now I am on fire for this movement!"

Behind me I hear Kyle searching for paper on the bus.

"Kyle, do you mind if Kelsey rides with us? I offered Kelsey's bus over to Mikaela."

He grabs paper for his clipboard and walks off the bus.

He nods, "How are you doing with everything Miranda?"

"I'm just happy to go back to our Haven in Big Sur and away from this mess. With more people we can make Jayne's plans a reality. It will get better."

"I sure hope so. I don't wanna be here any longer."

The woman and her two kids walk over. The Mom's still crying.

"Are you ready to go?" I ask trying to sound professional and caring at the same time.

"Please can we ride with you? Is that okay?"

"I do not see why not," I look to Kyle for an okay and he nods. "I just need your names please."

"I'm Lauren and these are my two kids, Hailey and Brendan," she starts to board as we take their names, but then I see her huge bag.

I throw my arm out, "I am sorry, you cannot take bags."

She jumps out of her skin like I had a gun in my hand.

"Why?" She asks.

"Ummm," I tried to think of the answer. "I guess so it does not get crowded in the shelter? That is what I was told to tell others. I am sorry but it is not negotiable. Also we need as much room as possible on the bus for people. Also everything you will need and more will be provided where we are going."

"I have some of my husband's belongings in here."

"The rules are strict." I avoid eye contact.

She places the bag gently on the ground by my feet, bends down, and kisses the top of it.

I watch the people milling around in the parking lot. Mikaela and Mark and Lilly talk to each individual and point them to different busses.

More people are coming up to me and Kyle. We get information and instruct them to squeeze into the back.

"Miranda," Kelsey walks around the line of people.

"Hey I know driving a bus is a big responsibility, but I thought it would be nice to be together right now. I hope you aren't mad at me."

"Of course not. I didn't want to drive that beast back on those terrifying roads especially full of people."

"Oh good," I feel relieved. "I have missed you."

"I'm glad we get to be together." She boards the bus.

Another family comes up. They try to take some bags aboard with them, but we have to tell them no.

"Thank you so much for saving us. The bags don't matter. Thank you, thank you, thank you. We're grateful for your generosity. We just want to get away from the chaos."

"We are the New World Freedom," I say with pride. "We are here to help. That is what we do. Go ahead and give your information to Kyle here."

A lone man walks up and bends to his knee holding my hand, "Thank you. I couldn't thank you enough for everything you've done. I can't live through another night like this last one. It's too much. I just want order. Anarchy is evil."

Another behind him lurches forward, "Yeah what he said. Thank you! My friends have been murdered by these people you call The Nothings."

Almost every person and family who came up profusely thanked us for saving them and sacrificing our time to get them. Although I was filled with joy at the thought of being able to save so many people and be a part of something amazing it started to make me uncomfortable. The people were filled with sorrow and pain and desperation. I felt like they were revering me as a hero, but all I was doing was driving them back. The more I was praised the more I felt like I shouldn't be, but at the same time I felt more empowered and important. I can see why Mikaela loved being here, but I would never say it's worth it.

"Miranda the bus is full," Kyle says.

"There are still people in line though."

"Send them to the other busses."

"Miranda," Isaac appears out of thin air.

"I didn't see you there," I say startled.

"There's a chance we won't be able to fit everyone. Don't let that information spread."

"We can't leave them though."

"We can come back for them at a later date, but we need to head out. We saved a lot of people today. Every bus has nearly a hundred people on it. Good job Miranda. You're an important part of our team. Tell them there'll be a second wave of buses coming," he bows his head slightly and walks off stiffly.

I was about to ask if that was true, but decided against questioning him. Jayne will send people to get the rest.

4

We drove away from the church leaving people behind, probably to die. It was heartbreaking. They looked like lost sheep in a slaughterhouse. A minute ago everyone was expectant and excited to be saved and now their world has been destroyed again. Hopefully the ones left behind are wrong about us not coming back.

I am sure we will be back. We will be. Somebody will be.

"What are we going to do for them?" Kelsey asks.

"Isaac told me Mikaela is leaving behind trusted members she recruited to hold their territory down. They are to gather more members for us and spread our word."

We get to the edge of the territory where the mile of spiked heads will lead us away from this nightmare. At least driving away I only see the backs of heads. Not that you could tell the front from the backs of the heads on some. I can almost fool myself into thinking they are road signs until vultures land and tear at the leftover stringy tendrils.

We drove for hours uninterrupted. We had to stop at several more gas stations on the way back due to the weight increase. Every time I expected to be attacked when Isaac and Kyle would figure out a way to extract the gas from the reservoirs. The last station had the words Order Through Chaos will destroy New World Freedom spray painted all over the place. On the walls, the floor, and inside the looted station.

The people on the bus stir nervously, but stay silent. They know we will get them to safety. Their faith gives me more faith.

It took a long time, but we eventually reached the northern expanse of Big Sur. We're back in the wilderness.

"Isaac to team," the radio buzzes.

"I hear you loud and clear. Over," I echo back. The other members give their affirmative as well.

"We're about to stop for the privacy drill. Over."

The busses stop.

I turn to face the terror stricken, hopeful faces on the bus.

"We are getting closer. We will be able to arrive this day. Everyone please stay on the bus and we will be back," I say. Kyle, Kelsey and I get off the bus and meet Isaac.

"They may not like this, but it's necessary to keep our location a secret," Isaac says.

"Let's just get them there. If they do not want to use the bags then they do not need to come," I say impatiently.

"That's the spirit," Isaac says flatly, but I can tell he was genuine. He walks to the back of his bus. The back of his is filled with supplies we will need so he couldn't fit as many people inside. He hands each of us a large black duffle bag.

We walk back onto my bus. The people look like lost children stuck in a hurricane without phones.

We're covered in dried blood and sweat and grime. To say the smell was thick enough to eat would be an understatement. I have to remind myself everyone here is running on no sleep and just experienced what I did. I only want to get back safely.

"Is everything okay?" Someone in the back asks.

Kyle nudges me.

"Nothing is wrong. I just need you all to do something for me."

"Of course," "Anything," and other murmurs of agreement resonate back to me.

"We need to protect our secret location so unfortunately I will need to cover your faces." I look at them trying to feel out their reactions like I have a choice. I reach for the duffle bag and pull ropes and black bags out to bind their hands and blind them.

They begin whispering to one another. The bus is getting loud.

"I don't think they like the idea of roped bags," Kyle says. "It looks like what you wear before you're hanged."

"No fuck."

"I don't want to wear that!" Someone yells followed by agreement.

"umm please-" I start, but I am drowned out by their shouts. I'm reminded of the shouts that came from below my stained glass Mary window the other night.

"QUIET! You will wear these or you will not come with us. We cannot risk one of you being a Nothing and knowing the way out so they can send for people to bomb our area. Do you want that? Do you want to risk a leak so we can be murdered in our sleep again? Tortured? Lose more loved ones? We need to hurry and get out of here. We are giant yellow sitting ducks."

Chapter 10

1

The Big Room went from accompanying several hundred to well over a thousand. There's still plenty of room to move around and still some extra chairs rest along the wall. It feels like I'm on an overcrowded television set and at any minute the director will yell CUT! and we'll return to our normal lives.

Jayne clonks onto her stage with the people who drove the buses. Mikaela might as well be glued to her side. The rest of her small counsel and original members are behind us on the ground.

"May I have your attention?" Jayne addresses the dirty, smelly, and worn out survivors. "My name is Jayne for those who do not know. Many years ago my partner and I learned about The Nothings and have been working tirelessly to prevent their destruction of our world. We held them off for a long time, but they had too many people who believed anarchy would be the answer to the world's problems. As we have all seen that leads to destruction, murder, and sorrow. So here we are today in the ingeniously designed Haven in the middle of nowhere so we can build society from the ground up. Nobody will find you here. We will not let them win. Those who they murdered will not have died in vain. Not only will we bring back civilization, but we will create a better one for everyone to live equally in. Many new people arrived today. I also understand none of you have had food since last night. We will eat soon. They are cooking up something delicious in the kitchen just for you. And do not worry for those who did not sleep on the ride over, your rooms will be ready . . ."

"I don't know about you, but I can't sleep without my hands tied and a sack over my face either," Kyle whispers.

"Shh," I repress a smile.

". . . with such a high influx of people so suddenly I am going to enact some new organization rules. I know you are exhausted, but my counsel members will be working profusely until everyone is settled in. Thank you for your hard work. Everyone here has the chance to involve themselves in the administrative work in this new revolution. Every single role is as important as the next though. Everyone will be assigned a job appropriate to their experience and interests. Of course, this is not permanent and you are welcome to move around to a different job after you go through the appropriate channels. We have to work together to create this space. As you can see I taped letters around the room so after you eat please go to the letter that corresponds with the first letter of your first name. I know that means families might have to split up for an hour or so, but it will not be for long. You will get clean clothes.

"One more thing before I depart. We are grateful for the new recruits. Thank you for trusting us. You will not regret it. We will provide a safe and fair world for you."

And on she goes, but I doze off having heard this before. I'm also exhausted. The repetitive words are starting to enter my dreams now so I don't feel as bad as before when I would doze away. It's so repetitive.

The room explodes in applause and hollers, jerking me out of my own little world I've started to create. The recruits are cheering even with no food in their stomachs and despite the trauma that crushed them since the attack. Their eyes are red and puffy and they look to be falling over exhausted and yet here they are ready to continue the fight for a better world. This world we are creating is magnificent. My smile booms at them smiling at us.

From here on out, anytime I have doubts I will remember this moment and remember how many lives I have helped save. I fill my heart with the sounds of their cheers. It feels good.

Jayne looks as radiant as ever in a black long sleeve shirt with black leggings and those short, but powerful black heals she always wears. They echo through the cave system when she is coming. Her leather jacket ties the look together making her look like a leader to rebuild a world that has turned to ashes. Her short black bob bounces sharply as she takes her leave from the stage. I have so much faith in her.

The people with ravenous bellies hurry to get in line along the side of our cavernous room. The members who were already here stand out of their way against the walls. Some of them are holding their shirts over their noses.

2

I'm sitting underneath the letters L, M, and N after dinner. I have three chairs set along the wall with boxes of supplies for the newcomers.

"Hey Miranda, looks like Jayne put us together for this task," Kyle walks over.

"Cool."

"I know you miss your boyfriend."

"I like working with you. Of course I miss him, but Rome was not built in a day?" I force a chuckle, but I feel more fake than I probably sound. "I have not seen him since we got back. Where is he?"

"You'll see him soon," he smiles.

I find comfort in his easy going nature.

"We are disgusting. I am covered in dried bodily fluids. Why can't we take showers before giving everyone else clothes and a room. They can wait."

"Yeah, you do smell like shit," Kyle laughs.

"You do too asshole," I laugh.

I see the woman I found in front of the gas station with her kids walking our way with kids in tow.

"Miranda and Kyle correct?" She slumps into the chair facing us.

"I wish we could have met under better circumstances," I smile.

Kyle barges in, "Unless your kid's names start with an L, M, or N they need to go to their proper station."

"The girl's barely a teenager and the boy is only eight. What do you mean? My kids aren't allowed to stay with me?"

"They'll be returned to you in no time. It's only for sorting so we can house and place you the right way," he answers.

"They aren't belongings." She stares at him for a few seconds, but she's exhausted and gives up quickly. "They will be housed with me right?"

"Yes Mam, but they still need to be placed into their job here."

"Their job?"

"I mean the intake will see where they'll be placed for our school we're starting and for their chores."

"They can stay together if you would like and take turns going to their stations, but it will take longer," I look at her drooping face. I feel terrible again. I know it's just the beginning, but people aren't part of a machine.

"Jayne was very strict about this Miranda and I really don't want to break any rules no matter how stupid they seem to us. It's bitten me before."

"No, it's okay," She says and turns to her kids sensing the urgency in Kyle's voice. To me, she sounds afraid. "Hailey, help your little brother get to his spot then go to yours. I'll find you afterwards."

They look like orphans during the war walking away.

"So tell me how old you are, who is a part of your family, who you want to be housed with and what your interests and talents are," I cross my leg holding a clipboard on top of a huge file of papers.

"I'm Lauren Tanner, 38 years old. My two kids, who you already saw, is who I want to be housed with obviously. I used to own a restaurant before the bombs came. I'm a good cook," She speaks with more than enough efficiency, but her eyes are looking far beyond us.

"So we already have a chef and his name is Charles Stroff. That's who you will work under. Any questions or complaints please go to him. As part of the new organization's rules, everyone who works in the kitchen will dress in forest green."

"I wasn't asking to be a chef," she says flatly.

Kyle stands and walks to one of the many boxes around us and pulls out three work outfits and other clothes in the color of forest green. He hands them to her neatly folded.

"What's this?" She asks.

"It's three outfits. Three pairs of pants, three T shirts, three button ups, five pairs of underwear and socks the same color, two bras, a pair of non skid shoes, two aprons, and hair ties. All in forest green. Also in that pile you have pajamas, workout clothes, and a pair of leggings and a shirt to lounge in. All in forest green," I say.

"Why's everything the same color?"

"It's a part of being able to organize everyone more efficiently so it does not turn into anarchy. You should hear Jayne explain it. She is a genius."

"What about warmer clothes for the winter?"

"The temperature down here remains relatively stable."

"We can't leave?"

"Of course you can. For the time being, it is not safe to leave the compound or more specifically the safety of our Haven until the chaos outside becomes manageable."

I can't tell if it is the exhaustion and grime, but she does not look grateful for us having saved her life.

"We would appreciate it if you would immediately change into your new clothes and bring us the ones you are wearing," I say.

"Why?"

"It is so anarchy does not take over and more people do not die. We need to be as organized as possible."

"We don't want what happened back in town to happen here. We need to make sure everyone does their part," Kyle says.

"And what's that?"

Kyle urges me to take this over. I shrug and look back telling him with my eyes he's got it. He seems to be better at enforcing the rules. Maybe I'm just weak or something in me is working against the movement like Jayne has told me before. Some of the evil is trying to influence me.

"We're rebuilding. And saving lives like your kids," he says.

"But not my husband."

I say, "I am sorry. I wish we could go back in time and we could have stopped those people from ever entering the boundary. That and much worse will continue to happen if we let The Nothings turn the country to anarchy. We will have vengeance for your husband. We do not want the same thing or worse happening to your children."

Lauren stares as if she's trying to see what else I'm not saying. The bags under her eyes weigh her head back down.

"You said gym clothes?" She asks.

"Yes. There is a large gym just inside hall Heaven or hall H. It is the large tunnel the UTV's go through to get in and out of here. It will be the first door on your left."

"And your room," Kyle pipes in. "You'll live down Hall Clarity in a family unit. There isn't a full bathroom. I know it sucks. There's a toilet however because you have at least two kids," he holds up two fingers. "The showers will be down the hall. Can't miss 'em."

"Will I have a place to cook?"

"The food will be provided through the kitchen you now work in. Any questions?" I ask.

"No."

"Alright. Have a good night's rest because you have breakfast to cook bright and early in the morning. Well not any brighter than normal since it is always the same brightness down here. Go ahead and head to the kitchen to see the schedule posted inside the door."

She leaves without another word.

The next person takes a seat and we go through the entire script again.

We continue these interviews until we have everyone documented, housed, and placed into a role.

I don't feel like a human at the end. I'm tired and overworked.

3

The next morning I wake up to Cody beside me. I snuggle closer feeling his familiar warmth.

"Counselor's dinner is ready in 30 minutes," Jayne's voice emits from the speaker above the bed.

"Oh my God! Cody, is it really already dinner time? What time is it? What day is it?" I smack my head into the bed side table trying to see the nonexistent clock.

"Wow, I feel stupid."

'It's fuckin' okay love. Only habit."

"Old habits die hard and apparently I can't even control my own body right now."

"Shhh babe, it's fine," He pulls me in closer rubbing my head gently and snuggling me harder. I relax back into his arms feeling safe and loved. He rubs the back of my head and plays with my hair. I start drifting back into blissful sleep.

"Mirandaaaa?" Kelsey taps on the door. "Can I come in?"

"Uh. Yeah. Sure come on in," I answer groggily.

She walks in with white pajama bottoms and a white cotton t-shirt that does nothing to hide her cute belly or what's left of it. I can see the outline of the plain white bra she was given. She looks angelic, like an old soft painting.

Kelsey's smiling, "Well looks like we slept the day away." She walks over and pulls on the covers playfully.

"Come on sleepy heads, let's go."

I let her pull the covers off of me trying to shake the grogginess.

"You're in black?" She asks. "I thought Jayne gave the counsel members white?"

The silky black gown I am in glides against my skin. It feels cool and soft. It has lace on the bosom and the bottom. It makes me feel pretty.

"Yeah she gave us new clothes as well. Her extra small counsel received black clothes." I am trying not to bring attention to how much nicer mine are. I feel valued by Jayne and like I am in a special position for something greater than I can imagine.

"You've always found a way to have it better."

"Darlin'. It just takes more fuckin' time. You did an amazing job. Ain't nobody to deny that, but Miranda has been workin' with us for about a year and I've a lot longer. Give it time," the way Cody grins it's obvious he knows he's handsome.

Cody sits up in a black silk button up and black silk boxers poking through the grey covers. Everything is grey in the room. The bed side tables, the lamp shades with their LED lights we can't turn off, the dressers and the bathroom fixtures. The only thing that is not grey is the navy blue curtain that cuts our bathroom off from the rest of the room.

They probably ran out of grey curtains when they built this place.

"Oh," Kelsey fiddles with her fingers. "I thought after this rendezvous I would be considered a close alibi."

"15 minutes," Jayne's voice transmits over the grey speaker.

"This would be a lot easier with a clock in our bedroom Cody." I expect his response to be, "Yeah, babe."

Instead he says, "Maybe in the future babe, but not now. Jayne doesn't like 'em."

"Why?"

"She doesn't want us getting distracted by unnecessary constructs." I know the last two words came verbatim from Jayne.

"What? Like the concept of time? That's supposed to distract us?"

"I dunno," he waves his hand shooing my question away. "Let's get dressed and rush over. We shouldn't be late. It was generous of her not to wake us and take a day or so off, but we can't be late."

"A day or so? How long has it been?"

"Hurry, Goddamnit," he smiles, but there's a flicker of annoyance.

I grumble my way out and throw other black clothes on and throw my messy hair into a bun jumping into the bathroom to look in the mirror. Yeah. I look presentable. Even good considering what we went through.

The three of us head down hall Aero joining other members in the white and black parade. Even our belts and underwear match our slick outfits.

Looking around the Big Room is shocking. Everyone is sitting for dinner in outfits of one solid color. The colors mix and match at different tables, but a pattern is starting to form. People of the same color tend to sit with each other. The other weird thing about the clothes is they are the exact same cut. Except for me and everyone dressed in black and white. How come I am allowed to have different clothes than everyone else? How did Jayne manage to find these? How did she get so many so quickly?

"Earth to Miranda?" Cody teases me. "Let's fucking go," he gestures to the rest of the counsel heading for hall Framing to Jayne's office for dinner. Before we can start walking again he pulls me in for a kiss.

"You have the cutest grin," I say bopping my nose on his.

I catch Lauren's eyes from the opening in the rock wall serving dinner in her forest green outfit. I cannot read her expression from here, but it feels off. Why would she not be beyond grateful by now?

4

As usual Jayne isn't there to eat with us. Dinner tonight consists of sautéed broccoli and onions with rosemary sprinkled mashed potatoes and freshly baked bread. It's not like we could have gone to a store and bought old bread. We even have butter to slather on it.

After we are full and happy she comes out of the almost hidden door behind her desk.

"It is good to see you healthy and alive especially those who retrieved those poor people from Santa Cruz. I see your bravery and I admire it." Jayne struts in her heels and sits on her desk.

"I heard there was some trouble on the way there and in the territory Mikaela made. A round of applause for Mikaela. She managed to make a base in that area and therefore saved many people in the process. She is a hero."

A polite applause murmurs through the room.

"What about Austin?" I say under my breath to Kyle next to me who passes the message onto Kelsey.

Cody turns around with a face that says, "What could you possibly be talking about that's so important you would talk while Jayne's talking?" I slump my shoulders feeling like a slapped dog.

"I would like to take our new small society a step further," Jayne smiles softly. "I think we should start having more fun."

We wait for her to continue.

"Well? What do you think?"

We keep waiting for her to continue.

"Well?!" She says louder.

"What do you mean exactly? That's sounding fucking rad J," Cody sits up straighter.

I look past Kyle to Kelsey and mouth, "J?"

She shrugs looking just as confused.

"I believe we should have more fun down here like I said. So many people have lost their lives and ways of living. Maybe we could start having some beer with dinner? I don't know. I do not want people to lose sight of the bigger project and start introducing substances, but a tightly controlled amount seems like a good idea. Let's hear your opinions since you are all considered my close counsel now with some of you being considered extra close to this movement. Those who are dressed in black that is."

She walks back and forth across her middle eastern rug already knowing our answers will be positive.

"Of course, unchecked, alcohol can lead to chaos and then to anarchy, but if we control it in just the right way we can use it therapeutically to relax the people here and maybe help form bonds and loyalty."

"That's fuckin' awesome! You're a genius!" Cody stands and slams his hands on the table, rattling us.

"Thank you, Cody."

Then more people start chiming in.

"Yeah, sounds awesome."

"I like it."

"I miss alcohol."

"This could be good."

"How are you going to control consumption though?" Lilly Whiteman asks. She is dressed in black jeans and a black blouse with her dirty blonde curls pulled back. She's picking at her thumbnail like it's the most interesting thing in the world right now.

"Well Lilly, I have a plan. It is important we control the amount exactly. I am serious about that. I would like to meet with my small counsel now. Everyone else can go to their homes. We have a big day tomorrow. Well; everyday is big when you are leading a revolution," Jayne says. She has the type of beauty that makes people want to listen to her talk.

5

"I got you something special for tonight," Jayne sits on her pillow in the warm circular room.

The room is full of soft candle light. The candles are on the floor and hanging in beautiful golden candle holders on the walls. My body feels warmer than normal. This room always makes me feel warmer compared to the rest of the cavernous space.

Jayne crawls to a chest along the wall. Her heels are off and laying stacked neatly by the door where the rest of ours are.

"I have wine and it is 30 years old waiting for this night," Jayne rummages in the chest pulling out little wine glasses and a corked wine bottle. It's a smaller version of the chest Isaac pulled his "tools" from down the staircase behind the bookshelf. They look a thousand years old. The portions are small because she only splits the one bottle between 10 glasses.

"Cheers everyone! To having the blessing bestowed upon us to change the world. We have a clean slate here. This is a rare opportunity and you get to be a part of it." Jayne holds her glass in the middle. We clink our glasses and sip.

"Thank you so much to those who helped with the last mission and specifically Mikaela." Mikaela's sitting by Jayne.

I used to be next to her, but now I'm one over. It's not like the seats are assigned. Mikaela just sat there before I did. I've been sitting there since the beginning though.

"We only have nine members at the moment so there is an opening for someone to join our small counsel."

I was about to ask what happened, but Cody placed his hand on my shoulder and I stopped.

"What happened to the other guy?" Lilly looks at her hands.

"Hello Lilly," Jayne smiles. "You always find a way to have lots of questions. I found out he was a supporter of the Order Through Chaos. At least it did not seem like he was actively against them. He had different ideals than us and I could not work with him any longer."

"So where-" Lilly starts.

"Another round of cheers for Mikaela here," Jayne holds her glass high demanding us to follow suit. She downs hers and waits for us to do the same.

"And another cheers. Cheers to the friendships we are making. Would anyone like to share?" Jayne asks.

I would answer, but I feel the most relaxed I have felt in a long time. I want to fall asleep. My head feels heavy, but in a good way. I let it fall forward.

"Cody what about you?"

"Yes J, I'd love to. The color coding idea. Brilliant. It'll be easier to get information now," Cody bounces on his cushion.

I can hardly keep my head up. Sleep starts to pull me over. The pillow beneath me feels nice. I just want to lay my head on it. I don't dare fall asleep while Jayne's talking though.

I shake my head trying to push the tiredness away.

Everyone looks as tired as I am except Jayne and Cody. Then Cody's head starts to sway back and forth until he falls asleep sitting. There's no anger from Jayne, only peace radiates.

The candle lights seem to dance across the wall more than normal. They flicker higher and wider than before. The soft yellow light begins to pulse slightly as if it was singing me a lullaby.

Only a few others are still awake. Some are laying on the floor now.

Jayne says to me, "You are valued and important. Together we will change the world." She reaches to squeeze my hand. That feels nice.

Her hands are foreign. I rub her fingers with mine feeling the delicate roughness of her calluses. I let my hands fall away from hers to my pillow. The pillow's even softer. The colors on the pillow are more vibrant and they seem to dance like the flickering of the candle light. I continue to rub the soft pillow.

In slow motion I see Jayne stand and then gently lay me on the floor.

I close my eyes.

6

I'm jolted awake at the sound of low rumbles and a gentle vibration in my room. The bright lamp that's always on flickers.

I flip over and reach an arm out for Cody, but it falls on the blankets. The low rumble comes again.

Then the lights go out. It's pitch dark. I can't see a thing. I reach for my phone under my pillow out of muscle memory forgetting we gave up our phones when we got here. The dark is foreign to me now.

It's menacingly silent. I'm trying to will my eyes to adapt to the darkness, but I can't see anything no matter how hard I try.

Did I fall back asleep?

"Miranda?" Kelsey's voice thankfully pops the silence.

"Yeah?"

"You're still there."

"Of course where else would I be?"

"I'm coming over now."

I hear her clumsily feeling around in the dark walking to our joint door. I hear the door open and close and her shuffling around and the sound of her hands brushing the wall.

"Ow!" Kelsey fumbles against the corner of the bed.

The moment she makes contact she wraps herself around me. I embrace her. Strangely, I feel more peace next to her than I have with Cody. She is my best friend and we have known each other for years. I hug tighter burying myself in her familiar bouncy hair.

"What's going on?" She asks.

We're holding each other like we would after watching horror movies as kids when we were too afraid to let go of each other for fear the killer would grab one of us.

The room rumbles and vibrates again and I don't know what's moving or what's just us shaking.

And then it's still again.

"Cody is gone," I say.

A red light flashes on casting everything in a hellish glow.

I look to the speaker above the bed where the red light is shining from preemptively sensing and wanting an announcement.

"Go to the Big Room immediately. Move slowly, but deliberately. Stay calm. Go to the Big Room immediately," Jayne's voice shuts off with a rough static filled click.

Kelsey is starting to sweat in her pajamas.

"Let's go," Kelsey whispers.

"We need to dress."

"Why?"

"We are counsel members. We need to present ourselves as such. If something is happening we cannot look disheveled." I feel the panic subsiding as I grasp for the inner control I have been working on since the trainings.

The floor glows red in the light making me feel like I'm floating in hell. I can barely see. I place an arm hesitantly in front of me feeling the empty space until I get to the plain grey dresser that's now a dark red. I don't let go of Kelsey's hand. I grab for black clothes, but everything looks red. It's not like I have other colors to get mixed up with.

"Miranda, I have to grab my clothes," she pulls away.

I grab her arm tighter. "I don't want to lose you."

"You won't. Why don't you come with me to get my clothes."

After we are dressed I place my right hand against the wall letting it guide me past Kelsey's door and to my front door to get my black boots on.

As I step into hall A my world is flooded with a more extreme hellish glow. The long tunnel feels like I'm creeping through the underworld. The emergency lights have replaced the bright white. It has turned into a mining tunnel instead of a medical wing.

A barely audible whisper of cries echos down the tunnel. I can't tell which way it's coming from.

7

The Big Room is as red as a fire trapped in a glass box full of continuous fuel. People are running. Shouts and screams come from everywhere. They sound like they could be above and below me. I'm floating in a bubble of panic.

A man carrying his small girl sprints behind me and across the room. He ducks under a lunch table and hides.

"You can't take my child!" A woman screams.

"Oh God we must be under attack!" Kelsey digs her nails into my bicep. I try to get loose, but she squeezes tighter and I'm glad she does.

I hear children crying. It's swirling around me throwing me into a tornado of desperation. I run to help, but after taking a few leaps this way and that way I realize the mass is our own people and I have no idea what to do. There's no one to fight, but there's so much crying.

"Gather the children!" Cody appears suddenly.

"What?! Why?" I ask.

"They gotta be protected. Grab em Miranda! Stop askin' so many fuckin' questions all the God damn time and do what the hell you're supposed to. GOD DAMN," Cody vanishes in the chaos.

"Please line up and take your children to the entrance of hall Evening. We are under attack. I repeat we are under attack," Jayne's amplified voice cuts the confusion for a brief moment, but doesn't stop it. She is on the stage looking as regal and well rested as ever even in this ominous lighting. She is a trance amidst this menagerie of movement.

A line of people hold their children leading for hall E. In this red glow everyone looks distraught and heavy, but as I look longer there are people who seem calm. It's every single emotion on an extreme spectrum.

Others are running back to their rooms down hall Clarity and Demo where the new recruits live. My own people are dragging them back like they're pigs in a slaughter house. Their screaming turns to pig squeals the more they're pulled and yanked.

It's hard to see in this light, but I know it's Cody pulling a young girl away from her mother's grasp. Without his dimpled grin he doesn't look like himself. His body is straining and I can't tell if it's Hailey's face because the red light distorts it making almost everyone look like a demon. The girl's cries turn to curdles of pain. They fling backwards away from the Mom. She runs over to them, but another member in white comes up and grabs the moms arms behind her back as Cody runs off with the girl. He runs past me and into hall E past the other parents with their children.

The line is longer than the people who are resisting.

"I do not want to cause panic, but we are under attack and if we do not calm down we will be lost and there will be nothing we can do to protect you," Jayne stands on the stage watching everything unfold below her. Her eyes are a light of their own. They look supernatural.

I search for the Dad and kid under the table, but they're gone.

A little boy tugs at my shirt, "Where's my Mommy?"

"There you are. You run fast." A person dressed in white snatches him up and places him at the head of the line.

The line's dwindling as the kids disappear down the tunnel without their parents. I can finally hear my own thoughts again. My ears are ringing and my head's pounding. I stand dumbly on the sidelines.

I'm going to hear about this later. My stomach starts to summersault as the distractions dwindle and I realize how useless and stupid I was during this. Where did my calmness I've been working on go?

In a blind worry, I join the others sitting and wait for Jayne. Some are slumped on the floor. The last few families still trying to argue aren't as fervent. They peacefully hand over their children until it is only one parent with their kid near hall E.

She's pleading with Isaac. He whispers something into her ear that makes her body go limp. She starts to protest, but Isaac shakes his head, cutting her off at once. She hands over her young child and finds a seat on a couch far away from Jayne and the rest of us.

A deep rumble vibrates the table under me.

The red lights turn off. It's black again.

I reach to either side of me for Kelsey, but the hand I grab isn't hers. They don't pull away though. It's not Cody's either.

My eyes aren't able to adjust. Light ceases to exist. I put my hand in front of my face and I swear I can see my fingers moving. Maybe there is some light bouncing off them, but when I put my hand on my lap my vision doesn't change. We're far away from any light penetrating this depth.

A few dull glowing red lights flick on where Jayne is standing on the stage. If the darkness has mirages then this is what they would look like. My vision is tunneled by the light source being so minute in such a vast space. It's like my body is being pulled towards her down this red platform. Jayne's a needle with hundreds and hundreds of individual threads forming their own light tunnels coming off of her. I don't want to look away even though I feel like I should be running, but where to?

I can see just enough to see it is Kyle next to me. I snatch my hand back. "I am sorry," I mutter embarrassed. I showed weakness.

"It's alright. I'm scared too."

Kelsey slips into the other chair next to me.

"I couldn't find you," she said grabbing my arm. I don't feel like I need to run anymore with her by my side.

The room is silent.

"We might be under attack. There is a decent possibility they did not see us flying over. We switched the lights and power off just in case. Our vehicles are hidden and as long as we stay quiet they should not find us. Those are military style planes and helicopters that have been flying dangerously low to the ground. Do not be fooled. They are not the military we knew. Those are The Nothings trying to locate any decent sized groups who are not being lead by one of their members. I wanted to start working outside. We need to utilize the land and farm our own food. Unfortunately we will have to wait on that. The only entrance and exit in hall Heaven the UTV's are in is going to be boarded shut for the time being to make sure the enemies cannot penetrate our Haven if they manage to find us," Jayne seems to give a rehearsed speech.

"If the counsel members could make their way to the front."

Something catches my shirt and I turn around to a woman with wild eyes. It's Lauren. She looks more terror stricken than the day I met her, but instead of her eyes being full of hopelessness there's a fiery determination that makes my skin tighten.

She leans in uncomfortably close. Her breath is unusually foul in a sick from fear type of way and her warm, moist breath pushes against my skin making it constrict as if my skin retreat if it hugged my bones tight enough.

"They threatened to kill . . ." She whispers shakily before immediately sitting back.

I want to ask her more questions, but I feel Kyle's fingers press into my lower back and Kelsey pull on me and I keep walking. I try to look back, but I'm swept away with the small crowd moving forwards.

"Chef Charles if you could take as many people you need from the kitchen crew and put together a breakfast for everyone that involves no electricity that would be great. The fridge and freezers are still operating, but try not to open them," She smiles at him making intense eye contact. She looks crazed. She looks beautiful.

Maybe it's the darkness and the red glow from the front, but it looks like he's blushing when he smiles back. She keeps his gaze until he breaks it and begins tapping people to go back to the kitchen with him. He seems bigger than before as he walks around. There is a new confidence in his steps.

"What about the kids?!" Someone yells from the back. I try to see who it is, but I am blinded from the red lights shining on us.

More red lights are turned on that illuminate where the noise came from. Then more are turned on and the space now exists as an inferno.

"We are keeping them safe. If we are attacked we will need every hand on deck to fight. To fight for equality and safety then everybody needs to do their part. Children cannot help and only serve as distractions. Do not worry for they are being well taken care of. They will be returned to you as soon as we determine it is safe. We will need to do our part to make sure that happens. One person can ruin everything for everyone here.

"Thank you for being understanding and cooperating. It does not go unnoticed. Nothing does."

Chapter 11

1

"Hey babe," Cody embraces me from behind and kisses my neck. "I've missed hugging your beautiful body."

"Stop," giggling I try to turn around to kiss him back like I normally would, but a sharpness travels through my body. I'm unable to move.

"I love ya so fuckin' much, you know that right? You're amazing."

"Thank you love," I finally turn around and place a big kiss on his soft lips and I immediately forget the rest of the world. It feels nice to have the lights back on and be in the Big Room with everyone.

"But."

"What?" I ask pulling away.

He pulls me back in and his voice deepens, "Obviously Jayne took notice you didn't help this morning. You just stood there lookin' horrified. I mean what the fuck Miranda? You looked like a dumb bitch. I went out on a limb for ya, but you couldn't lift a Goddamn finger when we needed you."

I try harder to pull away and manage it this time.

"It was so sudden. I have done everything else and more. Next time it will not happen. Please tell me she is not mad at me?" My heart switches to hard thumping. I try pushing on it, but it won't stop.

God, I'm so fucking stupid. I knew immediately after the chaos stopped I was going to be called on, but I hoped no one noticed me in the midst of it all. I was just one person in black pressed against the wall.

"I don't think she's mad, but she had certain expectations for ya. She thinks you can do amazing things if you only just fuckin' try."

"Her words, not mine love," he reaches for my trembling hands and kisses them.

"I promise I will. It will not happen again."

Cody pulls me back and kisses me on my forehead. He walks off towards hall F where Jayne's office is.

"I've been trying," I mutter to his back.

I feel like the entire room's looking at me. Nobody's heads are turned towards me, but that doesn't mean they aren't watching. Yeah, they're talking and reading and laughing with one another, but I can feel their eyes on me. I'm in everyone's peripheral vision. I look around for a place to sit when I see Kelsey looking at me. She looks worried, but it's directed at me. It's annoying.

I stand taller.

I walk over to her to the warmer section of the cave on the far side with rugs and wooden tables and couches and books. The light seems especially deceptive over here. It's as bright white as nearly everywhere else, but it is bouncing off these warm reds, yellows, and browns. It gives the light a delicate tone. It's like a cute bear cub, but its Mom is leering over. It does not feel particularly safe, but it is the most comfortable spot in this place besides that little round room Jayne takes her small counsel into at night. Jayne always says "It takes a while to feel the peace and comfort in a new and changing place."

"Hey Miranda, what happened with Cody?" Kelsey asks when I sit next to her on a soft brown fabric couch with red roses. Something you would find in your grandparent's home.

"It is fine really. How are you?"

"You can talk to me."

"I said I'm fine for fuck's sake!"

She pulls back as if I had slapped her.

Great. Now I feel like a dick.

"No no no I'm sorry. I didn't mean to snap at you."

I reach for her hand, but she walks away leaving me by myself.

I look at the rainbow of people in solid colors milling about. I would not have guessed this morning happened. People are playing board games in the maze of couches and rugs around me.

"Hey Miranda," Lilly is dressed in black. "Have you heard?"

"Heard what?"

"What's going on with the children," she's biting her nails.

"No I have not."

After a long pause Lilly begins, "Well the levels of this place go deeper and they were brought-"

I cut her off, "Were you told to pass this information onto me? Who said it was okay?"

"Oh . . . n-no one did."

"That is what I thought. Then you probably should not tell me. A need to know basis right?" I immediately regret saying that, but what if it's a test? I repeat in my head, only information on a need to know basis.

"My bad, I only figured since you were on the small counsel you should know," Lilly pauses and looks at her hands. "Don't tell."

"Do not tell what?" I say forcing a smile.

"You know the . . ."

"The what?" I say again raising my eyebrows. "Just be careful."

2

"All of us will have dinner together tonight. I was able to get my hands on some beer. It was not an easy task, but for everything you have all sacrificed for the movement I knew I needed to do something. This was not easy, but you are worth it. This will be a celebratory drink so even if you do not usually drink, grab one anyways because it is symbolic for the New World Freedom we are creating here. Thank you for all you do and enjoy," Jayne announces in the large room before getting off the stage and disappearing down hall F.

I am sitting at one of those high school lunch tables. The plastic ones that leave your butt sore. There's at least a thousand of us sitting in here now. The Big Room's so cavernous it doesn't feel like much people until I start counting them.

Kelsey, Kyle, Lilly, and Lilly's partner Mark is sitting with me. I don't know where Cody is.

"When will the kids get to come back? It has been a whole day and nothing has happened since this morning?" Kelsey asks. "I think the kids would be quiet if we told them to. It doesn't make much sense. Why exactly were they separated? What does that have to do with their safety? So we can focus better? Nobody can hear us down here."

I am about to tell her to shut her mouth, but I find myself curious and I look to Lilly. She looks back at me and must have assumed I was giving her a different look because she shakes her head.

"You shouldn't inquire about the happenings with other members. Ask Jayne if you want to know," Mark says. He's dressed in black, but still has the look of an IT guy mixed with a frat boy.

"Does nobody here know?" Kelsey asks looking at each of us in turn searching for any flinch of acknowledgment.

"Dunno," Kyle said trying to wipe a stain out of his white shirt.

"I work with them because Jayne trusts me. Lilly's down there too," Mark says.

I try to telepathically tell Lilly I want to know by making my face say "go on," but she looks more nervous than normal. She only stares at the table and pokes at the food in front of her. Her beer is almost half way done.

I shouldn't have said what I said earlier to her. Actually, no that was right because I do not need to know. If Jayne wants me to know, I will know. This way confusion does not spread.

Each of us has a black permanent marker dash on our hand from when we grabbed our one beer we were permitted to have tonight.

"Lilly-" I begin, but Cody walks up and sits on my other side.

"What the hell're we talkin' about?" His big joyful smile brightens the place up, but not as much as it did before.

"How great it is to have alcohol at dinner again. It is a touch of normalcy I did not realize I missed so much." I don't know why I just lied to him, but I have a feeling I'll pay for this later. He'll find out. God fuck me, why'd I just say that? It felt as fake as it sounded coming out.

"How would y'all like to help me with something?" Cody leans back.

"I would love to," I say too eagerly. "I would like to help. I have not been doing enough lately."

"That's good Miranda. And you four?" He asks, but it's not a question. They nod.

"Help me go around this room and just drink with other groups until you see everyone finish their drink."

"That's important?" Kelsey asks.

Cody's smile faltered for a second or maybe it didn't. Maybe he realized I lied to him? "Yes Kelsey dear. It's a symbolic gesture for our new freedom we're creating. Everyone has to participate. It's not optional."

"Sounds great Cody. I am going to head over there," I move away from his demeaning glare.

I look at my beer I haven't touched. I can't remember the other night when Jayne gave us alcohol. It wasn't much so it's not like I drank a lot. My stomach's feeling queasy near the bottom like it's trying to talk to me, but I won't listen. I look into my beer again and my stomach gets worse.

I must not want beer. Or maybe I just have no appetite right now.

I find a group with half full glasses and head for them. My stomach jumps again.

"Hey guys. My name is Miranda."

The small group is dressed in yellow; electrical, yellow green; sustainability like our solar panels and such, and two in light blue; medical. This is a smart group.

"We know who you are," the woman in yellow green says.

"Oh yeah? Well cheers to safety." I bring my full glass forward and we clink ours together. I watch them down the rest of their drinks.

I bring the glass to my lips, but I sneeze spilling my beer into an empty soup bowl.

"Oh my God, I'm so sorry," I frantically move to clean, but it landed conveniently in the bowl.

"It's fine," the guy in light blue says. "It happens."

"Thank you," I say uneasily.

I turn around with my empty glass and realize nobody's looking at me and Cody is on the opposite side of the room. Nobody saw except that small group. That's good, I don't think I can stomach anything right now anyways.

As I pass the lunch tables and walk through aisles of people, their heads begin to droop and talk is lowered to a murmur. It reminds me of last night. I'm beginning to remember, but there's a wall preventing the flood of information.

I let out a big yawn as I hear more yawns going around. They're infectious. I don't feel tired though. Not like I did the other night.

"I'm so sorry," I bump into a large seated man. He doesn't respond though and I see he's hardly awake. He's supporting his head with his large callused hand and isn't looking at anything because his expression's empty. A small smile touches his lips like he saw something silly.

The man next to him is closely inspecting the last morsels of food in his bowl like he's uncovering the secrets to atoms.

I notice more weird behavior around me. Some people are giggling then drifting into a waking sleep with their heads rolling down and back up.

I find my seat again, but only Lilly is back.

She has both her elbows on the table straddling her empty bowl supporting her head.

She turns her head to me and starts to giggle. It feels like she's looking at something on my face. I wipe at myself, but don't get anything and then she goes quiet again looking like she's about to face plant into the table.

"Miranda, the kids . . ."

"Yes Lilly, please tell me," I grab her wrists trying to shake some energy into her.

"You said no," She trails off on the "o" sound.

"Please tell me. I'm sorry. What is it?"

"It's bad."

"What is?"

"Hey Miranda?" Cody comes up cheerfully. "How're ya feeling?" He looks at me suspiciously. It's like he's studying my movements. I suddenly feel urgency to look as tired as possible. To mimic the others around me. As I learned from training earlier to blend in you have to start feeling the emotion yourself. I let myself fall into a role.

"Sleepy," I lean against my palm. I don't know why I lied, but it felt right in the moment.

"Yeah me too," He slumps besides me and leans against me.

Slowly, Kelsey, Mark, and Kyle return. More like, they barely returned. I decide to blend in and I consciously copy their movements and let my head drop.

"Your hair's so pretty," Kelsey plays with the ends of my hair.

Without me having to lift my head I hear the click clack of Jayne coming back.

"Hello everyone," Jayne's voice calmly projects from the stage.

I swear I'm not dreaming it. The lights dulled some. It feels more comfortable in here. Not so much like an underground laboratory. I feel myself truly becoming more relaxed but I'm not zonked out like the rest around me. The lights and having a full belly are relaxing, but I still have my wits about me. Looking at the weird faces people are making and the empty staring faces around me it seems like I'm the only one cognizant.

Kelsey falls onto my shoulder and looks at the high ceiling.

"The colors," she speaks in a loving way.

Cody's still leaning on me from the other side. I decide I need to rest my head directly on the table so it doesn't look like I'm supporting them. I lean forward and Kelsey and Cody lean into each other resting the sides of their faces cheek to cheek.

"Please direct your gaze to me in your own time."

Kelsey shuffles around in her seat and Cody lifts his head up. It's as if there are two strings attached to his eyelids. One pulling down and the other pulling up and they're in this monotonous and slow battle with one another. They're of equal strength so his eyes remain half open.

The sounds of sluggish movements bounce off the walls making it feel as if I am in an oiled bowl of snails trying to get out but I keep sliding back to the middle. I'm caught at the bottom between everyone. Jayne's waiting up there with uncharacteristic patience. It's not an irritated silence like she usually does, but a patient one.

"Thank you to everyone here. Each and everyone of you is noticed and admired," Jayne speaks. "Repeat after me, we are the New World Freedom."

Mumbles of "We are the New World Freedom," come from all around me. I channel my old training from before the bombs. I was told when coming to the Haven to blend in no matter what. If the cars were driving chaotic then drive chaotic. If everyone seemed calm and confused then do that as well. Match the speed of the cars around me. I'm matching the speed of those around me right now. I repeat the words in the same sloshy rhythm.

"Our actions will save the world."

"Our actions will save the world."

"Only through absolute control can we stave off anarchy."

"Only through absolute control can we stave off anarchy."

"More violence might be needed."

"More violence might be needed."

"We will work together without questions."

"We will work together without questions."

"I will report anyone against us."

"I will report anyone against us."

"I am valued and powerful."

"I am valued and powerful."

"I will listen to those in black."

"I will listen to those in black."

"We will save the world."

"We will save the world."

"Without each and every one of you this would not be possible. On the other hand one more life missing in the name of New World Freedom will not matter either. Remember that. You had a pleasant evening and will wake up in your beds. The end of this night was spent chatting with your friends about the love and dedication you have for this movement. You will think about this as you fall asleep tonight."

Isaac comes out of a dark corner across the room and starts gathering everyone in yellow. He leads them down hall C. Through my half closed eyes they look like ears of corn happily and drunkenly floating away.

Jayne's still standing on the stage looking at us. I let my head fall to my chest and float back up and float back down. I match the speed of the people around me. Some start giggling so I giggle and then go back to swaying.

Isaac's back in a short time and makes his way through the colors until he leads the counsel members to their homes down hall A.

3

The lights are as bright as always when I wake up in the morning. The grey stone walls bear down on me waiting for me to form an opinion of last night. It's like they're waiting in judgement.

I reach for Cody in bed, but my arm lands on Kelsey's stomach.

"Hey girl, Cody must have left before I woke up as always."

"Yeah I heard the door close a couple hours ago and didn't want to be alone. I hope you don't mind," Kelsey wakes up. Her eyes look refreshed this morning instead of exhausted. That eases my heart.

"I'm pretty stoked not to have to wake up to an empty bed again."

"I can't remember the last time I woke up with this much energy. My mind feels clean," Kelsey moves closer to me, our faces inches apart.

"I'm happy for you.

[pause]

"Now that I think about it I have been more energetic in a calm way since that night the small counsel had with Jayne a few days ago."

"Can I snuggle with you? I miss human touch."

"I would like that," I move closer to her until our noses are touching. I wrap my arm and leg over her as she does the same. We look like a black and white swirly cookie.

"How loyal are you to Jayne and the movement?" I ask.

"Why? I'm very loyal. I have no questions about it. Not any."

"What if it meant doing something you weren't comfortable with or seemed wrong in the present or what if it meant . . ." I trail off.

"I know it's wrong to say, but my loyalty is first to you. What are you talking about? I'm still your best friend."

Her soft tummy is pressed against my hard one. I only just noticed how much skinnier and fit she is now than pre-bomb. Her blonde loose curls smell sweet. She presses into me harder. My body relaxes and my skin feels tingly. It's not the same tingly nervous excitement with Cody, but one from feeling unconditionally loved by someone I've known for so long and knows me so well. I wish I could stay here with her until the world's normal again.

"I really love you Miranda," Kelsey whispers.

"I love you to," I say quietly. "Knowing I'm not just here for myself, but also you has given me a lot of strength."

I open my mind to her and let her in.

The front door bangs the wall. "Rise and shine ladies!" Cody yells energetically. "Let's go!"

My body jumps away from my mind for a second as I physically sit, but mentally I'm still wrapped in her arms.

Kelsey also manages to sit before Cody walks around the corner.

She abruptly puts her hand on my shoulder and laughs. "Miranda! You're hilarious!"

It takes me a second, but I start laughing too so Cody doesn't question us before I can think of something to say.

I'm laughing with her until it turns into a real genuine belly laugh. "Oh my God this is crazy!"

"What's so funny?" Cody starts to chuckle along with us. He sits on the end of the bed. "You've been getting more Miranda time than me Kelsey. I'm getting jealous."

I can't stop laughing to give an explanation. I feel elated. Even more so because Cody believes it's a joke and not just happiness my laughter is coming from. Finally, something I have hidden from him. It doesn't feel like much of a secret, but I trust Kelsey more than I do him and I feel more comfortable with her. I know she isn't hiding anything. It's not that he's hiding anything, he just won't tell me everything. Just as soon as I felt like I was flying I am crashing.

Cody is laughing full heartily with us now. He turns over on the bed on his hands and knees and tackles me kissing my body. "You're so beautiful babe! I love your laugh. I wish I could hear it as much as I used to." He hugs me moving the length of my body and twists around me.

Kelsey walks through our conjoining door.

"So what's so fuckin' hilarious?"

"I do not remember anymore. I am just happy you are spending time with me right now," and I mean it.

"I know I haven't been around much, but it's busy work saving the world babe."

"The world?"

"I mean the country. Get dressed. We've got a full day ahead of us."

The grey covers have been carelessly kicked off the bed. The ceiling and walls seem further away and I can breathe easier. Laughing is such a great release. I don't feel as claustrophobic.

I walk to the bathroom pulling the heavy blue curtain aside and I feel the cold smooth stone beneath my bare feet. I study my reflection.

There's a heat rising from between my legs. Who did that? Was it both of them? Do I just want genuine love and care that's reciprocated? Nothing needs to be sexual in any of this. I feel like Kelsey knows my soul and I know hers and that's all I care about right now. I'm always being told, it's easy to form wrong opinions when you don't have all the information. I am probably just being stupid anyways and should let the people in charge do what they need to and get out of my own head. I am being selfish focusing on myself so much when there are people out there in agony.

"Miranda let's go," Cody says outside the bathroom waiting by the front door tapping his foot cartoonishly to vividly show his irritation. "You're needed in the Big Room."

4

Lilly hands me a camera like one would pass a loaded gun, "Basically she wants pictures of everyone here smiling and having a good time."

"Sounds fun. What is she doing with it?"

"I'm not sure. I heard there'll be some kind of video. Maybe something like an on-boarding video? I've no idea.

"Oh and make sure to get people's names so the photos can also be put in everyone's records."

"Are you coming along?"

"Yeah I want to, but I also have to. I was told we can't interact with the other colors without another member of the counsel with us."

"Oh that's weird. Is it a trust thing?" I want to ask more questions, but I do not. I do not want to appear to question any of Jayne's decisions. I am just happy to be a part of a revolution. I think so at least. "I am sure Jayne has a perfect reason. It is not weird."

"Isn't it though?" She urges me to ponder my question further. She's chewing on her nails and looking at the ground.

"I do not know. Where do you want to start?"

"I'm hungry. Let's go to the kitchen," she looks up.

The traffic's chaotic as people grab for food and start their days. I snap a few pictures of people sharing a meal together. I am trying to find those with boisterous smiles that would push the feeling of happiness home in my pictures. People seem to be happy for sure, but the smiles are calm and content ones. Everyone looks more relaxed and almost elated. Even Lilly seems to not be such a tightly wound ball today. Jayne knows what she is doing. I mean just look around. Something wonderful is at play here. People are happy despite the tragedy in the world right now.

The kitchen is a landscape of stainless steel and forest green.

"Hey Miranda and Lilly. What can I do for you?" Chef Charles Stroff finds us the second we walk into the kitchen.

"I am taking pictures of everything and everyone today to document the happiness we are creating here Chef," I say.

"J is doing a great job at that isn't she?"

J?

"And we're pretty hungry. Anyway we could have some breakfast burritos? Possibly with bacon?"

"I don't know about the bacon, but if you don't tell anyone I can find you something real good," Charles is like a Grandma sneaking a piece of candy after bedtime.

Lilly waits for my reaction to see if I'm okay with breaking a rule. If I want her to talk again I have to bend the rules. Immediately, I am flushed with heat after asking for a special menu change.

"Sounds good," I say. My curiosity about the children is killing me and I believe Jayne when she says knowledge is only on a need to know basis, but I'm fully in this movement and I want to know more. How can I do more without knowing more?

He goes off past a crowded kitchen. They're like little trees standing over burners and flat tops pulling items in and out of ovens. A forest of workers around dangerous heat sources.

"Lilly, none of them look happy enough to take pictures of."

"They're focused on cooking. Maybe after the breakfast rush we could have a couple of them cook something small and joke around with them?"

"Yeah, I like that."

I bring the camera up anyway and take a few candid photos of the chaos in here. Lauren's throwing vegetables in the air sautéing them.

"Lauren!" I yell over the clanking of pans and ventilation fans.

"Hi."

"How have you been doing?"

"Surprisingly I woke up alright today. It's a nice change of pace."

"That is good.

[pause]

"Why do you think that is?"

"I feel different since last night. Not so ... angry. When do I get my kids back?" She turns the burner off and faces me. Her demeanor is calm, but now her eyes are raging.

"I do not know," I turn away feeling uncomfortable. Then I remembered her grabbing me a couple nights or so ago. "You said something the other night?"

"I did?"

"Yeah, when I walked up to go behind the stage you yanked my shirt."

"My memory of the last week is fuzzy."

"You said something about a threat?"

Lauren flicks her eyes at Lilly. It's like she's trying to read her mind to see if she can speak freely here. Lilly then looks at me with a similar look.

Everyone keeps looking at me expecting something. I feel important. People look to me to make decisions now.

I want to tell her to speak freely, but I am better in an observational role going along with what others tell me for now. I hope Lilly tells her it's okay. They both look nervous.

"It's nothing. I feel much better this morning. I know we have to work as a team to protect everyone and work against chaos. At least that's what I was thinking about last night," Lauren says. "We need our full focus. One person can ruin it for everyone," She speaks carefully.

"Got those burritos!" Chef holds out two plates of steaming breakfast burritos. I can smell the bacon and the cheese is melting out of the tortilla folds. "You'll put in a good word for me with Jayne right?"

"Oh God these are delicious," I say. Jesus, this is phenomenal. I get good food in Jayne's office, but this brings me back. I realize breaking little rules has a lot of perks just like being on the counsel. I need to be more careful. Oh well, I like this. I like dressing in black. I deserve it. I was made for it.

"Thank you," Lilly mumbles through a full mouth of food with cheese stringing to the burrito.

The Chef grins as he watches us eat his food. "You'll tell Jayne I helped as much as possible with those photos right?" He winks at me.

"Napkin please?"

He hands me a rag and I wipe the grease away and set the plate on his cutting board. I take the camera out documenting his smile. When I look down at the picture I realize Lauren's worry lines are so prominent they threaten to become permanent. When I look up she has the same small content smile I keep seeing everyone else wear.

I snap another picture of him with her in the background cooking. He laughs with all the attention we are giving him. This time she looks content.

"Is there anything else I can do to help?" Chef asks.

"No, you are wonderful," I say.

"That's good. I feel like some of the new recruits are contemptuous towards me. Some have more experience than I do."

"You're doing great. If anyone does or says anything you let me know alright?" Lilly says as if they're already friends.

I scarf my burrito down in a few more blissful bites. I notice a few of the cooks staring at us like hungry dogs. I can feel the eyes plastered to the back of my head, but the ones in front of me divert their gazes when I look in their direction. I look behind me and they look away too.

"Chef, what is with the . . . ?" I gesture around.

"They're exhausted and hungry," Chef's smile drops. He cracks his knuckles and makes himself busy while talking to us as if he is trying to cover up what he just said. "They're good, they're good." He smiles again.

"Come on guys! You're doing great! Keep moving!" Chef yells to the kitchen crew and they return to their chaotic dance of cooking and moving around each other.

"Why are they hungry?"

"Well, I was told they can't eat until everyone else does and some have been working this kitchen for at least five hours today. It's not that anyone is complaining. I promise you they're not. That might explain the looks. It's fine. Breakfast is almost over and they'll get to have a snack before lunch is in full throw. It's fine. It really is. There's just a lot of people here. We're all super happy about that because that's more people we can share with."

"Do you need more people?"

"YES, oh God yes we do."

"I will see what I can do. No promises," I say.

"It's completely fine actually. We're okay."

"Ummm, okay just let me know if you need anything."

He tries to cut a tomato, but the knife is so dull it only accomplishes smashing the tomato. Even I know to sharpen my knifes.

"Should you not sharpen that?"

"There's no sharpeners," he moves to another station with another knife and when he tries to cut broccoli it pushes on it more than it cuts it.

"Let's get pictures of the kids," I tell Lilly prompting her to tell me what she didn't the other day.

"We can't do that."

"Why?"

She glances across the Big Room to hall E where they are being protected. She doesn't say anything.

"Lilly?" I ask.

"Lilly?!"

"Yeah we can't do that."

"Why?"

"The video we're making with these pictures are for them."

"So that means we can't take pictures of them?"

"Oh my God," She slaps her hands over her mouth.

"What? What is it?"

"I wasn't supposed to tell you that. Please Miranda," She grabs me like she would a life raft. The way she contorts her face I know she's waiting for me to slap her, but I'm not angry. "Please don't tell anyone I told you." Her eyes search the room.

"I won't. It's okay," I pull away from her. "Why are you panicked? Talk to me. I want to hear what you were going to tell me about yesterday."

"It's a trap," Lilly says under her breath so quiet I can hardly hear her. She didn't say that to me, but to herself.

"Lilly."

"I don't know what you're talking about."

"Lilly I want to hear what you have to say."

"It's nothing. Look there's some light blues over on that couch. Let's go ask them how the medical equipment will do for them and maybe get pictures in their office." Even Lilly is referring to groups of people solely by their colors.

We walk over.

"Hi. I am Miranda and this is Lilly."

"We know," one of the three says.

"I was wondering if we could take pictures of you guys in the medical room? Maybe get some action pictures?"

"Anything you guys need. Follow me," the same one with a Midwestern accent leads us towards hall Heaven where the UTV tunnel is and the gym.

The guy pulls out a key and unlocks a box where he enters a long code. The polished stone door makes sounds of electrical bolts unlocking. He props the heavy door open. "That way others feel free to come in. I was just taking a break for breakfast." He walks behind the desk.

I seem to have stepped into the regular world again. This is like any other boring doctor's waiting room. Even the lighting is right. Which is to say the same as everywhere else down here, but it actually belongs here. Those old chairs with the dulling patterns on the fabric are here. Magazines are on the table and the corner has toys. Their light blue uniforms aren't the same cut as everyone else's clothes since they're medical scrubs. There's that cold sanitized smell with a touch of the earthy smell that penetrates the rest of this shelter. The other two medicals stay on the patient side of the desk waiting for us to say something.

"Would you like to take some pictures here or in the back medical rooms?" I ask

"We're not supposed to take anyone back there without running it through the top first."

"We are the top though."

"I mean I don't know if pictures should be taken back there."

"That's fine. How about the three of you stand behind the desk," I say.

"Oh and hold a teddy bear and some candy," Lilly adds.

"Alright smile and look like you are having a lot of fun," I say snapping the picture.

5

After spending the day taking pictures of the people in various colors Lilly and I walk down hall F to deliver the camera directly to Jayne per her instructions.

"Do I look like I fucking care? Why can't we do it right now? Give me one reason I shouldn't kill you right now?! What's your fucking game?" Jayne's voice muffles through her closed door.

I look at Lilly and her eyes are as big as mine. We're two mice caught in a kitchen, unable to leave, but we can't stay here. I can't seem to walk away though. Lilly shuffles to each foot again and again. She's gnawing at her finger nails again too.

"Canada and Mexico are already sending people over to help rebuild America and you expect me not to take action," Jayne says followed by a slapping sound and then a thud as if someone was pushed from a chair. Possibly the same chair I was held at gunpoint on.

At the loud sound, Lilly jumps and makes herself smaller.

The voice is muffled and I can hardly hear. I lean in closer until my ear's pressed against the door. Lilly hesitates, but follows my lead.

"The weapons aren't stable. I'm sorry. Please don't send me down there again. Let me work with them."

"We need to send them off soon. If we're to save the world then I need to at least control North America. We have a revolution to make happen," I hear the clacking of her heels on the stone floor and then muffled by her extravagant carpet as she paces. "Ian step over here will ya."

"Ian?" Lilly mouths to me.

"From Santa Cruz. Got the Wolf," I answer. "Baby face."

She nods remembering.

"No! Please God no!" The man yells. "Get that fucking monster away from me! Fuck!"

"Will you have them ready by tomorrow? I have my people already set up. They're waiting for the signal."

The man's sobbing, "Yes, yes, I swear. It won't be completely safe to do so, but they can be sent out."

"Good. Get yourself cleaned up," Jayne's threatening voice returns to her public one in one sentence. "And Ian, I know I do not have to tell you to make sure this place is spotless in an hour for the counselor's dinner."

The sound of her heels, like little rocks stabbing the floor in synchrony comes our way. I pull Lilly into the first door I see.

The locks on Jayne's door engage. The sounds of sliding metal and suction echo through to the room we're hiding in. The sound of those little pointy heels slapping the stone floor grows quiet as she walks away.

"Oh my God," Lilly says.

Unlike the Big Room, the private quarters, and any other public place the lights in here are off except for a blue glow behind me. I turn around to see what Lilly's looking at and it's security screens. They're recording from so many secret cameras I had no clue about. I'm absorbed in their glow.

The far left shows different parts of the Haven. There's areas I've never seen before. There's two different angles of the Big Room and inside the kitchen, but I also notice a lack of areas covered by the cameras.

"You see that?" I ask Lilly pointing at the kitchen screens. "There's a blind spot."

Cameras are placed at the entrances of each tunnel that branch away from the Big Room. The gym and the waiting room for the medical wing is online. The gym is full of colorful people.

"Have you been to the gym here?" I ask.

"Mark doesn't like women with too much muscle."

"What?" I start and quickly remember not to be bossy. "I still haven't been in there." I feel an especially strong push to get my strength up right now.

On the other side there's live feeds from outside. It looks like it's early morning though. We're about to have dinner soon. That can't be.

"Lilly the time doesn't match up."

Lilly spits a nail she chewed off onto the controls.

"Maybe they're not live videos. But the kitchen is obviously prepping dinner on the video just like they should be doing now," Lilly says.

"The pacing of our days is inaccurate. Look outside. Our body clocks are getting fucked with."

She doesn't respond.

"Lilly," she doesn't hear me though between chewing on her nails and staring at one screen in particular. Several screens show the children. The first one I'm drawn to shows a dark room with a large screen silhouetting children tied to chairs. They appear to be in a trance. The screen the kids are looking at is distorted on these cameras. I can make out images of fire and blurry images of people fighting or maybe being murdered? I'm squinting my eyes as if that could help the screen the kids are looking at become clearer. The words OTC,

Order Through Chaos, and The Nothings flash rapidly resembling a strobe light lighting the kids silhouettes and then making them disappear. It's like a haunted house. I try to articulate my horror to Lilly, but there's no speech that would do this justice.

I hear chatter outside, which knocks me out of my trance.

"Oh fuckin' hell what time is it?" I ask Lilly.

"What?"

"Oh yeah none of us have watches. We should have been able to hear her voice calling for dinner over the speakers, but they aren't in here. That means we've been in here for an hour. I think. Is no one watching these?."

"How are we going to get out without being seen? We can't leave. There's more videos we haven't been able to watch."

"Lilly what the hell's happening here?"

"I need to tell you something."

"I want to hear you, I do. We have to get out first though."

"We don't have much time before irrevocable damage is done," Lilly squeezes her fingers one by one. If she doesn't relax she's going to burst or just as worse look suspicious and make people ask questions.

The sounds outside are starting to dissipate. I press my ear against the door waiting for silence.

"Okay Lilly I'm going to head out first and if you don't hear me scream . . . umm . . .let's say "Hello guys!" then it's clear to run into her office."

"We could say we were getting pictures."

"No we can't do that. Think a little more. The pictures have time stamps for fucks sake. Let's say we were napping, no that's not it. Let's say we were in the kitchen again to get pictures of the dinner crew, but they were busy and focused we couldn't get any ecstatic looking pictures," I say. "Alright Lilly I'm going out first. If you hear nothing then come out."

I barely pull on the door and it squeals. I didn't have to wait for it to echo to know it was going to bounce off the stone.

Lilly gasps and my heart skips a few beats.

6

After a dinner of locally caught salmon smothered in butter, wild asparagus, and grains with fresh herbs Jayne walks in. The counsel continues to eat better than the Big Room every night.

"Could two of you help me pass the wine around?" Jayne asks.

Mark and Cody jump into each other. They were in the closest seats possible to her desk.

"Watch it fancy pants," Cody whispers annoyed.

"We're in the same clothes," Mark rolls his eyes.

"Unfortunately I have plans that are imperative to our survival happening tomorrow so I need to go, but feel free to hang out and drink a swig or two before going home," she makes eye contact with everyone as she walks. Her smile is beautiful. When she gets to me it does not feel like I am just another person to look at, but like she sees me and appreciates me.

"Miranda, Lilly, do you have the camera?"

Her floral perfume hits me as I hand it over.

"Thank you. You are valued team members. I have new responsibilities coming up and I want you guys to be a part of it. This world is coming together and we will be able to save so many lives and get society back on its feet. You two specifically are who I need."

Before she departs Jayne says, "Good night everyone. You are a part of something ground breaking." I can hear those little clonking sounds of her heels fading away.

I relax.

I look into the wine glass I was given. I saw what happened to everyone the other night and I know the same thing or maybe more happened to me the other night in Jayne's calming meditative room.

Lilly, Kelsey, and Kyle have already started drinking theirs. Mark and Cody seem to be nowhere in sight.

"Once again Cody disappeared without even telling me where he's going. I feel like we're growing apart. I don't want to say this, but . . ."

"Go ahead and tell us what you think." Lilly said the following sentence with abnormal intensity, "You can talk to us about anything. I promise."

"I feel like he brought me here and put me through this training not necessarily because he liked me, but because he believed in me. I feel like he chose me for this. It sounds conceited, but I was waiting for something to find me that recognized my strengths. I try my hardest at everything I do, but I have trusted everything without question. In the past, I yearned so badly to be recognized. I've always followed others. I'm sorry I'm going on a tangent and now I don't even know what I'm trying to say. I don't know what I want anymore. I thought I was meant for something grand like this movement. I wanted it so badly. Now that I'm here I don't think I was meant for that. Jayne did tell me if I ever felt this way it was because I was letting evil influence me. I'm not sure about myself anymore."

I wait for them to tell me I'm being stupid and sensitive.

I sharply inhale when I realize they are almost done with their glasses of wine. I don't know how to hide mine again. What will they do to us? What's in the drinks? Should I stop them? Is that the evil influencing me and making me believe delusional thoughts?

"I'm here for you," Kelsey reaches under the table and places her hand on my knee. Her touch makes me realize I'm holding my breath and I let it go.

"You can speak about anything to us," Lilly says gesturing to include Kyle. "Anything".

"How do you guys feel right now? Sleepy at all?"

"No, I don't think so. Are you feeling alright physically Miranda?" Kyle asks me confused.

"Yeah, yeah I am fine," I lean towards them. "Don't change your demeanor when I tell you this and do not look around. After I tell you this start laughing like I said a joke. Cameras are everywhere. I can't explain right now. Just don't drink any more wine in the future. These ones seem normal so keep drinking them. Don't attract attention. Alright lean back and laugh."

I throw my head back laughing utilizing what Kelsey taught me this morning. I sip at the wine slowly, worried if I drink it too fast the wine will turn into Isaac and realize my second thoughts and take me down the stairs behind the bookcase.

I keep drinking it with an orchestrated smile on my face. I feel a slight buzz, but that's it.

"I'm going to say this in a lighthearted way like we're talking about the delicious dinner we had so stay smiling. We need to find a way we can talk. Lilly I know you tried to tell me something and I scared you away, but too much has happened since then I need to know now. Kyle I think you kept getting cut off when trying to tell me something in Santa Cruz. Or was I wrong?"

"You aren't. There wasn't a place to say anything and the more time went on the more wary I felt about you.

[pause]

"Kelsey, can you be trusted?" Kyle asks her.

"Of course she can," I interject.

"What are you talking about?" Isaac stands over us.

Chapter 12

1

"Please report to the Big Room immediately. We have shattering news. Please move with efficiency. We are safe, but the world is not," Jayne's voice from the speaker above the bed wakes us up.

My cheek is pressed into her large breasts and I feel warm and soft covered in the blankets. I don't want to leave, but I feel rested and ready to continue forth.

"It's always something terrible happening all the time," I attempt a joke.

"Who knew an apocalypse would be such a burden," Kelsey leans in and gently kisses my cheek before getting up and leaving to her room to get dressed. It felt loving and romantic and motherly.

I go to shower, but the mirror stops me. At first glance I saw a stranger, but on closer look it's still me.

"Miranda let's go," Cody says with his head poking through the curtain. I jump. His body looks like it could run laps through these halls and it still would not make him slow down. He is buzzing. I can feel his overly intense energy bouncing off of me and the walls. He looks absolutely elated, but extremely serious and graven at the same time. It's intense.

"I did not hear you come in."

"You don't have time for a shower. Jayne needs all of us. I need to get everyone else in this hall. We really got to go," He runs back out.

"Hello Cody, it is nice to see you. Where were you? Oh you are happy to see me. How nice," I say to nobody, but myself.

I splash water on my face and throw my clothes on. I think about locking my door, but why? I don't live in the city anymore and Cody nor I have been locking it anyways. What is there to hide? Our nonexistent wallets, phones, jeweled watches?

"Miranda!" Kyle runs up behind us the second we step into the hall.

"How's it going? All things considered."

"You seem more relaxed."

"Yeah. I feel that way. I had some good sleep," I say thinking about crawling back in bed with Kelsey to go back to sleep and enter my dreams where none of this real.

"You needed it. I have a bad feeling today that's all."

More of the counsel members join us as we pass by their doors on the way to the Big Room. Any privacy we had to talk is gone.

Any lightness I felt earlier has now been buried deep under the heavy stone. Nobody says anything as we walk. I remember the conversation I heard the other day and dread lines the hall in front of me.

The Big Room is crowded with people. Not even the kitchen crew is working this morning. There is no smell of breakfast. It's just the cold damp forgotten smell of a cave and light body odor.

Isaac and Ian are pressed against the wall behind the stage talking. Another guy I do not recognize is in between them. It looks like his nose is broken and he has two black eyes. He's standing funny. Ian pushes into him with the side of his shoulder and the man straightens. The man grimaces. Ian pulls on his own shirt and tugs at his sleeves with quick and precise movements.

"Everyone please take your seat," Jayne amplifies. She looks strong standing there with her black hair in a straight line above her shoulders. She is not wearing those black heals, but shiny new black combat boots like the rest of us on her small counsel.

"I have grave news." She looks around the room letting silence do some of the talking. The counsel members and I stand behind her on the floor.

"Canada and Mexico have been attacked by The Nothings. Order Through Chaos, which by no means is any definition of order, has killed millions more. They destroyed cities, airports, and worst of all, nuclear bombs were used. Millions and millions of people have died early this morning and continue to do so."

I look for Lilly who is a few people over from me chewing on her fingers like she's starving.

I sink. It feels like I'm going to fall through the stone. This must have been what I heard about last night. I didn't know it would be this morning. My vision blurs and it feels like I'm walking through a spinning room as I try to stand straight and look professional. Little black specks appear in the corner of my vision.

My head begins to throb.

"This morning we found one of our own people down hall Heaven who managed to break the wooden planks we secured the opening with. That put each of our lives in danger. We heard the OTC in military style planes and helicopters not too long ago and today the same thing that happened in our country happened in Canada and Mexico, but worse. After questioning the person, we learned they are one of The Nothings sent to steal inside information. They wanted to reveal our location. They were told to set smoke signals once they found us and learned about our movement. It was smart we closed off the exits when we did or we would not be here now.

"The people who are down here are my closest members. We are training for the new world. There is more of us elsewhere across the country, but this location right here is where I hope to find my leaders to bring peace back. It hurts to find someone we have trusted to build our society betraying us. To discover he was lying since the beginning is especially alarming. To make matters worse this epitome of evil was someone I particularly trusted. He even traveled to Santa Cruz with Mikaela and Kyle-"

She left out Mikaela's partner's name, Austin.

"-to help save people. The movement and the powers to be are working through me, but I am only human and for that I apologize for trusting the wrong person.

"Please bring him forth. This man has contributed to or may be entirely responsible for some of your loved ones dying. Who knows what he made happen in Santa Cruz. Who knows what he left behind on his way back here so people could trace him. He is the reason your father, mother, husband, wife, children, and friends have been murdered and some were tortured as they laid dying with no help. I learned he was the sole reason the last attack in Santa Cruz happened. He wanted to make it seem like we could not protect you. He caught us at a weak moment, but we only continue to grow stronger. We have learned from this mistake and it will never happen again." Jayne's demeanor suddenly changes. She is holding herself like a different person. A fire's in her eyes I have seen before. I tried to forget about that first day in her office, but those eyes are unforgettable. Her eyes have changed and my memories are flooded by what happened. Instead of the graceful almost floating way of moving she has, it's a tad jerky now. Her body seems wider. Not fat, but like it's taking up more room. If someone told me that was a different person who just looked a lot like Jayne I might have believed them.

The counsel members around me are turning and I see Ian and Isaac push that man forward and then Cody of all people, grabs his arm and leads him through us and then in front of the stage.

"You promised I wouldn't die!" He yells at Jayne on his way up the stage. He turns to the crowd ahead, "This is a lie! I didn't do anything wrong! They're lying to you!" He's screaming while being dragged. He kicks Cody in the leg and runs through the crowd getting tackled by a random man in pink at the entrance of hall B.

"She's trying to kill you! She is-"

He's cut off when Cody catches up to him and yanks a gag he made from his own belt around his head. His teeth are protruding out making him look like a horse. He's still thrashing around trying to get loose, but Cody and a man in pink, security, hold onto him and walk him back. A person in the crowd spits on his face.

"You're evil!" I hear another yell at him.

"Why?!" Someone screams at him as they appear in front of the three and kick him in the groin. The person disappears back into the crowd.

The gagged man collapses as his knees give out, but Cody and the pink man snatch him back up. The crowd is in an uproar. A glass cup flies through the crowd and smacks the back of his head. It shatters upwards towards the dark ceiling and falls back onto the people closing in on him as they encroach the stage.

He's yanked onto the stage and forced to his knees. A loud pop rings out from him his legs. I think Cody broke one of his knees. He's sweating profusely and his hair is plastered to his face. He looks disgusting. The sweat is falling into his eyes making him blink rapidly. His hair is jagged. He looks like a villain. He starts shaking his head back and forth mumbling broken words through the gag.

I want to feel pity for the man but if he did that then he deserves everything coming his way. The crowd is screaming hate at him and I realize I hate him to.

"I am sorry you have to witness this, but who knows how many deaths this man was responsible for, like the massacre that happened in Santa Cruz the night before we brought most of you down here. If you were not there I am sure you heard about the outrageous violence. Here's to our loved ones who died from the OTC." Jayne holds her hand out and Ian hurries onto the stage dressed in an ironed shirt and perfectly combed hair. He proudly hands her a knife from his belt and then straightens his belt again.

Isaac strides up the steps with arms plastered to his side to stand on the other side of the traitor.

She nods to Cody and the pink man and they exit the stage and the pink man merges with the angry crowd. The pinks are the only color who never form their own groups. There's only a handful, but they are always spread out.

Cody smiles devilishly at Mark as he passes him.

Jayne grabs the man's hair. She pulls it upwards, the little brown ruffles popping through her strong slender fingers. He's no longer struggling, just sobbing. His hands aren't tied. They limply hang by his sides. She reaches her other hand high above her ahead with the knife gleaming in the bright lighting. The crowd is full of cries of "Vengeance," "Kill him, "Evil," and so forth.

In a theatrical swing she brings her arm down, but stops and gently places the blade against his neck. She takes a second to look in his eyes. His terror and pain stricken eyes stare back and she slides it across his sweaty skin. The blood jumps outwards with one final cry of salvation until it pours like syrup out of his neck. As the life leaves his body, the rest of his body goes limp until he falls forward in his own bath of blood. It continues to pour from him collecting in rivulets down the wooden stage until it trickles over the edge like a tiny waterfall.

2

Kyle slides next to me and whispers, "We need to get out."

I snap out of the humdrum of the ecstatic hatred around me realizing even if he did do that, how would they have proved it? And even if they did prove it, this is terror as well. You can't create more terror to end terror.

Jayne steps off the stage. Her hands are drenched in the man's blood. Ian runs along handing her rags and helping her clean her hands. He gently wipes her face as they walk away down hall F.

The crowd in front of me is one single frenzied unit. They are moving and reacting as one being. A few are puking, but those are the mouth of this creature. The ones in the middle who aren't moving or saying anything are the innards. There's people along the edges who are still cheering and crying out. Those are the fingers and toes of this monstrous glob in front of me. There's people sitting and staring in silence representing the eyes. Some are walking around and talking to everybody they stumble into. They are also the mouth while the listeners are the ears. It moves as one with a million things going on at once to make up the whole. Everyone is connected by their colored uniforms and when I look away and back again it's like they're individual cells. Each one performing a different duty in this mass designated by the color they are wearing. They don't seem like individual people, but cogs in a machine delegated by their colors.

And here we are separated from them dressed in white and black watching the colorful mass moving and breathing. Isaac is talking to Mark through the crowd then over to another dressed in black and then to me.

"Make sure the counsel members are gathered in hall H." He walks to the other blacks while we gather the whites.

When I walk through the mass of people I feel like I am penetrating something. I don't belong here. I feel uninvited. The emotions around me are full of zealotry.

I do overhear a few conversations about when their kids will be returned though. Mostly, the common emotion is one of unity and passion. They seem ready to fight. They're looking for an enemy and Jayne put one right in front of them making a huge spectacle out of it. They got off on it and they're hungry for more.

We walk past the gym on the left. There's a poster on the wall next to it I never bothered to look at. It's a schedule. A color coordinated schedule. Every hour different colors or portions of colors are scheduled to come here. That didn't use to be so. All the colors used to mix together.

    We pass the locked doctor's office on the right. All the light blues are in the Big Room right now. We keep walking through the tunnel until it is dark and nobody from the Big Room can see us. Five UTVs appear in the distance to take us the rest of the way. There is no more than forty of us so we can pile in the attached trailers.

3

We are in the oak grove where the cars were originally parked. It feels nice to be in the fresh air again. The cavern tunnels are so quiet and the way they hold sound is disorienting. They aren't just quiet, but sound goes there to die. Up here the birds are singing and I can faintly hear the ocean far off in the distance. I want to take my shoes off and feel the dirt and plants beneath my bare feet. Yeah the cold stone floors down there is earth, but it's not alive.

The wind brushes against my skin cooling me in the warm sun. It's not a constant temperature like below. There's fluctuations and changes even standing in one spot. Life means nothing is constant. A bug flies past and I probably feel the most gratitude than I ever have before towards a bug.

It's so nice after so long to see so much life. Especially without having to worry about completing a mission.

Some of the other members have not stepped outside since first going down there right after the bombs. One girl is sitting on the ground running her fingers through the dirt and another is leaning against one of the twisting oak trees with closed eyes.

A hawk sings its cry above us. I look at the blue sky to see it flying overhead with a glimmering red tail. I bet he knows how beautiful he is. He knows we are looking at him.

I trip over Lilly who's laying in the tall grass. She doesn't move.

I walk over to the edge of the oak grove to be on the open ridge. I see orange and blue flowers off in the distance. They call me towards them, but I have to stay right here for now. They make the mountain look painted. The amount of color is a stark contrast to the grey below.

There's a lone tree in the distance. My internal compass pushes me towards it. I feel compelled to investigate the tree on a ridge with nothing else near it. It's massive and its branches swirl in wild directions.

"Miranda!" Cody is by my side once again. He is always appearing and then disappearing.

"Hey," I force a smile out.

"Don't go off on your own or it could look like you're trying to leave."

"Am I not allowed to go off on my own?"

"Of course ya fuckin' are love. I gotta make sure it's safe to be in the complete open first. Isn't that obvious?" He smiles. What I thought was his charm is starting to annoy me now.

"I mean . . . I guess. Yeah."

He pulls me into a hug and kisses my neck. At first I want to pull away, but now I'm giggling. I just haven't seen him as much lately. It's not his fault I am feeling moody towards him. He is so cute.

I kiss him back.

"I love you babe. I really fuckin' love you."

For the first time since I told him I loved him first I find myself pausing. "Love ya too," I say quickly.

"I've something to show you. Follow me," He grabs my hand and hikes me to the painted part of the mountain leaving the group behind.

We walk through knee length grass. Little grasshoppers fly through the air as we walk on. Honey bees buzz pass in search of the next flower. The sun is stronger outside of the grove, but then the gentle breeze brushes it off keeping me cool and comfortable.

When the oak grove is out of site and we are in the middle of the imaginary painting I see Jayne sitting in an orange field of poppies. They look like little cups a fairy might use as a pool blowing sideways in the wind. The delicate orange petals are as much in tune with the wind as the bees are with their nectar. I walk further in front of her captivated by the beauty.

I am fixated on the bright orange flowers dancing at my feet. The wind goes flat and I feel the heat bear down on me, but it's nice. The Pacific Ocean fills my view going on forever and ever until it blends seamlessly into the blue sky. It's perfectly clear.

I saw this place's beauty on the way up here, but I was in such a crazed fight to survive I did not see any of it. On the way to Santa Cruz I was again too concentrated on surviving and not tumbling the big bus off a cliff.

Now I have nothing to worry about and I am above the world. I am standing on a mountain above the ocean. It's as if I could take a giant step forward and walk across the water to meet the sun.

That's when it settles in that the sun is too low in the sky for it to be the morning. And it's on the wrong side. It's near the end of the day. The time down in the Haven doesn't match the one up here. My internal clock is out of wack. Here we are with the time of the earth not matching the time underground.

"It is beautiful is it not?" Jayne walks up behind me resting her chin on my shoulder and leaning her head into mine.

Her approval fills me with joy. I turn my attention back to the beauty and grandiosity of the place. I lean onto her and she puts an arm around me. Cody steps onto my other side with an arm around me.

God does this feel good. I feel accepted and loved.

I let myself feel this moment and watch the blues of the ocean and sky complimenting each other. The green grass and blue and orange flowers on the mountain breathe with us.

Jayne turns me towards her and guides me to sit in the soft plush grass. Cody moves around me and sits so we are our own little circle on our own giant isolated mountain.

"Cody has been an invaluable member of this movement from day one years ago when he first started with all of this. I know he has been absent, but that is because he has been helping me and Isaac and some other people work towards a better future. When he came to me about a year ago and told us about you I was hesitant at first. Not because of who you are, but because you are new. I noticed you are an observer and great at going with the flow. You do not put up a fight when things are new to you, but instead you go with them. Not that you do not have fight in you because it's obvious you are a fighter. You like to wait to form opinions and weigh your options. Stop me if I'm wrong," She grabs one of my hands in both of hers and moves closer.

"You are so special Miranda. I notice you and I admire the way you travel through life. I want to know your opinion of where we are headed right now. I value it."

"What do you mean?" I ask.

"You know our goal is to create a fair world. Through more control we can have more freedom. Chaos and anarchy only results in violence and death and does not allow everyone to live out their true lives. If we can control the way society is structured then we give everyone a chance. Those with different talents have a chance to prosper. Do you have anything to say?"

"I am not sure. I mean I cannot wait to see this come to light. What about the rest of America? What about Canada and Mexico? What about the rest of the world? What happened there anyway?" I worry I'm asking too many questions. I don't think it's my place to ask, but she's giving me permission.

"It's a tragedy. I have my suspicions The Nothings are trying to take over the world. We have a plan though. It is not only us in the Haven. We are all over the United States or what used to be the United States. We have people in Canada and Mexico doing the same thing we are here. We are preparing the next group of leaders."

"Why couldn't you stop the same thing happening in Canada and Mexico if you knew about it?"

"Believe me we tried, but they evaded us at every turn. The best we could do was be prepared for the inevitable. We have the opportunity to build a new and improved civilization from scratch. We have to wait for the right moment though."

"Why don't we go out and rescue more people? Aren't we letting them die by not doing so?"

"It takes time and I have people in different towns and cities making their own boundaries like what happened in Santa Cruz. It is dangerous though. We do not know who is a member of OTC and it's sad to speak this aloud, but if people do not see the atrocities that result from chaos then they will not believe in our order."

"So you're making people desperate?" I can't believe that came out of me. I bite my tongue waiting for her to snap.

"No."

"I did not mean that."

"I am a safe person to talk to," She squeezes my hand and looks deep into my eyes. "I want you to speak freely and I want you to play a bigger role in this. If you are ready of course."

I want to give myself over to her and the movement. Jayne has a way about her that gives me faith.

I glance at Cody who nods and smiles.

"Yeah. I mean yes. What can I do?"

"I know you worked with children before the bombs. I heard you were a psychiatrist and I was hoping to utilize those talents."

"I would be honored." I'm excited, but my body feels queasy. "Honestly, I am feeling nervous right now. I am sure you can tell, but I am ready to help more."

"I would hope so. We do not have room for lukewarm people who aren't on fire for the movement."

"What do we do about the lukewarms?"

4

She didn't answer my question, but walked back to the group.

"I want to thank you all for your hard work and dedication. I have given each of you different tasks and you have all done them better than I hoped for. It is not safe to be outside right now, but I figured it was worth the risk to get you outside to experience nature and to look at what is to come. I plan on building homes up here so we can have our own little society to return to when we eventually spread out to the rest of the world. It may seem difficult right now, but our efforts will lead to a world that gives you the same feeling this mountain does. When you are feeling doubts, harness this feeling right here."

We watch the sunset together until the colors have stopped changing and we walk back in the dark.

I'm walking through the green grasses behind everyone. Jayne comes to my side and whispers, "I know I say this a lot, but you are doing amazing things here and I appreciate you. You're one of the special ones."

I can't help but blush.

She grabs my hand and holds me in place and let's the group walk on. "Can I trust you through and through with the children? The methods might seem odd, but I assure you this will all lead to a better world." She is standing close to me. Our chests brush against one another. It is electrifying to have her want to talk to me specifically.

"Yeah I am ready," My breathing is shallower and I don't feel like I can breathe fully with her this close to me.

She embraces me. I feel slightly uncomfortable. I put her on such a high pedestal and right now she seems so human. Almost relatable.

"Are you ready for possibly the most important task for building our society?" She asks.

5

When we return to the Big Room people have not started dinner even though it's night above us. The time jumps are messing with my head.

I go down hall Evening where the kids have been placed. Lauren and another woman are waiting by a large metal door in a metal wall separating the hall from the rest of the shelter.

"Where are our children?" Lauren asks.

"I am actually going down there right now to work with them," I say politely smiling.

"What the hell does that mean?" The other woman asks.

"Uh, I am sorry I cannot discuss anything with you."

"Those are our kids! I'm being worked to death and anytime I complain they mention my children. What are they implying there Miranda?" Lauren asks.

"I do not know what you are talking about. I wish I could help you. Whatever is going on I can assure you it is for the future of the world. I do not know everything either."

"The fuck are we doing in this cave?" The other woman asks. Lauren elbows her in the side. Hard.

"We're keeping you safe," I declare.

"What she means is I don't know what's going on above. And now I heard other countries are falling as well? Shouldn't we be with our children." It wasn't a question.

"I do not believe you guys are allowed back here," I tell them.

"But-" The other woman starts and Lauren pulls her back towards the Big Room and tries to walk away.

"I thought you said we could trust her," The other woman accuses Lauren who is still trying to drag her away.

"Shut up," I hear her say as they rush off.

I pull out my keys and unlock a small metal box to the right, which then reveals a keypad. I enter the long code I was told. The thing starts flashing red and counting down from 10. I enter it again and this time the door unlocks.

I walk through to an identical tunnel just as bright, but as I walk the tunnel gets narrower and narrower until it is the size of a hallway you would find in any home. This leads to a staircase carved straight out of the stone. The LED lights are in the staircase as well. An unlit torch waits on the wall. There's no railing. Just stone stairs with the stone wall directly on each side. I follow it down as it spirals. My footsteps echo through the spiraling staircase making a strange music.

It's eerie seeing such an ancient looking staircase with bright LED lights. It doesn't match. It's like I'm walking in another dimension where everything is just a little off. Maybe I am dreaming. A land of no shadows and where time has been warped. Ancient is added with the new. I follow it further, burying myself deeper in the Earth with each step. There's nothing else except the disturbed dust of previous footprints. The staircase is abnormally dry.

I continue walking downwards in a swirling pattern brushing my fingertips along the rough dry stone until the ground flattens out beneath me. The light has been sucked away. My silhouette is long on the dark flat floor in front of me. Then in a blink all the lights burst on. Must be motion activated. There's nothing here except another door at the end.

I was told this one will be different. I pull the key out that unlocks the little black box, but this time instead of a keypad it's a screen. Jayne told me everything was already set up so my handprint must already be programmed.

I bring my hand to press on the little dark screen expecting nothing to happen. The moment I touch it, it lights up and beeps and I hear several locks unfolding inside the hefty door.

Movement and laughter fills the space. Kids are playing. I am in some common room with couches and toys and rugs. The stone isn't as rough in here. It's been polished. The toys add bright splashes of color. Lilly and Mark are behind an ancient wooden desk.

The kids are dressed in grey.

A hallway lined with doors lead straight out of this room. The doors are made of wood and painted white. For a moment I forget I'm in a cave.

"Hey guys!" I walk over to them.

Lilly has dark bags weighing her eyes down and her fists are clenched, but she responds with a soft, "Hi."

"Hey Miranda," Mark smiles. He is sitting up straight and taking notes on a clipboard.

"So what do you guys have for me? What is the run down?"

Mark stands with his shoulders back. I have never seen him look so in command. "We need your help in teaching our vision for the new world. Follow me." He walks without waiting for my response.

I pass kids running and playing. Some are playing with dolls and cars and the older ones are sitting around talking child gossip I assume.

We pass a few doors until he opens the one he wants.

"This is the room that teaches the new ways. Once I see you can handle this, Jayne says you can work in the other room."

"What is the other room?"

"It teaches the old ways," He leaves as if he's the boss and when he's done talking there is no way there could be more questions.

A plain blue rug covers the ground and a television in the front plays a slide show of pictures. I recognize some of them as the pictures I took. Others are drawings of an outdoor community with people in the same colored outfits laughing and eating and working. It looks like an advertisement for a happy commune.

A paper rests on the table to the right of the door with instructions.

"Dear Miranda,

"This room is for positive reinforcement. You will talk one on one with kids about what they would like to do. You will dress them accordingly. When they do something right let them choose a small piece of candy from the box under this table. Give them a scenario where a loved one speaks ill about what we are doing here and let them play out what they would do. If they do not go to authority immediately then use negative reinforcement by withholding the candy. But by no means use punishment. Let them play with our future form of currency. Jobs they do will give them tickets for food, clothing, and entertainment. Let them spend it and each time they do give them candy.

"I believe in you,

"Jayne"

The door opens and a teenage girl walks through. I would know her anywhere. She's Lauren Tanner's daughter from Santa Cruz.

She's looking down twiddling with her thumbs.

"You are Hailey right?"

"Yeah."

"Lauren's daughter?"

"I'm a daughter of the movement."

She appears to be shaking slightly.

"This is the candy room right?" She asks.

"It is."

"Okay. I like this one." She looks up at me and drops her arms.

"I am Miranda. Do you remember me?"

"Yeah, you saved us from The Nothings. They killed my Dad."

"Alright, let's get started. First, how old are you? What are you interested in? What would you want to do for a living?"

"I'm 13 and I want to be an explorer."

I look at the list of jobs available on the page under my instructions. I cannot see where that could match.

"What about security? Sometimes they get sent out on missions?"

"Yeah I just like to find things. I found something here."

"What did you find?"

"Do you promise not to tell anyone? It's a secret. You can't tell anyone. My Mom told me to go to you if I need anything. That was a long time ago though. I haven't seen her in so long," she looks intense.

"Of course what would you like to tell me?" I'm wondering if she found a stash of candy or some other lounge room for the adults. My curiosity is peaked and I am excited to be working with kids again.

"I have to show you. But I can't show you here."

"Why is that?"

"Don't look, but there's a camera in the corner. It's my secret spot."

"Where do we go?"

"You have to follow me."

"Lead the way."

Hailey opens the door and peaks in both directions. When she is satisfied she waves me over. Her eyes are the same fiery eyes her mother has when she asks about her kids.

"Where are we going?" I ask jokingly.

"Ssh. Don't be so loud."

"My bad," I say taken back. She sure is a little explorer.

She walks to the end of the hall and pulls me into a claustrophobic janitor's closet.

"This is your spot you like to hide in?" I ask smiling.

"Don't be silly. Stop talking."

She moves a large rolling trash can and some brooms and mops out of the way then pulls on a set of shelves with wheels on the bottom. With care, she rolls it to the side leaving a small gap between it and the wall. A break in the stone wall stands out to me. She pushes on it and it opens inwards. It's not just dark inside, but like light has never been in there.

"Get in," She instructs.

"I don't know. We are probably not supposed to be down here. Everything serves a purpose and we do not need to know everything."

"I haven't gone down it. I just really wanted to show you. But you won't see the strange room it leads to if you don't go in."

"I thought you said you have not been down there."

"Can I trust you?"

I think about that for a moment. I want to impress Jayne and I want to be an invaluable member to the counsel, but I was told to work here and if I am to work here then I need to be there for the kids. I need to be someone they can trust. I should report this immediately, but something pushes me forward. I walk into the darkness.

"Yes you can."

"Pinky promise?"

We join our pinkies.

She walks in after me and pulls the shelves back and reaches through them to the rolling garbage bin and pulls it closer. She reaches for the wall and lights one of those torches I saw on the staircase earlier. She lights it with a butane lighter she picked from a hook beside it. She sticks it in her pocket.

"The tunnels mess with time really badly. Like a lot," she warns me.

I'm resting my hands on my knees since I cannot stand without bumping my head. She only has to dunk slightly. The stone is rough and pieces protrude from it waiting to break my head open.

"Follow me and be very very quiet."

There's no lights or wire running through, but yet there was that lighter near the front so it couldn't have been too long ago people were in here. My back starts to ache having to bend over so much. As we walk further, cold water drips on my nose and when I look above me I notice tiny little stalactites. I make a mental note not to stab the top of my head on those. I bend over more.

Eventually the ceiling grows in height and I can stand straight. For stalactites of that size to have formed this cave has to be at least thousands and thousands of years old possibly millions if it went through a dry spell.

I start panting and running out of breath. I listen for Hailey, but her breathing is normal. It seems like we have been walking forever when she stops.

"Is there enough oxygen?" I ask as if she's a cave scientist and not a child scrambling through dark tunnels.

"We've been going uphill."

The walls are further apart and I'm feeling less claustrophobic.

She stops walking. "We can keep going straight or there's a turn ahead to go left or right."

"Where have you been?"

"I've been straight and left. Straight is really scary. I want to go left."

"What's straight ahead?" I have a bad feeling, but my curiosity needs an answer to her comment.

"We should go left."

"Will you take me straight after we go left?" I regret I said that the second it came out of my mouth. I know there's a different type of darkness straight ahead.

The fire is flickering across her face distorting her features, but there's a deep fear. Not the nervousness I saw back in the study room, but something much deeper. Her pupils have grown darker and deeper. It's like there's something she saw that's now trying to attach itself in her mind that she's fighting with and I'm seeing a glimpse of it through her eyes.

"If that's what you wish." She keeps walking and then makes a left.

The walls start narrowing again and eventually I have to crawl. She's holding the torch with one hand and crawling with the other in front of me. We're ascending rapidly. I'm almost climbing now trying not to bump my head on the roof. A bump down here could mean death. I notice a light up ahead.

"Be careful. I have to put this out. Don't slip between the rocks. You must spread your body out." She rubs the torch on the rocks and the shadows come rushing back engulfing us in their darkness. The floor gets rockier and I'm still having to climb. I feel for safe hand holds.

Thankfully the floor starts to flatten and I'm not reaching up as much as I am reaching out now.

I know nothing can live down here, but scrambling in the dark fills me with terror of what could be lingering behind me or in the cracks my hands occasionally slip into.

I put my hand forward and fall. My shoulder stops me. My hand dangles in some unseen hole that as far as I know has no bottom. My other hand pushes my body back up and I carefully slide over the hole. The light ahead is getting brighter.

Hailey's waiting for me and when I reach her I can hear voices. I recognize some of them. I peak over a small opening. It's barely big enough for a small child to fit through.

It's the Big Room.

It's a long fall to the bottom.

All the colorful people are moving around. Most are in the lounge part of the room where the mismatching couches and chairs are scattered making a maze of "living rooms."

"How did you..." I begin, but Hailey pushes her hand over my mouth.

"Sound's amplified here," She mouths the words.

Lauren's in her forest green clothes and forest green apron and walks out of the kitchen and slumps onto a couch.

I feel Hailey tense next to me. I look at her and it seems like she's about to say something, but she relaxes again or more like her body deflates next to mine and the sadness is infectious. We sit for a while watching the people below.

Jayne comes in with Cody following her and walks up to a guy in light blue, one of the medical personnel, at a table and sits. When Cody sits next to her he slides his hand down the top of her back down her spine to the top of her butt. His finger slides along the rim of her black pants. She doesn't flinch. She's used to it.

The light blue is nodding and then leaves. He heads over to the couches and sits alone. He grabs a magazine, but his head never moves and he doesn't flip any pages. He looks like he's listening to the conversations around him.

He's spying.

Jayne and Cody go into the kitchen.

My heart feels like it's sinking.

I want to yell at them, but I can't. I feel helpless. But do I even have a right to be upset? God, I feel like I'm going to throw up. Jayne and Cody have probably been together this entire time. I never meant anything to him. It was all a facade. I'm so stupid.

Hailey taps my knee and nudges her head back towards the darkness. I feel like I'm breaking out of a stone sculpture. For a second there I felt like my skin was the stone around me stuck in a perpetual nightmare. I could see something awful, but I couldn't say anything and I can't ever say anything.

She's crawling back down facing me as she anticipates the steep part. I follow her.

Eventually the tunnel is flat enough that my thoughts of what-ifs are intruding again. We crawl in the darkness and once there's space between me and the all seeing hole I feel like I can breathe again.

She pulls the lighter out of her pocket and lights the torch again.

We're at the intersection once more.

"Alright can you show me what's straight ahead?"

"Are you sure? We've already been in the tunnels a long time and they might check on you. What are you going to say?"

"Just don't tell anyone I was here. Okay? Let me worry about it. Do you hear me?" God my nerves are shot through the roof. If I stop now, I won't come back here.

She ignores me and keeps walking.

There's no doubt in my mind I'm doing something dangerously wrong. Every time I talk to Jayne I want to do what she says. She has this way about her, this persuasion that makes me want to please her. Everything that has happened to me though is awakening something in me. What if I don't just go along with what she says? Cody told me that's actively working against them if I question them though. Doubt means I'm weak or at least that's what I was told. Ah fuck, I feel confused.

"You're smarter than you look," I finally say. "I'm serious though when I tell you this is wrong and if you or I get caught it's going to be bad. Do you understand that? Your secret spot will be gone."

"I was going to remind you, you can't say anything. I'm trusting you." She looks into the fire away from me looking like the same nervous little girl I knew before.

"It's our secret."

Her eyes change and she stares through the fire. Mentally she's gone somewhere dark. It's the same face she had when I first discovered her with a million yard stare being held by her crying Mother.

She shakes her head and walks back towards the janitor closet.

"Too much time has passed even if it doesn't feel like it. We gotta go."

"Hailey, can I meet you here tonight?" I think about the cameras, but nobody was in there when Lilly and I stumbled into that security room and I've never seen anyone coming in or out. Since the door is right next to Jayne's office I would have seen some sign that someone goes in by now.

"Yeah. I'm in cell B."

"Cell?"

"Yeah, they call them dorms, but we aren't allowed to leave them unless they come get us first."

"Who's they?"

"Mark and Lilly. Lilly's very nice though. She opens all our doors."

"What about Mark"?

That fearful expression returns, but she doesn't say anything.

6

Later in the night after dinner the small counsel participated in a small motivational meditation where we visualized the future of the new world together. Jayne told us we need to push our energy into the world to help in any way we can. I couldn't commit fully though to what she wanted. I pretended. I'm more confused and distracted than ever.

Cody's laying next to me in our bright room. He swings his arm over me across my breasts and snuggles in closer. He pushes his crotch against my waist. I feel him growing against me. Usually I would be turning towards him, but after what I saw I'm not feeling it.

"Babe you alright?" He whispers in my ear and starts kissing my neck.

I start relaxing and I let myself soak up his sweet kisses. He's moving over my neck and onto my cheek then onto my lips as he swings his body on top of mine.

A knock from our shared door interrupts us and Kelsey's voice cuts the action, "Hey guys, I'm not doing well. Can I come in?"

"Of course," I sit and pull my strap back onto my shoulder grateful for the disruption.

Cody audibly sighs like a child after a tantrum. He crosses his arms exasperated.

"Hey guys," Kelsey walks in timidly. "I miss my family and I don't want to be alone."

"Come and sit," I pat the bed beside me and push Cody as I move into the middle.

"I'm going to go do some work. There's paperwork that needs to be filled out and plans to sharpen," Cody says as he gets dressed. He doesn't seem to care about being naked in front of Kelsey any longer.

He checks his appearance in the mirror before leaving.

"When will you be back?" I ask.

"Tomorrow."

"What time?"

"Oh I don't know Miranda. God, stop fuckin' askin' so many questions. I'll see you in the Big Room for breakfast. Or not." He walks out the door.

"That was genius," I smile.

"What? Are you okay? He's being a major asshole."

"Unless you really need to talk we can, but I discovered something today and I was going to go further into it. I figured you used your sense of yours to know I needed you."

"Further into what?"

"You said you're loyal to me right? More than this movement?"

"Always."

"Do you want to go? This could potentially be dangerous. We could also stay and talk if you need to because I am totally completely fine. I am here for you."

"Where?"

"I can't really explain it. I have to show you."

"Sure."

"It could be dangerous."

"Let's go." She darts over to her bedroom and pops back in fully dressed while I'm still getting my shirt on.

"First I want to check hall F to see if anyone's in the video room."

"The video room?" She asks.

"Oh yeah, Lilly and I found this room with tons of screens showing different parts of the Haven."

"Oh God."

7

I tap on Hailey's door. For a second I get nervous she isn't going to answer and we're going to get caught, but then the door opens an inch. I look inside and it's the size of a closet. A small twin sized bed pushed against the corner with what color sheets? Grey of course. A tiny bit of space is on the other side of the bed where she can get up and nothing else. She's in her pajamas. They're also grey.

A flash of anger and worry fills Hailey's face when she notices Kelsey.

I wave my hands in front in a calm down gesture trying to tell her it's fine and let's go without talking.

We walk to the end of the hall and go into the closet and get into the tunnel. She lights the torch and we start walking. We don't dare talk until we reach the intersection where I can finally stand.

"Who's this?" Hailey asks.

"My best friend, Kelsey. She's okay with this," I look to her for help.

"Yeah I am. I want to see your secret spots. I can keep a secret. Miranda already told me about the Big Room overlook on the way here."

"Miranda can't keep a secret."

"Please Hailey. I wouldn't have been able to sneak out without either her or my boyfriend knowing and we can't let him know."

"Okay, but this one isn't a spot I like or want to be in. Once you see it you won't want to be here anymore. Or at least I hope. There's something evil in this cave. It goes deep. It's very very very old."

"I wouldn't repeat that to anyone. You can't say that about Jayne or the movement," I say.

"Just follow me."

We trudge forward with Hailey leading the way. The ceiling doesn't lower again. I'm praising whatever is out there because I don't think my neck or back can handle anymore hunching over today. The ground is rough with boulders and rocks we have to scramble over. We walk until we can't anymore.

Another torch hangs on this wall. It has to be covered in an inch of dust though. There's no lighter or boxes of matches next to it, but this little metal thing that looks like something that would make a spark when you hit it.

We've hit a dead end.

I look at the wall in front of us trying to make out some fracture line where a door could be, but I don't see anything.

"Where's-"

Hailey cuts me off with her finger pressed hard and fast against my lips. She looks upwards.

There's a small wooden latch.

"Listen first. Sometimes there's people."

We listen closely until we're sure there's no sound. The sound of our breathing is amplified. I feel like we could wake a mummy. I push on the latch, but nothing happens.

Hailey pushes me out of the way and drags a rock underneath it. She climbs on it and pushes at the corner letting it fall to the side. Her fingers move between the crack she made and she pushes it on the side scraping it hard against the floor above. What I thought was a latch is a wooden board with a large stone on top. Hailey pulls herself through it and helps us up.

I inhale sharply as the torch makes the room alive with its flickering.

"I've been here," I say to myself.

"What?!" Hailey yell whispers. "No, no, no, no, no please don't hurt me," She's backing up towards the hole.

"Wait stop I would never," I try to tell her, but she killed the fire.

"You can't find me without light," I barely hear her.

"I won't. I promise."

"Why have you been in this room?"

"It was a long time ago when one of The Nothings were captured and brought down here. That was the only time. I haven't been since. I hoped I would never end up in this room again."

I'm looking around for her, but I can't see anything. I feel Kelsey's hand reaching for mine and I grasp it firmly holding onto it as if it would give me light. Darkness underground is another kind of darkness. I don't think I'll ever get used to it.

"Do you know what they do here? Have you noticed people missing?"

"I have, but I was told they were sent on quests from Jayne."

The sound of a lighter flickering across the room catches my attention and the torch is ablaze again.

That's when I see the horror.

My hands slap my eyes and I nearly fall backwards shaking my head back and forth. "No that can't be it."

"Miranda, we need to get out of here," Kelsey roughly tugs on me.

I back into something soft that swings away and then hits my back and I have to stifle a scream. The back of my heel thumps something hard and there's a sloshing sound.

I turn around and it's a body hanging upside down. A bucket is underneath it filled with a dark syrupy liquid.

I reach my fingers into it wanting to puke the moment my eyes meet the dripping red on my finger tips. The smell of iron is unbearable. It smells like a butcher shop if it was never cleaned and humans were hanging instead of pigs and cows.

The room doesn't smell rotten though. It's like opening a bloody steak from the grocery store, but if you had a bath tub of the stuff. It's fresh. The entire room is full of bodies cut at the throat. In the middle is a table with a body on it covered in salt.

"It looks like they're preserving them," I say.

"Isn't this one of the counsel members Jayne sent to the surface to gather intelligence?"

I bend over the corpse.

"He used to sit at the same table as me. Why would they kill him?"

"More importantly why are they here and why are there buckets of blood under the bodies?" Kelsey asks.

"That isn't the worst of it," Hailey grabs our attention to the other side of the room. She's sniffling and trying to hold back tears. Her body starts to heave and drops to the floor. I run over and pull her to me wrapping my arms around her. Kelsey bends down as well and we hold her as she cries.

"I . . ." She chokes through sobs, "have . . . already seen . . . this, but it still . . . hurts." She buries her face into my chest. Her tears soak through my shirt. They don't stop. "I just want my Mom."

I look up and another girl about her age hangs upside down. The blood on her neck looks fresh. Barely congealed.

"What happened?"

"She tried to escape to get to her parents after stage two," She muffles.

"Do you know what they're doing with all this?" I gesture at the buckets circling us.

"There's more tunnels I haven't found. There's also that big one that goes right at the intersection."

"Miranda, what did you get yourself wrapped up in?" Kelsey asks.

"People use this room a lot," Hailey looks at the girl her age.

"I'm sure there's an explanation," I say.

"You need to be realistic," Kelsey says.

I can't believe I let myself believe them. They said they were good and warned me not to let evil inside. They said I was special and capable of so much. I had so much I could say, but nothing I could say would make any sense.

I wait until her sobs subside and she pulls away. We let her take the lead when she's ready.

We slide back into the hole and pull the board over it.

We don't say anything until the intersection.

"You said you can overhear people in there. Do you recognize any one of the voices?" I ask.

"Besides that lady who would blabber on and on, I haven't recognized anyone." Hailey's eyes are transforming into that glazed over look she had when I first met her.

I hold her hands, "Hailey stay with me okay? You'll be okay. Just do what they say. You're going to be okay. Just keep doing what you're supposed to do and tell no one what you've seen. Do. Not. Trust. Anyone. Do you hear me? Hailey do you hear me?"

She stares.

Kelsey rubs her back, "Hailey. It's going to be okay."

She stares.

"Your Mom, Lauren, is doing good right now," Kelsey tries.

That snaps her out of it. In the most terrified voice I've ever heard, Hailey says, "Please get us out of here."

Chapter 13

1

I'm sitting in the Big Room eating a rubbery egg breakfast with Kelsey, Lilly, and Kyle.

"Where's Mark?" I ask Lilly.

"He's down with the kids. Guys I have to tell you something," Lilly darts her eyes around the room chewing at her lips. "I have to say it," Lilly watches each of our faces waiting for a reaction that will tell her to stay silent, but we don't give it to her. "Something's bad. I don't know what it is. But something isn't right."

I had to strain to hear that last part. I must've look confused because she said, "You haven't seen it all Miranda. Just wait."

"I know," Kyle chimes in. "In Santa Cruz they started killing anyone who disagreed or wanted to leave or they would just," he lifts his hands and pops his fingers out, "poof."

He looks at each of us for dramatic pause. "They said they left the boundary, but I don't think so. I was powerless to stop it and I couldn't leave. And I wanted to believe," he said the last sentence with shame.

"I wanted so much," I say with the same shame.

I look at Kelsey who's already looking at me. We're wondering what we should say.

When half a minute passed and I didn't say anything Lilly blurts out, "Never mind. I'm just joking. I don't believe any of that. I'm happy to be here."

"Yeah definitely. Just a joke," Kyle forces out a laughter.

"Guys it's okay. Some strange things are happening here. We've seen it," Kelsey says.

They breathe deeply and seem to melt in their chairs when they realize we're okay with what they're saying. A stark difference from the stiff as a board demeanor they've had.

Lilly's nails are bleeding. They've been chewed as much as possible before the entire nail is gone.

"We're in this together," I say.

"Hello everyone," Jayne smiles from the stage and looks as professional as ever. When I look at her smile, I know it communicates, "Look what I have done for all of you."

People start clapping and the whole room erupts in applause.

She's been doing a lot of work with everyone recently. It's like when a politician goes to different cities, but here she's going around to different colored groups.

"Thank you, thank you guys. I am trying my best. Soon we will get to start building houses outside. For now I love the way our little society is coming together. I have loved listening to all of your ideas. My team is starting to make up blueprints and plans."

We look at each other confused. As members of her team, none of us have heard anything about this.

"I hate to be the bearer of bad news, but it's time to tell you. The entire world has gone to war. What happened in North America is now happening in other countries and bombs are flying. Small nuclear weapons have been dropped in some areas, but for the most part the countries are holding off on the ones that could bring the complete extinction of Earth. It is the end of times. Something greater and more powerful than us is reigning terror. A debt is to be paid to our Mother Earth and she intends to claim it. We have a chapel you are more than welcome to use inside hall Gathering. I didn't want to tell you about this too soon because I know some of you have your own Gods. We pray to the one God and the earth. I'm doing everything I can and with your help we can ask for atonement. Tomorrow we will have a big feast in Mother Earth's honor. All of us together in this room. I will announce it on the speaker system when the time is closer."

I'm waiting to see people's reactions, but they're hanging onto her every word and seem to be waiting to be told by her how to feel.

"It will continue to get better. I rescued you from the murder of The Nothings. I know some might have had a rocky start, but as we establish ourselves it will only get better."

I've become relaxed. I start clapping with the other people here. I feel good. There's a sense of unity in the air. I breathe more of it in with every sound of approval coming from those around me. My muscles are relaxed even with all that climbing and dunking and moving around yesterday.

I take another sip of my orange juice enjoying its flavor.

Wow, I have no anxiety left. She must be speaking the truth. Something she's saying is settling kindly in my stomach. I feel good. I finish off my orange juice and set it aside.

"This is weird," Kelsey whispers. She's sitting on the edge of her seat and clenching her fists over and over again. She does that when she's anxious.

"Hey relax, it's all good," I tell her.

"What?" She asks confused diverting her eyes across the table. "Are you okay?" She reaches for her glass of orange juice and drinks it.

"I hope to see you there today. Make sure to write your names in the log. Have a wonderful day," Jayne exits the stage.

Kelsey's muscles visually relax. Her shoulders fall from her ears and her jaw unclenches. She holds my hand.

"It doesn't matter," She tells me smiling a big goofy beautiful smile. Her face changes and her eyebrows furrow and then she relaxes again and then her eyes narrow and her eyebrows furrow more and she inspects her glass of orange juice.

"Miranda, this is it." She puts the glass in front me.

"What is?" I feel blissful.

"I feel good."

"I know. Me too. We've been too hard. We should listen to Jayne more. Anytime she's around she sets me at ease. I think it's the energy in the world making us crazy."

"Oh Miranda, it's the evil influencing us."

"You're so right. It's all so clear now," I say as if we just discovered the secret to the universe.

We start giggling.

"I feel good right now. It's the orange juice," She leans her head against my shoulder smiling. "That's why everyone loves her so much. The food is laced. We haven't felt it as strongly because the counsel members can get their breakfast and lunch to go from the kitchen so we don't eat what everyone else does. We usually don't get the juice because it's usually out by the time we get our food. I don't know. This is nice though. Maybe she's right." Kelsey smiles looking energized for the day.

We get up blissfully to start our responsibilities. I head for the children's wing ready to do what I'm supposed to.

2

"Miranda!" Mark stands from the desk in the busy lobby-like room. Children are laughing and playing, but there's also a few on the couch and floor with blank expressions. Their eyes look like they were ringed out.

"Hey Mark, we missed you at breakfast. Have you heard the news?"

"World War 3. Yeah. But America's already destroyed so we'll be safe. J told me already." He struts back over to the desk and trifles through a pile of papers pulling out a few packets.

There's another person saying J.

"You aren't scared? You aren't completely petrified?"

"I've been praying every night and worshiping. It's okay to relax. Jayne says we need to be healthy to help others. Have you gone to the chapel yet?"

"No."

"I've been going for weeks now. You need to go. It'll help. Worshiping God through the Earth gives back calmness and confidence."

"I will. What are those papers for?"

"I understand you only got that girl to work with the other day . . ." He's snapping his fingers and looking up.

"Her name's Hailey."

"Yeah, your paperwork was clean and thorough. She must have cooperated."

I feel like I'm being questioned. "Yeah, she did."

"That's a first. She's been nothing but difficult. I guess she doesn't need to do stage two then."

"What's stage two?" Before the question was half way out of my mouth I knew this was what Lilly must've been talking about.

"Follow me," He leads me down the door lined hall past the bedroom cells stopping at a door with a lock and code. The doors look the same. There's locks on all them, but this one also has a code box.

"I didn't see what you entered there," I say.

"Oh this one you don't need to know. I'll let you in and out. When you're ready to leave press the button inside there and it'll buzz me," He pats his side where a radio lives. That's new. He looks proud of himself. I'd like to wipe that look off his smug face.

The room is dimly lit. Two chairs with leather restraints for the hands and ankles face a large projector screen. What looks like cushioned clamps are on the top of the chairs. They're straight though, not like the curved head restraints I've seen in movies. The only light is coming from the back of the room above a mirror casting a yellow haze over everything.

I feel Mark's eyes on me waiting for me to fuck something up or give something away. He's watching me. He's jumping out of his shoes with excitement. It's something he's waiting for me to do.

Then it clicks.

I turn back to him, "I'm honored to do anything that'll help our movement. Especially now considering the predicament the world is in."

He deflates, but his grin that stretches too far stays.

"I'm especially grateful I get to work in the same unit as you Mark. You're so smart."

That makes him soar with glee. "Hey I'm a married man now," he straightens an imaginary tie.

"No no no. I wasn't saying-"

"I'm going to hand over two of the kids that have resisted treatment. The positive reinforcement of adding treats and approval didn't work on them. They don't understand the blessings we are bestowing upon them by allowing them to be here. The goal was to try to increase an almost patriotic sense of self. They didn't respond well so now they have to move to stage two.

"In this stage they'll be bombarded with images and associations on the screen. We'll use a combination of positive reinforcement and punishment. The positive reinforcement, where we add a stimulus to encourage behavior, will be minor shocks. We want them to experience terror and pain when they see the words "Order Through Chaos," "OTC," or "The Nothings" so they form an association now and not the hard way in the real world. You'll administer a shock when those words appear. If they close their eyes you will activate a loud boom sound that reverberates through their bodies as punishment.

"This is the first time implementing stage two. It's my own creation," he waits for approval. I don't need to say anything because he's already filling his head with admiration and cheer. I would only be background noise to his delusions.

When he's done he looks at me waiting.

I keep my face still. I'm not going to let him have a peak into my psyche. In my minds eye I rip the papers down the middle and start kicking the chairs over jumping on them and destroying the technology. I yank the screen down on top of him smothering him with it. I burn this place down.

Instead I nod my head and grab the paperwork he wants me to fill out.

"I'll be watching," he gestures to the mirror in the back.

3

Two boys walk in. The younger one is visually shaking and the older one is holding his face as strong as he can. His lips are pursed and his eyes are squeezed in a glare making a force shield nothing can penetrate and nothing can escape. He doesn't make eye contact with me. He's working on turning himself to stone. It breaks my heart.

The door slams behind them and I hear that sucking metal sound of the locks engaging.

"Daniel, sixteen years old, curses at counsel members and other workers, feeds false information to his little brother, speaks ill of God," I read aloud from a clipboard. The older boy's expression doesn't change.

"Jacob, eight years old, fed toxic information, only cries for his Mom, won't listen to the teachings."

"You're brothers?" I ask.

The older boy only tightens his lips more, but the small one, Jacob, nods his head.

"If you would please sit," I glance behind me at the mirror.

The little guy looks to his brother who stays rock solid.

"Please listen to me so we can get this over with," I mutter.

Daniel, the older brother, walks over and his little brother follows.

The video reel starts the moment they sit.

"Please place your hands through the straps," I say.

A video of families being shot down and people screaming over their dead bodies comes into focus. The shooters are waving flags with the words OTC on them. I press the remote and a shock shoots through the small metal plates beneath their wrists.

The boy lets out the saddest screech and rubs his wrists furiously.

The screen is alternating rapidly between dead bodies outside and pictures of the earth polluted by human waste.

"Miranda, strap them in now," Mark's voice fills the space.

I jump.

I head for Jacob and try to place his wrists in the restraints, but he's fighting me.

"Please. It'll be over soon," I say in my best soothing voice, but I know I sound scared.

He's shaking his head so fast I'm worried he's going to hurt himself. Violence and images and text are flashing behind me. I'm blocked from Mark's view crouching in front of the chair.

"You need to listen or you'll be punished worse. I'm going to attach these loosely. Okay?" I try to get him to calm down. "You'll only feel a minor pinch, but you need to react a lot okay?"

He stops shaking back and forth and looks at me with big round teary eyes. His lower lip is pouting, but he nods. He understands.

I strap his wrists and ankles loosely. I pull the head bars in only enough so he can't move his head side ways, but loose enough so it's not squeezing him.

Daniel looks at me. He's let his guard down in the confusion.

Bombs and machine guns followed by dying screams vibrate through the speakers traveling around my body. I feel it in my spine.

"Daniel, I'm placing these on lightly. React a lot when you feel a minor pinch. I'll get you two out of this. He's watching us," I close one of the cuffs loosely around his ankle.

I'm waiting for something to disrupt this process. Something the universe will send to make this stop. Where's the SWAT, the FBI, dumb luck? This is the time. I look around waiting.

Nothing happens though.

"The Nothings" flash in front of pictures of parents holding their dead children in strobe light fashion. I press the remote to send the shocks. I hold my breath hoping they won't give me away.

Daniel starts thrashing and half a second later Jacob thrashes and let's out a small scream then falls still panting heavily. I did loosen those straps enough right? Yeah, they're acting.

I expect something to bail me out of this, but nothing happens. The strobes and screams planting themselves inside my head. Flashes of gore and burning buildings, and smog ridden cities flash. "Order Through Chaos" is printed on flags and shirts of the people in the video.

I press the remote every time I see those words like I was told to.

I want to check on them, but Mark won't trust me if I do.

The movie stops and the lights return to the usual brightness.

Mark's messing with the locks outside.

"I'm going to get you out of this. Act the part. Please," I whisper in a hurry to undo their restraints. Trying to move fast enough so Mark doesn't see I barely strapped them in. We're all sweaty.

"I was unsure about you Miranda, but I think it's finally time," Mark's smile is empty and prideful.

I follow him out. Hailey runs up behind and snatches my head down to her ear, "The end of your hallway is a way to the tunnels."

I turn around, but she's already inside her room.

"What are you doing Miranda?" Mark asks already standing 15 feet in front of me.

4

I don't have anywhere to be until dinner so I decide to walk to the end of hall A way past my quarters. Kelsey isn't there just like I thought. She's been busy computerizing everything and logging data. Lilly's working with the kids. I don't know where Kyle is.

The doors stop appearing on either side of me. I continue walking down the hall with its brightly lit ceilings.

It keeps going.

The ground is getting rougher. The tunnel is also starting to get smaller. The walls aren't smooth anymore. The lights end 10 feet away. I keep walking. It feels like I'm stepping into a black hole shutting the door on the world behind me. The hall is shrinking. I can barely see anything anymore.

When I turn around and see the series of lights and smooth stone stretching out it looks surreal. If I ever have a near death experience then this is what the light and tunnel thing must look like.

I turn back towards the darkness you can only experience underground. The wall ends in a boulder pile. I feel around without my sight, but I don't feel any doors or latches. I check the sides and the floor and still nothing. I'm starting to hyperventilate. I feel stuck. I could just walk away.

I brush my hands across the boulders and near the corner I feel a small opening. I bend down watching the black in front of me and stretch my arms into it. It's small, but I can fit. I probably shouldn't be crawling through a boulder pile in a man made tunnel, but I have a new found strength in me. It's not the kind that was trained into me either.

I sink to my belly and drag my body further into the rocks. The thought of getting stuck flashes through my mind, but I push it out. I focus on my next move to get further in.

I'm halfway through when there's not rock brushing along the top of my head anymore. I carefully lift my head with a hand resting atop it so I don't die from a head wound.

More air! I crawl through and stand. I'm ecstatic moving around in the darkness. I can lift my hands above my head and it doesn't touch anything.

I feel for the walls next to me and sure enough there's a torch. I feel around for lighters, but I only find an empty hook. With my free hand I'm blindly brushing every surface.

Near my feet I feel a box. Matches! I strike one and it putters out immediately. They're old. I try again and it putters out. I try again and it works! The cloth at the end of the torch is still oily to the touch and it lights up pushing the heavy blackness away for the time being.

Stairs descend in front of me and a thin passageway stretches to the right. I go for the stairs.

I hear water dripping, but I don't see any. Every footstep echos through the walls making it sound like there's other people in here with me. The rock is full of fractures.

The stairs end at an intersection. There's three options. I pick the first one. I would try to guess my location, but I know by now our sense of direction is as useful as trying to navigate with only sound.

I walk through this skinny tunnel where my shoulders brush against the sides. At least I can stand. The torch flickers in a funny way as if there was less oxygen.

The light jumps off an earthy red paint instead of the grey rock. In large letters I read "THE EARTH NEEDS BLOOD." I walk further and more letters almost as tall as me read, "WE WILL RISE."

I look for more messages, but there are none.

A soft light glows ahead.

I put my torch on the ground letting it burn, not wanting to put it out. There's a small slit at eye level. I look through it and I'm looking down from the corner of a ceiling. It looks like the chapel Jayne was talking about. It's full of people. There's Isaac up front talking to a huge group of people. There's a stone carved tree taller and wider than he is behind him. Its branches wrap around the sides of the walls. There's three glass pillars in front of the tree. One looks to be full of dirt, another rocks, and another dried leaves I think. A woman in pink walks to the front where one long wooden bench separates the people from the elevated area. There's a golden goblet bigger than my head on that bench. The woman kneels in front of it and Isaac does the same, but elevated from the stage on the other side. He grabs the goblet's handles. His hands are turning white from the weight. He carefully tips it forward with two hands and a thick red liquid pours into the woman's mouth.

She returns to the pews. They aren't your red velvet benches normally in churches. They look handmade from redwoods. The wood is smoothed where people sit. Dried leaves and flowers lay over the benches. I recognize the blue lupines I saw on the mountain side. Tightly wrinkled orange poppies cover the ground beneath the goblet like a first snow. I don't recognize the other pink and white flowers.

More people make their way to the front and sip from that enormous gaudy cup. Energy fills the room. People start moving around more. Isaac puts on gentle music.

It's the same few lines over and over again. He starts singing along and encourages others to do so as well. Soon the entire room is singing those lines over and over again.

"The world is at its end," Isaac projects over the music. "Continue to sing so we may show our love."

He sings with them. A few people have one or both hands raised in the air in worship. Some have their eyes closed. Everyone is swaying. A few have their faces crinkled up like they're about to cry or something. Actually it looks like they're on the verge of an orgasm. Their mouths are in an "o" and their eyebrows are turned upwards in the middle. It's the same face I saw people making in church growing up.

"The Earth provides us with everything we'll ever need, but humans have destroyed her. We need to help clean the Earth," Isaac speaks on tempo with the music.

They keep singing the same lyrics with the same mellifluous tone over and over again.

"We've been working with other people around the world for longer than I've been alive. This is our time."

They sing and sway for what seems like forever. They're being hypnotized. At least a type of hypnotization. They're in a trance.

I leave to go deeper and it leads me to another room directly behind the chapel. I'm looking through a crack in the corner of the ceiling again. The voices are softer now. They sound like distant angels.

"Our group in Germany is telling the Nothing group to stop the explosions. They're backing out. All of them," Ian says to Jayne. It looks to be private quarters, but unlike Jayne's office and the smaller meeting room, it's not lavish. It's plain grey like mine and Cody's. It's the exact same layout with the bathroom, grey bed and grey dresser in front. The only difference is instead of a smooth stone wall to the side of the bed there's another carved tree. This one is covered in what looks like blood.

They're sitting on the bed.

"No! That isn't fucking possible! No fuck them!" Jayne screams pacing around the room barefoot.

He runs to her and wraps his arms around her, "Jayne sshhhh people might hear."

He pulls her gently back to the bed and straightens out her shirt, lingering around the collar above her breasts.

"The war's still raging. Enough people will die without the explosions," He says tugging gently on her collar.

"How are we supposed to have a congregation there if everyone backs out? That can't happen."

"Well . . ."

Her mood flips instantly to a joyful eagerness as she pulls her feet onto the bed into a kneeling position and faces him.

She runs her fingers through his perfect hair. He fixes it.

"We have our own weapons."

She leans into him. Her back is arched accentuating her round ass. Her toes curl into the blanket helping her keep her balance.

I mutter nearly inaudible, "He's so young though."

"But, we want to destroy as little of Earth as possible." He sits with perfect posture.

"Yeah I know. How am I supposed to do God's work when the devil is constantly inserting himself into the people I'm supposed to depend on," she sits back onto her knees.

"It's a part of his tests. We'll keep feeding the devil's life sources back into the Earth to God."

"Why didn't I find you sooner?"

"You found me when God willed it so," he wasn't joking.

Jayne leans back over and pushes her self close to his chest. He reaches out and pulls the hair behind one ear out so it matches the other side. He looks at her, but doesn't move. He looks to the side like he's waiting for someone to tell him how to proceed.

She reaches past him and dips her hand in a small gold bowl on the night stand and brings it back dripping dark red. He immediately grabs the rag next to it and holds it under her hand preventing spillage. She pushes it into his mouth and he sucks them clean.

He looks back over his shoulder at the tree, nods, and pulls Jayne on top of him. His harsh demeanor smooths and he's working around her body in a romantic way and not like he's much younger than her which he grossly is. He's touching all the right buttons and the clothes aren't even off yet.

She's being gentle with him and letting him take control. She rolls onto her back as he caresses downwards. She looks so vulnerable.

I'm watching them captivated by the sudden changes in their personalities. I remember I need to get back in time to arrive with everyone else for dinner. Panicky, I fall slightly forwards.

Their heads snap up and look around their room. It's Jayne who shrugs and pulls him back. I feel compelled to stay longer, but I walk away.

I hurry back the way I came pausing at the chapel. The music dies out and everyone's still swaying. Isaac opens his eyes and looks out as they slow to a stop and flutter their eyes open.

"That went by fast," I hear someone say.

"I wish we could do that longer," I hear another.

It's been at least an hour. I don't have a clock, but I know it's been well over an hour since they started singing. They lost all sense of time. He put them in some kind of trance and they don't even realize it.

"I feel rejuvenated," another tells their friend who nods in agreement.

It finally dawns on me that I've been being manipulated.

I want to scream down, "No fuck, you feel rejuvenated! They've been feeding you mind altering substances! Of course you feel relaxed! He put you in a fucking trance using meditation techniques and repetition." I realize I'm saying these words to myself. Fucking obviously I'm going to feel more relaxed down here. I repeated over and over again my love for God and the Earth and how I'll do anything that's needed. It has been plastered into my brain. I'm going to dream about it. I'm going to think about it. It's going to pop in my head randomly and and I'll think the song and the "sermon" or whatever the hell I called it had that big of an impact on me. It should've been so obvious.

I was the one that helped bring innocent people into this mess.

I walk away trying to work on my own breath. It's obvious the manipulation used when viewing a service like that from above. It's hard to decipher when you're in the thick of it.

5

New people are eating in Jayne's office at the massive redwood tables. The rings in each slab stand out especially vibrant today.

I drank some wine at dinner, but besides a slight buzz there's nothing more. I wouldn't have drank anything, but I feel like eyes have been on me. I'm feeling watched. It's the same feeling I got as a kid when at church they convinced me I was always being watched where if I do anything wrong or think anything wrong it will be known. It's hard to act normal. I can't get that song they were singing in the chapel out of my head.

"My heart belongs to God and the Earth,

"I will do anything needed,

"I give of myself."

Some of the new people eating with us were the people in that strange chapel I saw earlier.

"Hey love," Cody sits next to me. "How ya doin'?"

"Fine. I've missed you." Unfortunately, I have.

"I've been busy babe. I'm doing God's mother fuckin' work here," his smile still gets me. His words fill my skin with needles though.

"How is everyone doing tonight?" Jayne walks out of the door that blends in with the wall.

She's smiling. It's a dignified and professional smile though. Her black bob is no longer disheveled. I wouldn't have been able to guess what she was just up to.

"You will see some new people in the counsel today. I already gave them white clothes, but they will retain their former job titles and colors for now outside of this office. They showed exceptional promise. Their devotion impressed me. Mother Earth has provided this meal to us today. We take and never give back, but we're changing that."

When her eyes pass to me I feel penetrated.

"I want you to know that any doubts you feel towards this movement and specifically me is only the devil and other evils at work. It is because, I am eccentric. I dress differently. I wear my hair differently. I was raised in a large city across the seas so it is natural to be unsure of me. I am telling you, the evil is squeezing its way inside of you and when you have these doubts you know it's making headway and you need to push it back out. Do not let it win."

People are buying it. I was unsure at first, but I went along with it. When it's apocalyptic death or the promise of a beautiful future I think I know where I'm going to lean. Mostly, they saw something special in me. I accepted her immediately. I probably helped cement other's trust and devotion. I spoke passionately and even brought my best friend with me. Nothing's as it seems anymore. But then again, maybe it's evil seeping inside pushing the light away. Somewhere lost inside me I feel there's this physical spot that's getting gnawed on by my brain, heart, and gut, screaming at me to be careful.

"Things may seem funny or kind of wrong in the present moment, but it is all a part of the plan," she tells them. "Put your faith in the higher power that what is supposed to come, will. Nothing is easy."

"While we are all here I would like to promote one of the men on my small counsel to be one of my three closest allies," She nods to the back of the room near the bookcase. It's Ian and Isaac.

"Cody will you please come and join me up here. As a thank you for your dedication I am gifting you a Smith & Wesson .357 Revolver," she blocks our view of him bordering on seductive as she attaches a leather holster around his waist and slides the new gun inside pausing before taking her hands away. She whispers something in his ear that makes him hide a grin.

He's never made that face with me before.

Cody joins Ian and Isaac.

I catch Mark out of the corner of my eye. He's writhing in his seat. If his eyes could be the death of someone, Cody would have already died.

"One more thing. I know I said in the past it does not matter if you are religious or what your religion is. If it is not too much to ask for, then I would like all counsel members to start attending some of the chapel services. They run throughout the day. Those who are not as serious can come to the one held right before dinner. The three other services are for true beginners and anyone is allowed in there at anytime even when it is not occupied except for the service that comes after dinner. That is only for those who are truly devoted and I have pre-approved.

"Have a good night. Continue doing your jobs and report to the correct people. Miranda, can I talk to you before you leave?"

I lean over to Kelsey, "Grab Lilly and Kyle before they leave and wait for me down the hall."

I wait until everyone but Jayne and the three guys leave before I walk through the tall chairs across the red Afghan carpet in front of Jayne.

I expect her to say something, but she only smiles. She's waiting for me.

Finally I can't take it anymore and say, "You wanted to talk to me."

Each time I'm close to her, her skin is whiter than before. It reminds me of translucent milk.

"I wanted to see how you were doing. I'm aware there is apprehension lately. You have not been as attentive."

She waits for me to speak.

"No . . ." I begin, but her look cuts my facade I was going to start. "I just. It's just a lot in a short time."

"The universe has plans for you. I know it. If you follow God's path it will reveal itself in time. You are important."

I can't help myself but submit to a smile. The woman who watches over so many people is singling me out. I feel like I can do something great.

"Thank you," I say messing with a loose thread in my shirt.

"I've noticed you've been gone a lot."

I look at the three guys. I swallow.

"Cody has missed you, but I am so proud of you."

"What?"

"You have not gone unnoticed. Thank you for being so devoted with the children. They are our future."

"Oh for sure."

"I'm serious. This movement needs you".

She continues, "And one more thing." She pinches her fingers together showing me how small it is.

"Yeah?"

"I need Cody closer to me. I have new quarters for him that I can access without going into the main hall if I need him. Ian and Isaac are near me. Is that okay?" She asks like I have a choice.

I want to ask, "like how you and young Ian are?" But instead I say, "That's fine."

"I knew that would not be a problem. Your passion to this movement is wonderful. You have such an influence over others and as long as you are careful you will be able to use that for good. Be cautious. There will be a lot of temptations that will want to lure you away from good work in the world. And of course you will still get to keep your room with a bathroom and you can come visit him and stay the night when he gives you the go."

When he gives me the go?

He would love to think I'm at his beck and call.

"Okay," I say.

"Is this alright?" She asks again. Her eyes scan me like a machine and I wonder if they really can read me.

"Yes," I smile.

"I will see you later Miranda," She makes physical contact by squeezing my arm before she goes.

A part of me still wants to please her.

Her touch feels like a tornado siren.

6

I thought they didn't wait for me, but I find them a little ways down Hall A. They don't say anything.

They wait for me to say what happened.

Lilly's chewing on her nails. It's not unusual, but her gnawing's faster than normal. "Lilly you're going to eat your fingers off."

"You know, maybe Mark's plans to recruit the younger people and the kids isn't as bad as it sounded. I mean look how safe and provided for we are. The last I've heard from above ground is people are fighting. Everywhere." Her face is full of regret.

I want to scream. Now I have to worry about her talking too. Spouses have been turning against spouses and we're teaching the children to tattle on their parents.

"I'm sorry," she says.

I'm startled by how dejected her voice sounds and then I see there's a bruise on her neck her hair is mostly covering. I would have mistaken it for a shadow in any other lighting, but everything here's so bright. She has the slightest limp on her left leg. I don't remember that being there.

"Lilly are you sure?"

"Yeah I am," She looks around searching for movement even though everyone else has already left for their rooms a while ago.

"I can see the bruise and the way you're walking. If you believe in this movement, convince me."

She keeps walking.

"If Mark did this, say something. Anything."

She pushes out a purposeful cough, "excuse me."

"Are you able to get away from your place for the next few hours?"

"If we stayed in the common area. If not, no."

"I'll keep you updated." We stop at her door. I hug her tightly, "I'm going to learn more. Just hold on. Just hold on a little longer."

We walk the length of hall A in silence. Anyone could be listening.

"Should we really leave her back there with him?" Kelsey pronounces the last word with open disgust.

"I have a plan."

"I know you don't."

"Well, there's nothing else I can do right now. Do you have ideas or do you want to make that my fault too?"

"We can't turn on each other," Kyle says.

"Crawl through there," I point at the boulder pile.

I light the torch with the old box of lighters and tuck extras in my pocket just in case.

"Right up those stairs and down a way it leads to the chapel and I think to Ian's room. I don't know, but it had a stone tree engraved in the wall as well."

"What're you talking about?" Kelsey asks.

"You'll see."

At the bottom of the stairs at the intersection I'm trying to remember which of the three turns it was. I'm swinging the torch back and forth between them trying to recognize the tunnels, but they look identical.

"Do you know where you're going?" Kyle asks.

"Shh, yes she does. Let her think," Kelsey tells him.

"This way," I lead them down the hall that's straight in front of the stairs. The walls begin squeezing inward. The ceiling stays tall. This is it. I remember the long, tall, skinny, tunnel.

The dark grey cave is getting darker. Worry shoots through me when I look at my torch, but it's okay. It's burning just as bright. The ceiling seems higher. I can't see the top. I don't remember seeing it before though.

"What's this stuff on the walls?" Kyle says behind me. I turn around and he's grimacing while rubbing the wall.

He rubs it faster in a tiny spot and it's turning back to the dark grey of the rest of the rock. "It's some kind of paint," he says.

I hold the torch around me. The walls and floor are covered in it.

"Could it be blood?" Kelsey asks pressing herself against the back of me like a child when they see something large and unrecognizable.

"Let's go," I walk ahead knowing they'll follow. I'm the one with the light and I wouldn't want to be sitting in the dark in a possible blood cave by myself, but to each their own. Their footsteps are behind me.

I didn't remember that part, but I wasn't exactly concerned with touching the walls. We've been walking for quite a while.

There's a small light on the floor between two boulders the size of trucks. It's in the middle of the walkway, which has started to open up.

"It's the Big Room," Kelsey says.

"Not so loud," I tell her. "Let's keep going."

We tiptoe over the small gap. The tunnel continues to open up until we can walk next to each other.

"Okay this isn't the place I wanted to show you. I'm so stupid. I'm going to get us lost. We should turn back," I come to a stop.

"Stop saying that about yourself. I remember the way back. I mean, you already saw what you wanted to show us so just tell us about what you saw and we can go further and see what there's to see since you can't tell us since you haven't seen what we will see now," Kyle speaks incoherently. "Sorry. I talk too much when I'm nervous."

"It's alright Kyle. I do the same," I say.

We keep going.

The walls seem to evaporate leaving us standing at the entrance of a huge cavern. Stalagmites pierce the ground. I look above and five times as many stalactites hang down. I move the torch over the ground. "Guys it looks like some of these stalagmites were cut. See how they're flat on top and only a few inches off the ground?"

"I don't like the feeling in this place," Kelsey says. "Also, there's a weird smell like metal and something else."

We walk ahead careful with our steps. The ground isn't only bumpy with holes, but also wet and slippery. We nearly walk into a monstrous stalagmite because we're only watching our feet. I hold the torch up and follow it up and up. As the light travels upwards I see we're standing in front of a massive column. It goes up and up into the dark ceiling. I don't think if all three of us linked arms we could hug the spire.

Above my head the column seems to branch off. There's a central point that continues into the darkness, but there's more stone that branches off stretching their arms higher. There's tree limbs skirting around the stone up there. It almost looks like roots are coming down through the darkness. I can't tell in the dark and the distortion from the flickering red glow of my torch, but it looks like moss is growing above the central column. Much higher than any of us could reach even if I stood on one of their shoulders.

Kyle says, "It looks like it formed naturally. And phallic at that. Is that moss?! There's no way. We'd have to be just under the surface and there'd have to be sunlight. but I don't see any . . ."

"This is ridiculous."

"And it's real wet. Guys come touch this!" He walks around the back of it. "Oh holy fucking Christ Mary Mother of God that is fucked up. Nope. Nope. Yeah, I'm going to say a big nope."

We walk over to see what he's blabbering about. "Oh I'm going to be sick," Kelsey gags.

The torch casts a red glow on everything that isn't shrouded in shadow. What was hiding from us on the other side of this tree column is a body in Christ's pose. His feet are above my head or what's left of them. To say it looked like a dog chewed him up then left him in a bucket of water in the hot sun wouldn't do this decomposition justice. His arms are outstretched hanging from a wooden cross. Sneak peaks of his bones reveal themselves through too much hanging flaps of his discolored skin. Something's growing on him. His bones are black and almost fuzzy looking. They look like a spider's leg mixed with old chicken bone. The wooden cross is hanging by chains attached to something high up in the darkness.

Where an eye should have been there's an empty socket with a drooping brown bubble dipping below its chin. I swear I could see it swaying. It's naked. There's a hole in its stomach giving us a peak inside. A rib is protruding at a 90 degree angle away from his body. In the hole where we should have found a textbook picture of anatomy, it has collapsed and turned soupy. His pelvis has turned into microwaved human broth. It'd been slurped almost clean years ago. Some is still in there though.

"Why doesn't it smell?" Kyle asks.

"Most of the decomposition must have happened years ago or we wouldn't have been able to stumble our way over so easily without detecting anything. There's definitely moss on him. The Earth's taking over, but how?" I ask taking a closer step.

"There's no sun here. Nothing should be able to grow," Kelsey answers.

On the column, beneath what's left of his mangled feet is a large metal circle with an odd shape sticking out of the center. It shows symbols I'm not used to, but they seem to resemble our numbers. There's 12 of them. Beneath those, are 12 more symbols. The inner 12 resemble hieroglyphics. They're images, albeit abstract. I think I make out a flower. This one might be a dog or animal of sort. That one is surely a man.

"Is this some kind of clock?" I ask to myself.

Kelsey reaches over me to touch it. "Oof that's pretty sharp." She steps through us to get a closer look. It's at eye level with her. She brushes away the dust that's accumulated for who knows how long.

"Could be a few decades, could be hundreds of years judging by the dust on this thing. There's no footprints besides our own," Kelsey looks around.

"That doesn't make any fucking sense Kelsey. How can you not tell how old it is by that much? Which is it?" Kyle asks.

"I don't know. Both?" She leans back from it. "You take a look."

Kyle leans in closer. He brushes a huge pile of dust from it. He runs his fingers along the edge of it then places both hands on the outer edges and tries to shake and move it.

"What was this place used for before . . ."

Sounds of cracking rust and metal makes my head pound. "Stop you're about to break it!"

He pushes his entire body into it now and the sounds of hinges snapping pierces the air around us and then it moves. It turns like a wheel, but with resistance.

"This has to be some kind of clock guys!"

"But how Miranda? It doesn't resemble a clock. It doesn't look like anything electronic has ever been down here. It looks like a sundial."

"Well what the fuck are we supposed to do with a sundial in a cave Kyle? Huh?"

"I don't know. I guess you'll have to ask Jayne's God. Maybe they'll speak to you if you ask extra nicely."

"You know what Kyle?"

"Guys stop it! This place is terrifying enough without you two getting into it. I've never seen you guys talk to each other like that," Kelsey says.

I turn away ignoring him.

"Besides all this rot the air seems to be clean. There's no bugs and it doesn't smell. An overwhelming smell of iron makes me want to gag though. I don't think I would have been able to smell anything else," I say.

Kyle reaches up and smacks the bottom of the cross. It hits the column making a solid thump reverberate through the room. I jump out of my skin spinning back around. The sound violently smacks around the cavern's structures swirling around the room until the sound hits us again in an echo. The chains rattle and creak as years and years of rust are awoken.

A sudden sound of metal chains clangs against each other higher up. The chains must have hit other ones because now they're creaking and rust and dirt are falling. The sound continues to spread above us as chains hit others out of view that hit others slowing their momentum until there's a soft whining from the entire ceiling. It get's quieter and quieter until the silence bears its weight down upon us.

Part of the man's hand above us crumbles like dry cheese off his bones thumping onto the toe of my boot. It sticks to it until I kick it off. Flicking the piece of hand was like flicking food off something. I look closer at the man and although his skin has been rotting away for some time it looks like a boy. Not even a teenager yet. His stature is short now that I'm studying it.

"Why the hell did you do that?" Kelsey seethes.

"I wanted to see what happened."

"And?"

"Well judging that we're inside a cave, I don't think we're in a rusty abandoned chain factory so that rules out the obvious."

"When was the last time someone was here?" I look at the body.

"I don't think he's going to answer ya," Kyle replies.

"Shut up," I say punching his arm. "That was kind of funny."

"Can any of you read this?" Kelsey's nose is an inch away from the lettering on the rock.

I walk to her casting more light on the wall.

"Is it Latin?" She asks.

"No. I know a little bit of Latin, but this isn't that. Look closer and you'll see it isn't the right alphabet. The symbols seem to purposefully mimic ours." The wall is a mixture of paint and carvings. The words are painted and it looks like multiple coats. Breaking the script down the middle is two carved lines that swirl in tighter and tighter meeting at the center. They're inside a large, upright rectangle. The carving only has a depth of a centimeter or so, so it can't be a door, but I still want to try.

I place my hands on it and push. Then push again and again. Huffing, I try once more. I only disturbed some dust.

"Miranda what are you doing?" Kelsey asks.

"I think it's a door."

"That's only a petroglyph. It's a shallow carving see?" She pushes her finger in the "crack" of the door.

I feel like something's almost happening.

"It's only more rock," she tells me pulling her finger out.

I follow the line of the "door" looking for any discrepancies all the way to the floor. A large crack runs between the wall and the floor like a miniature mote. At least an inch across and a few inches deep. Dark red bathtub lines stripe the inside of it showing where liquid used to sit. I follow the crack along the wall. I disappear behind an exceptionally large stalagmite when I realize I took our only source of light with me.

"Miranda what the hell!" Kyle yells in a whisper.

It doesn't feel right to be too loud. Especially after the disruption Kyle made with the chains. I have a feeling I might wake something if I'm not careful. I can tell we're all feeling a similar way now.

"Sorry. Come over here, I think I found . . . something."

We walk along the rough limestone wall. We're still following this gap, which hugs the edge of the large room. The flicker from my torch makes the cave formations look like they're breathing. We pass the large doorway we entered through and the gap continues on.

"That's manmade," Cody states the obvious.

We follow the wall.

"There's more holes all over the place. Are there more tunnels Miranda?" Kelsey asks.

"I don't know. Probably just crawl spaces, but one thing I know now is to never underestimate the slightest crack. Even the smallest hole in a cave could lead to a huge undiscovered cavern."

We go deeper and further away from the door and our exit. The stalagmites are getting tighter. Not as many have been cut off over here. They stand proud.

The wall's now covered in paintings and a few carvings. There's crosses mixed with other symbols. Balls that appear to be the Earth are scattered about. A mushroom cloud? They're randomly placed.

"These are from different times than the ones earlier," I say getting a closer look at the different styles of craftsmanship, paint, carving, and erosion.

"Look at these," Kelsey squats near the gap.

As I squat, my eyes follow an image of little figures falling off one of the earth drawings and ending above the gap. The word "BLOOD" is printed throughout with different paints and in different languages. Blood is written in Spanish and Latin. I can now assume the other languages also say "blood." I recognize the characters in one! It's the same as the paint on the large rectangle near the column.

"Do you guys have a pen?"

"No."

"Nope."

"Memorize the letters then."

We study the wall for some time. I feel satisfied and step back and so do they. Without saying a word we start tracing the gap again.

We make it back to the giant stone tree thing. The body is still swaying slightly. The little bit of skin left dangling is reaching for the rest of itself decomposing slowly towards the ground. A deep stain streaks down the back of the corpse leading to a gap similar to the one that traces the entire room. The gap surrounds the entire column.

I get on my hands and knees. I lean closer to the gap under the body by the tree. A little closer. I lower my head to the floor.

"Miranda. The fuck you doing?" Kyle asks.

I sit startled by his voice, "What? I was looking."

"No you weren't just looking. You had your eyes pressed into that gap. Then it looked like you were about to lick the inside or something," Kyle's face is paler than usual.

"That's stupid, I wouldn't do that," He looks at me bewildered. "I don't remember that. Kelsey?" I look to her to confirm he's joking. She only looks at me sorrowfully.

"Let's go guys, I feel like we're being watched. This place is doing weird things to my head." I glance back over my shoulder at the carved door I couldn't get to budge with the strange characters.

7

I notice a lot more paths on the way back with skinny, but obvious openings. They seem to be angled outward from that creepy room. Explains why I didn't notice them on the way up.

"I was supposed to take a left," I tell them when we get back to the stairs. "Let's go real quick."

We peak into the crack that reveals the chapel.

"Have either of you been in there?"

They shake their heads.

I'm looking at the tree carved in the stone along the back wall with more interest now. I feel a longing to go towards it. It seems to be a bastardized copy of the naturally formed one back in that creepy room.

"Do you think Jayne and them know about that room?" Kelsey asks.

"I'm not sure," I answer. "There was no sign anyone has gone in there for a looong time. And I'm pretty sure they only started utilizing this space as the Haven not even a decade ago."

The doors to the chapel are thrown open and people come flooding in. A lot of them are in dark green. They're kitchen workers.

"What are they? Wait, is this the first service? The one after breakfast?" I ask them whispering feeling the panic fill my chest.

"Fuuuuck, what time is it?" Kyle asks.

"We haven't been gone that long. We left right after dinner. That means it had to have been over 15 hours. If breakfast is done we are dangerously late."

I slow jog as I try not to trip on anything.

8

I hurry to the children's wing being careful not to sprint through the Big Room. Blending in. I'm so focused on blending in I barely notice what's not right next to me. I pass noisy construction on one of the walls of the main room. There's members harnessed from the ceiling chiseling at the stone.

I unwillingly stop as my curiosity is peaked. I can vaguely see an outline of a massive tree. Every time they smack the wall I think of the tremors before an earthquake.

I don't have time to question what they're doing.

I go to the children's wing.

The second I'm out of sight I soar down the stairs and to the locked metal door.

"You're late," Mark says without looking away from the kids. He's sitting behind the desk writing notes as usual and then watching and then writing and then watching and then writing.

"I slept in," I lie.

"You didn't."

"Yeah I did." My heart sinks and my skin heats up. My body's screaming at me that we got caught. I feel compelled to be honest so this feeling can be over. I stand my ground.

"You weren't there when I went for you. Where were you honestly?" His eyes narrow suspiciously. "I didn't go to Cody nor Jayne nor anyone for that matter so you owe me now. Things are . . . umm . . . sharp today. I wanted to give you a chance to explain yourself before I got everyone else worried."

"I did sleep in though," I'm hoping all to God, well not God that's for sure, that he'll tell me more information I can work off of.

He squints his eyes. "You didn't though. Where was your friend Kelsey? What're you two up to?"

My vision wants to blur. My body calls to rest on the couch behind me. I want to tell the truth about what I've found so I can stop feeling this panic, but that would be far worse.

"It'll be better if you come clean immediately."

In my sleep deprived mind I almost consider it. "We were at Kyle's," I finally say.

"Why? You know it's the unspoken rule not to socialize outside of the Big Room?"

I look to my side as if I could turn my eyes all the way around and my brain could tell me what to say.

"Well?" He presses on.

"Sex," I blurt out.

"What? Wait what?" He talks as if it's a struggle. Like I surprised him with my answer. He was ready for something. He looked hungry to catch me. Now he looks disappointed.

"Yeah. We had sex."

"What about Cody?"

Without thinking I know my response, "He's having sex with Jayne and who knows who else. We might as well have an open relationship by now," I can see this is bothering him.

"Yeah, I've known about him and Jayne for a long time now," I haven't though. "Especially lately. I'm cool with it though."

His mouth falls agape like a toddler who is told no for the first time. He looks at me wide eyed.

This is working.

"Yeah they've been fucking. A lot. It's almost spiritual the way Cody describes it to me."

He throws his head to the side looking away horridly uncomfortable. He clears his throat like he's going to say something, but doesn't.

"Yeah, he tells me about it. Apparently they talk about the other members especially the small counsel and who deserves to know what," I can tell the more I talk, the more uncomfortable he's getting. I can feel myself getting carried away. If he tries to get proof I'm screwed, but then again I might be telling some of the truth.

He's holding his hands up in surrender like a cartoon. "Okay. Yeah I get it. Sex is happening here. You have work to do."

"I know they talk about you," I say before I can stop myself. I have power over him. I can't believe something so simple is working on this psychopath.

"What?! Like what?!" The entire room falls silent and everyone's staring at us.

"I mean I don't know for sure about that. Forget I said anything. I didn't realize you'd get neurotic. I guess I can't talk to you honestly." God, this feels good baiting him like this.

"What? No! No. No." He gets quieter, "Thank you, I appreciate your honesty. I'm going to go to . . . the . . . ummm . . . bed. I meant bathroom. I have to shit," He runs out.

Why haven't I behaved like this my whole life?

Well, it's dishonest. I feel gross even though he deserved it.

My shirt's being tugged. "Ma'am, Ma'am please." A young boy looks up at me with watery eyes.

"Yeah?"

"When do I get to see my Mommy?"

My feeling of control and power blinked away as fast as it came. Now I feel inadequate. "Hey, I know you," I say.

"You were there when Daddy died."

Children's sadness is the worst. "You're Mom is Victoria. You're from Pacific Valley nearby. I remember you," I squat to his level reaching out for a hug. For a moment I thought he'd start crying again and run away, but he fell into my arms and then cried.

"Do I have to watch those scary videos again?"

I walk over to the desk and see his name along with a few others for stage two treatment.

"Well sweetie, Mark never gave me any paper or directions for today so it looks like I'm the only grownup today."

The relief that fell out of this tiny little boy was heartbreaking. How can someone so young be so stiff?

I look around the room for Hailey. She's not here so I go down the hall trying to remember which room is hers. There's a lot. I feel guided though. I have this inner confidence I've never had before and I choose one. No indecisiveness, just decision. It's Brendan, her younger brother, on her bed sobbing.

I run to him crouching, "What happened? Where's Hailey? Are you okay?" I pat his arms and chest looking for any injuries.

He sniffles trying to repress his cries, but then his lungs burst with air again and he cry screams.

I sit on the bed and hold him until he's able to speak. "Hailey's in trouble. Big Trouble. Mark yelled. A lot. She ran fast. Some older kids blocked him in the hallway. He didn't see where she went. Then he looked. And looked. And still no Hailey. Where's my sister Mrs. uh . . . Where is she? Is she dead? Like the others?"

"You can call me Miranda. I think I know where she is. I need your help though. Can you do that?" I'm asking an eight year old for help.

"Yeah," snot bubbles cover his lip. He lets them hang.

"Okay how good are you with time?"

"What?"

"Do you know how long a minute is?"

"Yeah."

"Can you count out 60 seconds over and over?"

"Yeah."

"Good after 30 minutes if I'm not back I need you to go to the room at the end of the hall. It's a cleaning hall. I need you to bang against the rock in the back. There'll be a shelf, but it'll be moved away from the wall. I need you to bang against it loud. Got that? Sit here and count to 60, 30 times. Keep track on a piece of paper how many times you count to 60 and count slowly. Okay?"

"Why?"

"Time is weird." It's the same explanation I would have given an adult. Time is funky enough down here, but in the darker tunnels it's nothing I recognize.

"I'll be back."

"With sissy?"

"It's a possibility." I wasn't going to lie to him.

9

I walk down the tunnel to the intersection and head for the room with hanging bodies. The place where I essentially helped Jayne and Ian torture and murder that man.

I stop and listen just like Hailey showed me. I'm looking up at the rock through slats in the wooden panel.

"Grab the buckets," a muffled woman's voice commands.

Heavy steps trickle bits of dirt on my face. Clunky boots are moving around. More than two people.

"Guys come on, let's hurry." That's definitely Jayne.

The clank of a large bucket hits the floor right above sprinkling dirt on my face. I hear liquid slosh out and splatter right above me.

The boots move to the other side of the room. Definitely two people and Jayne. They get less clumsy with each bucket. Every time they put a bucket down, it's the solid thunk of heavy metal on metal. Back and forth and back and forth. If it was my guess, I would assume they're literally dragging their feet. It takes forever for them to walk, grab, drop, rebalance, walk back, clang the bucket down and do it all over. I feel itchy. I need to keep moving. They're taking forever.

The sound of an engine starting explodes the quiet space. Sounds like a UTV. The rumble as it drives away confirms it's one of their UTVs. I only knew about the stairs to Jayne's office through the book case and this hole in the floor. Apparently there's another exit in that room. Eventually the rumbling gets quieter until I can no longer hear it.

I stay and listen a while longer though. It's silent.

I push the wooden door with its big rock sitting on top of it, but it won't budge. Hailey did it easily. I bend my elbows and push harder this time making sure to keep my back straight and nothing. My heart seems as loud as that UTV and I'm alone in this creepy place with no Hailey to admire her bravery or Kyle to make stupid jokes or Kelsey to give me courage. The opening won't budge.

Okay, stand back and think.

Hailey is shorter than me so she wouldn't have been able to reach it let alone push on it. I lower the torch and remember the rock she was standing on. I push it over. Standing on top I push it again. And still nothing.

I place my hands on it and start pressing in different spots starting form the center. When I'm nearly done with my spiral I touch the corner which makes it pop to the side. My fingers are able to fit in the gap and I push it over.

It feels like I'm going through a portal as I raise myself inside the room. The buckets of blood are gone like I thought. Only half of the bodies from last time are here. Roughly five of them are hanging backwards facing the wall. In front of them painted on the stone is a large cross.

The one with long brown loose curls is as naked as the others, but she's still dripping blood from the side of her neck. It feels like a minute passes between each drip and I stand there mesmerized listening to the splashes on the dark stone.

"Miranda."

I jump around so scared that my body might as well be projecting its own light from the energy of my shaking. I'm a glowing target. I throw the torch down.

Oh God. There's someone in the staircase watching me.

"What are you doing down here?" The silhouette asks.

"I . . . umm . . . I . . . wait. Cody? Is that you?"

He steps out of the shadow letting the fire light his face. The red glow makes his light hair look like it's on fire.

"What are you doing here? How'd you get in?" He looks at the huge wall that's missing. The UTV's tracks go down it. There's a gap in the wall where the "door" must slide behind.

I catch myself from looking down trying not to give it away.

"Miranda. Don't make me ask you again," he takes a step closer.

"Stay away," I tell him holding my ground firm.

"Miranda. What do you know?" He takes another step forward and his chest bulges.

"I said stay away," I jump to grab the torch and I wave it in front of me as if he were a bear.

His right hand starts to twitch and I see he's thinking about pulling his gun. His face furrows like he's about to make a quick decision and just as he pulls the gun from his hip, I lunge the fire into his face.

"AAAAAH! You stupid cunt!" His pistol flies across the room smacking into a soft body. He scratches at his face. The flames lick into his hair and I jump onto him crashing us onto the stone. I cover my body over his face extinguishing the flames almost immediately. The damage could be worse.

"You're going to be sorry now," he says through clenched teeth. He's breathing uncomfortably loud. Is it from smoke or anger? He pushes me aside and in one swoop I grab the torch off the ground and swing it against his head. He falls unconscious immediately.

They're going to be back soon. I need to hide him. I can't put him down my hatch though or he'll find where it goes when he wakes up. The faint sound of an engine far in the distance reinvigorates me. I look around the room at the piles of rocks along the edges. Come on, where's another entrance? The engine sound is closer.

I try to lift him up to drag him up the stairs, but he's too heavy and drops to the ground like a sack of rocks. I slide his belt off and put it on myself. I grab the pistol and slide it into the leather holster. That feels more like it.

The ground beneath me starts to vibrate. The engine's getting closer.

I grab his arms and drag him to the latch. I never closed it, thank God, I wouldn't have had the time to open it again. I stick his feet inside the hole. The engine is getting loud. It's close. I push on his shoulders until his body slides in and thumps to the ground below. I jump in afterwards and yank the hatch shut.

Not even a minute later, I hear voices again.

I set the torch on the ground. I drag him by his feet. His shiny leather boots reflect the fire. I drop him and go back for the torch and move it further down the tunnel then go back to dragging him. I repeat this until I get back to that janitor's closet.

The door slides open. "Hailey?" Brendan asks timidly.

"How'd you know there was a door?"

"Hailey showed me. She told me not to tell anyone. Is that man dead?"

"He's only sleeping."

I back into the metal shelving trying to drag Cody. It rocks back and forth, but Brendan's little arms shoot out and balance it.

I rush through the hall and pull Cody's body into the first room I see.

It's dark. I can only see what the bright hall lights from outside the room illuminate. Tons of filing cabinets stand guard along the walls. Old tables and chairs. Desks and shelves with odd curiosities on them.

I place him down and close the door behind me. I examine my key ring. I try the one that's supposed to lock the kid's rooms from the outside. It works.

"Where's Hailey?" Brendan's standing behind me. A few kids stop at the other end of the wall and peak at us. The moment they catch my gaze they disappear. I pull Brendan by his soft hand back into the closet.

"Why didn't you knock on the door when the 30 minutes were up?" I ask irritated.

"It hasn't been 30 minutes."

"What do you mean? That took forever though." Why did I trust an eight year old?

"It's only been five minutes," he says.

"That's physically not possible."

"No look," He pulls out a piece of paper and on it are almost five rows of 60 dashes. "I counted the number and put a mark down at the same time. I thought I did good."

"No, no, no you did," I lean down allowing us to be face to face. "Please I want you to continue to do this. So you can help me find your sister."

10

"Don't let me stay more than 25 minutes okay?"

"Please bring my sissy back."

I pick the torch up and head off towards the Big Room overlook where they're chiseling some tree into the towering wall. The constant hum of their work disappears in places and comes back incessantly in other places. There has to be hundreds of passageways I don't know about.

It only just occurred to me I have the torch from this entrance. Where's Hailey then?

A faint scream echos through the tunnel. I think it came from ahead. I pick up my speed. I trudge higher in elevation. I can feel my breath becoming shallower. The cave is getting bumpier. I'm getting close to standing above the Big Room. I can see the light ahead of me. I'm almost there. I just need to reach that light and look down and I'll know. I walk forward barely giving attention to the boulders becoming more hazardous. The light is beckoning me.

I hear another scream, louder this time, but from behind me.

I start heading back when I notice a crevice in the wall. I know I need to go through it. I push the torch into it first and when I don't feel a back I try to slide my body through. My body gets caught half way in. There's no way I can squeeze through.

I strain my eyes trying to see what's further in the crevice. I almost turn back when something not of this world pushes me in. It felt like a wind. For a second I'm sandwiched between the stone and I can't take a full breath in, but on the exhale I fall to the other side. I fall directly on the torch extinguishing it instantly.

A clanging echo swims up the tunnel and into the crevice. Brendan. There's no way. 25 minutes couldn't have passed. I just went back inside.

"Hailey?" I ask tentatively.

Rustling sounds come from everywhere, near and far at the same time. The sound of a clock ticking is faint in my head.

Something else is in here with me. A painful nerve travels down my spine and into my stomach making it rumble.

Something brushes my fingers and clasps onto my hand. I stifle a scream. It's squeezing my hand painfully hard

"It's me." It's a girl's voice, but it's not Hailey's.

"Hailey?"

"He's in here."

More rustling comes from nearby. Then it sounds like "he" is directly behind us. I spin around still sitting on the ground clutching the dead torch in my free hand.

"Don't move," Hailey's voice sounds like it's coming from a long distant call out at sea.

Sounds of light squishy footsteps get closer. The sound of hot laboring breath comes from my right. The hand that grabbed me dissolves away. I stay perfectly still. Not daring to move a muscle. Wet drips and a panting sound is close on my left side.

A booming thunder pushes me backwards. Hailey lets out a small scream right beside me, but scurries away. In an instant, a presence is in the exact spot Hailey was in. It's that tension or energetic feeling I have when I'm close to someone, but it feels evil and I'm all alone in the dark.

The sound of a suction popping loose happens in quick succession followed by grippy wet footsteps. The sounds fade away, but now the sound of hot breath surrounds me. I don't move a muscle. I don't dare turn my head.

Then silence.

Directly in front of me I hear, "Miranda" followed by something reaching mindlessly in front of them until they feel something solid. In this case that solid is me and Hailey grasps at me.

I pull her with me as I stand. With my other hand I continue to hold the extinguished torch. I back up until I hit rock. I pull Hailey closer while tracing the rock with my hands.

I pull the lighter box out, but Hailey smacks them out of my hands. I feel her voice in my head saying no.

I bend down to pick them up, but she's pulling me. I stick the torch between my legs and reach again extending my fingers as much as I can since she won't let me fully bend down. She has a death grip on me. I find them and stick them back in my pocket.

I feel a crack, but when I stick the torch inside it hits rock.

"Shhh."

I take a step forward and crunch a small pebble. A low roar rises from the floor to surround us in sound. Something evil latches itself in my brain.

I continue brushing against the wall desperately trying to find the exit.

I find a crevice that's promising. It's nearly a foot in thickness. I slide the torch inside trying to be silent and it doesn't get stopped.

I pull Hailey in front and guide her body in sideways. She resists, but I push harder. Not daring to make a sound, she allows me to push her through.

I follow.

First thing I do is take the box of old matches out and light the torch. I push the darkness back into the crevices. I push that penetrating evil presence out to follow the darkness.

"You saved me." Hailey has dark purple bags under her eyes. She looks skinny and malnourished. Her hair's in giant nests. "Thirsty," she barely says.

"In a few minutes I promise," I grab her hand and we get the hell away from whatever that was.

"How long has it been? I've been in there for at least a week. How am I not dead? I've had no water or food."

"It hasn't been that long," I say.

"No. I've been hunted for at least a week."

"Hailey, it's in your head. You're safe now."

"Are you another trick?"

I grasp her shaking body and hold firmly until she stops jerking.

"How long has it been?" She murmurs.

"Let's just go."

She stumbles forward, but I catch her and wrap an arm around her.

11

"Hailey!" Brendan tackles her. "I have water. You told me you needed it and I got it. I heard you calling in my head." He pushes a huge cup into her hands.

In the bright light I can see her veins, but only for a second and then her skin looks normal again. There's still dark circles under her eyes, but they're not sunken or bruised and her weight is back to normal.

"How'd you?" I start to ask.

She keeps drinking the water. "How'd I what?"

"Do that?"

"Do what?"

"Your skin. It changed."

"I don't think so."

"You looked like you were actually in there for a week, but its only been a day and now you look normal again."

"Brendan how long has it been?" Hailey asks.

Thinking about the time jumps make my chest tighten.

"It's been 10 minutes since Miranda left."

"No how long was I gone this time?" Hailey asks.

"All night long. It's the middle of the day."

"That was the worst trip yet."

Brendan hugs his sister and she leans into him exhausted letting her little brother support her.

"Brendan, wasn't that you pounding on the door to tell me half an hour was up?" I ask.

"No."

"What was it then?" My eyes are huge and my knees start to shake. "I feel insane. Wasn't I gone for hours?"

"That wasn't me. It was only 10 minutes."

"Then where did that pounding come from if it wasn't you telling me the time was up? It must have been the construction. I haven't heard that noise from them, but it has to be it".

"You saved me," Hailey stands up straight. "I'm sure you've noticed weird time in the light. The dark areas are way worse. It plays tricks on your mind and messes the time up."

"What was that back there?" Now that I'm somewhere relatively safe my body begins to shake and gives out beneath me. I can't shake the terror I felt while inside of that room. It's like a piece of it is still in my head hiding in a fold waiting to come back out.

"The dark tunnels play tricks on your mind. This cave makes you loony. There's things I can't explain."

"Jayne's faith? Is that what you're talking about?" I try to comprehend what Hailey's saying.

"I don't know. I've been exploring these tunnels forever now, but every time I come back the time's different. Once I stepped inside for 20 minutes and when I opened the door again it had been over 12 hours. I would've been in there longer if Brendan didn't come get me. He's been my guardian angel."

Chapter 14

1

I'm sitting at one of tables in the Big Room with Lilly, Kelsey, and Kyle. Mark sulked off the second I got there.

"He demanded me to go with him," Lilly says.

"I'm happy you stayed."

I remember weeks ago when I passed all of this construction and barely noticed except for the near constant hum through random spots in the tunnels. I hadn't had much time to look though because I had to get down to the children's wing and work. Now to see the stone tree almost complete is something else. I haven't been able to escape the terror from that day. Oddly enough, I feel an excitement towards the completion. A yearning to be near it.

I feel queasy from Jayne not letting anyone eat the last couple days.

"I'm starving," Kyle says.

"I've never gone this long without eating," Kelsey says.

"My body can't fast. My blood sugar's too low," I say.

"I haven't been able to focus on anything. Everything's been more intense," Kyle's watching the kitchen door waiting for it to open.

"The fast's done weird things to me. I'm more susceptible to what's around me," I say.

We're watching a group of people dressed in grey, chisel and hack the wall behind the stage. They're carving the largest relief sculpture I've ever seen. Its grandiosity shadows most real trees. There's a magic in it. I'm sure we all feel it as it's built before our eyes. They've been working non-stop day and "night." Other areas of the Haven have been put on hold to give more hands to this to anyone who's remotely capable of working.

Some of the workers are attached to chains by their harnesses hanging above the floor working on the outer branches.

"Look out below!" A woman yells from a couple stories up as a chisel hurtles to the ground. It clatters loudly, narrowly avoiding someone walking by.

She's been working on the finer details of one of the outer branches. She lowers herself by pulling on one of the chains connected to her harness.

"They'd normally be connected by rope right?" Kyle asks.

"I think you're right. The chains are weird. Do you think they know about the room we found?" I ask.

"Nah. There wasn't any signs of anyone else being there for decades, if not centuries," Kelsey says.

"What are you guys talking about?" Lilly asks. "Oh shit. Mark's walking towards Isaac and Ian. I'm gonna catch up with him. Sorry," Her face wrinkles in regret.

"Hold up," I grab her arm.

She glances nervously in their direction. "I can't talk to you guys."

"No matter what happens from here on out during the big dinner tonight, keep your thoughts your own. Nothing can take over your own mind fully without your permission." She runs off the second I let go.

"That was a new bruise on her neck."

"We can't let her go over there," Kyle says.

"What do you suggest we do?" I ask.

"Calm down guys. Our time will come," Kelsey says.

The hoard of forest green kitchen crew people flood out pushing carts full of tiny plates.

"Wait to eat until everyone has a plate in front of them," Jayne says from the stage as she watches the construction. She's how I imagine the Egyptian pharaohs looked at the pyramids when they were almost finished.

Lauren sets a small plate with a tiny steak and a pile of sautéed green beans with fresh herbs in front of me. "How are my kids?" She asks trying not to break flow.

"Good. They're smart."

"Smarter than me." Then she's almost inaudible, "Don't eat that or not all of it. I know you're starving, but don't. Whatever you can get away with." She places more plates in front of people then heads back to the kitchen.

"Wait, I didn't hear you," I try to call out to her, but I can't be too loud or I'll attract attention.

"Can I sit here?" Victoria from Pacific Valley plops down. "Where's my daughter Miranda?"

"So everyone knows I've been in the children's wing?" I ask.

"Yes. You've been working down there for a while now so it's pretty obvious. Tell me please," Victoria crosses her arms. I feel like I'm being reprimanded.

"He's good. Healthy . . .

" . . . How's your devotion?"

She chews on her lower lip and glances at Jayne across the room, "Oh good, very good. When does my son get to join me?"

"You know if you aren't that devoted . . ."

Kyle and Kelsey both place a hand on me.

"You can be honest with me. I'm a safe person. I'll save you and everyone here . . .

"I mean alongside Jayne with the help of God and Earth." I said the last part looking away hoping she picks up on the cue.

"Yes. Thank you dear. I'm saved," She hurries away.

"Be careful," Kelsey tells me. "You need to reign it in."

An hour goes by where the same melodic music with the same couple cords are playing seamlessly on repeat. Even the air feels different now. I'm entranced by watching that tree be built out of the stone.

"Hello New World Freedom. My people. The kitchen will now pass out a spiritual drink. We do not have as much of a religion here as we do our beliefs. Religion is not enough to describe it. It might sound peculiar unless you have been attending enough service, but there is sacrificial holiness in it. We are more spiritual than religious," Jayne says.

I expected sounds of confusion, but most people seemed to understand her perfectly. I've been working such long hours in the children's wing I haven't been to services.

"It's been carefully crafted. The main thing I ask of you during this group bonding experience with our Earthly God is that you think of our Earthly God. Think of your faith and where you stand within this planet. How you have been spared from the evils of the world. Nobody is surviving out there except for other shelters like us. We have been connected all across the world. There is an entire community waiting to embrace each other when the chaos ends. It's a small percentage of the population unfortunately, but by number it's a lot of people. We have an entire loving population waiting to embrace us and the others to start rebuilding this world.

"As you eat your food take deep breaths and calm your mind. Think about how you were saved. How I personally will continue to help save you. Feel the power of our God moving through you. He knows everything and as a branch of him so do I. We use this knowledge to help everyone. The more you allow yourself to feel God's love the more influence and love you will receive in this world.

"This will be an intense experience. It will feel like days. Maybe even weeks to some. It is a fast course to concreting a relationship with our God."

The same massive gaudy goblet I saw in the worship room is sat between us, the enormous one that was made for a giant. Another one is placed further down the table. It's painted gold and has a cross on one side and a tree on another with red stones lining the top of it. It's so tall I can't see into it unless I stand up.

When the last goblet is set down and the last plate passed out, the kitchen crew sits at their own table already filled with the goblets and plates. I don't see Lauren with them.

"Reach into your cup and pull out what's inside," Jayne says as she paces across the stage, but since she changed into boots I don't hear the click clack of her heels anymore. She walks quietly now.

I reach my hand into the goblet and pull out a giant railroad nail the size of my forearm. It's dripping in blood. It's heavy and slippery. The liquid's thick and makes a silky sound when it slides in my hands.

"Is this real blood?" I whisper.

"These nails are representative of the people who have had to die for our God. Many made this same sacrifice. Tonight we remember those who died for us. Their life forces were given back to the Earth so we may live." The lights dim. "Look down at your nail and feel the blood around it. They did that for you! Are you going to let their sacrifices be in vain! Will you be lukewarm in your faith or will you be on fire for God! You know the most dangerous devotees are the ones who are lukewarm. They believe they are tight with God and do not need to do anything to improve. All they want is the security of going to heaven, but they are WRONG! There is always room for improvement. You must save others when you get the chance. Help convert them so they do not burn in misery for the rest of their lives. You may think lukewarm is good enough, but I tell you, you will be surrounded by evil forces writhing in agony for eternity if you are not on fire. Lukewarm is the work of the Devil. It is false security! Doubt is an evil infection. I am here to save you all. People suffered horrible fates so you could walk around today without worry of God's wrath."

My heart's speeding up as I hold the nail and listen to her sermon. I can feel my heartbeat through my wrists, thumbs, neck, forehead, ankles, and chest. An overwhelming feeling of sadness and guilt shadow me. I feel like I'm responsible for all the suffering in the world suddenly. I've allowed so much to pass by while I lived comfortably.

Jayne has always had a way with words and having nothing in my stomach is making everything she says more intense.

The energy of the room is a vortex and as Jayne continues to preach, the vortex sucks me in deeper. I try to separate myself, but there's an emotion infecting everyone here. I can't stay away from it. I'm getting swept away in the moment with everyone else.

So much of what she speaks is true, but so much of what I've discovered is evil and I don't know what comes from where and what comes from the movement and what comes from the devil himself. I know I need to stop something, but what?

I feel this horrid heaviness washing over me as I look at the nail. The blood drips down my arms. It was driven through the tendons in the wrist and the ankles. They suffered. Just like that man we saw in that room. I look at the tree and my gut does somersaults. I want to puke, but my stomach's empty.

"Please eat the food provided. You will need your strength especially after having fasted for days."

I poke at the meat with my fork inspecting it. I'm so hungry. I nearly inhale the vegetables. I know there's going to be something in the food or drink tonight, but besides the fact I'm starving I have to blend in. Just like I was trained to do. There's no way I can lie tonight.

"Eat slowly as you are introducing food back to your body," Jayne says.

I slow down, but it's not easy.

A line of people dressed in dark red march out of hall F.

"Nah, I don't believe it," Kyle says.

"It's true. It's the other small counsel Jayne's been spending time with," Kelsey says.

"I heard rumors there was rituals going on with a smaller group, but I didn't know if it was true," I say.

"That's why she hasn't been calling us up so much. Why do you think you've been able to work with the kids without interruption," Kelsey says.

A few members dressed in black and a handful of white are in the line that's spreading across the room. They have dark red belts on their waists.

I'm poking at the last bites of my food wary of what may be inside them. A member in dark red coughs behind me.

"You need to finish," he says.

I eat the last bites. Immediately my body feels better. It's a high in its own. It hasn't been long enough for anything to kick in, but after not eating for so long, the food in my stomach feels abnormally intense.

The dark red man walks to someone else, coughs, watches, and moves on to the next.

Isaac and Cody carry a screen onto the stage. They turn on a movie where a man is on the verge of collapse as he limps through an angry mob with a massive wooden cross on his back. The crowd spits on him and throws rotten food at the gashes on the actor's back. It's absurdly gory.

"Those who sacrificed their lives and their pride so we can live on this Earth in peace did it all for you! It is all your fault what they had to endure!" Jayne's pace quickens and she waves her free arm over her head.

On the screen men violently throw the man onto the cross they made him carry for miles. They drive enormous nails through his wrist and ankle tendons similar to the ones we're holding now. The man's sobbing, but he still has love for the people in front of him who curse him."

I feel overwhelming sadness.

I start to sob and I clench the blood drenched nail to my chest. I can't help, but be fully absorbed in this moment. The torture and pain those people went through is unbearable to think about. Others are sobbing around me.

"I'm so sorry!" A person one table over cries out.

"I didn't deserve their sacrifice!" Another sobs.

The collective energy in the room's rising. Kelsey and Kyle push their finished plates to the center. Others are doing the same.

"You caused this torture because of your sins!" Jayne speaks with conviction.

I bury my hand in my arm crying harder than I ever have before. The violence on the screen is too much. The man on the cross who's dripping blood as people are throwing moldy food and their human waste at him continues to say, "I forgive all of you."

I feel guilty. I've been lukewarm. Oh God, the guilt feels terrible.

A clear cup of dark red wine, I'm assuming, is placed in front of me by a member in dark red.

I pick up the nail again. I can't believe these were driven through people who only wanted to love them.

"Now it is time for our holy drink. We are going to go on a quest together where time is an illusion. You will do inner work, but also feed off the people around you. Call unto God and remember him during this. Do not let the deaths of your loved ones from the war be in vain. They sacrificed their lives so you could be here today. This is your one on one time with God. He will speak to you individually. Keep your mind focused. If you feel yourself getting distracted come to the front and sit on the stage here where Isaac will lead a meditation the entire time. We also have Bibles up here if you feel the need to read. Love to you all. Focus your mind and breathe."

A member in dark red walks gracefully on stage and presents Jayne with her own clear glass.

She holds it up in a toast to us all and starts drinking.

"Keep your minds strong," I tell Kelsey and Kyle. "She can't force us to believe something we don't want to. You can go anywhere in your mind. Find your happy place and build walls. You can build anything you want there. Add a fucking telephone if you want and maybe we can call each other. Add a window, a heater, A/C, whatever you want. Make it comfortable and make it yours, but don't let it be penetrable. Put a lock on it and swallow the key so nobody can go inside your head."

"Miranda I'm scared. The fasting and the video and the bloody nail. It's all too much," Kelsey says.

"You're the strongest person I know. I'm sorry for ever doubting you."

"Shit's gonna get weird," Kyle drinks his.

We don't have a choice. Where would we go? There's no way out.

"Focus your mind on your happy place," I say.

"Well time to drink the kool aid," Kyle tries to smile.

"Not funny," I say.

"You said to find my happy place. There's jokes in mine."

Kelsey and I drink.

Sweet iron and strange flavors.

Here we go.

2

"Feel free to sing along. I encourage it," Jayne nods and someone turns on that same repetitive song I heard in the chapel. New speakers must have been installed because the song comes from everywhere at once, not just from the stage.

"Don't," I say. "It's a way to hypnotize people. You won't notice how much time passes."

"How do you know?" Kyle asks.

"The church I grew up in would do this in service and also on these weird retreats. I'm sorry. I should've seen the warning signs. I only wanted to feel special."

"It's not your fault," Kyle grabs my hand. "We'll get out of this. Stay strong. Your words. Positive thoughts."

At least half of the room moves to stand and sing in front of the stage where the enormous stone tree's been completed. I thought Jayne had a strong presence, but that tree stands with overwhelming, immense power.

Members in dark red who didn't eat or drink are cleaning up the meal. They inspect every glass to make sure they were emptied.

Mine was emptied. So is Kelsey and Kyles. We're blending in, but what will the damage be? I can't think like that. Nobody can change your mind completely. I'm building my fortress inside my head. It'll be so strong that even if someone could take over my body I would be able to hide inside my mind, inside my little room that'll be my fortress with all the information I don't want anyone to know. They may get the other files, but anything I don't want to be revealed will not be.

I concentrate on my old home I shared with Kelsey. I concentrate on the hikes I used to go on. I concentrate on real trees made of bark and leaves. I think of sunsets and sunrises. I put everything I love and everything I need to hide inside our old home and build an unbreakable shield around it. I expand my dome of safety to include nature to add a stronger protection layer. I run around the perimeter with a chain several times and lock it. I swallow the key. I sit under the oak that used to be in our front yard and center myself.

"God loves you. He sacrificed his children for you," a soft voice comes out of the speaker eerily in time with the music.

Don't let that in.

I see my old house. The sun is pouring on me. Birds are chirping. I just went on a nice long hike. The trees are my fortress. They provide protection and will not let anything penetrate my field. They're my protectors. I think of the grasshoppers and the butterflies dancing around me. I concentrate on the sky and make shapes out of my imagined clouds.

I go over this world over and over again cementing it in my brain.

My hands appear to have their own heartbeat now. I can see the little lines so clearly. The lines start to subside to the edges of my hand and I feel like I can step inside.

The table has a breath of its own. My shirt's breathing. They're reminding me to breathe slowly.

I look at my friends. They look beautiful.

"Accept God into your heart," the speakers project.

Everything's breathing with me. It's beautiful. I wish I could change the music, but I can't control everything. I'd love it if I could, but that's not how the world works.

More people are getting up and moving around now. The singing crowd expands. The energy they're creating over there is astounding. Over there seems like miles away.

Some leave the singing heap and head for the couches and rugs. The lights dim significantly.

"That's better," I smile relaxing in the softer light. "Not too bright and not too dark," I say dreamily.

"People died so you could have this moment," the speakers say with the beat of the music. It's quieter than the lyrics, but easy enough to make the words out. It's like a voice whispering in the back of your head. But it's not in my fortress. I won't let it penetrate.

"Want to go to the couches?" Kelsey asks us breaking the thoughts Kyle and I were fixated on.

"Sounds lovely. As lovely as the woman swimming with me in my bright blue lake in my happy place. Sounds as good as the soup my Mom's bringing me in my happy place. I wish I could taste it in real life. Man, that would be soooo gooood right now. Do you guys like soup? It's nice," Kyle continues to talk about his happy place while playing with a tag on the bottom of his shirt.

I can't help smiling and giggling at the way he talks. It's nice to sit back and listen. I like people who talk a lot about nothing. It's comforting.

I feel weird as we make the journey across the Big Room to the couches. My feet feel like they become one with the floor with each step melting further downwards, but the Earth is holding me up. My version of Earth. Not their bastardized version of God and Earth. I breathe. Positive thoughts. I can always address this later. The walk over is a trek and so much time passes. I have a destination in my mind. That couch. It's going to be nice to get there.

It feels like it took half an hour to cross the room. It probably took a minute. I'm proud of myself for making the journey. I'm with the couch now.

Everything's more vibrant now. We sit on a couch that's covered in roses. Something you would find in your grandmothers house. It's soft. The flowers are breathing and outlined in more colors than normal.

I look at the tree carved from stone. It's beautiful. Its branches are waving in the wind and giving me a gentle light show. The builders are gone, but I swear I can hear the sounds of chains from above. I can't see them because they've been pulled up into the darkness. I look back at my hand and it's not just breathing, but swirling now.

"God saved you all from the horrors of the present day," the speakers pour the sound from everywhere making it feel like I'm in a bubble of inescapable sound.

"Guys, check this out," Kyle says. He joins his fingers in front of his face and starts waving his arms making it look like a snake. "Wild right?"

"There's hundreds of copies of your hands," Kelsey's smile is huge.

A dark red walks over to us. She's like a cherry with arms and legs and says, "Hello there, I want to remind you to focus inwards on your journey with God. You wouldn't be here without him having seen something special in each of you. Here's some bibles." She hands one to each of us. She believes she's spreading love and salvation. You can see the authenticity and how much she cares. I want to hate her, but I understand. She just wants others to have what she thinks she has. She believes she's saving us from damnation.

It feels funny to hold it. It's not so bad, just a book we've all had and probably all read portions of. It's just paper. Toxic paper that leads to toxic things. A sexist text full of horror and pain. Yeah, I'm gonna stick this somewhere else. I slide it out of our little "living room." The dark red cherry woman is gone.

"Yo get rid of mine as well," Kyle hands me his and so does Kelsey. "That lady looked like a bird. What kind of bird?"

"A dumb one," I giggle.

We share a secret laugh like we're the only people in the world at this moment then we drift into our own worlds again.

Everything around me has evolved from breathing to swirls and morphing. I can hardly decipher where the couch ends and the floor begins let alone where my body ends and the air starts.

"Accept God. Accept this. It feels good," the speakers continue in time to the music.

I trace my finger in the air watching the fingers that come out of it.

A light blue walks over to us.

"You're a wave from the ocean bro," Kyle says.

"Niiice," he walks away.

"You know, everyone's just trying to do their best," I say.

A blood curdling scream bursts through the sounds and movements. I look above us, but I can't make anything out. It's dark, but it's also full of colors. I can't believe I was in the shadows of the stalactites before, invisible to those below. There could be someone there right now.

Jayne steps up, "Keep relaxing and concentrate on God and Earth and everything they provide. That was the devil trying to distract you. Just like in life you have to hold tight to your devotion." Her voice sounds like butter. "We have devoted people coming around the room. They are vessels for God to work through. They are here to help you. Please feel free to call one over if you would like that."

When I look at Jayne she becomes a screen and then that screen gets smaller and she's inside another screen and then in one fell swoop she's inside a hundred identical screens moving further away.

I sit back and close my eyes. My eyelids burst into a thousand colors and patterns. There's a castle in the distance with magic and worldly food. I stay under my tree in my fortress though. That sounds nice over there, but I like this spot. The movie on the back of my eyelids is enchanting. Mandalas form inside the clouds above the castle until the clouds are mandalas. Flowers line the pathway and smile at me.

"Relax into it and picture the cross, our God, and the Bible," the speakers instruct.

I almost do. Crosses appear on the backs of my eyelids like doors with the mark of the beast trying to burst into my mind. They turn bloody and I squeeze my eyes until they pop open. My world is turning upside down, but I know if I close my eyes the world won't tip over, but I can't let the beast inside. I think about my tree.

I go back to the entertainment my closed eyes gave me. Everything's colorful. I'm sleepy, but I'm not truly tired. I'm floating here and there laying on this rose, grandma couch.

The blood curdling scream penetrates the room again. I burst my eyes open and look up. It's coming from up top. The one thing that doesn't seem to be messed with right now is my hearing. The movement of everything swirling and morphing into each other is puttering out, but only slightly.

Then it clicks.

"That's Hailey," I sit up straight and look at Kelsey lying on the floor next to me and Kyle lying on the other side of the couch with his legs draped over my lap.

"Please excuse me," Jayne starts.

"It's all a lie! Human sacrifice! Jayne's evil! Those she works for is evil!" The screams come like a dagger from the ceiling trying to assassinate Jayne's lies. The daggers are slashing people's beliefs and connections they were forming over hours and hours during this intense time.

The sober dark red sheep start panicking. They become frantic.

"She wants blood! You drank human blood! That wasn't an animal, that was human blood! Possibly your friend's or even your child's! I've seen the bodies they drained!" The voice from above screams.

The visuals and strange ways of thinking aren't going away, but rather they're integrating into my reality. I'm starting to feel normal again. Or more like the intense part of the experience is fading, but nothing looks as it did before. I look at my hands and they aren't opening into a dream of their own. They're only breathing slightly now. They must have had a great time. Too bad I can't ask them.

The hymns are turned up and it blasts through the speakers. Instead of quiet hypnotic music, it's like turning a lullaby your Mom used to sing to you to max volume in the middle of the night. It sounds like the speakers might burst or if they don't then my eardrums will burst. They've turned it up so loud I feel like I'm in a horror movie where everything that's meant to be comfort is teetering on madness.

I can hear Hailey screaming down, but I can't make out any words. The music's going to make us all deaf. I cover my ears and I scrunch my face for hope if I squeeze it hard enough any holes that could let music in will close.

"It's loud! It hurts!" Kelsey tries to scream over the music while pushing her way in between me and Kyle. We squish together on one half of the couch. We're also each other's safe spaces now.

I hear a pop and the music is slightly quieter. Then another pop and it's quieter. And pop. Pop. Pop. Pop. Pop. Until the only speaker that's still playing music is the one on the stage.

"Find a way up there!" Jayne screams. "Now!"

The chains are lowering. Dark reds are tripping over harnesses.

Jayne's panicking. "Go!" She yells at the people struggling with connecting the chains to their harnesses. She spots Isaac and runs over.

"Isaac handle it!"

He gets up without an expression and jogs with his arms straight by his side down hall F.

There's no more screaming and although I can't see her, I know Hailey's disappeared. Ever since going in the dark tunnels with her the first time I have a connection with her I can't explain. I can almost hear her thoughts sometimes. It's like the cave walls echo my footsteps back to me as her voice.

The lights return to normal. As bright as ever.

3

Jayne's dark reds are passing out sandwiches and water.

I'm still sitting on the couch with Kelsey in between me and Kyle. We're pressed against each other. The swirling movement's coming to rest into the places I knew before. My hands don't appear to have a mind of their own anymore. Everything has more life to it. The couch we're on isn't moving or breathing anymore, but the colors are more vibrant. It's like there's a life inside it even if it isn't normally detectable.

There's a few pinks, security, on the couch across from us crying. One has his hands together in prayer. A lot of gibberish, but I can make out some of the words.

"Don't worry God, I know that was the devil himself trying to ruin our connection at the end. My devotion's strong. I am on fire for you. Especially now, after seeing how he works against us."

A few counsel members in white walk by in a daze. None talk to each other, but they talk nonetheless. "Did you feel God's presence?" "God was next to me singing." "The more I sang, the more I felt God." "God guided me through the night." "I felt light and airy singing." "God revealed amazing things to me." "I can still feel the magic in my head. God is within me now." "I will never be lukewarm." "I can't wait to do that again." "I need to feel that connection again." "I have no doubts." "That helped our relationship." "I had doubts, but not anymore."

They walk aimlessly with stupid smiles and "revelations." And off my hope goes to extract the truth from the lies for the people down here.

"I feel different," Kelsey says.

"Yeah, me too," Kyle responds.

"In what way?" I ask.

"I'm more energized now. My head feels clearer. I barely have any doubts now," Kelsey says.

"Doubts about what?"

"Something's seriously not right down here. This is more than a mere religion. This is a cult. I need answers."

"Yeah," Kyle adds. "I did what you said Miranda. I didn't let my mind concentrate on what Jayne wanted. I created my own place in my head and made the experience mine."

"GO AWAY!" Someone screams across the room.

I search for the noise.

"NOOO I'll serve you! I swear!"

Underneath a lunch table, a woman in the fetal position rocks back and forth holding her head like all her thoughts will pour out if she doesn't. She's muttering something, but I can't hear.

"Is that Lilly?" Kyle asks.

"Oh my God."

"Get out of my head! NO! Stop! Don't kill them!" She crawls out from underneath. She's straining to get out as if something's holding her leg. She grips her leg under the table with both hands and yanks.

She stands, but her body flails backwards and her head hits the other table. She stumbles. She stands. Blood's dripping down her face.

She flings herself forward and runs. Screaming the entire time. She runs for the stage barely keeping herself upright. She flies across the room as if a huge gust of wind blew her forward. She lands face down near the stage. Jayne and others are telling her to calm down. A circle of people are surrounding her on the ground talking in calm voices. Too many calm voices sounds like a nightmare though.

I start to get up, but Kelsey shoots her hand out and yanks me back.

In a burst Lilly pushes her way out and runs around the room screaming again.

"Get out of my head! You don't belong there!"

She's searching desperately for something. She looks under a table and then another and runs back to the couches and targets a brown one with roses. She yanks and chucks its cushions across the rug. She pulls on the carpet corner looking underneath and crawls beneath it and to the other side. She's positioned to sprint, but stops for a second as she locks eyes with me. She huffs and without taking her eyes off of me, runs with crazed intensity directly at me.

Her eyes are pink and blood shot. Her hair's flying behind her in matted clumps.

She's so close to me now. I don't know what to do.

She flies forward smashing her face against the thin carpeted floor beneath me inches away from the couch. The way she fell without sliding or moving at all made it look like she was tackled, but nobody's on top of her.

A dark red pool spreads beneath her. We fall to the floor around her. I grab her face.

"Lilly? Are you okay? What happened?" I say.

"Come on girl, get up," Kyle adds.

"Say something, goddamnit," I shake her.

Kelsey rolls her over. The rest of the people close in.

Several of her teeth had fallen out on the rug. A gash on her forehead broke some of the thousands of vessels protecting her brain and blood pours out. She blinks it away.

"Miranda," her hoarse voice is full of terror. She's so scared. "Closer."

I lean in closer. Blood spittle splashes my face when she coughs, but I don't flinch away. Her breathing sounds like someone had crawled into her body and is pushing her throat against her windpipe making it nearly impossible for her to talk.

"I saw it."

"What did you see?" I ask.

"They're recreating history. It showed me. Trees and blood. So much blood," Lilly's breathing becomes shallow. She coughs again spraying me with more blood. I lean in closer.

"What do you mean?"

"You need to stop the cycle. This cave is full of answers, but you need to listen. Keep your mind closed, but stay open," Lilly's shivering.

"Get out of the way!" Jayne thrashes through the crowd. She pushes me out of the way. I fall into her blood. Kyle pulls me up and holds me when he realizes I lost the strength in my legs.

"What did she say to you?!" Jayne screams at me. It isn't the way she yelled at me the first day in her office. She's desperate.

The words don't reach my lips. I try to say them, but they catch in my throat. Lilly silently mouths, "I'm so scared. Help me."

Jayne's about to scream again, but then her face changes. It looks calm again and in charge. "Miranda I need to help her. I will do everything I can for every single person here." She's feeding off the attention. Everyone's watching the spectacle. "What did she say to you?"

I try again and it gets caught in my throat. I decide on the lie. "A bunch of gibberish. She couldn't say anything clearly."

Jayne looks at me. Those eyes are penetrating, but I keep my walls up. I keep my mind closed. She isn't able to unlock it.

She turns back to Lilly. At that moment, Isaac and Ian push through the crowd and help Lilly to her feet. Surprisingly, she walks fine. It looks like she'll be okay. They walk with her to the front, behind the stage, and in front of the enormous stone tree.

We follow.

That's when I notice the gap on the floor stretching the entire length of the cavernous room.

"It looks like what we found in that chamber, but even bigger," Kyle gestures to the gap.

Jayne, Isaac, and Ian surround Lilly as she's pressed against the tree. Her lips are moving, but I can't make out anything she's saying.

Someone in the crowd screams, "The devil's inside her!" People are shoving each other to get a closer look like selfish circus goers when something goes terribly wrong in the arena. They feel an urge to get closer to the tragedy.

"The evil is within!"

"Stop listening to her!"

"She's possessed!"

Jayne turns around looking over her "congregation." She never glances at us. She walks on the stage and grabs the microphone and walks back down holding the chord so it doesn't snag.

Lilly looks slightly better. She isn't bleeding anymore, but she's pale. Her head's swaying and she looks to be further from reality than when she was running like a madwomen.

"I regret to tell you this, but the evil near the end swooped inside of our member, Lilly. She has served us well," Jayne stands in front of Lilly while Isaac and Ian hold her shoulders up. Ian tucks Lilly's hair behind her ears.

"No it didn't! She's fine," I yell. I'm muted by the other's screams. Jayne heard me though. She looks directly at me.

"I can tell you are all devoted or you would speak against me right now. It is not uncommon for evil spirits to jump out of one person and into another. If we sacrifice its host, it will become weaker."

God, I feel so fucking helpless. I can't say anything or they'll say the demon jumped into me. My face is burning. I want to run at her, but I can't. I'm stuck in place. My nervous system is screaming fight or flight, but I'm not allowed to move.

"Through her infected blood we'll give back to our God. Back to Earth. We show our true devotion today. She tried to ruin everything we are working for. The holy tree will experience its first life force today . . ."

"Drop the chain!" Jayne yells. She's feeding off the energy of the room. She's on a roll and nothing will stop it.

A loud chain drops violently from the ceiling so high in the shadows you wouldn't have known it was there even in this bright room. It clangs and rattles and drops within a foot of her head.

I grab Kelsey's and Kyle's wrist and pull them backwards into the mob. The maniacal sheep don't notice us. Their eyes are fixed on Lilly. People in the back are on each other's shoulders or they're standing on chairs and tables.

Once we're through the crowd I hug the side of the wall and head to hall Evening.

"And with this sacrifice we profess our love!" Jayne shouts like a preacher yells when he has his congregation under his spell.

Lilly's screams are like a gun blasting through the room followed by a gurgling sound and then silence. I hear the chain slowly roll up.

The crowd's in an uproar behind us.

I look over and she's being hoisted into the air naked. She scrapes against the tree. Her neck was cut and the blood scrawls down the tree's trunk.

We walk into hall E and thank, not God that's for sure, that my keys and passcodes and prints still work.

4

We run down the stairs to that dark stone room outside of the children's wing. The lights don't turn on like usual. The only light comes from the staircase.

"My key isn't working," I say.

"What's wrong?" Kyle asks.

"I don't know. Everything else worked. This should work. What the hell?!" I kick the door. I try the lock again and again as my frustration grows.

"Why are you trying to get inside?"

"What?" I turn around and see a dark figure in the corner of the rough stone room.

"Who are you?" Kelsey asks.

The dark figure glides forward in the darkness until he's in the dim light. He locks eyes with me.

"Mark," I say.

"My partner just died. I thought Lilly was your friend and you run down here. Why?"

"They murdered her Mark. Did you see that?" Kyle asks.

"What did you do to her?"

"Nothing. She went on her own and left us before the ceremony. She left to go to you. What did you do to her?" I ask.

"No! What did you do?!" Mark's become belligerent. "I've been nothing but loyal to the movement. I've strained my brain over coming up with ideas. The children's experiments were mine! I'm creating kids so devoted they'll be the best soldiers in the movement. That was me!" He's waving his arms sporadically and with each turn of his head, sweat sprays off. He's pacing while pointing at his chest. "It was me! Doesn't Jayne know! I showed Ian and Isaac! It was me! I would have shown Cody to, but nobody's seen him. What's going on there Miranda?! They think I did something! They knew I was envious of him! Is that why they killed her?!"

"What do you want?" Kelsey asks.

"I want this utopia I was promised! Why does nobody appreciate me?! Why did Cody get promoted and not me?! What's he doing that I'm not?!" He runs at me. His foul breath mixes with mine. I gag.

"What? Do I disgust you Miranda?" Something desperate's rotting inside him.

"I don't know," I shriek against his wrath.

"You know what I found?"

"No," I look away. I won't lower my head in submission but I can't look at him directly.

"Well, I found Cody of all people. In my area of jurisdiction. The area Jayne put me in charge." He's stabbing at his chest with his fingers as he paces. "You know what that stupid idiot did?! He locked himself in one of my rooms! He came down here to check on MY work and locked himself in. Well if you ever want to see your precious Cody again you better listen to me."

He turns away from us. I reach into my pants where I hid Cody's gun.

"They'll hear," Kelsey says.

"What?!" Mark turns around. He looks like a monster. His lips are pulled back exposing his teeth like a rabid horse. "What did you say?" He looks like some biblical beast.

He stomps over smiling and dripping drool. He walks closer to Kelsey until she backs up and hits the wall. He places both hands on either side of her head. Slobber falls out of his mouth and falls on Kelsey's chest. He presses into her. "What did you say?" He asks. He presses into her harder.

"I didn't," She squeaks.

"Who do you think you are?" His nose is touching hers.

I silently walk behind him with the pistol held high and I bring down the butt onto the top of his head. He drops immediately.

"Fuck yeah Miranda!" Kyle runs over.

"He's going to wake up," Kelsey says. She looks down at Mark's body. "This is for Lilly you fucking scum bag." She lifts her heavy boot above his head and stomps on his face.

And again.

And again.

And again.

And again.

And again. All of her anger she has ever stifled in her life is coming through her now.

"AAAAH! You son of a bitch!"

Kyle and I pull her away from him. She's breathing hard and continues to stomp the floor, but there's nothing beneath her boot.

"It's okay. Shhh. It's okay," I embrace her. She keeps stomping. Her face doesn't look like it belongs to her anymore.

Kyle slaps her hard against the cheek.

"What the hell?" She asks. She looks at the mangled remains of Mark's face. He looks like she stuck him in a blender then tried to put his face back together. She looks at Kyle confused.

"You were a badass. That's all you need to know. Let's get in," Kyle searches the corpse. I turn Kelsey away gently. He pulls out a key ring from Mark's pocket followed by a hard kick to his gut.

I unlock the box. I enter my credentials that are thankfully still working. We're in.

5

The children's wing is normal except there's no adults.

"Is there anyone else that comes down here regularly?" Kyle asks me.

"Not that I know of. Lilly and Mark are both dead now."

"Why are they staring at us?" Kelsey asks.

"Well, we look like savage dogs bursting in breathing hard splattered in blood. That might be it," Kyle says.

"Miranda," Brendan, Hailey's little brother, walks over.

"Where's Hailey? Is she alright?" I ask.

"Who are they?" He points at Kelsey and Kyle.

"Friends. You can trust them. Where's Hailey?"

"Her room. She said his voice told her to go to her room and wait."

"Who's he?"

"The boy."

"What boy?"

"The one who was sacrificed thousands of years ago."

"What?"

"Follow me."

We walk down the hallway lined with doors.

"Hailey. They're here," Brendan lets us in.

"Hailey? I brought Kelsey and my friend Kyle with me. He's cool," I sit on her bed where she appears to be sleeping under dark grey blankets.

"Hailey?" I lay a hand on top of her.

"Mom was singing with them. She believes. I watched her pray," Hailey mutters. Her voice is rasp like she's been crying a while.

"She wants you guys back."

"I hope so, but she is one of them now . . ."

"Did I at least help? Did I help anyone?"

"More than you know. Some only blamed it on the devil, but there were plenty who were quiet. I couldn't read them, but silence doesn't mean they believe," I say.

"It means they don't have the balls to do anything. They're sheep."

"They aren't sheep. It's much more complicated than that."

"Did he cut the music?"

"Did who? Wasn't that you?"

"No, it was the boy. He spoke to me in my head. Similar to that monster you saved me from, but he felt good. He's stuck."

"Where's he stuck?"

"I don't know. He said a big room. He also told me there's a lot of big rooms though and several more like his. He's on a tree."

"Oh my God. I think we saw him," I look at Kelsey and Kyle who look equally as freaked out as I feel.

"We need to get out as soon as possible. Has anyone been murdered on a tree yet?"

"Why?" I have a feeling I already know where this is going.

"That's a yes."

I look down.

"It's already started then. More will die in the next few days. That doesn't count the blood they already collected," Hailey says.

"Then what? What are they doing with it?"

"I don't know."

"How? Why don't you know?"

"I wasn't told. Nobody knows. Not even he does."

We're squeezed in Hailey's tiny grey room.

Hailey sits, "I think there's a tunnel that connects everything. I can't leave my Mom though. If we escape she'll be punished and chained up. That's what Mark would tell us. The only thing about the tunnel is . . ."

"Yeah?" Kyle asks.

"Not every place will have a door or an opening or even something you can squeeze through. Some only have a small crack to look into. I think I found the beginning of it, but I don't know for sure. There's so many turns."

"A labyrinth," Kelsey states.

"We need sleep. We can't keep going like this," I say.

"No you don't. I'm really serious. When I step into the tunnels I can stay awake for days. Or at least what I think is days. Sometimes the time goes fast, sometimes slow, sometimes normal. I can't figure it out," Hailey says.

"Is Cody awake?" I ask.

Someone knocks on Hailey's door.

Brendan opens it. "What are you doing?" I lunge for the door, but it's already open.

Daniel and Jacob, the boys from stage 2 of Mark's training, are there. "What? I recognized the knock. Sheesh," Brendan says.

"There's a guy making a lot of noise in the back room and asking to be let out," Daniel, the older brother, says.

"Cody?" I ask

"Hey, you're the lady that saved us."

"I only tried my best not to hurt you."

"No lady. You saved our lives. There were kids who went in there after you left that came out dead.

"Anyways, what do we do with him?" He looks at Hailey like she's the one in charge.

He's become so normalized to this terror. I should have been able to save the others.

"What do you think?" Hailey asks me.

"Huh?" I look up and shake my head. "He could be useful later on. Obviously, Jayne admires him for some reason and you could use him for bargaining if it comes to it," I can't believe I'm bargaining my ex. "He has to stop making noise though."

"I'm on it," Daniel says.

"Wait, what are you going to do? He needs to be okay if Jayne's going to trade him for anything," I say.

"I have this stuff Mark used on us to get us to shut up," Daniel and his little brother leaves.

6

"Brendan. I need you to wait here to warn us if anything happens. If something really bad happens then you go inside the tunnel and stay put. Okay?" Hailey pleads with her little brother, but she's reluctant to leave.

"Got it. I love you," his round eyes are wet.

"I love you too. I'm going to get Mom back."

We enter the tunnel. Brendan rolls the shelf back in front of it.

We turn left towards the Big Room look out. The ceiling remains high, but the walls compress the further we go. Hailey's leading the way with the torch. She knows these tunnels well by now.

"It's right after the walls start to open up again and right before the floor turns into loose rock."

"Here . . .

"Miranda you saved me once from here, but I was able to get in and through it and back out last time on my own. This room gets inside your head. I was stuck for at least a week. I know you said it wasn't a week, but it was. You just don't understand." She looks at Kelsey and Kyle and waits until they seem to take her seriously. "You need to stay quiet. If you hear any noise you need to be as still as a statue. Don't breathe too hard. Do you hear me. This room really fucks with your head."

"How still do we need to be?" Kyle's acting like it's a joke.

"As still as a statue," Hailey presses on.

"I should move?"

"What? No."

"Kyle stop it," Kelsey smacks him.

"This is really serious. I'm going to put the fire out. We need to join hands. We can't lose each other," Hailey stares him down. "No matter the terror you feel, do not let go of each other."

She rubs the torch on the ground and our reality is back to black.

I reach for her hand and for Kelsey's behind me. Hailey squeezes in through the crack pulling me after her. For a moment I'm stuck halfway again and panic starts to rise. It's like my body's inflating.

"Relax. It's okay. Remember to breathe," Kelsey squeezes my hand.

Exhaling, I slide through. Kelsey and Kyle squeeze through.

It's dark, but I can feel the ceiling's high above me. I know I don't need to worry about hitting my head, but there's rocks and other cracks on the ground waiting to grab my ankle with their awakened claws and pull me down. I close my eyes so at least it's my own decision not to see anything. I let Hailey guide us. We're inching along the wall.

Kelsey or Kyle trips over something and the sound reverberates through the hollow space. Hailey stops immediately clutching my hand tightly. I do the same to Kelsey passing the intensity to Kyle. Something scratches my head and I nearly fall from the shock, but I catch myself when Hailey squeezes my hand. My breathing sounds like a choir, but I know I'm breathing slowly and evenly so it can't be as loud as it sounds to me.

My breath gets louder. I know I'm not changing anything. I'm still breathing slow and steady, but it gets even louder which makes me want to panic which makes me want to start breathing and moving. The room starts to fill with my breath. I can feel the wind it's starting to make. It's swirling around us. It's blowing through my hair. I can't make it quieter. I hold my breath and a sound of thunder goes through my ears. I grab my head in agony.

Now it's silent. I listen for any noises.

I wait for Hailey to move, but she doesn't.

My head's starting to pound from not breathing. I try to let a small inhale of breath in, but it comes swooping in all at once in a breath I know for sure was loud.

Hailey yanks on my arm and runs a few paces before stopping again.

The sound of something scurrying along the floor picks up speed and hits the wall where we were. Dirt should have fallen, but nothing falls and barely a sound is made.

"Talk.

"Talk.

"Talk. Say something. It will make the silence better."

"Talk.

"Talk.

"Talk," a voice repeats itself inside my head. It's quiet in here. I can't hear myself breathing. What if I'm not breathing anymore? I feel the dreadful urge to talk.

Kelsey pushes into me slightly causing me to push into Hailey who pulls me to the ground. I lean my head onto her trying to detect what she's doing without letting go of either arm. She's swinging her head like a grandfather clock. I nudge her with my head, but she only continues on until I feel her rocking side to side.

Kelsey pulls on my arm as she stands and lunges forward. We nearly lose touch, but I grab her harder. She lunges again and slips beyond my grasp and her footsteps thud across the floor past me. That scurrying sound follows her and then that same noise is coming from every direction towards me. Fingers brush against my empty hand.

They grasp my fingers. It's Kyle's.

"Talk to me.

Talk.

Talk. I have your hand. Don't you want to run," The voice rings through my head.

I try to let go of the hand, but another arm snatches my elbow still. If it was the voice it would have let me run. I push my head into Hailey until she stops swaying.

She moves silently forward hugging the wall. I want to pull away and find Kelsey, but I know not to. I hear unnatural wet sounds nearby like a cat gorging itself on a slimy mouse, but amplified. I turn towards it with my eyes wide open, but I can't see a thing. The thing's eating. It got Kelsey! Those sounds are it eating her!

"Talk to me. I'll stop. I promise.

Talk.

Talk.

Talk."

It's a trick, I repeat to myself like a mantra.

I let Hailey lead me. She pulls me into a long skinny corridor. I pull on Kyle's hand guiding him in after me.

Hailey lets go and lights the torch.

"We need to go back. We need to get Kelsey. It was eating her," I'm panicking.

They look at me like I've gone insane.

"What are you talking about?" Kyle asks.

"It has her. She ran off. Why aren't you guys taking me seriously?"

"Miranda. I'm right here," I turn around and Kelsey holds my hand.

"What the fuck. Where'd you come from?"

"What do you mean? I was holding your hand the entire time."

"The room messes with your head. Like I said," Hailey says. "Do you see that sliver of light?"

We follow Hailey.

The ceiling gets closer to us as we reach the light. It's a long crack along the ground. We bend down to look inside. It's the kitchen.

"It's Mom. She wasn't here last time," Hailey says. "Mom! Mom! Mom!" She whispers loudly.

A member in white with a dark red belt walks by. He stops and looks around. He pulls a radio off his belt, but then puts it back on without saying anything. He waits there and then walks on. He has a pistol on his side.

"You need to be more careful," I say.

"This is my first time seeing her this closely since we were separated. I need to talk to her."

Lauren, dressed in forest green, stops directly beneath us. She's chopping something. We're looking at the top of her head. "Mom," She tries again, but quieter.

"Hailey?" She looks around frantically. She looks at the member in white and goes back to chopping. "It's all in my head. It's all in my head," She says to herself.

"Mom please, it's me."

Lauren ignores her daughter.

"Mom. I'm finding a way out. I'm in a series of hidden tunnels. Don't do anything drastic. Me and Brendan are safe. I'm with Miranda and a couple others. Do you remember her? I'm going to find a way to your room. If not I'll find another way to contact you."

Lauren nods.

"Let's keep going. It looks like she didn't get completely turned by Jayne. She was probably doing whatever was necessary to get to you and your brother," I say hoping that was the truth.

We're crawling over loose rocks now.

"Watch your heads," Kelsey says. "Actually it might be a good idea to wrap our shirts around our heads like helmets."

I turn around to see her and Kyle wrapping their shirts around their heads. Kelsey's white bra glows in the torch light.

Hailey and I do the same.

Not a minute later I smack into something hanging from the ceiling. I reach for blood, but there's none. It only hurts. The shirt worked.

The tunnel's closing in tighter from all sides until we're on our bare bellies. I don't notice the scratches. My adrenaline's high.

"Are you sure this is the way?" I ask.

"No," Hailey calls back.

The sound of a train coming roars in the tiny space. The entire place starts to shake and I feel rocks beneath me begin to move. I don't know what's under us. It could be a thousand foot drop.

"What do we do?!" Kelsey yells.

The train's blaring its deafening horn and the engine's getting louder. It's getting closer. I can't do anything but lay here with my hands over my head. I'm trapped.

"Keep going!" Hailey barely makes a sound over the oncoming train.

I'm crawling as fast as I can. My head continues to lightly bump the low ceiling. If I didn't put the shirt on I would be a bloody mess by now if not passed out.

The train pushes out its longest and most screeching whistle yet. Screams come from everywhere. The tunnel sounds like the inside of a drum now. I keep crawling until I fall a foot. I was sure that drop was going to be the end of me.

It's silent again. Kelsey falls in after me and then Kyle. I stand up shaking in the small room we fell into.

"There's an extra torch!" I say running over to the wall. I grab for it, but it disappears. "Where'd it go? You saw that right?" I look at them for validation.

"What the hell was that?" Kyle asks. "What the fuckity fuck fucking fuck is this place?"

"Food!" Kelsey runs to the other side of the wall grabbing at the air. She drops her arms in defeat. "It's gone."

"There's a TV!" Kyle runs to the center and sits. He's using an imaginary remote. "There's nothing good on.

Wait! Where did it go?!"

"Mom!" Hailey runs and crawls into a hole dropping the torch before she disappears.

"Hailey wait!" I pick the torch up. Three different holes tunnel away from here.

"The food! It's back! There's burgers and hot dogs and Mac and cheese!" Kelsey's grabbing at the air. She looks to be piling food onto a plate. She's in ecstasy as she's shoveling air into her mouth.

"Guys, there's doors on two of these holes," I say turning back around to see Kyle angrily flipping through the "channels." He seems to decide on one.

"You didn't have to do that," he's crying.

"One hole without a door." I open the one on the left and music fills the space. Rock music I used to listen to nearly everyday pre-bomb is flowing out. I close it in a hurry. That's not real.

I open the one on the right skipping the center one. The door on the right is an exit! "I found the exit! Guys look! Blue Sky! There it is!" I start crawling through, but I feel a light touch on my ankle that makes me stop.

"It's not real. Your friends need you. Hailey's in the middle tunnel alone in the dark. Stay focused. Everyone needs you," a boys voice softly floats into my head.

I squirm back out. Kelsey's on the floor rubbing her belly. She looks too full to move even though she didn't eat a bite.

"Oooooh. I think I'm going to be sick. I ate too much," She rolls over on her side. I swear I can hear her belly gurgling.

Mark's in the fetal position sobbing. "They didn't have to kill that character off. The directors should fucking die. That's not okay." He tucks his head into his knees.

I pull Kyle up. It's like he doesn't see me or feel me pulling on him, but he follows my guidance nonetheless. I lead him to the center hole and start pushing him into it until he starts crawling on his own.

I turn to get Kelsey. She's dry heaving on her hands and knees. "Too much food, but it was sooo good."

I pull her up and just like Kyle, she mindlessly follows me. I push her through and follow them.

I crawl through with the light, which leads to a long tunnel of normal height. Hailey, Kelsey, and Kyle slump against the wall and stare up at me with huge uncertain eyes.

"What happened?" They mutter.

"I don't know, but we need to keep going."

7

Doors of every shape and size line the tunnel. Some are on the ceiling and some are on the walls. They're wooden with old metal fixtures.

The first one we come to is a small square door in the ceiling. Only a foot across. It looks like it should be deteriorating, but it's mummified.

"Hailey, get on my shoulders," Kyle bends over.

I'm reminded of her age once again as she effortlessly pops up.

"Well, what do you hear?" He asks.

"Someone praying, I think."

He puts her down.

"Let's open this one," Hailey puts her hand on a door that's taller than me and wider than all of us put together. I press my ear against it. I don't hear anything. I barely open the door. Its hinges screech. It reveals a stone slab behind it. Looks like the kind to roll over. I squeeze my fingers into a notch in the side and I pull it along the wall. It opens to a small bedroom. The door's an entire wall. A small grey bed and a wooden dresser painted grey is beside it.

"Is anyone living in here?" I ask.

"Look," Hailey points under the bed. "There's boots."

We hear talking outside of the door and slink back inside lugging the stone door shut. It closes with a loud thump. The talkers enter the grey room.

"What was that noise?" A man with a squeaky voice asks.

"No idea. Who cares man. Worship's soon and I'm not gonna be late. They've been giving out the fun stuff almost every time now," another man with a forgettable voice responds.

"You buying that shit bro?"

"Nah, I just like the shit they give us. I don't do all that breathing bullshit. I just close my eyes and go in my own world. I guess you could call that meditative."

They laugh.

"Same bro."

We walk on.

"That was a good sign right?" Hailey holds the torch. I gave it back earlier.

"They also don't sound angry with the setup though," Kyle says.

"They will be," Hailey says.

"You have such an ominous tone towards everything for a kid."

"I'm not a kid. I'm 13. Trust me, they'll get angry. They need to. I guess Jayne had some truth in that "on fire" crap. We need people really angry if we're gonna end this."

We stop at a tall skinny door and hear people praying. A small latch above us has the sound of people praying also. A large latch above us has the sound of someone praying. A door on the left has the sound of a man praying and so does the next door on the right.

We frantically pass the doors stopping briefly to listen at each one.

"We must be in hall Clarity or Demo. That's where the newer recruits were moved to. I would have recognized the voices by now if they were in the small counsel," I say.

"Guys hold up," Kelsey calls us back. Her ear's pressed against a short wide door. "It's a woman saying Hailey over and over again."

Hailey runs into Kelsey. I lean in. "Hailey, Hailey, Hailey, please find me. Hailey, Hailey, Hailey, please hear me. I need to go soon. Hailey, Hailey-"

Hailey swings the door open and pulls the stone aside. The entrance is blocked by a bed. "Mom! It's me!"

Lauren's trying to drag the bed while we push on it. It's heavy, but it starts to slide and eventually we can squeeze in.

Lauren grabs Hailey and swings her in the air. They're both crying. I tear up too. It's the kind of hug that happens when people didn't know if they would ever see each other again. The kind you see after disasters or when men and women come back from deployment. Although it's a reunion, it's an intense feeling of pure sadness.

We're in a large room with three beds. Two of them have been empty for some time now. And a toilet in the corner with a grey curtain around it.

"How'd you find me? What's going on?" Lauren asks Hailey. She narrows in on me, "You." She points stepping closer. "It's all your fault we're in this mess."

"Whoa now," Kyle steps between us. "You came into that shelter in Santa Cruz of your own free will. You also don't strike me as stupid so you at least had an inclination of what was going on there. You were wise to distance yourself, but you still took advantage of the protection because you knew it was best for your kids. You also could probably guess if you stayed put you would've all been murdered. And not necessarily by outsiders. She did what she thought was right and so did I and it probably ended up saving your life up to this point."

All the energy Lauren mustered escapes her. She looks weak. Her arms hang limply and the effort she takes to blink seems like too much. Looking at her I realize how tired I am. How tired we all are. We have large dark circles under our eyes, which is only amplified by our ghostly pale skin. We haven't seen the sun in so long. Kelsey's roots are darker than the rest of her blonde hair. She's usually outside gardening or sitting watching birds and without the sun her hair is darkening.

"I'm sorry," Lauren starts.

I cut her off, "It's okay."

"Where's Brendan?"

"He's safe Mom," Hailey says. "We're trying to find a way out or answers or something. Something much larger's about to happen. I can feel it. We need to stop it from happening."

"They're going to expect me back in the kitchen in a couple hours."

"How long has it been sense they murdered Lilly?" Kyle asks. "Also mind if I?" He gestures at the toilet.

"Go for it," Lauren says. "It's been. I would say at least six days."

"What?! No, oh God. Hopefully Brendan went into the tunnel or everything's normal. I don't know. I wouldn't be able to hear any warnings, but I think I would sense if something really bad was happening over there," Hailey rambles. "What about the time it was since we saw you in the kitchen?"

"That was a few minutes ago. Why?"

Kyle walks back, "No fucking way. Not after what we went through."

"What are you guys talking about?"

"Time's really funny in the tunnels Mom. I can't explain it. Have they done anything else since then like what they did to their friend?"

"No."

"Anyone gone missing?"

"No."

[pause]

"Actually, yeah there's been a few people I've stopped seeing, but nobody says anything about it so I assumed they got moved to a different area. Socialization between the departments are seldom."

"We have to keep going," I say.

"I'll go with," Lauren says.

"Actually," I look at Hailey, "I'm sorry, but we need your Mom to do something else. It just occurred to me.

"Lauren, I need you to learn how many people are devoted, how many people don't care. The ones that are just here for safety and food. And most importantly the people actively against what's happening. Those who have had their kids stolen from them would be a good start. But they also might be harder to learn the truth from. Can you do that?"

"I can't go with you?"

"No."

"You'll keep my kids safe?"

"With my life."

"If it has to be done to get out of here."

"Be ready when I need you. I don't know how we're going to get out of this, but be ready."

8

As we walked down the hall it shrunk in size until only one person could fit at a time. We arrived at the top of a spiraling staircase.

"Do you mind leading?" Hailey hands me the torch.

"Are you okay? I mean, everything considered?"

"I want to step back and let you lead."

I hold the torch in front of me and take the first hesitant step down the stairs. They're rough, but solid. It feels ancient. They smell like the past. It's not the smell of a cave, but of a community long ago whose smells were trapped in this staircase. The flickering of the flame pushes back the darkness making room for us to descend. The darkness closes back immediately like we were a submarine traveling through the deep ocean. We disturbed the air for a second just like the submarine does the water, but then everything flows back to normal like we were never present. The light is our submarine; if we step outside it we could die.

"This is taking forever," Kyle complains.

"Don't be such a baby. We haven't even been going down that long," Hailey says.

The further down we go the smoother the stones look as if they were worn down. I brush my finger along the wall expecting to collect centuries of dust, but dust would mean activity and life. Caves are sterile environments. Nothing moves this far below ground. Nothing can live this far down. Just smooth rock sliding under my finger from millions of years ago when this cave was formed by rushing waters, then stairs were carved, then abandoned with who knows what in between.

We continue walking in silence. Our footsteps sound muted. I'm aware of the crackling in the fire, but it seems to be hushed. The space doesn't believe we are here or I don't think we're really here.

We continue to climb deeper into the Earth.

I watch my feet as I step down.

"I hate to annoy, but this is going on forever. It's making me nervous," Kelsey interrupts the silent descent.

"I'm sure we're almost there. Right Hailey?"

"My legs are getting tired of this motion."

And on we go.

We step and step.

I'm tracing my finger along the forever curving wall.

I start to thump against it. It's almost melodic.

Thump . . . thump . . . thump thump thump.

Kyle starts to clap softly along to the beat I created.

Hailey starts to whistle.

Kelsey steps with varying pressure adding to our beat.

We're creating a song together. Unlike the other rooms that amplified sound to no end, this staircase seems to suck our sound from us. It sounds hollow and empty, but it's nice to create sound. To make some permanent presence in here before it swallows us. This skinny, claustrophobic staircase truly is like dipping into the deep ocean and nothing noticing you. Are you truly there if nothing is altered? If no sound penetrates the space around you? If no footprints or particles of sand are moved?

It's like when I've been driving for hours without stopping. I go into an auto pilot consciousness and when I eventually stop the car, the world doesn't stop moving with it. For a few seconds the world continues to glide past me as my eyes adjust away from the constant movement of the vehicle. I'm waiting for the staircase to end. We still haven't discovered another room or any alteration in our environment.

The staircase tries to suck our creation away, but we keep making sound expanding the space this darkness is making for us. It's difficult to keep with the beat, but without speaking we know we need to make our presence known here. Instead of being still as a statue we need to move and make noise or we will be turned to stone. An invisible urge comes over us to persevere, but the staircase's silence is alluring. The more noise we make it seems like the more light the fire creates therefore creating more space for us to travel through.

"These are a lot of steps," I say dropping my hand from the wall cutting the music off. "My knees are achy."

"Why don't we rest a while? I'm getting sleepy," Kelsey says.

"That doesn't make sense. I'm draining, but these caves have let us retain our adrenaline since we got in here. I only felt exhausted at Lauren's," Kyle says.

"Let's keep going," Hailey says.

And on we go, deeper still.

"No this is bullshit! We should turn around," Kyle snaps.

"And go where?" I ask.

"Well, where the hell are we going right now?"

I don't need to say anything to tell him we don't have an ending in mind. We're just going.

I sway the torch in front of me with each step I take furthering me away from the surface. The walls dance from the fiery light bouncing off of them. It's creating its own art so effortlessly. The fire must be so comfortable sitting on the stick. It doesn't have to worry about getting people out of a weird cave. It gets to sway and swoosh any way it wants. It does its job and that's all it needs to do.

And on we go descending the stairs.

I stop abruptly. "What was that?"

"What?" Kyle asks.

"Did you not hear something like a whisper?"

They shake their heads no.

"No, there's something."

"You've lost it. I regret to tell you, but this time none of us are hearing nothin'. This tunnel's empty," Kyle says. "Unnaturally empty. Even for a cave."

"It's in my head. That's it! I need to listen inside."

"Turn," a voice says.

"What?"

"None of us said anything," Kelsey looks concerned.

"Turn around," the voice continues.

"It says to turn around."

"He," Hailey corrects me like she was correcting a mispronunciation. "He sounds like a boy right? Was it a kind voice or was it bad?"

"Kind!"

"Turn around or be stuck descending forever," the voice rings louder in my head. I need to make sure this isn't a trick, but I don't think any of us can keep going down this staircase any longer.

"We have to turn around," I squeeze past them in the tiny space trying not to hit anyone with the fire.

"Fuck that! We've been descending for God knows how long. Going back up all those steps and through all that again will destroy us," Kyle's becoming flustered.

I walk up the staircase. I know Hailey and Kelsey will follow me. Kyle will follow because it's either that or be left alone in the dark.

I climb a few steps and then I'm at the entrance to a room several stories high.

"What the hell man?! Why can't these rooms just not fuck with my mind?!" Kyle says to no one.

I walk into the long room. We head for a large relief sculpture on the opposite wall. I trace the torch as high as it will go. I can barely make out any shapes above this thick barrel of protruding stone.

"It's a stone tree!" Kelsey exclaims.

I step back and hold the flame as high as I can reach and I can see the bottoms of the branches snaking along the wall.

"Do you hear that?" I walk back to the tree and press my ear against where the trunk meets the rest of the rock. "Guys, I hear voices."

They rush over pressing their ears to the wall.

". . . have five escapees this morning. After speaking with them, we learned they were going to sell our information and tactics to The Nothings!"

Strangely, the speaker isn't Jayne. The voice reminds me of Mikaela. She's yelling like a preacher, but I can barely make the words out.

"That's fucking Mikaela," Kyle says. "I know. I had to work with her and watch her go crazy with power."

"What's she doing speaking? Do you think it's the Big Room on the other side?" I ask.

"Of course, she's now speaking on the microphone. If there was one thing that cunt loved, that was speaking to an audience. I don't now how she swindled Jayne into letting her speak . . ."

"That makes perfect sense actually. How am I still putting Jayne on a pedestal. I still wanna believe in the movement. This isn't fair. I could have ran away long ago, but I stayed because I believed in Jayne. This isn't fair. It's not fair," Kyle slides to the ground and leans against the stone tree.

". . . sacrifice . . ." Mikaela's voice caught our attention.

"Oh no." I strain to listen.

"Their blood will run down this tree and into the river around the room. The gap along the perimeter might be the biggest in history and maybe the biggest in the world compared to other shelters, but we will fill it. This is a long standing religion and we will make a stance with our group that is on fire for God! We will give back to the trees. We will fuel God!"

The crowd's cheering. The crowd's also shouting angrily. I hoped those were aimed at her and the counsel, but they're directed at the people who tried to escape.

"Please don't hurt us!" One of the members yell.

I don't recognize the voice.

"Please! I promise you, we don't know anything about The Nothings! It's all a lie! I swear!" another is pleads through their cries.

"You admitted it. You admitted working for them. It's over for you now," Mikaela says calm. The kind of calm a leader has when they know they have the power and they can say whatever they want and nobody would dare challenge them.

"NOOO! We didn't confess! Everyone listen to me!" The voice is drowned by the devotees cheers and yelling. "Jayne, Mikaela, Isaac; They all lie! Listen to me!" The person keeps trying.

Mikaela laughs and the devotee's stop shouting.

"I promise you I know nothing of any of this! We didn't confess! You know what I think?! I think the New World Freedom is The Nothings. These people that are about to MURDER us are the Order Through Chaos! That's what I think! They aren't saving y-" A gun shot goes off.

"Order Through Chaos will stop at nothing to end us! We are everything they are not. They send people in to do the devil's work. I have heard God speak to me through prayer. And so can you. You can ask him yourself to absolve you of any doubts. You are the chosen ones to carry out this message," Mikaela sings out soaking up the attention. The devotees cheer her on. "The more you show us, the more Jayne and I will need you to be part of the inner group and then you will have a direct hand in saving the world.

"First, we need to show God that we are devoted. Then he will send his guardian angels to protect us as we move out of our Haven and join with others." An eruption of loud cheering follows.

"Now!" She yells.

The sounds of chains being unrolled is mixed with the cheers and shouts of a manipulated congregation. They drop to the floor in a clunk that rings out doom.

The rest of the attempted escapee's agonizing screams penetrate through the rest of the noise as they call out for mercy. The damned scream fuck you and shout about lies and deceit.

The chains are moving again, presumably upwards. The victims go silent, but their silence is replaced with the devotee's shouts like nobody paused for a breath after their death. I can picture them now, hanging on chains dragging against the stone tree. Their throats are cut and blood's pouring down the grey rock and into the "river" of blood.

Hailey runs to the opposite side of the room to retch.

I go after her, but I left my torch leaning against the stone tree. The shadows are long, but dull as I head to the stalagmite she ran behind.

"I can see! It's not just the glow of the fire, but I can see the back of this stalagmite and other shapes that should be cast in complete shadow right now!" I yell.

"Oh my God. Where's that coming from?" Kelsey runs down the long skinny corridor.

"Don't trip! It's only faint!"

Hailey stands up and runs after me as I sprint the entire distance of the chamber as if I'm running the long nave of a church. Ian's close behind Kelsey. We slow down as we get further away from the fire because although we can see, it's like turning off the lights and shutting the windows in a house. It's dark, but it's not a complete absence of light anymore.

We turn our heads towards the ceiling. A small dull light in the corner shines with salvation.

"We only found another room. That's it," my body deflates. "We need the torch if we're going to continue on." I walk back.

"It's not the right color. It's yellow, not bright white. It has to be a real exit," Hailey fills with joy.

"There are rooms down here with yellow light and candles. It doesn't mean anything."

It takes forever to walk back and grab the torch and return to the group. We're so close, yet so far away.

"Where's Hailey?" I ask.

Kyle points at the light. Hailey's climbing the wall on a swinging ladder. She's at least 20 feet in the air now. She disappears through the opening. I hold my breath terrified she rolled into Jayne's weird ass "meditation" room or her office or the chapel, God forbid, or something worse.

I wait for the nightmare to be revealed.

"I'm out! I'm really out! Get up here!" She pokes her head back in.

I feel like I'm in a dream or a slow motion movie. I climb the ladder. It's swinging and creaking. I normally would have guffawed at the notion of climbing this. Heights make me shake, which tricks my balance, but after everything I find myself climbing the rope ladder. I'm terrified and I want to shit myself, but I'm not shaking. I'm focused.

I reach the top and my hands brush grass as I grasp for a hand hold. I can't see anything, but the beautiful blue sky. I reach blindly and grip onto what feels like wood to either side of the hole.

I pull myself through enough to see I'm at the base of the largest oak tree I've ever seen. I grab the root base and drag myself out.

I slump over the base of the enormous tree.

"I feel grass!" I roll away from the hole and rub my face in the vegetation. I hit the ground and turn over on it relishing the feeling of living plants.

The smell of the earth is orgasmic. Not the cold, sterile, old, stale smell of the cave, but the rich fullness of soil that's teaming with life. I relish in the fact little bugs and microbes are beneath me.

Kelsey tumbles out the base between two log sized roots.

The sky's so blue. I stand in the light. In the natural light. A butterfly flutters past me and there's deer in the distance.

Kyle crawls out.

I can breathe again.

"Hands in the air!" A bullhorn blasts as a swarm of people in varying uniforms come flooding out of the nearby oak grove pointing guns at us.

Chapter 15

1

"Hands in the air I said!" A man yells into his bullhorn.

"Please don't hurt us," I plead.

"Oh my God. Jayne was right. It's The Nothings. They're pretending to be the military. Why'd we leave?" Kyle asks.

"Silence!"

People wearing varying official uniforms surround us. Some are in camo. They're bearing a wide variety of patches from different countries. There's plenty of American flags on chests, but there's also the Canadian flag, the Mexican flag, and the British Flag.

A man with an American patch and a thick mustache walks in front of the man with the bullhorn and says, "The Nothings are down below."

"What are you saying?" Kyle throws his arms out.

"Miranda, I don't understand," Kelsey mutters to me.

I glance back at the oak where we climbed out from between it's roots. My stomach sinks to the floor. "There has to be some misunderstanding," I say.

The bullhorn guy says, "Hands up!"

"They go by other names too. We saw you come out of the ground. We've been searching this countryside for months to no avail. Who are you? Are you one of them?"

I take the lead, "I'm Miranda. We aren't a part of that group. I mean we were. Yes. But no. We aren't. We escaped."

"You escaped?" He asks suspiciously.

"Please listen to me. There's some fucked up shit going on down below. We need your help."

"I don't believe them Miranda," Kyle says.

"Are you really claiming they," I point to the ground, "are The Nothings? That isn't possible."

I look at the uniformed people expecting someone to tell me the truth, but they avert their eyes.

"They're lying," Kyle says.

The man scratches his mustache ignoring Kyle. "You're in shock."

"To hell I am," Kyle waves his hands. "You're lying. I met members of The Nothings and they were not the same!"

"Did they say they were members of The Nothings or did your leader tell you they were?" The man asks.

His question silences us.

He continues, "We know this is a cult that's been around for hundreds of years. We already initiated the shut down of two other camps. We know what they've done and what they're planning. We know they were responsible for the bombs inside the US."

"Responsible for the bombs! Ah Jesus Christ," Kyle says.

"Is the world over? Is it World War 3?" I ask.

"No," The man laughs. "The world's fine, but America is not. We've been able to keep this cult at bay in the other countries. We've been working tirelessly for the past ten months."

"Ten months?!" Kyle yells.

"My arms are getting really tired," Hailey says.

"You can put your arms down."

"No they can't," the man with the bullhorn says.

The mustache man only has to give him a look. "You can put them down. My name's Henson by the way."

"Ten months? That's not possible. It hasn't been that long. A few months at the most."

"I understand this must be very confusing for you. It's not uncommon. We plan to infiltrate the Haven. Will you help us?"

"Will anyone get hurt?" Hailey asks.

"Unfortunately, that's a risk. It depends entirely on what they do."

"You can't hurt anyone!" Hailey runs over, but she's stopped by a woman who sprints up and shoves her away from him.

"I'm sorry little one. We can't take too many precautions. These are dangerous people as I'm sure you're aware of."

"I'm not little," Hailey mutters.

"We know they stock pile weapons. How many or how dangerous is unknown," the man continues.

"I don't know all that about the weapons, but there are innocent people. A huge wing is full of children. That girl you pushed," I glare at the woman, "-has her Mom and little brother trapped down there. Both innocent."

"How did you find a way to escape?"

"Dude, that's a long story," Kyle walks over, but stops when several officers step towards him.

"Will you help us then? With your help we may see this to the end with limited fatalities," Henson looks at me.

"We barely know how we got out. It's a labyrinth. I do know of another entrance though."

"Where is it?"

"I don't know where it is from here because I don't know where we are right now."

The man steps so close I can smell his aftershave. "How do I know you didn't know we were coming and this is a trap?"

Kyle clenches his fists, "You fuck heads are interrogating the wrong people! We're running out of time. They're sacrificing people. Did you hear that? Sacrificing! How do we know you're who you say you are? That's exactly what Jayne and Mikaela taught people. That The Nothings, which could be all of you," Kyle dramatically points at them, "-are trying to get inside and kill everyone. How do we know to trust you?"

"Well, I don't reckon you have a choice right now if you want to save your friends. I can't do anything to convince you I'm not lying. I see that your friend here," He glances at me, "is hiding a pistol in her waste band right now. Any of us could have killed her, but we didn't."

"Now are you going to help me or what?" He asks me.

"This is exactly what we were warned about. That The Nothings dress up as the military, but it's false and you would be here to kill us. They just found people who were working with The Nothings - or so Jayne said. How do we know you aren't?" I ask.

"Obviously you're terrified," The man softens. Not by much. "The Nothings are down below. It's the same group. I know nothing I could say that will make you believe me. Your leader isn't lying though."

"What?!" Kyle flails his arms in the air.

"I mean your leader isn't wrong that there were people who were a part of The Nothings or New World Freedom that were dressing up as the military. They did that so you wouldn't trust anyone."

"I'm not sure."

"You said people are getting sacrificed. This is urgent. I won't let this happen again."

The man with the bullhorn blares, "How do you know this isn't a trap Henson?"

"Will you turn that damn thing off Parker?"

"But sir," he begins without the bullhorn.

"I'm not having another massacre on my hands like what happened in Idaho. Do you not see these fucking people Parker? They look scared shitless. Look at their eyes for Christ sake if you don't believe me. They don't look like the leaders we've captured in the past. They're pale and sickly looking. They're not a threat. Do you see how bony they are?"

"We could die," Parker says.

"So could the hundreds down there."

"Over a thousand," Kyle corrects him.

If I don't make a decision soon I could potentially cause the murder of more people. But, if I'm wrong then I could potentially kill everyone like Jayne said would happen.

Finally I say, "Well you could climb down the way we came up. There's a shared wall between the room we were in and the Big Room."

"The big room?"

"It's this enormous room. Like a common space. Food and speeches and well, anything. Can't you blow up the shared wall and storm in?" I ask.

He sighs a breath of relief, laughs at the sky, then turns his attention back to me. "Well you must not be very high in the ranks if you think that's a feasible option. They not only have weapons, but they also have small time terrorist toys such as loads of poisonous gas. They also have arms out the wahoo. So no we cannot take this base by force especially if what you're saying is true, that there's children and innocents down there. We can't risk killing any more than we have to. I'm not gonna let it happen. Hopefully no one at all will die if we can help it. We need to be smart."

"What do we do then?"

"I think I have an idea, but you'll have to go back down there with us."

"I mean I can try, but honest to . . . well honestly I don't know how we got here. The cave fucks with your head and time's distorted and your own reality's pulled and squished until you aren't sure what's real anymore. I'm wondering if I'm still in the cave and this whole conversation isn't real."

Henson turns around, "See Parker? You can't fake that kind of trauma and fear."

Henson looks at us with sorrow, "That's commonly seen in people who've spent a long time in caves."

"No. That's the thing. We weren't down there that long," as I said that I knew it wasn't true by the expression on their faces.

"Don't give us those pitying looks," Kyle huffs, but his weariness makes his voice come out as a struggled whisper.

"We're going to have to take our chances. The thing about caves, besides the guarantee that getting lost and starving to death is the most probable possibility, is there's always more passages."

"It's a long fall to the bottom. You have to climb an old rope ladder." I can already feel vertigo rushing back and my face flushing.

Henson nods and grabs the roots to either side of the hole and lets his feet dangle until he finds the rope ladder. He looks up, "Alright who's coming? I need at least five soldiers with me. I would appreciate it if you guys would come down with us. If not, I can make do with a few more of my men and women."

"I'm going," Hailey says immediately.

"How old are you?" He sticks his head back out.

"18. Why?"

"Is that true Miranda?" He asks me.

I nearly correct her, but decide better. "Yes."

"If you say so. What's your name little fire ball?"

"Hailey."

"And what about you two?"

"Yeah, alright, fucking fuck me am I right? I'm Kyle. Let's get back down to those demon filled tunnels."

"I'm Kelsey."

"Are you coming sweetie?"

"Don't call me sweetie . . ."

"Yes. I'm coming."

"Thank you Kelsey," He respectfully nods.

I'm moving a lot slower than I was. The exhaustion's hitting and it's hitting hard. Have we slept? Would I even know if I slept down there? I slug my way to the bush feeling a hundred pounds heavier even though I know I must weigh next to nothing. Kelsey's lost any extra pudge she used to carry. We look terrible in the light.

2

"Are you guys tired anymore?" I ask once we're back inside. A small taste of freedom and now we're here again.

They shake their heads, but they look apprehensive to go any further. In fact all the soldiers seem to have caught the weight of this place.

"Are we going to come up with a plan?" Hailey asks.

"You're quite the brave one, aren't ya?" Henson asks.

"What in the actual?" A woman is looking at the tree sculpture with her headlight. She looks down and follows the wall until she hits a huge pile of boulders leaning against it. Directly next to the thinnest part between here and the Big Room. She inspects the ground closer. "What's this?"

"What's what?" I walk over. I'm surprised Henson let me keep my gun in my pocket, but it's not like I can use it down here anyways unless I want to alert every living and non-living soul trapped down here of our presence. Also, with this construction going on I don't want to make any extra loud sounds that could cause a collapse.

She holds her finger up caked in thick blood. "It's some channel carved into the floor," She says.

"If there's wet blood then it must be flowing from the Big Room. There must be an entrance," I say as we crowd around her.

"How did we miss this?" Hailey asks.

"The boulders are blocking any entrance we would have seen," Kelsey places a hand on Hailey's back.

"How do I get out of this room?" Henson asks.

"We came in through a stairwell of sorts," I say.

"Where?"

"It's right there behind you," I say as I look around them and see the stairs are gone. Nothing is there, but a thin fracture in the rock.

"Are you alright to continue forth Miranda?."

"It was right here," Kyle slaps the wall. He tries to push his arm through the fracture, but to no prevail. "I swear it was here," He looks crazy as he continues to slap the wall. "It was right here."

"We can work with this," the woman at the boulder pile says.

The small channel encircles the entire room just like it did in the Big Room and just like it did in that ancient room we found with the dead boy.

"I can have sleeping gas sent down here. We can pump it through this hole or drain or whatever the fuck it is that leads into this Big Room of yours. It won't do any good if we can't find a way in first though," he looks at me, Kelsey, Kyle, and finally Hailey. "One of you needs to find a way in."

"You said the kids have their own wing right?"

"Sort of. You need credentials to get in and it's possible they blocked mine by now."

"What about Mark's master key to the wing?" Hailey asks.

"Once they discovered his dead body with the missing keys there's no way they didn't reprogram the security systems."

"They could have been distracted though."

"Get it from Jayne or Isaac. I'm sure they have something. At the very worst, cut off their hands to use as finger prints along with any keys they have," Kelsey says.

"Well, damn Kelsey," Kyle says.

"What? They're going to be passed out anyways. Who cares if they lose their hands right?" Kelsey looks at Henson for support.

He nods.

"The kids won't trust you without me," Hailey says knowing I was already going to be the one to volunteer.

"Why would the kids trust you?" Henson narrows his eyes, "How old are you really?"

"Yeah I'm younger, but I'm the one who discovered the tunnels. None of this would be possible without me. You and all your fancy soldiers would still be up there twiddling your thumbs."

"You don't need to convince me. You can go."

"How?" She asks. At times she seems beyond age like she has the life experience of a 50 year old. At other times the way she asks questions is how a girl would ask her parents for help on something she couldn't understand.

"You know these caves a lot better than I do. You can figure it out," Henson says with a gentle paternal tone. "When you get into that room, what you call the Big Room, give me a signal so I know you're ready. I'm going to get those gas masks sent down here."

"I'll yell out, "Jesus is Father," Hailey says.

"Won't that get mixed in with the other religious zealots?"

"It won't. Nobody says that. I've heard them snap at people for saying that because they say Jesus is not the Father."

"Won't that make you stand out?"

"It'll sound like the other shouting."

"One moment," Henson marches to the ladder and returns with boxes of masks and gas canisters. "Don't forget the goggles."

I turn back to where the stairs used to be. "How the hell did we get in here? It couldn't have disappeared. We were probably delusional when we got in and forgot the way," I say.

"There's more ways," Hailey says.

"How do you know?" I walk to the boulder pile.

"The boy told me."

"There's got to be a way a through these boulders."

I crawl into the first hole, but it's a dead end. I shimmy back out and try for a long crack, but it's also a dead end.

I squeeze into a small opening at ground level.

"Hailey follow me, but be careful. These rocks are balanced precariously on each other."

We could grab the wrong hand hold at any minute and the earth would tumble inwards. It feels like the rocks have been waiting to wake up and fall.

"Wait, where are you?" Hailey asks. "I can barely see anything."

"I'm coming for you," I shimmy backwards and stand up and climb into another skinny hole. "I see you, just back up and then follow me closely. Watch for the drop."

The boulder's are covered in dirt from the erosion that caused them to collapse in on each other long ago. It doesn't feel natural. No stalactites have formed. It feels fresh.

"Hailey, this collapse was caused by humans."

"You're right. I bet a hall collapsed. It must've been huge. There's so many rocks."

"It could still be unstable."

We crawl downwards through any space we can squeeze through.

3

"There's a light's over here. It might just be my imagination. It's extremely faint," I say.

I can hardly see her, but there's enough light to see her carefully trying to move forward without bumping other rocks. A scraping sound comes from above her and she freezes.

"Hailey! Get over here!"

She looks at the dust that's circling the air above her. I can taste it.

"Move!"

She can't hear me over the noise that resembles a mud slide before it breaks. A deep rumbling in the Earth. The rocks are waking up angrily as they scream at us.

"Move!" I yell.

The boulders begin to move.

"Hailey! Your Mom and brother need you! Fucking move!"

Instead of moving the obvious way towards me she takes the closest route, which causes her to squeeze through two boulders that may also collapse on top of her. She's stuck in the tiny gap between them.

I lunge at her amidst the dust and rumbling sounds. A large boulder above me drops a millimeter. More rocks above it are beginning to move.

"Breathe in!" I yell.

I yank her through and she tumbles on top of me. The rock above where she was immediately collapses closing the space we were in.

The dust settles and it's quiet again. "We're stuck," I say.

"There's light," Hailey points above us. "I can see light."

"Let's do this slowly."

We brace ourselves against the rock where light's seeping around its edges. My veins bulge as I push against it.

With our combined strength it slowly creaks open. Light floods into our rock hole. I'm barely able to squeeze through, but there's something massive in the way.

"It's the underside of a couch," I whisper.

"What do we do?"

The whole is too tight for her to crawl up and help me. I squeeze my arms through and pull on the front edge.

It screeches.

The couch moves on it's own.

"They found us," I say.

"What?" Hailey asks.

"What the hell?" I hear above me.

A face looks down at us, but the light makes it a silhouette.

"Do we call out for Henson?" Hailey asks.

"Hailey?"

"Mom?"

Lauren grabs my arms and pulls me through. She practically throws me aside to help Hailey through.

"Oh my God. You're still okay. It's been so long. Where'd you go?" Lauren asks Hailey.

"It's a long story. Can anyone see us?"

"Everyone's at the tree."

"Use your shirt as a mask Mom and get as close as you can to the children's wing as fast as you can."

"Be inconspicuous, but don't go yet," I add.

Hypnotic worship music surrounds us. They're singing the same three lines continuously. The lights have been dimmed and the focus is on the tree. The red emergency lights are pointing at it. A few stragglers sit with lost expressions on the couches and tables.

I make a mental note of this couch so I don't forget it just in case.

We're holding our respirators and goggles. We're terribly obvious, but even the people further from the stage never take their eyes off the spectacle at the tree.

Lauren tackles her Mom, but Lauren makes the hug short and with difficulty she lets go immediately. "I love you so so much baby, but it'll attract attention. We've already caused too much movement back here. Miranda, I've collected a lot of people like you told to me to," Lauren says.

"Gas is going to be released shortly. It's not lethal, but we will need extra hands. I need you to tell your top 10 most trusted people what's happening," I explain.

"What's happening?"

"There's people above who are going to rescue us. Remember to tell them to tie their shirts like a mask, but not until they see something happening. After that, get to the children's wing immediately."

"I love you baby. I'm so proud of you," she turns to Hailey.

"I love you too Mom."

Lauren walks with a normal gait up to a person across the room at a lunch table. I wouldn't have guessed anything is off looking at her.

"I'm going to get as close as I can to Jayne. You're responsible for keeping an eye out for Ian and Isaac. Do not engage with them. Here's a knife just in case." I say trying to read Hailey's face as she stares at the congregation. She doesn't look lost anymore. She's determined. "I still have Mark's master key, but I'm assuming they know he's dead by now."

"Let's go," Hailey has hatred in her eyes. "I'm ready to leave this fucking place."

I squeeze her shoulder and hope she's mentally ready for this.

I walk into the crowd losing sight of Hailey and Lauren. I push through the mass. I'm starting to sing along with them so I can blend in. There's something about singing the same thing while surrounded by the energy that's now filling this room. It's relaxing and oddly safe feeling.

"I need Alissa, Micah, and Lauren to come forward," Jayne's voice breaks the song. The trance is ending. That was going to be our main cover up.

Two strangers walk towards her and so does Lauren.

Alissa's the first person to arrive. She's smiling and looks at Jayne lovingly.

"God needs you for our purpose," Jayne tells her once she's on stage with her.

I'm filled with dread. My stomach sinks. I want to puke.

"Anything. Of course, you have my full devotion," She actually bows.

Ian and Isaac step onto opposite sides of the stage and pick her up. Her love flashes to fear.

They walk her to the stone tree.

"Wait! NO! I've been nothing but devout. What are you doing?!" She screams and kicks at them to no avail.

"You want to serve our God, this is how," Jayne says.

"No! Do you see this?!" She's addressing the room now. "I've been good! I'm devoted!"

Isaac slaps her in the face. Hard.

"You have started to doubt and it's infectious. Before you are wasted away into the Devil's hands though, God wants you. You have been chosen because you are special," Jayne grasps the microphone with two hands. "NOW."

Two chains drop from the ceiling and loudly clatter onto the floor echoing around the Big Room.

Isaac picks them up and fastens two hand sized hooks onto the ends. As he does this Ian forces the woman's shirt off. The crowd moves in closer. He rips her bra off.

Isaac stabs the metal hooks into her back and she lets out a blood curdling cry I'm sure the people above ground can hear. Ian silences her by slicing her throat.

An unseen person pulls the chains slowly upwards along the tree. The slice in her neck sprays blood until it gently pours down the trunk until it flows into the small trench that stretches the perimeter of the room and into the neighboring room.

I try to get closer, but the crowd becomes one tight moving entity. I can't move.

Hailey's on the edge of the crowd opposite from me. She's close to Ian and waiting for me, but there's no way I can get closer to her. Ian pushes past her and smooths his shirt where it wrinkled from their touch.

I can't make out what's happening.

They have the other guy and Lauren. They're dragging them to the tree.

I yell at the top of my lungs, "Jesus is Father!"

Nobody looks my way in the chaos, but Jayne locks eyes with me from her stage. The most anger and evil I've ever seen fill Jayne's eyes. And they're directed at me.

She knows.

I've been missing and she knows.

I pull my mask on. Jayne takes a deep breath in ready to scream into the microphone, but the smoke pours around the stone tree and into the room. She's interrupted by the crowd's sudden confusion. She turns back to me and takes another deep breath in, but her speech is slurred.

A few people in the crowd drop to the floor. More people drop. I can finally move, but I have to squeeze my feet between limbs so I don't step on the solid mass of people.

The people Lauren warned are running towards the back of the room tying their shirts around their heads as they sprint. Lauren's able to get loose as the people holding her drop to the floor.

Jayne's eyes are huge as she realizes what's happening. She doesn't break eye contact with me until she drops to the floor.

I lunge through the falling bodies towards her. Members in dark red try to grasp at my ankles from the ground, but their hands fall short as they fall unconscious. I pound onto the stage and my ankle's pulled out from under me. I fall over Jayne who's barely cognizant, but she has a small medical mask on her face. She's grasping for my mask. I pull my knife out and stab at her wrist. She screeches as she yanks her hand back. I kick her face trying to knock her measly cloth mask away. She passes out immediately.

I wish my knife was sharper, but it'll have to do. I position myself in front of her passed out body. Her beautiful black hair's covering her eyes. I grab her hand, stick my knife to her wrist and close my eyes as I cut. It won't cut the bone so I cut the skin and muscle around it. I stand and press my boot into her wrist. I can't do this. I close my eyes. I remember the people she's killed. I remember how she manipulated me and took advantage of my stupid need to feel special. I remember Lilly. I remember the bombs. I remember Victoria's husband from Pacific Valley. I open my eyes and I pull on her hand until the bone breaks under my boot.

I pull her shirt off to use as a tourniquet. I don't want her to bleed out. I want her to pay for what she's done. Also, Henson told me not to kill anyone if possible and I'm happy listening to someone who doesn't want to manipulate and hurt people.

I leap off the stage with her hand in mine.

4

I run with Jayne's hand in mine followed by Hailey, Lauren, and two guys Lauren warned. We make it to the last room before the children's wing. The same room we killed Mark in. It's just as dark as it always is especially after having gone down the brightly lit stairs.

"It feels more foreboding than normal," I say.

"This is how locked up you kept them?" Lauren asks.

"It's fucked," the guy with a shaved head says.

"The veiled threats of hurting my children was enough for me not to try anything," Lauren says.

My eyes adjust to the dark.

"Mikaela?!" I see her come towards us out of the darkest corner.

Her eyes are bloodshot and she's blinking too rapidly. She gently tucks her hair behind her ears repeatedly, but the rest of her movements are twitchy.

"What are you holding there?" The little light I have to work with bounces off the sheen of a large knife.

Hailey steps behind me and grabs for her Mother.

Mikaela's face is more sunken than the rest. I don't know how she's still standing, but devotion gives people superpowers.

Mikaela stops to stand by two other men who were blocking the door to the kids.

"Are you going to say something?" I ask.

"Where have you been? I heard you were a member of The Nothings and Isaac had to take care of you. Why are you down here?" She tucks an imaginary loose strand of hair behind her ears. From the amount of sweat and grime that's plastered her hair back I don't think it's going to fall loose.

"What are you doing here?"

"I am supposed to get these doors open no matter what it takes, but it has been weeks. They have Mark and Cody! They're keeping them alive, but they will kill them if we manage to get this door down. At least that's what they keep saying."

"It's Hailey! Don't open the doors! We're coming for you!" Hailey yells from behind her Mom. Muffled sounds come from the door, but I can't hear anything unless I move closer to them.

"What are you going to do when you get in?"

"Fucking kill them!" Mikaela shakes her head and stabs the air and slices the knife down and around her body. One oily strand of hair fell in her face, but she didn't notice. "They took two of Jayne's most important assets. How the hell did children do that? They are all guilty! Guilty!"

"They're kids."

"Who are keeping our people hostage! Where have you been?! Did you help them? Is Jayne using you for some secret mission she didn't tell me about?!" She extends her arm pointing the knife at us at the bottom of the stairwell, seethes, and lunges at me.

I fumble for my pistol and right before she reaches me I manage to whip it out.

BOOM!

"I didn't have a choice," I whisper.

The people behind me push to the side. I look down at her body. It's still breathing. It stops breathing. Her soul escapes, but her eyes are still looking at me. She looks bewildered.

The other two men draw their guns, but little Hailey and one of the guys we came with tackles them.

BOOM!

My ears are ringing. I know panic is about to steal my wits. Who got shot? Hailey lays on top of the man she tackled while the other two men are choking each other. Hailey is thrown off and the guy crawls to his gun that flew from his hand. His face has a bloody gash in it from where Hailey slashed him. He has several stab wounds as blood pours onto the floor into an unbroken trail behind him.

BOOM! I shoot him.

I could have slit his throat or stomped his face, but I wasn't ready for such an intimate kill.

"AAAAAH" Hailey screams. Lauren's already at her side when I reach her. I expect to see a bullet through her chest. I can't tell where the entrance wound is. She's covered in blood and I don't know what's hers or the man's. I tear her shirt off. My hands are slick with blood as I search for the wound. My finger slips into a small hole in her shoulder.

"MOOOOOM!"

I wrap her torn shirt around her armpit.

"Will that stop the bleeding?!" Lauren cries.

"You stay and make sure she's okay. I'm going in," I say knocking on the door. "It's Miranda."

I hear sounds of kids talking and furniture moving.

I go back for Jayne's hand I dropped at the staircase and unlock the door using her prints. I push it slowly as not to startle the kids anymore than they are.

The kids stand far away from the door. They don't know if they should trust me.

"Where's Hailey?"

"Brendan?" I search for him.

The kids part down the middle and Brenden walks up to me. He looks at the blood and pushes through to see his Mom crying over his sister.

"What did you do to her?" His bottom lip quivers.

"It's only in the shoulder. We're here to save you! We have to go right now though."

He throws his body on top of her. Hailey cries out, but smiles when she sees it's Brendan.

"Are you dying?" He asks.

"No she's not going to die," Lauren sobs.

"I'll be okay," Hailey says weakly.

Daniel and Jacob, the two brothers I saved from Mark's torture, tackle me against the wall as they hug me. They don't care about the blood I'm covered in.

"Where's Cody?" I ask.

Daniel pulls back.

"Well . . . ummm . . ."

"Say it," I demand. The exhaustion's starting to come back.

"He isn't doing too good. It was hard to keep him alive, but we did it like you said to so we can bargain with them."

"What's wrong?" I hold onto Jacob who hasn't let go of me.

"He smells really bad. He's got these holes full of puss and green and white squishy stuff," Daniel says.

"He's infected."

The old me wants to go in and save him, but instead I say "Get the kids. We're leaving this God forsaken place. We don't have time for him."

I address everyone, "Listen up. A gas will be released from above that makes people pass out. We need to get out of here so they can implement the next part of their plan and rescue your parents."

"Are my parents alive?"

I can't see who asked the question, "I don't want to lie to any of you. Your parents should be alive though. We'll pass them on the way out. They'll look dead, but I'll need you guys to follow me. Take your shirts and soak them in water then tie them around your faces to use as masks."

A girl asks, "Can I get a shirt from my room?"

"We can't risk losing another minute. Nobody's going to care sweetie. Everyone go do it now!"

They run back inside using faucets and drinking fountains. I notice colored smoke seeping through the water sprinkles on the ceiling.

"GET THEM ON NOW," I pull my respirator back on. The door starts to close. I push against it, but it's heavy and automated.

"GET OUT! If your masks aren't wet yet just put them on, it's better than nothing," I strain against the door. A few of the older kids run over and help me.

My feet are scraping against the floor moving millimeter by millimeter. I put one leg up on the door frame. The kid's are rushing through. There's only a foot of space now. The kids continue to fall through. There's only six inches left. My bones are straining under the weight.

The last kid tries to squeeze through, but he gets stuck. Kids are pulling on him. The door closes another millimeter.

"Breathe in," Hailey says as loud as she's able to.

The kid pops through tumbling to the ground.

I let it slam shut.

"We need to get out of here. Do not stop. For anything. Okay?" Little nods of agreement ripple through the crowd. "Don't look for your parents. You can't help them right now. It's a non lethal gas, but if you breathe it you'll pass out with the others. My job's to get you out."

"Oh and do not take those masks off," I say.

5

We sprint up the stairs and through the tunnel. The power's been cut. None of the locks or doors or security measures are on. We're able to get to the Big Room effortlessly.

A thin smoky haze floats in the room. Bodies are piled on top of each other as they sleep.

I run for the kitchen as it's the farthest away from the shared wall with the other big room. A few kids run off to their parents, but I can't slow down or all the kids will pass out. I don't know what'll it be like if Jayne and the dark reds and other devotees start to wake up. I need to get them out of danger.

We run into the kitchen and huddle in the back farthest from the smoke and the wall where nobody can see us.

"Kill them all! They're all traitors," Jayne must have woken up. We huddle tighter together as if making ourselves smaller would make us harder to find.

Nobody answers her. She's barking orders at sleeping bodies.

"I'm on it!" Isaac yells and a few more answer his battle cry.

"What do I do?" Someone asks.

"You go! Go do! I don't know!" Isaac responds.

BOOM! BOOM! BOOOOOM!

The wall's blown to pieces.

More sleeping gas is released.

Chapter 16

1

I'm sitting in the grass on top of a mountain in the middle of nowhere with Kelsey, Kyle, and the kids. Lauren, Hailey, and Brendan are sitting with a paramedic. They're crying and laughing. Hailey's wearing a camo jacket one of the soldiers gave her. Her shirt bandage has been replaced with actual gauze. If they aren't hugging then their arms are touching. They don't want to let each other go.

The last group of kids are hoisted out of the hole. They struggle over to us. Several of them are laying their heads on me.

The rescuers rigged a contraption that lowers into the hole that's able to hoist several people at a time. They were able to make the hole larger, but not by much or the risk of the entire room collapsing would've been too great.

I didn't want them to hurt the tree either.

The kids around us are watching the military waiting for them to start bringing up their parents. Most of the kids have put their mask shirts back on. The others moved them to the tops of their heads. Their joints protrude and their almost fluorescent skin hugs their bones. I get up to find sunscreen for them. I've only been out for 15 minutes and I already feel myself burning. I know how long it's been because I asked for a watch and someone lent me one.

"Where are you going?" Jacob asks.

"You can come with me if it's okay with your brother." Daniel doesn't nod, but joins us. He doesn't want to leave my side either.

A small group of sleeping members in handcuffs supported by a soldier are hoisted through the hole. The men and women gently drag them away. Jacob and Daniel take off. The other kids rush them as well. One girl who found a feather and stuck it into her shirt hat finds her Dad. The rest head for the hole.

"Please stay away from the hole. It's unstable and we need room to get everyone up safely," Parker blares through his bullhorn. They sulk back to where I'm sitting. I pass a few bottles of sunscreen around, but they don't care so I get up with Kelsey and Kyle and in our utter exhaustion we help the kids apply it.

It takes the rest of the day to pull everyone up. The medics are busy. None of the people who were sacrificed and murdered were parents. Every child that's still alive is reunited with their parents. Except for the kids who were murdered.

Ironically, the parents who lost their children are dressed in dark red. They're still groggy, but as reality sets in they start to panic.

Kelsey pulls me and Kyle in. We lay back in the grass letting the military take over all responsibility. I never want to let them go.

Although the adults are only just coming back to consciousness and are handcuffed, most of them are smiling. We're relieved. We're safe. Others are crying and others are still mostly passed out. Some of them are praying to I don't know who.

When the most dangerous members were brought up, I told the soldiers who loaded them into a box truck. I don't know everyone though. I could be sitting across from a devout follower who'll continue to spread the word. I know it's an armored truck, but a vehicle of any sorts seems too mundane to hold Jayne.

Parker, the guy with the bullhorn, passes out snacks and water bottles. Piles of blankets are stacked in the med area. People are laughing again. The laughter might be hesitant with heaviness underneath it, but it's there and that's all that matters right now. Trauma covers this day with a thick fog, but the sun shines through at the taste of freedom. Although I'm sure we're all uncertain about the status of the world, where we're going to go, if this actually means the end of this nightmare or not, but I'm gonna let myself enjoy this moment. I lay back. I'm not nervous of bugs any longer. I welcome the bite of a little bug that's alive. The cave was devoid and it actively sucked our lives away.

A redheaded solider is hoisted out of the hole and she says, "The base is empty."

Acknowledgements

      Writing is thought of as a solitary practice and for the most part it is, but I couldn't have written this book without the following people:

    My Dad, Adam Opava, who I dedicated this book to. You were with me every single grueling step of the way to see this book finished. When you were busy and had no time to spare you still edited pages and brainstormed ideas and technicalities with me. You are my rock.

    My Mom, Tonya Welch. You have always full heartedly supported me and with great enthusiasm. In my darkest moments of self doubt your shining smile was there for me. We've grown together during the toughest of times.

    I wouldn't have the strength I have now if I didn't have my Mom and Dad as role models. You taught me to rise up. You taught me it's okay to cry and then how to dust myself off and come out stronger than before.

    My partner, Christopher Ray. You never complained when I would go on 12 hour writing stints and abandon all housework, cooking, and even myself. You always picked up the pieces. You were also the hardest on me and I mean so hard I wanted to pull my hair out and scream sometimes. You pushed me to be better and I'm so grateful for that. I wouldn't be the writer I am today without you.

    My brother, Caleb Opava and my sisters, Hannah Welch and Elizabeth Welch. You were always so patient and loving with me when I would become a writing hermit. Each of your unique personalities inspire me.

    The Handy Family. You gave me a job in the wild land of Big Sur and mine and Chris's own little tiny home facing the ocean where I fell asleep to the sound of seals barking. I couldn't have had a more perfect place to bust out my debut novel.

    All my friends in Big Sur. You were also so patient and loving with me even when I would disappear off the face of the cliff. You're the most beautiful people I've ever met.

    Henry Miller Library. Reading at open mic nights gave me confidence. Being surrounded by creativity and my friends was the energy I needed.

    My friends, family, and other supporters. Thank you for believing in me especially when I didn't believe in myself. This list is not in order because without you I wouldn't be able to write as much as I do. Your engagement on social media gave me the needed boosts of "I can do this."

Big 'Ol Blueberry Bertha the Van, my '93 Chevy van. You gave me rent free shelter out in the wilderness allowing me to write full time.

Stephen King. You're my favorite author. Your imagination with words and stories inspired me to start writing again.

The manipulators in my life. This is a funny thank you, but the book wouldn't have been possible without y'all.

Megan Noel Opava attended a small town church in the deep south where manipulation and cult practices took place which inspired the psychological aspects in *The Secrets We Carry*. She received a degree in Neuroscience and a minor in Art Studio from the University of Florida. She has never lived in one location for more than three years at a time. She continued that lifestyle by converting an old van named Big 'Ol Blueberry Bertha the Van and living and traveling in it off and on. She has more books that address the human psyche on the way.

Made in the USA
Columbia, SC
30 July 2023